BORN THE SAME

BORN THE SAME

ANTONY DUNFORD

This edition published in Great Britain in 2023

by Hobeck Books Limited, 24 Brookside Business Park, Stone, Staffordshire ST15 0RZ

www.hobeck.net

A CIP catalogue for this book is available from the British Library.

ISBN 978-1-915-817-14-3 (pbk)

ISBN 978-1-915-817-13-6 (ebook)

Cover design by Jayne Mapp Design

Printed and bound in Great Britain

ARE YOU A THRILLER SEEKER?

Hobeck Books is an independent publisher of crime, thrillers and suspense fiction and we have one aim – to bring you the books you want to read.

For more details about our books, our authors and our plans, plus the chance to download free novellas, sign up for our newsletter at **www.hobeck.net**.

You can also find us on Twitter **@hobeckbooks** or on Facebook **www.facebook.com/hobeckbooks10**.

For Conor Reid
Welcome to the world

PART ONE

CHAPTER ONE

"DON'T SHOOT, I'M A JOURNALIST." COLM HAD DREAMED OF saying those words for real since he was at school, since he'd heard them in a film. Not in English, but in a local language. A dream of standing in some remote part of the world beyond the threadbare blanket of law and order that comforts the fortunate, where survival in the moment heightens every sense. A dream of men and women screaming, guns waving and firing in the air, where no one knows what is going to happen next. Until "Don't shoot, I'm a journalist" brings calm and trust, a trust in a quest for truth.

That was the dream. In reality, Colm was standing less than a kilometre from his office in the centre of Dublin staring at what looked like a pebble.

At first glance, and it did not warrant a second glance, it was small, about the size of desiccated apple. Light brown in colour, its surface was scarred like pumice or a sponge. Perhaps the whole thing was porous. It sat on a piece of paper in a wooden case, the glass lid propped open for the occasion. Had he seen it on the ground, he would have dismissed it as a bit of sandstone. If he even noticed it.

'Is that it?' he asked, his pen hovering over a blank page in his notebook.

Doctor MacMahon nodded, smiling broadly. 'Isn't it amazing?' she said.

'That's part of a bear?'

She nodded. 'Part of the patella. That's the knee.'

'And why is it amazing?'

'Because of these.' Doctor MacMahon, her hands protected by latex gloves, picked the bone up and turned it, pointing at a series of straight lines marking the surface. Colm leaned forward.

'They look like cuts.'

'They are. Cuts from a stone knife. This animal was butchered.'

'And that's the amazing thing?'

Doctor MacMahon was oblivious to Colm's tone. She had enough enthusiasm for them both.

'Not just that. We've had the bone carbon dated, technology that wasn't available when it was found. This animal was butchered around twelve and a half thousand years ago, which means people have been living on Ireland for more than two thousand years longer than anyone previously thought.' She paused, as if to allow herself time to contemplate the enormity of her own words. 'It's been verified by three different labs,' she added. 'Two here, one in the UK.'

Colm grunted and made a note. He found it difficult to share her enthusiasm. As headlines went, this hardly career-making stuff. *Hey, remaining newspaper readers of Ireland, you know that date you weren't aware of and wouldn't have cared about if you were? Well, it turns out it was wrong.*

'People ate bears?' he said.

'They might have. They certainly used their bones to make

tools, and their skin to make clothes. Bear teeth have been found with holes drilled through them, which suggests they were used in a necklace, as jewellery.'

Doctor MacMahon placed the bone back in its case with a gentleness bordering on reverence. Colm shivered. The museum's stone floors, and high ceilings kept it cool, even in August. Not that Dublin in August was particularly warm.

'There were bears in Ireland?' Colm asked, for the sake of something to say.

'Oh, yes. That's rather interesting, actually. Please, follow me.'

She led the way out of the storeroom, up some stairs, and along a corridor, emerging onto the balcony inside the rotunda. The vastness of the space and the architecture of the building impressed Colm far more than the little piece of bone had. Doctor MacMahon was oblivious to her surroundings. She talked as she walked.

'Genetically the Irish bears were a cross between the European brown bear, and the polar bear. Closer to the polar bear than the brown bear. In fact, until a few years ago it was thought that all living polar bears are descended from the Irish brown bear, thanks to analysis of mitochondrial DNA. But that's now disputed. The Irish sub-species was cut off by rising sea levels when Ireland was formed around sixteen thousand years ago.'

'Ireland had its own bear? And that bear was the mother of polar bears?' Colm said. This was more interesting. Everyone knew what a polar bear was.

'Ireland had its own species of bear,' Doctor MacMahon said. 'That it was the ancestor of all polar bears is now not believed to be true.' She had led him from the rotunda and through an innocuous-looking door into a corridor of glass with offices either side. She entered one of the offices through a set of double doors. It was a large, open-plan workspace filled with desks, chairs, filing cabinets, shelves, papers, samples, computers, academics, curators, assistants, and the strong smell of milky coffee.

Stopping at a desk bearing a plaque with her name on it, Doctor MacMahon leant forward and wiggled the mouse attached to a laptop. The screen came to life. She typed in a password, then navigated her way to a file and opened it.

It was a picture of a postage stamp blown up to fill the screen. "45p" in the right-hand corner. The main event: an artist's impression of an Irish brown bear.

'This was done as part of the "Extinct Irish Animals" set of stamps in 1999, along with the giant red deer, the woolly mammoth, and the wolf.'

Colm leaned his hands on the back of a chair and stared at the image. He vaguely remembered it from his childhood.

'It's extinct?' he said.

Doctor MacMahon nodded.

'About three thousand years ago.'

'Why?'

The doctor shrugged. 'Hunting. Habitat loss – all the forests were cut down to make way for growing crops, grazing cattle. The usual, since the arrival of man. The same thing happened in Britain, and in most of Western Europe. And North Africa. Anything larger than a badger was driven to extinction, unless it was edible and could be farmed.'

Colm nodded and made another note. She waited whilst he wrote. When he looked up, she was smiling at him.

'I know this won't be a big deal for most of your readers,' she said, 'but in terms of our understanding of the pre-history of Ireland, it's the biggest discovery in years.'

'I'm sure some of our readers will find it fascinating, Doctor MacMahon.'

'Please, call me Maggie.'

'Thank you, Maggie,' Colm said. He shook her hand and left.

———

The Archaeology building of the National Museum of Ireland was on Kildare Street. About ten minutes on foot from the office, if Colm cut through the grounds of Trinity College. With the walk there, thirty minutes with Maggie, and the walk back, he'd managed to fit the whole interview into his lunch hour. He spent the walk back trying to imagine the places he was seeing thousands of years ago. Had this really been a forest?

He stepped out of the elevator, nodded a "how-are-ye" to the bloke on security, and headed for his timeshare desk.

'They call it a "lunch hour", old man, but that's just a vestigial expression. Nowadays that's shorthand for "pre-processed sandwich at your desk whilst still working",' his boss, Neale, greeted him as he walked onto the news floor. Neale was always half joking. Which meant he was also always half serious. He was also still typing. Colm had rarely held all of Neale's attention.

'I was working,' Colm said.

'On what?' Neale's fingers flew over the keyboard. Colm had a momentary image of Neale sitting in front of a mechanical typewriter whilst wearing a green visor, a cigarette dangling from one corner of his mouth, punching the keys in brow-wrinkling fury.

'Press release from the NMI. Archaeology. Carbon dated a bear bone. Proves people were in Ireland two thousand years earlier than we thought.'

'Whoop-di-doop, what a scoop. That's going to send the circulation through the roof. I'd stop the press, if we still had a press.' Neale's tone had changed. 'I need twelve pieces from you today. You can't spend an hour on one.'

'There's a hook.'

'I'm still listening,' Neale said, though the speed at which he continued to type suggested otherwise.

'There was a bear. The Irish brown bear. It was a sub-species that only ever existed in Ireland. It was related to the polar bear. I thought I'd do a piece on the bear.'

Neale hadn't stopped typing, but he'd slowed.

'And what happened to this bear?'

'It's extinct. Hunting and habitat loss. Three thousand years ago.'

This time the typing did stop.

'I'll stick it in Breaking News... Seriously, you want to do a piece on how great it is our ancestors hunted the local bears to extinction? If it was still around and there was something we could do about it, maybe you'd have a story. But who wants to know about something they can't do anything about?'

The typing resumed.

Colm shrugged, left Neale to his two half worlds, and wound his way across the news floor to his timeshare desk. Which was occupied. By a woman, slouched in the chair, googling "influencers" and sending Instagram posts to the local printer. His laptop had been unplugged from the monitor and shoved to one side to make room for hers.

'It's second Wednesday, Bron,' he said.

'"Second" is a relative term, Colm,' she said.

Bron Jones. Degree in journalism from Bristol, personality from North Wales out of season, self-awareness of a communicable disease. The person Colm shared a desk with. She had it Monday and Friday, he had it Tuesday and Thursday, and they alternated Wednesdays. It was his Wednesday. Wasn't it?

'I've been here all morning,' he said. Argue possession from the playground perspective.

'And then you left,' Bron said. A-ha! She had tacitly acknowledged possession was a valid argument. She was sending things to the printer. When she went to pick them up, he could resume tenancy.

'Here you go, Bron. Hi, Colm.' Deirdre, an intern, handed Bron her printing, smiled warmly at Colm, and glided away.

'I was planning on working from home this afternoon, anyways,' Colm said.

'Not going to be around for the announcement?' Bron asked.

'What announcement?'

Bron lowered her voice. 'Rumour has it, more cuts.'

Colm lowered his voice to match, though he couldn't keep the surprise out of it. 'What's left to cut?'

'Us, eejit. The staff.'

A door slammed. The editor's office door. It was slammed by a woman, her face as determined as flint only not as warm. She marched across the office so quickly all the papers on all the desks were blown about. Or would have been had it not been for the clear desk policy.

'Wonder what she's so delira and excira about?' Bron said, mimicking Gay Byrne without any trace of self-consciousness.

The woman was Aileen O'Connor, the paper's award-winning war correspondent. She'd been in the business more than thirty years, reporting from every major conflict since Grenada in eighty-three. Her coverage of the Iraq wars was one of the reasons Colm had become a journalist. That she had covered them for this paper was the main reason he was here and not at a TV station or news agency. When she slammed doors, it did not mean she was delighted and excited. It meant that somewhere people were dying.

———

'I'm home!' Colm called as he opened the front door.

There was no answer. Unsurprising, as their car wasn't on the drive.

He put his laptop in the dining room and went to make coffee. As the kettle boiled, he looked out of the kitchen window, at the fields beyond the garden. A combine harvester made its way across them like a giant beetle, harvesting early to reduce the risk of mould after the grey, warm, wet summer. Had that field once been a forest? A forest roamed by bears?

He took the coffee to the dining room and sat down in front of the laptop.

'Shoot me, I wanted to be a journalist,' he muttered, and started to type.

CHAPTER TWO

'SOMETHING SMELLS GOOD, SO,' NIAMH SAID. 'AND DON'T SAY, "Thank you, I just had a shower".'

'Are you saying I've become predictable?' Colm asked, meeting her in the hall and greeting her with a kiss, his hands going to her belly. 'How have you both been this day of grand shite?'

'I'll pardon you not to be cursing within earshot of our child,' Niamh said with mock solemnity. 'At least not until they're a gobby little teenage fecker and we've washed our hands of them. And we're fine. You? The usual?'

She dropped her shoulder bag to the hall floor and followed him into the kitchen.

Dinner did smell pretty fine. He was feeling good about it. Cook the onions till they're practically black, that was the secret.

'The usual,' he said. 'Though I did learn about the Irish bear.'

'What was that?'

'A bear. Lived on Ireland and nowhere else. Only died out about three thousand years ago.' He saw her expression. 'Well, I thought it was pretty cool.'

'They still not given you anything meaty?'

'No. And there's an announcement. Supposed to be this afternoon but delayed till tomorrow. Redundancies, according to Bron.' And Bron was always bloody right.

'You should take it. You're so miserable there.'

Colm stirred the lamb while Niamh flicked through the mail he'd left on the table. She dropped the lot into the recycling bin.

'I thought about it. But there's no point. I haven't been there long enough for a pay-out. If I do leave, I need another job first. Especially with Junior there likely to have expensive tastes, like their mother.'

'Their mother earns enough to look after both of ye, and you know it, Reid,' Niamh smiled. 'This isn't about money, is it?'

'No. No, it isn't about money.' He stirred the lamb in the pan.

———

They ate at the dining room table, Colm's laptop still on beside them.

'I've three pieces to finish,' he said, by way of apology.

Niamh looked at her watch. 'And I was back late,' she said. 'It's coming up to nine. If this job isn't about the money it needs to be making you happy or it'll rot ye.'

Colm nodded and took another mouthful.

'It's all I can see,' he said. 'I've wanted to do it for so long I never thought about doing anything else. It's just so different now. Technology changed everything. Positive side, if you write the greatest story ever everyone in the world can read it within five minutes. Negative side, no one needs to move to find anything out. They just find the nearest person to the event who has a mobile phone, get them to film it, read a bit of background on Wikipedia, and a story that once took a month to pull together goes from concept to headline in half an hour. My dream is a corpse. Or at best a ghost.'

'That can't be universally true. It might be a trend, but not an absolute. Change doesn't happen that way.'

'It's happening that fast. Everything decent goes to the old guard. Here, Aileen bloody O'Connor, have another award,' he muttered.

'Yeah, yeah, don't shy. You idolise that woman. I swear, if I ever came home and found you in bed with her, I'd be relieved you'd finally got it out of your system.'

Colm looked up, eyes wide.

'Really?' he said.

'Just you try it, Mr Reid,' she smiled at him.

He smiled back.

'What are you going to do?' she asked.

'I don't know.

―――

Thursday was one of his days for the timeshare desk, so the alarm went off at the unwholesome hour of six. Beside him Niamh was missing, her side of the bed already cool. He found her in the kitchen, standing by the microwave, reading a report from her work.

'Couldn't sleep,' she said, as he kissed her neck and she continued to read.

He filled the kettle.

―――

The commute was surprisingly crowded considering it was school holidays. Perhaps the mediocre weather had led to more people staying in the city than usual. Whatever the reason, Colm was later getting to the office than he had intended, and the announcement was already underway.

The news floor was full. Fuller than he could remember seeing it. The Monday and Friday tenants were all there, as well as the Tuesday and Thursday tenants. There were some faces Colm didn't recognise at all.

The editor was speaking. Sean O'Sullivan. Proper journalist. Facts, Accuracy, Truth. FAT. He used it in a little speech he gave to all the new recruits. Been with the paper longer than Aileen O'Connor. Would listen to anyone; could tolerate change as long as it improved things; when he saw something stupid, he called it stupid. Colm liked the man.

Sean was standing in the middle of the crowd. His deputy, Kevin, and a couple of faceless suits Colm assumed were from the newspaper's new owners, were standing next to him.

'He's not said anything real yet,' Neale whispered as Colm stopped next to him. 'But he's building up to something, that's for sure.'

Colm heard a noise behind him. Someone had knocked a bag that was leaning against a desk leg, and it had flopped to the floor. That someone was Aileen O'Connor. She had her coat on and, ignoring the crowd on the news floor, she walked through reception to the elevators. Before she closed the door behind her, she looked back and caught his eye. He felt his insides do somersaults. She held his gaze for just a moment, then nodded slightly before resuming her walk and closing the door behind her. Colm was wondering what that meant, when a change in tone drew his attention back to Sean O'Sullivan.

'...these trends are challenging to say the least. We must adapt or the paper won't survive. To that end, there are to be some changes.'

The changes were delivered with the cheer of a church bell sounding midnight.

Sean himself was stepping down. *Bong!*

His replacement wasn't to be his deputy, as was tradition, a new person appointed by the owners was coming in from outside the paper, someone who had done well managing content on a platform, whatever that meant. *Bong!*

A voluntary redundancy package was on offer for a limited time at very favourable terms. The individuals whose roles it applied to would be contacted personally. *Bong!*

The lease on this building would not be renewed, and a more cost-effective premises had been secured down in Blackrock. A small suite for executives would be retained in the city centre. *Bong!*

Colm had stopped listening. The changes were so fundamental that whatever was left would take years to re-form into a functioning entity. The heart of the paper was being ripped out. Its purpose was morphing from a place that generated knowledge to one that moved data. With each new announcement, his dream of being a *real* journalist lurched further from realisation, closer to oblivion in the coldness of the waking world.

Neale nudged him. Sean was making one last announcement.

Aileen O'Connor, after thirty-three years with the paper, would be leaving in February. *Bong!*

But this wasn't the same as the other announcements. It didn't fit the pattern. This wasn't a change forced on the paper through necessity. This wasn't in the script either – the faceless suits close to Sean scowled disapproval as he spoke.

Leaving in February. Six months away. For someone of her seniority, that would be her notice period. If she had been made redundant, they would have bought out her notice period. Which meant she hadn't been fired. She had resigned. Colm heard Neale let out a long breath.

Sean reminded everyone that, if the option of redundancy applied to them, someone would be in personal contact. Then he thanked everyone and turned away. The announcement was over. The white canvas of silence on which he had presented his words was replaced by the grey of worried muttering. The crowd started to break up, groups heading to the kitchen area, the desks, reception, the lifts, the stairs. If Colm knew some of the older staff, the sub-editors, the managers, they'd be in a pub within ten minutes digesting what they'd just heard. The younger ones, like him, were in the main heading back to their desks. They'd be more afraid of redundancy than of the changes to the paper. They'd pretend it wasn't happening until that personal contact Sean had mentioned reached them.

Colm was at his desk, laptop plugged in and booting up, when Kevin, Sean's deputy, appeared beside him.

'Sean would like to see you in his office,' Kevin said.

Personal contact.

CHAPTER THREE

THE WALK ACROSS THE NEWS FLOOR TO SEAN'S OFFICE WAS through a distorted world. Colm passed groups of people whispering, but their voices seemed too loud, the faces that turned to look at him too large, the stares too sharp. Everything was an obstacle; a chair pushed back too far; a bag forgotten; a laser printer knocked out of position. And his head was throbbing. Was he about to lose his job? If so, why was he first? The faceless suits had only just left. No one else had been in to see Sean since. Colm wouldn't come first on any general ranking – most recently employed, alphabetically, lowest paid, longest serving, reverse-alphabetically, highest paid. He was none of those.

He knocked on Sean's open door.

'Come in and shut it,' Sean said. Colm looked blank. Did Sean mean keep quiet? 'The door.'

Colm recovered and shut the door behind him.

'Sit.'

Colm sat.

Sean handed him an envelope. It felt too thick to be an HR1. Not redundancy, then.

'Your next assignment,' Sean said. No messing. He picked up a piece of paper with an article printed on it.

'What?'

'I read your piece on the bear. Brief, but poignant. Already getting a lot of views on the website,' he said, then read from the piece of paper in his hand. '"Our ancestors didn't have our advantages. Whoever killed the last Irish bear could not have known they were doing anything other than feeding and clothing their family. We have no such excuse." Challenging. Controversial. Worthy of a follow-up. Which, thanks to that old Sally, serendipity, arrived a couple of weeks ago.'

Sean swung his laptop round so Colm could see the screen. 'Read it.'

It was an email from someone named Kennet Haven, writing from a conservancy in Kenya. A long email. Colm read on. This Kennet Haven was planning an expedition to a place called Garamba National Park in the Democratic Republic of the Congo, in Central Africa, to look for evidence of a species of rhino, the northern white. The species hadn't been seen in the wild for a decade, not since 2006. Kennet Haven hoped to find any surviving rhinos with a view to later capturing them and taking them back to Kenya to protect them and save the species from extinction. He was looking for journalists to accompany his expedition and raise awareness of the rhinos' plight.

'We learned yesterday that no other news organisation is sending anyone. They all think it too expensive or too dangerous or both, to send someone to look for something that, in all likelihood, isn't there. Anyone who does go will scoop,' Sean said.

Colm stared at Sean. No redundancy, then.

'The new editor also thinks it is too expensive. He's not worried about it being too dangerous. But he doesn't take over until tomorrow. By which time I am hoping you'll be on a plane.'

Colm didn't know what to say.

'It will be just you. No camera crew, no guide. You'll have to make your own way to the national park in the Congo. Kennet Haven will meet you there. The return ticket is valid for a month.'

Sean nodded at the envelope Colm was holding. Colm tipped it up. It contained another envelope, and a paper wallet that in turn contained six plane tickets, from Dublin to Paris, from Paris to Kinshasa, which Colm knew was the capital of the Democratic Republic of the Congo, from Kinshasa to Dungu, which Colm had never heard of, and then the same trips in reverse. The outbound tickets all had dates and times on them. The flight from Dublin to Paris left in five hours.

'My wife is pregnant,' Colm managed.

'Talk to her, then. But Colm, this might be the last international story this paper investigates first hand. Ever. Do you understand?'

'I do, sir. I'll call her right now.'

And Colm did, sitting in Sean's office. Niamh answered. Colm explained.

'Go,' she said.

————

Five hours was tight. He had to get home, which was an hour and a half in the opposite direction, pack, then get back into Dublin and out to the airport.

The train back was on time but seemed slower than an arthritic snail. Colm felt so many emotions at once. He tried to unravel them, to order them. The trust Sean was showing in him, the last throw of the dice of old journalism from a career journalist, and the dice he had thrown was Colm. It was a burden, a weight. He'd longed for an assignment like this, but not like this. Not on his own, hurled into a place he'd heard of but couldn't

imagine. Colm had never been to Africa. He'd only been outside
Europe twice, once on a cruise to the Americas with his parents
as a child, and once to India, to the wedding of someone he'd
worked with. On the India trip he and Niamh had been taken
everywhere by his former colleague's younger brother. He'd not
been to many places inside Europe, either. He didn't speak any
other languages. Well, he'd studied French at school, and Irish,
but not with any real direction, enthusiasm or result. They were
just subjects he'd had to pass, not skills he'd thought he would
ever have to use. They spoke French in the Congo, didn't they?
Though who were "they"? Was that everyone, or just some
people? It had been a colony, a Belgian colony. He remembered
that much from History. And the inhabitants had been treated
so badly by the colonists, as slaves, as property, as nothing more
than disposable tools used to rob the country of its resources.
But that was all he remembered. He knew nothing about what
the country was like now. The burden of trust, and the burden of
lack of knowledge.

There was a third feeling he unpicked from the knot in his
stomach. Fear. He was afraid.

Before he realised it, he was home.

The first problem was what to pack. He googled the weather
in the Congo. Hot and wet. Always hot and wet. His wardrobe
could handle wet. This was Ireland, after all. It wasn't as well
adapted for hot. He did his best.

Getting the train back into Dublin and then a bus out to the
airport was going to cut it too fine, so he raided the cash he kept
in his sock drawer and called a taxi. It seemed to take forever to
arrive. When it finally did, he jumped in the back with his bag.

'Dublin airport,' he said.

'When's your flight?' the driver asked. Colm told him. The
driver swore and pulled out of the street at speed.

He got to the airport less than an hour before the flight to

Paris departed. Mid-afternoon, and the crowds were a mix of tourists and business folk. He went upstairs to departures and queued to check in. He'd brought seven changes of clothes. He assumed that, were he to make it to the park, regular laundry and bathing would be in short supply, but he'd accepted a reduction in personal hygiene in exchange for a lighter bag. He kept tapping the pocket his passport was in to make sure he'd not forgotten it. The queue was moving slower than he thought possible. He was sure he was going to miss the flight.

But he checked in with thirty-five minutes to go. Boarding hadn't started. He still had security and passport control to clear, though, and that could take longer than check in. He walked quickly to the entrance to security. As he reached it, he heard running steps behind him, and someone drew level, joining him in the queue.

He had to look at them twice to be sure he wasn't seeing things.

Aileen O'Connor.

'You're brave, Reid, I'll give you that,' she said.

Aileen bloody O'Connor. Wait, brave?

'Know what government advice is for citizens considering travelling to DR Congo right now?' she asked.

'No,' he said.

'"Don't",' she replied. 'That's why they wouldn't send me. I insisted on security. Additional cost made the story non-viable. Feck 'em. Let them count their beans. The truth is worth more. You're brave. What inoculations have you had recently?'

'Er... I went to India last year.'

'Good. That'll have given you the basics. Hep. A, hep. B, tetanus, malaria. But no Yellow Fever?'

Colm shook his head.

'Mandatory for entering the DRC. Got your visa?'

'Visa?'

'Didn't think so. They didn't give you time. They didn't think. Don't know what it takes. Here.'

She handed him an A4 folder about five centimetres thick.

'ICVP - Yellow Fever vaccination certificate. It's mine, so if they check closely act like a sixty-five-year-old woman. Try not to catch it. Visa in your name. I have an old friend at the embassy. Stick it in your passport before you land. My notes on the LRA, SPLM, M23, FDLR, UDRC, Raia Mutomboki, Maï Maï Sheka, Maï Maï Kifuafua, LDF, FDC, FPC, FRPI, and a couple of dozen others. That's by no means all of them but it covers the main ones. You're not going to find any rhino, but if you get there, you'll find out that "there" is one of the most dangerous places on the planet. Stay close to the rangers or the army or whoever it is this Kennet Haven has convinced to escort him. If you do run into any rebels, make it clear you're a journalist. None of them have killed any journalists as far as I know. And learn all you can about South Sudan.'

That was a lot of information to take in.

'South Sudan?' he said.

'Too right, Reid. What Kennet Haven neglected to mention in his email, and the reason that every other journalist he contacted has turned him down, is that the last sighting of northern white rhino in the wild was not in Garamba National Park in the DRC, it was over the border in what was then Sudan and is now South Sudan. Garamba is incredibly dangerous, but at least the DRC now has a reasonably stable government and an effective army, and the park itself is patrolled regularly and in force. South Sudan, no such luxuries.'

'The LRA, M23... they're all...?'

'Armed insurgents. Rebel groups. Living in the jungle in remote camps, emerging only to attack anyone who has something worth stealing. Some have political aspirations to a greater or lesser degree; some simply don't want to be part of a state. It's what America would look like if the Federal structure collapsed. You can have that line, if you get to write the story.'

Colm swallowed.

'Why are you helping me?'

'There's a story here, and that story must be written. If they won't let me write it, then I'll help you write it. Find its heart, Reid. Find its heart and bring it home.'

She put her hand on his arm, looked him in the eyes, nodded once as if satisfied, and walked against the queue and out of his sight. The man behind Colm in the queue coughed deliberately, and Colm hurried to catch up with the woman in front.

CHAPTER FOUR

THE LAY OVER AT PARIS-CHARLES DE GAULLE WAS SEVENTEEN and a half hours. Sean hadn't paid for a hotel room, so Colm had to spend the night in the airport. The flight to the DRC, leaving at ten in the morning, had a stop in Brazzaville and wouldn't reach Kinshasa until eight in the evening. Colm didn't want to sleep through the night and then spend the day cramped in a plane seat, so he determined to stay awake in the airport and sleep on the plane.

He found a gate in terminal 2C that was closed for refurbishment. It was only two minutes' walk from a café. He bought an Americano with an extra shot, then sat on a chair at the closed gate, put his shoulder bag on the chair next to him, and sent Niamh a text message. She replied almost immediately. *Baby fine, mummy fine, daddy better look after his finely sculpted arse.* He smiled dumbly at the words for a whole minute. Then he put his phone away, stood up, and started to pace, papers from the folder Aileen had given him in one hand, the coffee in the other.

As he paced, he read.

The LRA. Lord's Resistance Army. Once known as the United Holy Salvation Army, and then the Uganda Christian Army. Stated aim to rule Uganda according to the Ten Commandments. Recognised internationally as a terrorist organisation responsible for more than two thousand deaths, more than three thousand abductions, and the displacement of close to half a million people. Believed to once have numbered hundreds of armed men. Believed to be operating in South Sudan, and to cross into the Garamba National Park in the DR Congo periodically to poach wildlife, especially elephants, for their ivory.

He flicked through the rest of the papers. There were similar details on forty different organisations.

Aileen had been researching this for years.

Colm had a moment of self-doubt so deep his head began to spin. He leaned forward and placed hands on his thighs. He was so unprepared. Last night he'd been complaining that the local stories he was being given were beneath his abilities. This night he had a real story and was convinced it was beyond his abilities.

He shook his head to clear it. He needed to focus. He felt like this sometimes when he encountered something previously unknown to him. The volume and complexity of the detail overwhelmed him. He became convinced he could never grasp it all, never understand it. But he knew now, as he'd got to know himself objectively, that he could overcome the detail through application and immersion.

He drained the coffee in a single go, dropped the cup in *une poubelle*, which his memory insisted on telling him was French for a dustbin, and moved onto the details of the next organisation.

After an hour he stopped pacing and sat on the floor, spreading the sheets around him, putting them in piles.

Aileen had included a map of the northeast Congo basin,

showing the lines of the Central African Republican, South
Sudanese, Ugandan, Rwandan, and Burundian borders. She had
shaded many of the areas where the groups had been known to
operate. Colm found a pencil and over the next few hours made
some amendments based on his reading Jaysus, Garamba
National Park was a battleground. Many of the groups were
known to be near it and had raided it in recent years.

What Aileen's notes didn't tell him about was the Democratic Republic of the Congo as a country.

He noticed the sun had risen. He looked at his watch. It was
eight in the morning. An hour and a half before boarding.

He gathered his papers and packed them into his shoulder
bag. The walk to 2E wasn't long, but he wanted to go via the
terminal bookshops and see if he could find a guidebook that
mentioned the Democratic Republic of the Congo.

There was only one, a thick volume entitled simply *Africa*. In
the thin chapter dedicated to the DRC, a section titled "How to
Get There" could be roughly summarised in much the same way
Aileen had summarised the Irish government's advice to its citizens: "Don't go". He also saw a copy of Conrad's *Heart of
Darkness*, though it was in French as *Le Coeur des Ténèbres*. He
didn't buy either book.

He found the gate his flight departed from, located a wall
socket, plugged his phone in to charge it, and googled the DRC.
After France, it was the most populous French-speaking country
in the world. The first thing he looked for was customs. How do
you greet people? Do you shake hands?

Ne tirez pas, je suis journaliste. Don't shoot, I am a journalist.
He muttered it under his breath like a prayer.

———

The Air France flight to Kinshasa departed more or less on time and was more or less full. Colm had an aisle seat in economy. For an eight-and-a-half-hour flight. Ten, if you included the hour and a half on the ground in Brazzaville. He was too young to have ever travelled business class for work, so he didn't miss it. But he'd heard enough stories of Aileen O'Connor escaping warzones in the luxury of a flying armchair and an all-inclusive flow of alcohol to imagine the difference.

Before the instruction to switch off all mobile devices came, he sent a text to Niamh.

Leaving France. The next time I set foot on the earth I will be in Africa.

Her reply was almost instantaneous. *Be safe.* And a heart emoji. He switched off his phone.

The seat next to him was taken by a younger man, early twenties, dressed sensibly for the heat of Kinshasa, though the weather app on Colm's phone had told him it was actually warmer in Paris than Kinshasa that morning. The man was reading a bible. If there was one type of person Colm found more boring than those who didn't go to church, it was those who did. Oh, god.

'Where are you headed?' the young man asked. English. Sounded like he was going to be cheerful. For ten hours. Double god.

'Garamba. Garamba National Park,' Colm said.

The person in the window seat was a woman, older. She reacted to the name, looking sharply at Colm, but then away, out of the window at Paris falling away beneath them.

'You're Irish?' the young man asked. Colm nodded. 'Is that near the airport? That place you're going?'

'Garamba. No, I have to take another plane, and then I'm getting a lift,' Colm said.

'I'm going to join a mission,' the young man said, without

being asked. Colm nodded, smiled a little. Settled back in his seat. Regretted not buying a book, any book. The young man kept talking. 'In a place called Dungu. I have to get another plane as well, but I might get a taxi. My dad says you're usually safer with taxis. My name is Jack. Jack Luckwood.' He offered his hand, easy from right to left. Colm shook it awkwardly, left to right.

'Colm. Colm Reid,' he said.

'Gollum?' Jack asked. Colm sighed.

'Colm,' he said. 'As in "column", like "Callum", but with an "o".'

'Sorry, very rude of me. Colm,' Jack tried again.

'Think nothing of it,' Colm said. In the absence of a book to hide in he closed his eyes. Something the young man had said was niggling him.

'Why are you going to... wherever you said you were going?' Jack said.

Colm considered pretending to be asleep, but it had only been a minute since he had last spoken, and he didn't think he would get away with it yet. He opened his eyes again.

'Garamba. I'm a journalist. I'm joining an expedition to look for rhinoceros.'

'That should be easy, shouldn't it? There must be loads of them in Africa,' the young man said. The woman on the other side of him shifted in her seat and looked at him.

'Not as many as you'd think,' Colm said.

'Well, I hope to see some. They told me Dungu is busy at the moment, at the hospital where I'll be working, that is. But I'm sure I'll have days off to see animals in the wild. I hope to see a hyena. I know most people want to see lions and elephants and rhinos, but I like hyenas. Their laugh is something wicked.'

'Are you a doctor?' Colm asked, for want of something to say.

'Not yet. Well, not really. Not at all. I'm just going to help teach the children.'

'Teach them what?'

Jack was about to open his mouth when he turned to his right, as if suddenly aware of the woman sitting next to him. Perhaps she had made a noise, but Colm hadn't heard it. The woman was staring at Jack without subtlety. Jack seemed to wilt a little in her gaze.

'Er, hello?' he said.

The woman was older than Colm, in her forties, he guessed. There was grey in her tight-curled hair, fire in her dark eyes, and very dark brown skin that contrasted dramatically with Jack's pasty pale hand on the armrest next to hers.

'You can't take a taxi,' the woman said. Her voice was rough, her accent Gallic.

'I'm sorry?' asked Jack.

'You can't take a taxi from N'Djili to Dungu,' she said.

'Where's, what did you say?' said Jack.

'N'Djili,' she repeated. 'The airport in Kinshasa.'

Colm was very conscious of the length of time it took Jack to respond. He could hear the rush of the recycled air from the vent above his head, the murmur of other passengers ahead and behind, the bright questions of the steward with the drinks trolley asking people what they wanted in French and then in English. Jack swallowed, as if suddenly shy.

'Why not?' he asked.

'They are three thousand kilometres apart. Paris and Moscow are closer together. They are in different time zones. But that is not the reason.'

'What is the reason?'

The woman held his gaze. Jack seemed to get smaller.

'Because Dungu is in the middle of a war zone,' she said. 'The hospital is busy because it is full of wounded. There will be no time to teach your bible. You'll be too busy staying alive.'

Colm watched Jack's face. The young man had no frame of reference, nothing that allowed him to process this information.

'A war zone?' he echoed. Then he blinked. 'I'm Jack. Jack Luckwood.' He offered the woman his hand, awkward, left to right. She hesitated a moment, then shook it gracefully.

'Odette Wemba,' she said. 'Doctor Odette Wemba.'

'What, a real doctor?' Jack asked, in evident awe.

'My PhDs are in Economics and Environmental Science,' she said. 'I am not a medical doctor. I work for the government.'

'War zone?' Jack said again, as if prompting a polite conversation.

'The northeast of the country, on the borders with Sudan and Uganda, is overrun with rebel groups. Many groups fighting for many different things. It is a very dangerous place. Volunteers are sometimes killed. You are very brave to be going there.'

Doctor Wemba's summary for Jack was so like Aileen O'Connor's that Colm momentarily wondered if they'd been briefed by the same person or read the same articles. Then he realised, no, they'd simply reached the same conclusion from the same data. He'd spent the night reading the same data, and he had reached that conclusion himself.

Doctor Wemba seemed content to leave it at that, sitting back in her seat and taking a copy of *The Economist* in French from the pouch in the seat back in front of her, opening it at the editorial, and starting to read.

Colm felt a chill down his spine. Not because he was flying into a war zone; that he knew already. It was because he thought he'd worked out what it was Jack had said that niggled him. It couldn't be... He reached under his seat for his shoulder bag and pulled it up onto his lap. He rummaged through the main compartment, taking out the neat A5 ring-binder in which he had filed his tickets. Dublin to Paris. Paris to Kinshasa. Kinshasa to... Dungu.

He looked at Jack, who was still staring at Doctor Wemba, perhaps trying to process the words "war zone".

There were bound to be plenty of flights three thousand kilometres across the DRC to an isolated town in the middle of a war zone, weren't there? But it was a false hope.

'What sort of journalism do you do?' said Jack.

Double god on a tandem, Colm thought.

CHAPTER FIVE

'IT'S QUITE ALRIGHT, REALLY,' COLM SAID, IN A TONE THAT would have told anyone with half a gram of self-awareness that it very definitely wasn't quite alright, and they'd be best leaving him alone for a while. Three years should do it.

'Please let me wash them when we get to the camp,' said Jack, stumbling out of the plane behind him.

Can't wash my shoes, Colm thought. He swapped his rucksack to his other hand and slung it over one shoulder. Jack had a smart yellow suitcase on wheels, completely useless on rough ground, and it bounced, and dragged off the slippery grass, almost tripping him more than once in the short walk from the plane's door to the shelter of its wing.

Dungu airport was a strip of grass cut out of the jungle. After fourteen hours flying and two stops for fuel, just as the twelve-seater plane made its final bank before coming into land, Jack had thrown up over Colm's trousers, bag, and shoes. Colm's dominant memory of his first steps in the mighty rainforest at the heart of the great continent of Africa would forever be the smell of vomit.

And water. He knew from his pre-flight google that the Congo was a huge river, the second largest by volume in the world after the Amazon. He knew it drained a basin four million square kilometres in area, which, as Aileen bloody O'Connor's notes had told him, was bigger than India, and eighty-five times the size of the whole island of Eire. But even so, he'd not been expecting this much water. The pilot had pointed out the land-marks on the descent, and the landmarks were mostly rivers. The airport was on the north bank of the Kibali River, which ran into the Dungu River, forming the Uele River, which in turn flowed into the Ubangi River, which eventually flowed into the Congo itself. And the Kibali was met by dozens of smaller channels and streams. And it was raining.

Which at least helped wash away some of the smell.

'I'm not going to your camp,' Colm reminded Jack.

'Oh. No, no, you're not,' Jack said, appearing crestfallen.

There'd been four other passengers. Three of them had already disappeared. The fourth was a tall woman with shoulder-length braided hair. She was dressed like a soldier, in dark fatigues and heavy boots. Colm had smiled at her once during one of the fuel stops but she had not smiled back. She had a duffel bag slung across her back and was waiting by the tail of the plane, seemingly oblivious to the rain.

Colm crouched under the shelter of the wing, his own bag on the ground between his legs, and looked around.

In every direction there were trees. A circling wall of dark green, towering above everything else. There were cries he didn't recognise. He guessed they were made by birds. Or perhaps monkeys. There was the occasional sharp ping of the plane's engine cooling, almost inaudible beneath the dominant noise – the rain. The rain drummed on the plane's body, on the ground, on the trees, on everything, as if it would never stop.

At one end of the strip was a shelter, a shed without walls, just a corrugated iron roof held up by wooden struts. The noise of the rain on the metal was thunderous. And halfway between the shed and the plane, a distance of perhaps three hundred metres, a giant walked towards them through the downpour.

'Colm Reid?' the giant boomed. He pronounced Colm's name correctly, but with an accent. Not French, though. Scandinavian.

'Kennet Haven?' Colm responded, leaving the shelter of the plane's wing and taking a few steps towards the approaching figure.

They met in the open and shook hands in the rain.

'Call me Ken,' Kennet said.

'Call me Colm,' Colm said.

Kennet looked past Colm at the woman by the plane's tail. She was walking towards them.

'Fatou Ba?' Kennet said.

She nodded. They shook hands. Colm and Fatou shook hands. The three stood in a triangle for a moment, as the rain beat down. Who was she? Was she a journalist? Sean had said there would be no other journalists.

Kennet was enormous. Two metres tall, or close to it. Colm wasn't short, but Kennet had more than twenty centimetres on him, and was at least twice his weight. Fatou was as tall as Colm.

'Very brave of you both to come,' Kennet said. 'Let me take your bags.'

He took Fatou's duffel from her shoulder and picked up Colm's bag from beneath the plane's wing. It didn't look much bigger than a purse in Kennet's huge hand. He passed Fatou's duffel into the same hand as Colm's bag, leaving his right free.

'He with you?' Kennet asked, looking back at Colm and nodding towards Jack who was standing close to the body of the plane, shrunken, as if trying to give the rain less to aim at.

'No, he's heading to some mission,' Colm said.

'Ah. There's a Jeep out front for you,' Kennet called to Jack, pointing in the direction of the shed. For a moment Jack just blinked at him. Then he walked over to the trio, his yellow suitcase bouncing and dragging awkwardly through the mud.

'Is he alright?' Kennet asked.

'A little travel sickness,' Colm said, more kindly than he felt.

'Ah. It will soon pass.' Kennet slapped Jack on the shoulder so heavily he nearly knocked the lad over. Jack turned even paler. 'Get going. You don't want to be outside for too long around here.'

'Hyena?' Jack said, almost hopefully.

'Soldiers,' Kennet said. 'Rebels. Many sightings near here this last month, the rangers tell me, impossible to know whose side they are on or what they want. Doesn't matter. They all shoot first, ask questions at your funeral. Which they don't hold.' Kennet laughed, as if the threat of death before rebel guns was no threat at all. He was so large Colm could almost imagine that was true.

Jack stared at Kennet. Then threw up again, onto his own suitcase this time.

———

A vehicle was waiting for them on the other side of the shed. A battered old Land Rover, door windows long gone, flatbed protected only by a tarpaulin stretched over four poles, three of metal and one of wood. The steering wheel was on the left-hand side of the cab. Colm had forgotten that most of the world drove on the right side of the road. There was a man behind the wheel, and another in the back. Both wore dark camouflage fatigues like the ones Fatou was wearing, except theirs were worn and repaired, heavily patched. The man in the back had a gun in his hands. Colm didn't really know guns, but he had seen enough movies to recognise an AK-47. He was, he learned later, wrong. It wasn't an AK-47. It was an AR-15.

'This is Hannington Banze,' Kennet said, gesturing to the driver. 'Deputy warden, veteran of Garamba, seven years in post, survivor of many a firefight, and recent recipient of a medal for bravery. It is our honour that he has taken time out of his busy day to greet you. And that is Kwame Ilunga, one of the Garamba rangers.'

'Good to meet you,' Colm said, extending his hand towards the windowless door. 'I'm Colm Reid. Please, call me Colm.'

'A pleasure to meet you, Colm,' Hannington said. Raindrops splashed from their handshake. 'Please call me Hannington.'

'*Bonjour*,' Fatou said. 'Fatou Ba. *Vous pouvez m'appeler* Fatou.' It was the first time Colm had heard her speak. Colm didn't have the most expert ear, but he guessed she was a native French-speaker.

'*Bienvenu, mademoiselle*,' Hannington replied, shaking her hand. '*Enchantée* Fatou.'

Kwame nodded to them, not taking his hands from his weapon.

Kennet tossed the bags in the flatbed and walked round to the other side of the cab.

'Get in out of the wet,' he laughed.

There was no getting out of the wet. If the rain hadn't already drenched Colm to the skin, which it had, the humidity would have soaked him from the inside out. He was sweating like a racehorse. All trace of Jack's vomit was gone, at least. A hundred metres away, Colm saw the young man climbing into a dirty white Jeep with a red and white logo, partially obscured by mud, on its door. He was dishevelled and soaked and looked thoroughly miserable.

Fatou climbed into the flatbed after the bags. Colm did the same, worrying that she'd made it look much easier than he had.

'Let me move that,' said Hannington, leaning behind him to pick up a second machine gun that lay on the bench seat Colm was about to sit on. Hannington tucked the gun on his other side against the door. Kennet got in the front next to him.

'First time in Congo?' Hannington asked. '*Premièr fois au Congo?*'

'First time in Africa,' Colm said.

'*Oui,*' said Fatou.

'What do you think?' Hannington said.

Colm thought. Most of what he'd seen so far was airports and airplanes. He'd spent the trip from Kinshasa staring out of the window at trees, rivers, and grasslands. He'd never seen so much green. Villages, towns, farms were like scars, but little ones, scratches from a bramble. Eighty-five times the size of Eire. Inconceivable.

'Weather's like Dublin,' he said. 'Glad I didn't come in the rainy season.'

Hannington laughed, a rich sound that Colm found warming. Hannington started the engine.

A packed-earth track led through the jungle for a hundred metres before joining a tarmacked road.

'This looks fresh!' Colm said, with more surprise than he'd meant to show. 'The road surface, I mean.'

'It is,' said Hannington. 'Has to be replaced every two or three years. Just washes away. Without it the park would be lost. The army needs the road.' Colm looked ahead along the tarmacked surface, and then behind them. The road was almost dead straight in both directions, disappearing into the trees as the land rose and fell.

'I heard there was some trouble here recently. Made the news,' Fatou said, speaking in English for the first time. Her voice was soft, though she was almost shouting over the noise of the engine and the rain.

'That would be two months ago. Twelve men killed in a fire-fight with Sudanese rebels. We lose men in fights with poachers regularly, but it only makes the international news when our dead are in double figures,' Hannington said, then fell silent. Colm looked at the gun propped on the other side of the ranger, then at Kwame beside him. Kwame was watching the road behind them, his eyes alive, his finger resting on the trigger guard.

The jungle they were driving through was immense. It was like a wall, forty metres tall, impenetrable to light before you'd gone four metres from the road. Huge trees from which grew other plants, vines, creepers, ferns. Colm had hoped to see animals and birds, but so far, he'd only heard them. It wasn't surprising. The vegetation was so thick they could be within spitting distance of an army, and they wouldn't know it.

Every few kilometres, Colm saw people walking along the side of the road, just off the tarmac. Women, rather. No men. Baskets or bundles on their heads, kept in place by a single hand, walking through the rain. They appeared to have come from nowhere, and Colm couldn't imagine where they were going. The rain kept falling.

'The main park station was destroyed in a battle some years ago. That's a little further, up in Faradje. It's been rebuilt now. That's where the main squad of rangers is based. We're heading for Nagero, not as close to the border, less risk from incursions,' Kennet said. 'About a hundred kilometres from Dungu. This road runs almost all the way there, so we'll make good time.'

Ahead of them Colm could make out a stall on the side of the road. He got a good look at it as they passed. A young woman sheltered beneath a large blue golf umbrella behind boxes of fruit – figs, dates, avocados, and possibly limes or oranges. The umbrella had been tied to a signpost. The sign read. "R420. Aba, 200km."

'What's Aba?' Colm asked.

'A town. Nearest sizeable one to the border with South Sudan,' Hannington replied. 'This road runs all the way there. It's also the southeast corner of Garamba.'

'Where is Garamba?'

'About thirty kilometres from here. Though we are going to Nagero. That is another fifty kilometres.'

Colm did some quick calculations in his head. 'The park is one hundred and seventy kilometres wide?'

Hannington shrugged. 'About that.'

Jaysus. It was more than half as wide as Ireland.

'How many rangers protect it?' Fatou asked.

'There are a hundred and eighteen of us now,' Hannington said, a hint of sadness in his voice.

They drove on.

Fatou had taken out a phone and was videoing the rainforest. Colm glanced at her, took her in. Her clothes, and her boots, especially her boots, weren't just unpatched, they were practically new. The fatigues bore the memory of creases in the sleeves and trousers, and the soles of the boots hardly wore a scratch.

Colm felt the vehicle slowing. Ahead the road was blocked. Piles of sacks either side of the tarmac, then white-painted planks on sawhorses across it. Armed men stood in front and behind, all looking at the approaching Land Rover. As roadblocks went, it was ineffective – they could have driven through the planks without accelerating. But Hannington had raised his hand in greeting and brought the vehicle to a stop two carlengths from the barrier.

One of the soldiers, a blue obelisk-shaped insignia of a single spear over crossed tusks underlined by yellow and red sewn to the shoulder of his uniform, stepped to the window and spoke to Hannington in rapid French. Colm caught the occasional word, but otherwise it was too fast for him to follow. The tone was friendly, though, and after no more than a minute the soldier waved towards some others and the planks were removed, allowing Hannington to ease the car through the roadblock and pick up speed once more.

'Is there a problem?' Kennet asked Hannington.

'Hopefully not. That's a long way from here,' Hannington replied. Kwame seemed to grip the barrel of his machine gun a little more tightly.

The forest began to retreat, the world to expand. The road ran through a wide area of grass and bushes. The forest suddenly almost half a kilometre from the road. Colm could see fallen trees, thick broken branches. Hannington slowed as the tarmacked surface was broken on the right side of the road and pulled over to the left to avoid it.

'What happened here?' Colm asked.

'Elephant,' Hannington replied. 'Some of them are moving south to avoid the dangers of the park. They make their own roads.'

They turned off the R420 after a hundred kilometres. By that time the trees had thinned further, giving way to grass, like the overgrown lawn at Colm's parents' house. Except here the grass was often taller than him.

Single-storey buildings were dotted here and there either side of the track. Some looked well-tended. Some looked abandoned. Some were burnt out.

They passed a sign. "Garamba National Park. World Heritage Site. Anti-Poaching Zone." It was rusting.

A hundred metres further on, the grass to the left of the track gave way to trees again, and a hundred and fifty metres after that forest rose in front of them once more. In those hundred and fifty metres nestled the ranger station. It was a compound surrounded by a three-metre wall of logs topped with razor wire. Trees had been cleared to form a space thirty metres around the wall. At the far corner of the compound was a

wooden lookout platform protected by log planks on two sides
and a sloping roof of leaves above. The whole thing put Colm in
mind of a prisoner of war camp in a film. Hannington drove
through a gate that was guarded by two men with machine guns.

'Welcome to Nagero station,' he said, stopping the Land
Rover next to three other vehicles, another Land Rover, a Toyota
Hilux, and a Jeep, all similar in age to the one they were in.

There was a single storey building in front of them. A
covered veranda ran all around it, or at least all around the two
sides Colm could see. On it, in a straight-backed chair, someone
was waiting. Colm could see a pair of feet, bare and dirty,
stretched out towards the rain, but the rest of the person was in
shadow.

Kennet opened the door, climbed out.

'*Jeg fant dem,*' he called.

The figure in the shadows stood up and walked along the
veranda towards them until Colm could see them.

It was a woman. She was wearing a short-sleeved khaki shirt
and khaki trousers. Her feet were bare, and her trousers rolled
halfway up her calves. She had dirty-blonde hair tied back in a
ponytail. Her skin was pale but for the right side of her face.

The right side of her face was a mess. The yellow of old
bruising clashed with the angry red of healing tissue. And there
was a grubby bandage on her right arm that stretched from wrist
to above the bottom of her shirt sleeve. Her face was neutral,
neither welcoming nor hostile.

'Jannika, this is Colm, from the *Irish Telegraph*, and this is
Fatou, from *Le Post Du Soir*, in Belgium. Colm, Fatou, this is my
sister, Jannika,' Kennet said before Colm and Fatou had got out
of the car.

As Colm dropped from the Land Rover it stopped raining.
Just like that, as if someone had turned off a tap. He was still
soaking wet, so it didn't make that much difference, except the

sudden absence of the noise was dramatic. For a split second he felt crushed by a silence such as he had never experienced, before the apparent absence of noise was replaced by the sound of the rain forest. The calls and cries and creaks had been there behind the rain all along but muted by the deafening fall of water. Now they were the dominant noise, and they were beautiful. Colm stopped to look around at the trees, none of which were closer to him than sixty metres, his mouth open, just listening.

'*Enchantée, mademoiselle* Haven,' Colm heard Fatou say. She was looking at the woman Kennet had introduced as his sister. The woman, Jannika, was staring back at Fatou.

Colm stepped towards the veranda and raised his hand in greeting.

'Call me Jane,' she said. Her expression did not change.

CHAPTER SIX

THE VERANDA ONLY RAN DOWN TWO SIDES OF THE MAIN building. Kennet, carrying Colm and Fatou's bags, led them to a long table with a view of the gate. The table was surrounded by stools made from slices of a tree trunk, roughly hacked by axes, but polished by use.

Hannington left them and went inside. Kwame crossed the packed earth, its surface still awash with rainwater, towards the men guarding the gate.

'I'll organise some refreshments,' Kennet said, dropping the bags on the table.

Jane hadn't followed them, and Colm suddenly found himself alone with Fatou. She was looking about her, taking photographs with her phone.

'My paper said this assignment was too expensive and too dangerous,' Colm said. Fatou nodded but didn't reply, stepping off the veranda and walking towards something that had taken her interest. Colm couldn't see what. He leaned against the table, his hands behind him. The tabletop was five centimetres thick and planed from a single piece of wood. It was very solid. More solid than he was used to wood being. Colm looked about him.

As well as the two on sentry at the gate, currently in conversation with Kwame, there were other rangers in the compound. Colm could hear men talking inside the building behind him, a mixture of French and another language he didn't know. Loud voices and laughter came from a series of low buildings along the perimeter fence. A lone man, a large, heavy-looking machine gun in his arms, crossed from one building to another. Colm could hear the *buk* of chickens and the *meh* of goats. He could smell the moisture in the air, feel it running down his skin. It was drier than it had been on the road, when the forest was no more than four metres away, but it was still hot and humid. Even the light was different, the sky more blue, colours at the same time brighter and more washed.

Colm was here. In Africa. In the Democratic Republic of Congo, the DRC. In Garamba National Park, World Heritage Site, Anti-Poaching Zone. This was it. This was his chance.

For the moment, he wasn't quite sure what to do with it.

Hannington returned with a tray loaded with drinks: a bottle with a label that read 'Primus', and several bottles of Coca Cola. Some things were the same wherever you went. Except these were all labelled "*Partagez un Coca Cola avec* Colette."

'Help yourselves,' he said, placing the tray on the table and taking the beer.

Fatou took a bottle. 'Who is Colette?' she asked. Hannington shrugged.

'We get what we can get,' he said.

'Do you have water?' Colm asked.

Hannington looked around at the muddy, rain-soaked ground, the buildings with water running from the roofs, dripping through the veranda, and laughed.

'I think I can find some,' he said.

———

A few minutes later they were sitting at the long table, Kennet, Colm, Fatou, Hannington, Kwame and one other man. Kennet stood up.

'Lady and gentlemen, I believe you all know each other except Tony here.' He gestured to the man Colm had not met yet. 'Tony Kanagi is the Chief Ranger at the conservancy I run in Kenya.' Tony nodded to Colm and Fatou. He had evidently met the others already. Kennet continued.

'I would like to thank Hannington and the rangers of Nagero for agreeing to my request to take us into the park and show us where the last northern white rhinos were seen in the wild, and for welcoming us to their station with the warmest hospitality. And I would like to thank our representatives from the press for taking the time and expense to join us on this journey. I am very excited about the possibility of finding rhinos in the wild here.'

Very formal, the start of business.

'There are no rhinos,' Hannington said. 'I told you this before you came here, my friend. I told you again when you arrived. I told you again this morning when we drove to pick up our friends here. It is the saddest truth that weighs on my heart, but the rhino are gone. Now we must worry about elephant and giraffe.'

'Come now,' Kennet said. 'It is a very big park. How can you be sure?'

'One moment, please,' Hannington said. 'Fetch the map, Kwame.'

Kwame entered the building and emerged a moment later with a piece of board about a metre square with a map of the park pinned to it. It was covered with different coloured pins and had pieces of paper tucked around the edges. The papers had writing on them. To the southeast, one read "LRA", to the northwest "pastoralists", to the northeast "South Sudanese", to the southwest *"bâtards avides"*. Colm had a vague memory from his schoolboy French that *"avide"* meant "greedy". His schooling hadn't included the word *bâtard*, but he could guess.

'What are they?' Colm asked.

'Those are some of the armed groups that keep turning up in the park,' Hannington. replied.

'Bâtards avides?' said Fatou.

'Poachers in it for the profit,' Hannington explained.

'No, the pins,' Colm said.

'Those are poaching,' Kwame struggled for the right word, 'incidents. Blue pin, an animal died, we didn't catch anyone. Yellow pin, an animal died, but we caught the men who did it. Green pin, we caught the poachers before they killed anything. Red pin, rangers died.' Colm counted the pins of different colours. There were fewer green than blue or yellow. And many red.

Double god.

'What is there?' Fatou pointed, circling a group of pins with her finger. She was right. About half the pins on the board were in that group. Colm looked a little closer. Most of the yellow and blue pins were clustered around a line, with more south than north of it. Above that cluster most of the pins were green and red.

'The animals are mostly in the south of the park, around the Garamba River, here.' Hannington traced the line on the map. 'There are far fewer animals left north of the river. The rhino used to live here,' Hannington went on, touching the map even further south than the river, 'but not any more.'

'Tony is a tracker,' Kennet said. 'If there are rhino still in the park, he will find them.' Tony was frowning as Kennet spoke.

'I appreciate your faith in me, Mr Haven, but if there are

rhino still in the park the Garamba rangers would already know,' said Tony, with a nod to Hannington.

'It's a very big park,' said Kennet again.

Tony shook his head, but before he could speak Hannington interrupted, an edge to his voice.

'You must listen to me. There are no rhino in the park,' Hannington said. 'No longer. When I was young, my first year, two people, a South African man and his British wife, lived in the middle of the park here.' He tapped close to the centre of the map with his finger. 'They looked after the rhino, nursed them, helped them when they were sick, for nearly twenty years. The rhino had been almost wiped out more than forty years ago, and this man and this woman brought them back until there were more than thirty animals.

'But then in 2003 there were peace talks in Sudan. It sent the poachers into a frenzy. That year men on horses killed half the rhino in the park and took their horns. Most of the rest of the rhino were killed the year after. Only five were left when the fighting started up again in 2005 and the conservation efforts ended. The last time anyone saw a northern white rhino in the wild in Africa was ten years ago, from a helicopter, and that was not in the park. These are big animals; they leave wide trails. They weigh two tonnes. The ground is soft. They leave deep footprints. The males mark their territory with great dung heaps. If there were any rhino in the park, we could possibly miss them for a month, maybe three, perhaps at the extreme, a season, but no longer than that. We have not seen them in more than ten years.'

Colm felt the weight of finality in Hannington's last sentence.

'It's a big park,' Kennet repeated, but with less conviction this time.

'It is. Over five thousand square kilometres,' Hannington said.

Double god, bigger than Donegal.

Everyone was silent around the table. Water dripped somewhere. Fatou was the first to speak.

'Why are we here? What is the story?'

'It is Mr Haven's story, but this is our part in it. Tomorrow we will go to where the rhino were last seen in the park,' Hannington said. 'You will see what is still here, and we can tell you what was here before. We will leave early; we will drive as far as we can, and then we will go on foot. We will be at least one night in the park, perhaps more, depending on the rain. That is the story Mr Haven wanted to tell. That is the only story there is to tell. This is where they were.' He tapped the map.

'Depending on the rain?' Colm asked.

'Too much rain and we may have to travel many kilometres out of our way to find safe crossings of the bigger rivers and the angrier streams. It can add days to a safe journey,' Hannington said.

No one else spoke. Colm heard the tick of a clock in his head. His life had been conditioned by too many films. At the same time, he felt as though he was being watched. He looked over his shoulder.

From the corner of the building Jane Haven was watching them. Watching Kennet. Colm couldn't read her expression.

'Now,' Hannington said, 'Kwame, would you be so kind as to show our two guests from the press around our home? Tell them our stories. Ask them what their readers are doing to prevent extinction.'

Kwame nodded and stood up.

'Please,' he said, gesturing for Colm and Fatou to follow him.

CHAPTER SEVEN

Kwame led them across the compound to the gates, where he greeted the guards and carried on out into the park. Once past the fence he turned left, in the opposite direction to the one they had arrived from and walked for a hundred metres along a packed earth trail, created by vehicle tyres. The track ran beside the compound's wooden fence and then turned nearly ninety degrees, heading roughly northeast until it disappeared into the undulations of the earth. Kwame stopped where the track turned.

'We are here at the start of Garamba. That way,' Kwame held his arms out at ninety degrees to each other, his left pointing northwest, and his right northeast, 'is mostly grassland and savannah until the border with South Sudan. The rhino lived that way, maybe sixty kilometre into the park. Too close to the border, too far from us.' He rotated his body ninety degrees, his left arm now pointing northeast, his right southeast. 'That way is mostly forest for a hundred kilometres. The border of the park, and of the country, is in the forest sixty, sixty-five kilometre that way.'

Colm looked. Fatou took photographs with her phone.

The forest intimidated Colm. It was still the source of noise. Birds, monkeys, possibly other things he couldn't even imagine. He had the feeling that things – creatures, perhaps even men – were hiding in the trees, waiting for him to step into them, to get lost, to fall within their power. But the grasslands looked equally menacing. The grass was waist high, more than capable of concealing plenty of dangers. A breeze ran across the surface of the great grass sea sending ripples through its blades, ripples that were only interrupted by the gash across the surface left by the track.

The track. The track made by the wheels of vehicles. Man-made vehicles. The track was the only thing he could see, standing with his back to the ranger station, that was evidence of man. He had grown up in towns and cities, where it was unusual to see things that weren't evidence of man. Even growing things were contained and maintained. Here was the opposite. Even where the wheel-ruts were deepest, Colm could see grass-shoots. If the track wasn't driven every day, it would be consumed by growing things in no time at all.

He looked more closely at the grass between the track and the forest. It looked different from the grass on the other side of the track. More tended, less wild, for two or three hundred metres. The more tended strip was no more than fifteen metres wide.

'Is that a runway?' he asked.

Kwame looked at where Colm was pointing.

'Yes. We clear it when needed. It used to be used for aerial surveys of the wildlife populations, but since 2010 they have mostly used army helicopters for the surveys. For safety.'

Fatou had walked into the grass and was staring out into the park. She was looking at something moving toward the horizon.

Colm followed the direction of her gaze. It looked to be a herd of cows. Big cows. With horns.

'Buffalo,' Kwame said, following her gaze.

Colm took out his phone and took his first photo, of Fatou's back as she stared across the grasslands at the crowd of black specks in the distance.

'We will see them more closely tomorrow. Come, I will show you the station,' Kwame said, and turned back to the gate. Fatou watched for a minute more, and then turned and followed him. Colm took one last look across the grass that stretched to the hills on the horizon, before doing the same.

'How many rangers are based here?' Colm said, stepping quickly to avoid a chicken running across his path. Fatou took a picture of the bird.

The compound was about ninety metres by eighty, with bunk houses, goats, chickens, a water pump, a kerosene-fuelled generator, and a heap of solar panels that hadn't yet been installed.

'A donation,' Kwame had said, pointing at the solar panels. 'We don't know how they work.'

'I can take a look if you like,' Colm had said.

'Are you an engineer?'

'Self-appointed DIY failure,' Colm said, with a smile.

'D-I-Y?'

'Do It Yourself. Tell me about something no one nearby understands, and I have to have a go. Until I reach the edges of my own incompetence, break something, and have to look at the manual. Then I call an expert. My wife thinks I'm an eejit.'

'What's an eejit?' Fatou said.

'Sorry, an idiot.'

Kwame grinned.

'I knew a man like that once,' he said. 'A very nice man. A dear friend.'

'You knew him? What happened to him?'

'He thought he could work out how to disarm a grenade by pushing a twig into the hole where the pin used to be.'

'And he couldn't?'

'No, he couldn't, but he was crouching over it and still trying when it went off. His body absorbed the blast. He saved the lives of four people. I take food to his family.'

A silence had followed this. Colm eventually broke it, keeping his voice soft.

'How many rangers are based here?'

'There are twenty-three of us. Three eight-man shifts, or two twelve-man shifts when we have a patrol in the park, like now. Then the deputy warden. And me.'

'That's twenty-six, not twenty-three,' said Fatou.

'Last month there were ivory poachers. They were well-armed. They killed six elephant and three men.' Facts. Kwame said these things as simple facts. Colm paused to write this in his notebook. Kwame kept walking, pushing open a gate into another part of the compound. This gate was reinforced with heavy wood, thicker even than the main gate. The padlock was on the inside and boxed in metal. Colm followed him. Fatou photographed the gate and then followed Colm.

'Hannington said twelve rangers were killed two months ago,' Colm said, hoping he didn't sound like he was questioning the veracity of Hannington's statement.

'At another station. We have been lucky. No one has attacked Nagero for many years. They have to cross the park to get to us, and their reach has grown smaller as the army patrols have increased. Our danger is in the park, when we patrol.'

'Who are "they"?' Fatou asked.

'Whoever. Groups of men. From DRC, from Uganda, from Rwanda, from Sudan. They disagree with someone, they get hold of some weapons, they run into the jungle where no one can find them. They need money, they attack the mines, they attack the villages, they attack the animals. I see lion take down buffalo. I see buffalo drive off lion. They need to survive. I see men, they need to survive too. But men don't stop. Men don't just take enough to survive. Men take everything.' Kwame shook his head. He looked at the ring of keys he was holding.

'Why do you do it?' Colm asked.

'Do what?'

'Be a ranger, when half the world is out to kill the animals you protect and will kill you when you try and protect them.'

Kwame selected one of the keys on the ring in his hand and unlocked a padlock on the door of a shed. Stepped inside. Kept talking.

'Half the world is not out to kill me or the animals. Just a few men, a minority, whose lives are different from mine, though we were born the same,' Kwame said.

The room Kwame had entered was the armoury. Guns arranged down both sides, one type down one side, one type down the other. There were many. Behind him, Colm heard Fatou gasp.

'Tell me what I'm looking at. I'm not an expert in guns, despite the accent,' said Colm.

Kwame turned to him. 'What do you mean?' he asked.

Colm stared. Realised he might be the first Irishman Kwame had met.

'I am sorry. I am used to... I am from Northern Ireland. There was a stereotype. A prejudice. I wear it sometimes. We had a civil war. Colonial.'

'We've had a few of those,' said Kwame, turning away. 'To the left, mostly AR-15s. Donated. And the AK-47s. Confiscated. They kill people. To the right, the elephant guns. They can kill elephant. Confiscated.'

There were about thirty AR-15s. They were all the same. A similar number of AK-47s. The elephant guns came in a variety of sizes and shapes. Colm counted quickly. There were at least a hundred. Some looked high-tech and practically brand new. Some looked like museum pieces. Fatou's phone clicked as she photographed everything. Colm wondered if she knew she could turn the click sound off.

Kwame led the way out of the armoury, locking the padlock behind Colm. His heavy boots thumped the packed earth of the ground. Ground that had been slick with mud only a few hours earlier and was now barely damp. Colm continued to make notes.

'Why do you do it?' Colm asked again.

Kwame stopped walking. They had reached another wooden structure within the inner compound. This was made of logs, logs halved and layered. It was rugged, tough. Colm imagined it could withstand a hand grenade or two. Kwame had the keys to its padlock in his hand. He turned. Looked Colm in the eye.

'To protect and provide, my friend. I have a family. A wife, a daughter, a son. My daughter will be a ranger. My son will be a reader, a thinker. I provide for them. I am paid to protect. But I have to protect. If I don't protect the animals of Garamba, who would protect my family?'

Colm scribbled, furiously, but neatly. Great stuff.

'You say your daughter will be a ranger. Are there women rangers?' Fatou said.

'There are many women rangers, in South Africa, Zimbabwe, Malawi, Tanzania. But not here, not out here. Women don't do so well out here, in uniform. Too many...' Kwame's voice trailed off.

'How old is your daughter?'

'She is six years old.'

'What's her name?'

'Lucia,' Kwame said, keys still in his hand, a few centimetres from the lock.

Colm returned his gaze.

'That means light, doesn't it?'

'It does. And light brings hope,' Kwame said with a smile. He turned and unlocked the door. Colm scribbled.

'We store these here until the government can take them away and burn them,' he said, flicking a light switch that looked as if it had come from the 1920s. The bulb overhead was less bright than the remains of the daylight that poked through gaps in the log walls.

The room was a cube, two metres by two metres by two metres. And it was filled with elephant tusks.

'On the black market the ivory in this room is worth fifteen point six million dollars,' Kwame said. 'We killed thirty-seven men taking it back. We lost three men and twenty-six elephant. Fifty years ago, there were twenty thousand elephant in the park. Now there are less than fifteen hundred. Without a miracle, the rest will all be dead before the end of my life, unless my life is short.'

Colm gulped. Stepped into the room. Squatted. Reached his hand out. Touched a tusk. Breathed. Breathed.

'Like the rhino,' he said.

'Like the rhino,' Kwame said.

Colm put his hands round one of the tusks. It was thick, his hands unable to reach all the way around it.

'How heavy are these things?' he asked.

Kwame shrugged.

'The big ones, twenty, twenty-five kilo,' he said.

Colm ran his hand down the ivory. He noticed something near the bottom of the tusk and bent to examine it. It was a mark cut into the ivory with a knife and then coloured in with charcoal. 2407.

'What's that?' he asked.

'Catalogue number. Every item is catalogued. So we know if they go missing.'

'Does that happen?'

'Not since we started cataloguing.'

Colm stood up. Looked at the hut. Fatou was turning as she captured the tusks in a single panoramic shot. For the second time Colm took his own phone from his pocket and took a photo. He put the phone away and squatted again, returning his hand to the nearest tusk. Elephants. Twenty-six elephants. Killed for their teeth. He looked up at Fatou. Her eyes were glistening. She was making notes on her phone, her thumbs tapping the screen.

Kwame gave them a few minutes, then ushered them out, locking the door behind them.

'You should keep those switched off,' Kwame said, motioning to their phones. 'The only place to charge them is here when the generator is running, which is usually only in the evening for the lights and to charge the radios. And keep them in plastic bags so they don't get wet. Otherwise, they will get wet.'

Colm nodded. Fatou looked startled, as if the possibility of not being able to charge her phone when she needed to hadn't occurred to her.

'Let me take a look at those solar panels,' Colm said.

Kwame smiled.

CHAPTER EIGHT

'WHY ARE YOU DOING THAT?'

Colm looked up. He was sitting cross-legged on the ground by the short side of the veranda of the main building, close to where Jane Haven had been sitting when they had arrived. It was Jane Haven who had spoken. She was standing over him at the top of the step with the sun behind her. She carried two long guns, one strapped over each shoulder, their barrels crossing behind her head. A bird, broad wings, short tail, hooked beak, flew overhead between her and the sun. To Colm, there was a moment in which she and the bird were a single silhouette. Then he blinked, his eyes watering at the strength of the light. The bird flew on, Jane took another step, and the image was gone.

Jane was also carrying a four-litre water bottle. The top had been cut off roughly to turn it into a small bucket. It contained a number of metal objects that Colm realised were related to the guns. Ammunition clips, a silencer – was that the right word? Or was it a suppressor? Or were the movies wrong about both? A long-distance telescopic sight. Or was that called a scope? And a bottle of what looked like oil.

'Doing what?' he said, looking down at his hands, which held an old screwdriver and a length of wire.

'That?'

'Trying to get them working,' he said, nodding at the solar panels laid out against the wall of the compound. A chicken had laid an egg on one, and the raindrops were splashing off all of them.

'Not like that, you won't,' she said.

She put down the container and slipped the two rifles from her shoulders with swift shrugs, laying them on the veranda's wooden boards. She stepped down and walked to him. She took the screwdriver from his hand. She picked up the power inverter, scowling at it, the healing side of her face blushing red as she did so.

Colm looked at the two guns lying on the veranda. They were different from the ones in the armoury, at least to his untutored eye. They looked... clean. The rain huddled together in drops on the metal. They were freshly oiled.

'What are you doing with the guns?' he asked.

'Deputy Banze asked me to clean them,' Jane said, without looking at him. She was lining up the power inverter and tracing the cables back to the panels. It took Colm a moment to remember that Deputy Banze was Hannington.

'What do you do?' Colm asked. 'For a living,' he clarified when she didn't answer straight away.

Jane was concentrating on the component in her hands. Without giving any indication she was paying him the slightest attention, she said 'I'm a teacher.'

———

The evening meal was served at the long table that filled most of the veranda down the front of the main building.

Hannington, his guests and most of the rangers in the station ate together. The food was brought out by women and children, some families of the men, many from the houses scattered around the station, outside the wall. The men were introduced in rapid succession, so Colm only managed to catch half the names, and of those he did catch he knew he wouldn't remember which name went with which face. It always took him five or six meetings to fix a name to a face.

The conversation was jovial, light. Occasionally the great boom of Kennet's laugh echoed around the compound away over the fence.

The food was served on metal plates varying in age from not too old to ancient. The one Colm was given had a dent in it that looked suspiciously like the work of a bullet. He didn't think about it for long, though, as the food was delicious. Goat. He had spent an afternoon on an island in the Caribbean once, a stop on a cruise with his parents that his mother had won in a competition or something. He remembered the afternoon on that island for two reasons. One was because, despite it being cloudy, he had been horribly sunburned; the other was because of a goat curry they were served. It had been heavenly. The Garamba dish was more of a stew than a curry, and it was even better.

The other portion on the plate he didn't recognise. It looked like cabbage but tasted nothing like cabbage. There was a metallic hint, reminiscent of spinach, and a smoky taste, and a suggestion of fish.

'What is this?' he asked, holding up a forkful.

'Pondu,' Kwame said. 'Cassava leaves.'

'Um. Good.' Colm ate the forkful, dropping some down his chin, though he didn't know what cassava was. He made a mental note to look it up.

After they had eaten and the dishes had been cleared away,

most of the rangers, including Kwame and Tony, disappeared to their bunks or, if they were local, to their own homes. Hannington, Kennet, Jane, Fatou, and Colm remained. Hannington produced a chessboard, laid it on a slice of tree trunk, and began to set up the pieces. Colm drank from a bottle of water. He'd never been anywhere so humid. He was struggling to remain hydrated.

Kennet was looking in the direction of the park, though the wall blocked his view. He had a beer in his hand, and he seemed lost in thought.

'I have never seen a rhino,' Fatou said to no one in particular. Colm looked at her but said nothing.

'They were beautiful,' Hannington said. 'Funny, greedy, sometimes bad-tempered, usually gentle. They were such surprising creatures. They get sunburn, that's why they bathe in mud, to protect their skin. The mud is sunblock. They are gone and it is a terrible loss.' He stopped talking for a moment and blinked. Fatou was watching him with rapt attention. Hannington shook his head.

'But we cannot change what has already been done. We can only change what has not yet been done. Tomorrow, as well as taking you to where the rhino once were, I shall take you to see some of the animals that are still here,' he said. He resumed setting up the chess pieces.

Suddenly, from beyond the walls of the compound, came a sound that made Colm freeze. It was a repeated roar that was constantly cut short. It was much louder than the insects and the birds. Colm saw Fatou tense. He felt his skin prickle.

'Is that a lion?' he said, standing quickly.

Hannington smiled. 'A monkey.'

Colm didn't relax, not immediately. The sound had unnerved him. He did not know this place.

'Wow,' said Colm.

He was standing on the ranger station veranda, bottle of water in hand. Two of Hannington's rangers had just closed up the compound, shutting the gates and threading a thick chain through the logs, which they secured with two heavy padlocks. Then the sun had gone out.

It was spectacular. One minute it had been day, the next minute it was not.

'Why did you say that?' Hannington asked. The chess board lay ready on its slice of tree stump. The board was made from a single piece of dark wood, the white squares painted on with a thick, chalky paint. The pieces were hand-carved from two different woods by many different hands, or one very inexperienced one.

'The sun set so fast.'

Hannington looked up and shrugged. 'That is how fast the sun sets,' he said.

'Where I am from it takes a lot longer,' Colm said.

Hannington looked at him. 'I can't imagine that,' he said. Then he motioned towards the board. 'Do you play?'

'Badly,' Colm said, still staring at the place where the sun now wasn't. The remaining light came from a weak bulb hanging naked from the underside of the veranda's roof. Colm moved the stool he was sitting on to be opposite the ranger. It took a lot of effort. The stools were heavy. He looked up at the bulb.

'You might get some more reliable electricity tomorrow.'

'You have done well, my friend.' Hannington looked out to the far side of the compound where the sixteen solar panels were sitting in the dark, angled towards the east, awaiting the morning sun.

'I think they were charging,' Colm said, 'It wasn't me, not really. It was Jane.'

Hannington nodded, lifting the chess board, tree stump and all, and placing it directly under the light bulb. The light cast faint shadows of the pieces, each one different.

'She's a strange one,' Colm said, quietly, looking towards the end of the veranda where he had last seen her sitting. 'Do you know how she was injured?' He raised his hand to the same side of his face as Jane's bruising and healing wounds.

Hannington looked up.

'I asked her that,' he said.

'What did she say?'

'Accident at work.'

Colm blinked. 'She said she is a teacher.'

'In my experience, schools can be dangerous,' Hannington said, with surprising solemnity. He waved his hand at the stump Colm had moved to the other side of the board. Colm smiled and sat down.

Hannington took a white pawn, concealed it within one hand, put both hands behind his back, and brought them in front of him again, fists tight.

'Black, or white?' Hannington said, grinning, his teeth brilliant in contrast to his skin.

Colm laughed and tapped Hannington's left hand. It was empty.

'You are black, my friend,' Hannington said, and made the opening move.

Colm made an answering move, sitting under the bare electric bulb surrounded by the sounds of insects and raindrops.

CHAPTER NINE

'AGAIN, I MUST SAY CHECKMATE,' HANNINGTON SAID, offering his hand.

Colm shrugged and shook it. 'Best out of seven?'

'Another night, my friend. Tomorrow we are heading early into the park. You will not sleep well, so best to start trying soon. Kwame, please show Colm and Fatou to the luxury suite.'

Fatou was sitting at the table staring into the night and the rain.

Kwame came over with a torch.

'The luxury suite is this way,' he said, a smile in his voice, pointing his torch across the compound beyond the solar panels. The torchlight bounced off too many raindrops to show what he was pointing it at. He stepped into the rain and set off at a run.

Colm followed, hearing Fatou behind him.

'Suite? As in a living room and a bathroom and one bedroom? For the both of us?' Colm said.

'We are not together,' Fatou said. Kwame didn't seem to hear.

Kwame's torchlight flashed off the solar panels and then moved on. Colm had to remember where they were to avoid walking into them. The torch beam was erratic. After another few steps, the beam flickered across the outline of a hut. Kwame went straight for the door and pushed it open. Colm and Fatou followed him.

Colm realised the beam was erratic because Kwame was laughing.

'Living room and bathroom! No, my friends. This is the luxury suite because the mosquito nets don't have holes.' Kwame used the light of his torch to switch on a storm lantern. It was brighter than either the torch or the bulb on the veranda.

The room it revealed had four low beds with mosquito nets hanging from rods about a metre and a half above them. Colm's bag was on the floor next to one bed, Fatou's next to another opposite it. Against one wall was a trolley with what looked like cutlery on it. Next to the trolley was a glass-fronted cupboard, bottles and cartons on its shelves. On the top of the cupboard there was a cardboard box with a red symbol on a white background stuck to it. Colm recognised it. The symbol of *Médecins Sans Frontières*. Doctors without borders. Not cutlery. Surgical implements.

'This is the hospital?' Colm asked.

'The luxury suite!' Kwame said, looking like he was about to start laughing again.

Kwame explained where the sinks and latrines were, then left them to it.

Fatou ignored Colm and dug into her duffel, pulling out a washbag.

'I'm going to wash. I'll take this,' she picked up the storm lantern. 'When I come back, you go.'

Colm nodded. Fatou and the storm lantern, the only light, disappeared into the rain.

Colm sat in the dark. The rain pounded on the roof. There was no light at all. He held his hand in front of his face but could not see it. A cliché made real. It was possibly the first time in his life he had been in a place this dark.

The noise and the dark were hypnotic. Sensory deprivation, that's what it was called. People paid money to lie in tanks where they could see nothing and hear nothing but white noise. Here he got it for free, sort of. And he was melting hot and sitting on the edge of a bed so low it was like a child's.

Like a child's.

He hadn't thought about Niamh and their child since he'd got off the last plane. Niamh's face filled his mind. She was smiling.

'You always know the right thing to say to me,' she had said to him, more than once. Which was bollix. He managed to say the right thing to her perhaps one time out of three. But she always heard what he meant, not what he said, even if he hadn't worked out what he meant himself.

'Go,' she had said.

Sean had said 'Call her,' so Colm had called her.

'Hi, sorry, I'm at work, they've offered me a trip to Africa, to the Congo, to look for a species of rhino that's probably extinct. I'd be away for a week at least, I think, and—'

'Go,' she had said. Just like that. In that one word the tone of her voice was so full of excitement. For him, for his opportunity. Not for them, or for their child. In her voice he heard how excited she was for him. In that tone he heard telling him that she would look after herself and their child until he got back, that was a given, that he was not to worry, 'Go.'

He felt so full of love for her his eyes filled with tears. His best friend.

'All yours,' the sound of Fatou's voice hit him at the same time as the sound of the opening door and the light from the storm lantern. He was blinded by the light and shaken by the sound. Niamh's face flashed in his mind as the lantern's light flashed in his eyes, then he squirreled away his thoughts of her to revisit later.

He took the lantern from Fatou. He used the light to find his washbag. Unthinking, he stepped out into the rain.

He ran to the building Kwame had told them had the sinks and the latrines. He relieved himself, though he figured he'd sweated out most of his excess moisture as his piss was but a trickle. He wet his flannel and washed his face, his armpits, his chest. Within a second of each wipe new sweat oozed out. He cleaned his teeth. He picked up the lantern and ran back.

All was quiet in the hospital hut. The light from the lantern showed Fatou as a bulge under a mosquito net. He took off his shoes, peeled off his soaking trousers, hanging them over the end of one of the unused beds in the vain hope that they would dry, and wormed his way under the mosquito net on his bed. He reached out, switched off the lantern, and then fumbled the net into place by feel.

The rain thundered on.

He lay there. He turned his head towards Fatou whose bed was on the other side of the room. It was totally dark. He could see nothing of the bed, let alone her.

'Fatou?' he said.

There was no reply.

He lay there. The rain thundered on.

After a few minutes he remembered Hannington's words. 'You will not sleep well.' The rain was so loud. He was used to rain, but not like this. The rain itself was heavier than anything he could remember, and he was in a log hut with a corrugated iron roof. Hannington's prediction felt like a certainty.

But there was a rhythm to the rain. As he listened, it seemed to get quieter. Not because it was falling less fiercely, but because it was becoming normal. He was getting used to it. And the dark was so dark that even with his eyes wide open he could see nothing at all. He closed his eyes and felt the rhythm of the rain fill him. The heat and humidity were intense, but the lack of light, and the beating of the rain were calming. He felt himself starting to drift.

'What did you do wrong?'

For a moment he thought he had fallen asleep, that he was dreaming. Then he realised it was Fatou's voice, from across the hut.

'Sorry?' he said.

'To be sent on this assignment. What did you do wrong?'

It took him a moment to understand what she had said.

'I- nothing. This is an opportunity for me.'

She didn't respond.

He waited, found himself counting in his head. One, two, three... sixty-one, sixty-two... When he reached a hundred and eighty-one, he stopped.

'What did you do wrong?' he asked. She didn't reply.

The rain pounded on.

———

Colm awoke from the deepest sleep he could remember. He felt like he had been asleep for hours. But it was still completely dark. He'd been woken by a sound, but he couldn't remember what it was. Then it came again.

It was a horn. A vehicle horn. Someone was pressing on it. Paaaaarp. An old vehicle. It sounded a long way off, but it was competing with the rain, which was still very loud. He sat up.

'Did you hear that?' Fatou's voice came out of the dark.

'Yes,' he said.

He heard her moving.

'What are you doing?'

'Going to see what it was.'

Colm shook his head. He fumbled with the mosquito net and managed to open it. He found the storm lantern and switched it on.

Fatou was sat on the side of her bed lacing up her boots. Colm stumbled out of his bed and found his trousers, which were still as wet as they had been when he'd laid them out to dry. He put them on, then his shoes. Fatou had already picked up the lantern. She had a notebook in one hand which she was trying to tuck into a pocket. He turned back to get his, fumbling for it in his bag in the dark after Fatou had left the hut. He found it, and a pen, and followed her.

Over by the gate men with torches were moving frantically. Colm saw Hannington, heard him barking instructions, though he couldn't hear the words over the rain. The chain was removed, and four rangers pulled the gates open. A Land Rover rolled through.

Fatou ran to the veranda of the main building, and Colm followed, splashing through puddles, keeping his notebook dry by leaning forward and shielding it with his chest. Fatou had stopped under the veranda and was watching the commotion at the gate. Colm stopped beside her.

The gates shut behind the Land Rover, which drove surprisingly quickly towards and past them, stopping close to the solar panels. Only one headlight was working. Men Colm hadn't seen before ran through the rain to the vehicle. Two of them ran away from it again, to the hut Colm and Fatou had been sleeping in. They disappeared inside, re-emerging a minute later with a flat thing carried between them. Colm realised the flat thing was in fact two things. Two stretchers.

CHAPTER TEN

Colm and Fatou watched through the rain and the shadows, by the light of a headlight and wildly moving torches. Two men were pulled out of the Land Rover, lain on the stretchers, and carried into the medical hut.

Other men were running through the rain between other huts. Hannington left the guards at the gate and strode towards Colm and Fatou, passing them with a nod, his face serious. Colm was struck by how young he looked. He had not noticed it before. Though Colm had noticed recently that an increasing proportion of the people he met looked surprisingly young.

'What's happened?' Colm said.

'Two of my men were shot by poachers,' Hannington said without looking back or slowing his pace.

The activity in the compound intensified. Colm realised the rangers were preparing to send out another vehicle. Guns and ammunition were being loaded into the Land Rover Hannington had used to pick Colm and Fatou up from the airport in Dungu. Eventually eight men climbed in – two in the front, six in the back – and the vehicle started to move. The gates were unchained and opened, and the Land Rover disappeared through them into the park. The gates were closed and locked behind it.

Colm felt his skin tighten, a feeling, as if part of him had sensed someone were close. He looked behind him. Jane Haven was standing half in shadow, only a few centimetres away. She had must have watched the patrol leave. Her eyes were moving, as if she were watching everything that was happening in different places simultaneously. Fatou noticed Colm turn and turned too.

'Do you know what happened?' Fatou said to Jane. Jane shrugged.

'The patrol found tracks. Followed them and walked into an ambush. There was a firefight, and they got away with two wounded. They were lucky.'

'How many men attacked them?' Fatou was taking notes.

'They didn't see. At least five.'

'How long ago?' Colm said.

'Early afternoon. They were on foot a long way from their vehicle.'

'Who told you all of this?' Fatou asked.

'No one. I listened to Deputy Banze report it on the radio.'

'How badly are the men hurt?'

'One will be taken to the hospital at Dungu in the morning. The other is less serious. They will treat him here.'

'And why did the other car leave?'

'Three men from the first patrol are still out there, tracking the poachers. The second patrol went to find them and bring them home.'

Jane turned and stepped into the building.

'Where are you going?' Colm said.

'To get some more sleep.' Her voice came out of the darkness, eerily loud.

Colm realised that, at some point in the last minute, it had stopped raining again.

———

Colm woke to find what sounded like the loudest bird in the world calling in his head, though he soon realised it was actually somewhere outside the hut. Its cry went straight through him, vibrating his bladder with an urgency that made him need the latrine. He jumped off the bed and entangled himself in the mosquito net he had forgotten was there.

As he disentangled himself, he realised the net wasn't the only thing he had forgotten. The hut had several windows he hadn't noticed in the dark. Daylight was now falling through them, showing the other three beds, all occupied. On the other side of the hut there was no movement from Fatou and one of the two men who had been brought in during the night. But the man in the bed next to his was awake and staring at him.

'Who are you?' the man asked.

Colm, slightly conscious he wasn't wearing his trousers, hopped out of the net and tried to offer his hand to shake, almost over-balancing.

'Colm Reid, Irish Telegraph,' he said.

'Agoyo. Garamba ranger,' the man said. He had raised one hand. Colm lowered his. The mosquito net on Agoyo's bed was between them, a suddenly impenetrable barrier.

Agoyo was lying on top of the bed in sweat-and-blood-stained t-shirt and shorts. One leg was heavily bandaged. He lay back against the thin pillow.

'What's the Irish Telegraph?' he asked.

'A newspaper. I am a journalist.'

'Ah,' Agoyo said.

Colm didn't know what to say. The man had been shot in an

ambush in the dark. Colm hadn't covered any violent crime stories before. He had no frame of reference. He improvised.

'How bad is it?' he said.

Agoyo closed his eyes. 'It is not bad. I was lucky.' He opened his eyes and propped himself up on an elbow, looking at the bed diagonally opposite him where his colleague lay. 'Erik was not as lucky.'

The bird outside the hut was calling again. Somewhere behind it, Colm could hear men calling, and an engine starting.

'Have you been shot before?'

'Three times. I don't recommend it.' Agoyo sank onto his back and stretched his arms.

Across the hut Fatou had sat up and was working her way out of her mosquito net. Colm looked around for his trousers.

———

The sun was high in the sky, but according to his watch it was only ten past six in the morning. Though his watch was a time zone out. Ten past seven.

The sun.

It was still not raining.

He stepped out of the hospital hut, closed his eyes, breathed deeply.

The air was fresh, as if it had been steam-cleaned.

He opened his eyes. Wisps of mist hung beyond the compound walls. The air shimmered as sunlight passed through the moisture.

Without the background noise of rain, the insects appeared emboldened, redoubling their efforts. He could hear sounds more distinctly and now he realised that not all the noise he had assumed came from insects sounded like insects. The high-pitched twee-twee-twee was similar enough to crickets for him to be sure of that. Some of the lower pitches sounded more like frogs. In a place this wet he presumed there would be frogs. It sounded as if they were everywhere.

Playing over the rhythm of the frogs and insects were the melodies of the birds. The sounds travelled high in the air from the tops of the trees. They were bright and welcoming to the dawn. Colm took it as a personal greeting.

Fatou came out of the hut and stood beside him.

'Have you been shot before?' she said, in a tone that made him doubt whether or not he had asked Agoyo the right question.

'No,' he said. 'First time I saw a real gun outside of an airport was yesterday.'

He crossed the yard and stepped onto the veranda of the main building. Between the building and the gate, preparation for their expedition was underway. Two vehicles were being loaded by Hannington's men, helped by some of the children who had brought the plates to the tables the night before. They were carrying rucksacks, food, water, guns.

Hannington was talking to Kennet, looking at a map spread on the hood of the Land Rover that had come in last night. Colm could see the headlight that hadn't been lit had been shot out, and there were several bullet holes along the passenger side.

Jane Haven was watching Kennet from the veranda. Colm could only see the undamaged side of her face. She turned to him as if she'd been expecting him at that precise moment. Fatou stepped past him.

'Good morning,' Colm called to Hannington. 'Any breakfast?'

'Of course, my friend,' Hannington said, noticing him. 'There is some on the table. My victory feast, but you are welcome to it.' He laughed. Colm took a moment to realise Hannington was referring to his victory at chess. Colm smiled. 'You will need your strength for your journey into the park.'

'You're not coming with us?'

'No, alas. Two of my rangers were shot. I have others hunting the men who shot them. I need to send others to the hospital. I have reports to write. I cannot leave the station today. Instead, I send Mak, you will be in good hands.'

On the table a breakfast of mostly fruit was laid out. Fruit juice, fruit slices, whole fruit. Three rangers were eating. Fatou sat down and started to eat.

'Any coffee?' Colm said to no one in particular.

One of the rangers lifted a cup and pointed through a doorway.

Colm went to the doorway and looked inside.

On the floor was a kerosene stove with a kettle on it. Next to that was a coffee pot with a filter attachment. The pot was half full.

Colm couldn't see a mug. He went back outside.

'Is there a cup I could borrow?' he said. The one ranger facing him looked up, his face questioning. Colm remembered the common language was French.

'*Une tasse?*' Colm guessed.

The ranger half-smiled and pointed at an empty cup on the table. Colm took it, shook it out, wiped it out with the edge of his shirt, and went to pour himself a coffee. He was secretly pleased. His schoolboy French was proving useful for the first time in his life. And the coffee was delicious. He raised his cup to the ranger who had pointed it out.

'*Delicieux!*' he hazarded. The ranger nodded.

CHAPTER ELEVEN

Even on a tarmacked road the ride from the airport had been bumpy and uncomfortable. Compared to the drive into the Garamba National Park it had been like floating on a bed of air.

The track, where there was a track, was never flat for more than a few metres. The land fell away to the southwest and was cut by a network of rivers and streams, like veins in meat. The Land Rover and the other vehicle, the Jeep, tilted forward and back, side to side, often both at the same time. Half the time they were up to their axles in water.

Colm was exhilarated – and scared. As they forded a stream, the fast-flowing brown water battering them from the side, his head told him the rangers knew what they were doing, they did this all the time. His instinct for self-preservation, on the other hand, told him they were about to be swept away and he should jump for it. Then the front bumper rose out of the water and up a bank so steep he could only see the bonnet through the windscreen. It tilted up and he could see the sky for a moment, before it tilted back down, and they were heading for more swirling water.

He held on.

They drove for two-and-a-half hours like that. Then they stopped.

The sudden absence of motion made Colm feel seasick. He leaned forward on the bench seat, his elbows on his knees, and breathed until his head stopped spinning. Even so, when he stood up, the Land Rover felt like it was still moving.

The others were already unloading and preparing to continue on foot. The party going into the park numbered ten: Jane, Kennet, Tony, Kwame, Fatou, Colm and four other rangers, including the one who had pointed out the coffee. His name, Colm had remembered on the journey, was Makur Kibwana.

'Call me Mak,' he had said.

Mak was one of Hannington's sergeants, and, in Hannington's absence, he was in charge. Two others were to stay behind with the vehicles.

Mak and Kwame unloaded rucksacks and guns, handing them out. Colm was given a rucksack. It was heavy. He put his arms through the straps and pulled it on. He lengthened and tightened the load adjuster straps until the weight was evenly distributed across his shoulders and back. It was well-packed, nothing dug into him too uncomfortably. But he worried about the weight in the heat. Sweat was already prickling on his back.

The stopping point was a spit of land above the confluence of two large streams. The one they had crossed was relatively mature, flatter, and fordable. The one in front of them younger, steeper, and more aggressive, and too much to contemplate with the old engines. It was easy to cross on foot as a tree trunk had been dragged into place to form an effective bridge. Where it had been dragged from was not clear, as the land ahead and below them looked to be mostly grass, the only trees that were visible being short and slim.

This, it turned out, was an optical illusion caused by the height of the grass. After they had crossed the trunk single file, climbed to the top of the bank, and dropped down the slope on the other side, Colm adjusted his perspective. This grass was taller than any he had seen so far. It was taller than him, taller even than Kennet.

'Elephant grass,' Kwame said. 'We must be careful.'

'Why?' Colm asked.

'Elephant!' Kwame grinned.

'I have not seen it this tall in Kenya,' Kennet said, following Kwame along a broad path into the grass.

'What made the path?' Jane asked.

'Antelope. Buffalo. Elephant,' said one of the rangers, whose name Colm couldn't immediately remember. The man pointed at a large circular impression in the earth, the grass within it torn and crushed. Jane knelt to examine it, her hand putting it in perspective. It was the size of a large dinner plate.

'That's an elephant footprint?' Colm said.

'Yes. They are like a fingerprint. Different for every elephant. Shoulder height is five point eight times the diameter of footprint for bulls. Five point five for cows. This is a big bull. Three metres tall.'

Colm knelt next to Jane to take a closer look. Much of the print was difficult to see because crushed grass had sprung back up, but the size was clear and the edges mostly distinct.

'This was made since the rain stopped,' she said.

The ranger nodded. 'He is less than twelve hours ahead of us,' he said.

'How do you know that?' Colm asked, impressed. The ranger shrugged, as if it were obvious.

Jane stood up and looked about her, as if expecting the elephant to emerge from behind a clump of grass.

Eight of them continued into the grass. The ranger – Colm now remembered his name was Mola – and Tony led, then Jane and Kennet, followed by Fatou and Colm, with Kwame and Mak in the rear. Mak had sent the other two rangers scouting along the edge of the grass at ninety degrees to the path taken by the rest of them.

They followed the elephant's tracks through the grass for another hour. Colm found the distorted scale eerie. It was like being miniaturised and dropped onto the lawn back home. All he could see were the men in front of him, Fatou beside him, the occasional pile of elephant dung swarming with flies and crawling with maggots, and towering grass. He felt trapped, claustrophobic. The feeling was made worse by the sound. Since they had left the trees well behind, the sound of birds and monkeys had gone. Insects still trilled and creaked, but their calls were muted by the thick grass. The most dominant sound now was the grass itself, whistling and rustling as the wind played with it.

But the country kept changing. The further they walked the less tall the grass grew, and soon they could see over the top of it. A little after ten thirty in the morning they stopped on the side of a small hill that rose from what was otherwise a surprisingly flat plain, a savanna of grass and shrubs, the occasional line of trees following the courses of rivers and streams.

'Rest, ten minutes,' Mak called.

'How much further?' Colm heard Kennet ask.

'Another hour, hour and a half,' Mak replied.

Colm looked around him. The morning was beautiful. The smell of the grass and the water had lost its dominance as he had grown used to it, but it still felt fresh and – he couldn't think of the word. Alive? Young? Untouched? Everything he could see was green. Nothing was moving other than them.

'Where are we going?' he asked.

'To the last place the rhino of Garamba were safe,' Kwame said.

CHAPTER TWELVE

IT FELT A LOT LONGER THAN AN HOUR AND A HALF. DESPITE its unfamiliarity, the landscape rapidly grew repetitive, and to Colm's disappointment, very little in the way of wildlife chose to show itself.

The monotony was broken not by an animal, or a bird, but by a building. They could see it for thirty minutes before they reached it. It was like something out of another world, another time.

Colm's first thought was that he'd stumbled onto the set of *Gone with the Wind*. The building was a house, four storeys tall, in a style he associated with movies set in the nineteenth century of America's deep south. Two verandas surrounded it, one on the first floor, one on the second. A square tower rose out of the roof, two tall windows on each side, with a spike at its pinnacle pointing to the sky. The whole thing was painted green. Some of the windows in the main building were broken.

The tower made it different from a colonial-era American plantation owner's house. It was like a spiked helmet on the top of the building. Definitely not the same as the ones from his movie education.

As they walked closer, through long grass that reached his waist, he could see other buildings behind it. Single storey, mainly. A taller structure some way behind that looked like a barn. A clutch of trees in rows, like an orchard. Corrals, fenced areas, just visible above the grass.

At two hundred metres Colm realised the place was a ruin. It wasn't that some windows were broken, it was that most windows were missing, and the rest were broken, some with the neat round punch holes of bullets. But the closer they got, the more the size of the place impressed him. It was enormous.

Even closer, Colm realised the wood was green not with paint but with moss. One of the outbuildings had partially collapsed. Bars were missing from the fences. The orchard was wild, with grass growing everywhere. A small tree was sprouting through one of the windows in the helmet-like tower.

Something about the building had made the whole party more cautious. They were walking towards a place of ghosts in an abandoned land. The rangers, and even Jane, were carrying their guns as if they were expecting shooting to start at any moment. Fatou, Colm was pleased to see, looked as nervous as he felt. Of all of them, only Kennet seemed comfortable and relaxed.

Kwame and Mola were at the front, focussed on the ground and all around them, alert as deer. The rangers were approaching the building as if it were filled with snakes.

The building was towering over them now.

There was a skeleton in one of the corrals. Its skull, one leg, its spine, and one side of its ribcage lay together, as they would have done when the animal was alive. The other half of its ribcage and its other three leg bones were scattered across the corral, if they were there at all. Colm guessed it had been a horse. Perhaps a donkey.

'What is this place?' Colm asked Mak, quietly.

Mak moved close before answering.

'When it was built, it was someone's hunting lodge. A rich white man. It was empty for many years. In the nineteen eighties the park took it over, fixed it up. This is where the conservation team were based. Thirty years ago. This is their headquarters. From here the rhino were brought back from the brink, before the brink came again and they were all killed.' Mak pointed past the house in the direction they had been walking.

Colm looked where Mak was pointing. It was just more grass-land, green and empty.

'What happened?'

'Men on horses with machine guns. Crossed the Garamba River in the north, followed it to here, where the animals were, and started shooting. They killed twenty rhino and a thousand elephant in 2004 alone.'

'A thousand elephants?'

'In one year.'

Colm couldn't get his head round the idea. He'd seen elephants in the zoo in Belfast. Two of them. They were big animals. And those had been Asian elephants. African elephants were even bigger, weren't they? Didn't they weigh four or five tonnes? A thousand of them?

'A thousand,' Colm said again, rather louder than he intended.

'Shhhh.' Mak put his fingers to his lips. He was staring ahead, crouching, and raising his gun to his shoulder. Colm followed his gaze. Kwame was waving in a downward motion. Mola was split-ting away from him, heading in a wide arc around the overgrown building. Jane Haven, intent on something on the ground in front of her, suddenly started moving quickly in the opposite direction to Mola. Tony followed Jane.

'This way,' Mak said. He led Colm, Fatou, and Kennet

towards a ditch, and dropped down into it. Colm followed him, pausing when he saw the thick red mud at the bottom, until Mak pulled him forward and he stumbled into it with a splash. The mud reached his knees.

Fatou jumped in behind them, quite gracefully and without complaint. She slipped into the mud almost silently. Kennet followed. He was less graceful, making a huge splash. Colm saw Mak wince and peer with concern over the lip of the ditch, his hands tightening on his gun. He turned to Kennet and lifted a finger to his lips before looking back towards the buildings. Kennet raised a hand in apology and crouched down.

Colm eased himself up the side of the ditch until he could see over the edge. The buildings looked unchanged. Kwame, Mola, Tony and Jane had vanished.

'What have they seen?' Fatou whispered.

'Tracks,' Mak said.

'Of what?'

'Men.'

'What do we do?' Fatou asked.

'We stay here' Mak's hands gripped his rifle, and his finger was inside the trigger guard. 'We wait.'

Fatou nodded.

'Why does Jane have a gun?' she asked.

Kennet looked at her.

'Why do you ask that?' he said.

'You don't have a gun. You're a conservationist. She said she was a teacher.'

'Ah.' Kennet paused and looked away, very briefly. 'She has some experience with firearms,' he said. 'We used to hunt elk with our father in Norway.'

'Why don't you have a gun?'

'I don't like them.'

CHAPTER THIRTEEN

IT WAS KWAME WHO CAME TO TELL THEM IT WAS SAFE. HE seemed to materialise out of the grass, appearing suddenly and coming towards them. It took him ten minutes to reach them, walking slowly, turning and covering a two-hundred-and-seventy-degree field of vision systematically, rifle raised.

'It looks like they're gone,' he said. 'You can come out.'

Kennet pulled himself out of the ditch, slipped, nearly fell in again, steadied himself, and then turned to help first Fatou and then Colm up. Mak had moved faster than Kennet.

'How many?' Mak said.

'Three or four, Sergeant. They camped here last night, in the building. Headed out the way they came, northeast, a few hours ago, since the rain stopped.' Kwame pointed.

'Are these the same men who shot Agoyo?' Colm asked.

'Why did they go back the way they came?' Fatou said at the same time.

'We should follow them,' Kennet said.

Mak looked at all three of them in turn, letting his eyes rest on Kennet the longest, then turned back to Kwame.

'Radio it in, then take Mola,' he said. He raised an arm and made a sweeping circle. 'At least a kilometre. We'll move slow, meet at the ford.'

Kwame nodded, turned, and walked away, still vigilant.

Mak inhaled, exhaled, took a couple of steps, then spoke.

'They're not the same men who shot Agoyo, those men were fifty kilometres away when these men were here.

'I don't know why they went back the way they came, but we've found poachers sheltering here many times. It's the only building in thirty kilometres with a roof. It's practically a poachers' motel. In fact, that's what we call it.

'And no, Mr Haven, we're not following them. I have been instructed to ensure the chances of you and your guests being shot are kept to a reasonable minimum. Let's go.'

'Can we see inside the building?' Colm asked.

'We don't have time for that,' Kennet said.

Mak looked at him, then back at the rotting edifice that rose from the earth like a decaying tooth. He nodded to Colm.

'We will wait out here,' Mak said. 'Be careful. The wood is rotten. Take a stick.'

'A stick?' Colm said.

'To test the floor in front of you, to make sure it is safe.'

Colm understood. He looked around. The nearest trees were in the orchard on the other side of the house. Fatou had understood as well. She walked to one of the corrals and scuffed around on the ground with her foot before crouching down and levering a fallen fence post out of the grass. The grass held onto it for a moment, and Fatou put more effort into freeing the post. The grass won. The post, rotted through to the core, disintegrated in a shower of splinters and Fatou was left with a handful of bits.

'Perhaps it's not that bad. Did the poachers have sticks?' Colm said.

'They had guns,' Mak said.

'Good point,' Colm said.

'Could we borrow yours?' Fatou asked. Mak shook his head.

It took Colm and Fatou ten minutes of rummaging through the outhouses and in the orchard before they both had something sturdy enough to test the floors. Fatou found an iron bar, rusted and unwieldy, but fundamentally still an iron bar. It had possibly once been part of a wagon. Colm had a fresh branch from a tree. He had broken it off then stripped away the leaves and smaller branches and twigs to leave a staff about two metres tall and fifteen centimetres in circumference at its widest. It would do.

'We need to be moving in ten minutes,' Mak said. He was waiting with Kennet and Tony about a hundred metres northeast of the building. Colm realised he hadn't seen Jane since the brief scare when they'd first arrived at the building.

'We'd better be quick,' Colm said to Fatou. She looked at him and nodded. He jogged towards the steps to the main door, but slowed to a walk when he realised how slippery the ground was and how heavy his staff was. He could hear Fatou following him.

The steps up to the first veranda were worn but solid, more than a hundred years since the trees they were made from were felled. They were slick with moss, but the staff helped with balance. Colm climbed them with care, the thunk of Fatou's iron bar sounding just behind him.

The veranda was empty but for moss and dead grass. It was broad and commanded spectacular views across the grass plain towards the river. Colm imagined women with parasols and men in pith helmets taking tea on the terrace whilst watching rhinos and elephants in the water. Twin visions of lost history, only one missed.

Fatou walked past him and stepped through the main doorway into the building's dark interior. Colm took another look out over the grasslands, empty but for Mak, Kennet, and Tony, then followed her.

Inside the light was different. Much darker than outside, and not as green, because where daylight couldn't reach, the moss didn't grow. But there was something unexpected. Glints. Glints of gold.

The main door opened into a square hall two storeys high. A staircase rose to the left and went up two sides of the square until it reached a landing that ran around the other two sides, a curiously asymmetric design. Doorways off both the level Colm was on and the side of the landing above him let in light from outside, filtered by any surviving glass. And this light was picking out gold, tiny flashes playing off the walls here and there, like fairy lights. The whole place felt even more other-worldly. Colm stared.

'*Les papiers peints*,' Fatou said from somewhere in the gloom ahead of him.

Colm played her words in his head. The papers paints? He moved closer to where a flash of gold had shone from the wall and spotted the glint again. It did look like gold. Metal, at least, buried in what looked like grey mush. He poked it with the end of his staff. The grey mush came away and the fleck of gold fluttered to the ground. He understood. Wallpaper. With some sort of gilt thread running through it. The paper had turned to mould, and the gilt had survived untarnished somehow.

Colm moved on to the doorway of the first room to the left off the main hall. The door was missing, and just the hinges remained. The room was large with a high ceiling and huge rectangular windows facing south and east. The windows were broken or gone completely, but otherwise the room was intact. There were no holes in the floor, though that didn't mean it would carry his weight. There were bullet holes in one wall, and the paint or paper that had once covered it had rotted or been consumed by bacteria and fungi. There was nothing inside the room. Even the ghosts of the ostentatious furniture Colm imagined had once dwelt here had long since fled.

Not quite nothing. There were small lumps on the floor over by one of the glass-less windows. Prodding the floorboards with his staff, he edged towards them. As he got closer, they started to play with the light. As soon as he could see them clearly, he stopped.

They were like pebbles on a beach, like smooth stones and wave-worn shells. But they weren't. They were broken bits of glass and old bullet casings. There was a dark stain on some of the boards. He laid down his staff and took out his phone, switching it on. His battery was ok, still at sixty per cent. He took a photo from where he crouched, looking up at the empty, ornate window frames, with the shattered glass, bullet casings, and blood stain in the foreground. He looked at the picture on the phone once he'd taken it. It made him shudder. He switched his phone off, put it back in its plastic bag, and put the bag back in his pocket. He picked up his staff and turned and walked to the doorway.

As he reached it another light, very different, hit the side of his face. He turned towards it and put his hand in front of his eyes even as he closed them. Someone was at the top of the stairs, with a torch pointed right at him. Whoever it was started down the stairs. Colm gripped his staff, trying to open his eyes but finding them still blinded by the torch. He wondered where Fatou was.

The footsteps on the stairs stopped very close to him. He sensed the torch beam lower, and slowly opened his eyes. Fatou was in front of him, no more than two metres away, also shielding her eyes from the light.

'There is nothing here,' Jane's voice said. 'We should go.'

———

Kwame and Mola were waiting for them at the ford. Mola was on his feet, rifle in his hands, alert. Kwame was on the ground a little way off, water bottle in one hand, an energy bar in the other.

'Did you get lost?' Kwame said.

'Took them a while to find a stick,' Mak said. 'What did you see?'

Kwame got to his feet. 'Nothing new. Four men, for sure, came from there,' he pointed to the east of northeast, 'sometime yesterday, camped in the motel, left early this morning the same way. Straight line, not carrying anything heavy. Two pairs of boots, two pairs of feet. Perhaps they were just after bushmeat.'

'Coming out of the park?' Mak said.

Kwame shrugged.

'Did you call it in?' Mak asked.

Kwame nodded. 'Hannington wasn't there. The patrol is still in trouble, he's taken more men.'

Colm looked at Mak. Mak was thinking. Perhaps trying to work out what all this information meant. Colm looked at the ford.

Here the Garamba River was about thirty metres across, but shallow and lazy. The mud at either edge was churned by the passage of feet, and the majority of those feet were not human. Colm crouched to examine their tracks. Hoof prints mostly. Some sort of deer, perhaps. And others he didn't recognise at all.

'Don't get too close to the water,' Kwame said, earnestly. Colm looked up. Kwame was pointing to one of the prints Colm hadn't recognised, a bit like a human hand but with shortened fingers and sharp nails. 'Crocodile.'

Colm stepped back, suddenly, as a spasm of panic jolted him.

'Would they...?'

'Oh, yes,' Kwame said. As if the moment had been rehearsed, something large and heavy splashed in the water somewhere out of sight upstream.

From that point on, Colm made sure one of the members of the party with a gun was between him and the river at all times.

'Let's get going, we're losing the light,' Kennet said.

'No,' Mak said. 'I cannot risk your safety with four unidentified men so close. We will head back to Nagero and return on a better day.'

'We are so close,' Kennet said. 'I must insist we finish what we set out to do.'

'With great respect, Mr Haven, you cannot insist. And we will finish what we set out to do, just not today.'

His mind made up, Mak snapped into action. He spoke to Mola and Kwame in a language Colm didn't know. He had read that there were more than two hundred languages spoken in the country, four of which were national languages, but the names had been new to him, too unfamiliar for him even to remember the words much less guess which one he was hearing. He would ask. But not now. Now, they were heading back the way they had come. Kennet looked unhappy, though he was trying to hide it. Colm thought through the angles of this turn of events. Sudden change of plans due to the presence of criminals with guns. Alien to Colm, just another day at the office for the rangers of Garamba.

CHAPTER FOURTEEN

COLM FELT ODDLY DISAPPOINTED AS THEY STARTED BACK. They'd not got to where they had intended to go, and they'd not seen anything on the way, so he knew there was nothing to see on the way back. A seemingly endless sea of thigh-length grass changed swiftly from an unspoilt and beautiful landscape to an irritating obstacle. The backpack he was carrying did nothing but get heavier. And he remembered Hannington saying they'd have to spend a night in the park, which he was not looking forward to.

He was lost in these thoughts when he realised someone was walking next to him and keeping pace. It was Fatou.

The party was strung out. Mak and Mola were perhaps a hundred metres ahead of Colm; Jane and Kennet seventy-five metres behind; Tony and Kwame another fifty metres to the rear of them. Despite no one being close enough to hear them, and the background noise of the wind in the grass, Fatou continued staring ahead as she spoke, as if she didn't want anyone to realise they were talking.

'Didn't you find it odd?' she asked.

'What odd?' Colm said, but he wasn't listening, because Mak and Mola had stopped and were crouching, watching something ahead of them. They didn't signal, so Colm assumed it was fine to continue. He walked slowly forward, watching the area of grass that he thought Mak and Mola had reacted to. It looked just like all the rest of it.

Then he saw a movement. There were animals in the grass.

Colm stared. They were big. Half a dozen of them, half a kilometre away, perhaps less. They looked like deer, with graceful, curling horns. He crouched as he walked, creeping closer to Mak and Mola. The closer he got, the more animals he saw. The six largest were around the edge of a group of smaller ones. Or perhaps some were large but lying in the grass rather than standing. One of the larger animals seemed to look right at Colm and he froze. But then it lowered its head and came up with a mouthful of grass.

'What are they?' he said, when he was close enough to be heard.

'*Waterbuck*,' Mak said. 'A species of antelope.'

'What are they doing?' Colm asked.

'Eating. This is how they feed. The sentinels watch for predators. The others feed.'

'Predators? They're as big as horses. What can threaten them?'

'Leopards, hyena, lion, and some cheetah, all would have a go at a waterbuck, especially a young one.'

'Lion?' Colm looked behind him, expecting to see a lion big enough to take down a horse with horns like swords, creeping up on him. He saw only Jane, who was almost next to him, and then she stepped to one side, and he saw Kennet, Kwame, and Tony behind her. He looked back at the herd.

'I can't see any young.'

'They hide them. If they are threatened the herd will stampede and draw the predators away. The young will be in the thickest grass. They are almost impossible to find, even if you know to look for them.'

Mak said something to Kwame, who nodded and set off in a direction at ninety degrees to the one they'd been travelling in.

'We haven't startled them, so we can rest here. They are good lookouts. Let's eat.' Mak took off his backpack, leaned his gun against it, took out a water bottle, and drank.

———

After water and a meal of dried, smoked fish, they shouldered their packs to resume their march.

'Two more hours, then we make camp,' Mak said, looking at the sky. He led them in the direction he had sent Kwame, moving nearly a kilometre off the route they'd taken on the way in to give the waterbuck a wide berth. For their part, the waterbuck eyed them warily but didn't move.

Colm found he was enjoying himself again. The smoked fish he'd eaten had been unfamiliar but full of flavour, and it had boosted his energy. But the main change was the waterbuck. He had never seen a waterbuck. In fact, he wasn't sure if he'd heard of them before. Either way, here he was, walking past a herd in its natural habitat, and the herd didn't see him as a threat. It gave him a warm feeling. He watched one of the sentinel animals with a smile as it watched them in turn.

Suddenly, the big antelope turned, ears twitching, nostrils flaring. All of the animals moved their heads in one direction, then, in one movement, the whole herd bolted.

'Something spooked them,' Kennet said. Colm had worked that out.

He was thinking lion. He was looking around for lion. He felt something touch his arm. He jumped. It was a hand. Mak.

'Lion are nocturnal,' Mak said, as if reading his thoughts. 'Mostly,' he added, with a smile. 'It could be nothing. It could have been us.'

'I heard gunfire,' Jane said. 'Automatics. More than one. In the distance. Difficult to judge direction.'

Mak turned to her.

'Are you sure?' he asked.

Jane nodded. 'I think it came from that way.' She pointed in the direction they were walking. 'I heard it. When the wind changed, just for a moment.'

Colm noticed that the waterbuck had run in the opposite direction to the one in which Jane was pointing.

Mak muttered something under his breath. He looked behind them, back towards the colonial building, now long out of sight. The running waterbuck herd was still visible.

He turned and looked in the direction Jane had pointed. The way they were heading. There was nothing out of the ordinary. Grass, a few bushes, the occasional tree. No life. No sound other than the wind in the grass.

'Kwame,' Mak said quietly, before beckoning to Mola, who had his back to him. 'Mola!' he hissed.

Colm noticed that Mola had been facing, by his reckoning, due west. Tony, gun across his chest, was facing northeast. Turning, Colm saw Jane, gun also ready, was facing east. And Mak, looking in the direction Kwame had gone, was facing southwest. Kennet, Fatou, and Colm, were in the middle of the diamond they made, protected by the rangers in the same way the waterbuck sentinels had protected the smaller ones and the young.

Mola walked briskly to Mak keeping an eye to the west. The two rangers spoke briefly, before Mola set off in the direction Kwame had taken perhaps half an hour earlier.

Mak motioned to Colm, Kennet, and Fatou to follow him towards Jane and Tony.

'Can you all hear me?' Mak said.

Tony and Jane looked at him briefly, nodded, then resumed their vigil. Mak himself, once he had seen he had their attention, took to looking west, in the direction Mola had been watching, as he spoke.

Colm decided someone should be on the lookout to the southwest and was slightly annoyed to notice Fatou had already thought of it. He selected a line south of southwest and watched that way, both hoping and dreading he would see something first.

'There are four men somewhere northeast of here, unless they changed direction significantly from their tracks of this morning,' Mak began. 'There were poachers west only yesterday, the ones who shot Erik and Agoyo, at least five, not the same group as the one to the northeast. They are still a problem – Hannington has taken more men to support the patrol. Both of those groups could have turned this way, but for either of them to make it as far as the edge of the sound of gunfire in that direction –' Mak emphasised with a wave of his hand '– by now is unlikely. It could be a third party we know nothing about.

'If we are lucky, the shots Jane heard were made by rangers. If we are not lucky, we have armed hostiles on three sides, and the fourth direction is one in which we do not want to go. We proceed on the assumption that we are not lucky. Kwame is scouting a new route. Mola has gone to bring him back. We will move very slowly until we reach them. Then we will hear what they have to say, and I will decide what we do next.

'Follow me, say nothing, stay low, lie down if I do this.' Mak repeated a hand-signal he'd shown them the day before. 'Let's go.'

CHAPTER FIFTEEN

THE NEW MARCHING ORDER WAS SINGLE FILE, TEN PACES apart, with Mak in the lead, then Colm, Fatou, Kennet, Jane, and Tony bringing up the rear. Six people, three guns. Colm had a good view of what they were walking towards, especially when the fall of the ground meant Mak wasn't directly in front of him. He guessed that anyone they were walking towards would have a good view of him, too.

They walked in silence. In effective silence, at least. The ground was soft, and the grass lush, so footsteps and leg movements made little to no sound, and the constant wind in the grass sea made more noise than they did. Colm was tense, but his tension was slowly enveloped with a feeling of anti-climax, as minute after minute went by with nothing changing at all. Five minutes, ten, fifteen. Thirty. An hour. The ground undulated a little, and the wind blew patterns in the grass. Once, somewhere not quite straight ahead of them, he saw a bird in the sky. It was probably large, though it looked tiny at this distance. It circled, lower and lower, then disappeared.

Colm caught sight of Mak's face whenever the ranger turned

his head. Mak looked worried. The only Garamba ranger left in the party leading five non-Congolese in the middle of the park with up to three groups of armed men potentially close by – Colm would have worried too if he'd been in Mak's boots. But everything Mak did was decisive. Colm took a lot of confidence from that.

As they dropped into a shallow valley, Colm glanced behind him. Fatou caught his eye briefly then looked away. He didn't think she was avoiding his gaze, just wanting to stay on the lookout. He saw something in her eyes he hadn't seen before. He didn't think it was fear.

Behind Fatou came Kennet, who was actually smiling. He seemed lost in thought, his eyes cast towards his left, roughly southeast, though Colm wasn't sure he was seeing anything. The big man had a hand in a pocket, an oddly casual gesture in such a potentially dangerous situation.

Briefly silhouetted against the valley ridge, Jane and Tony were mirror images of each other, watching in different directions, their guns ready to raise and fire. But there were differences. Jane seemed more tense, like a – what was the expression? – like a coiled spring. As if the slightest noise might set her off. Tony looked just as ready, but not as tightly wound.

Mak raised his hand. The signal to stop. Colm did so and crouched down.

Mak was on the edge of a ditch at the centre of the shallow valley. There was the sound of running water. A stream. Mak slipped into the ditch, disappearing for one, two, three, four, five seconds, then reappearing on the other side and climbing the bank. He waved the others forward.

Colm followed Mak into the ditch and up the other side. The water at the bottom was lively but barely fifty centimetres across and less deep, easily stepped over. The notable feature were the boot prints. Two sets in addition to Mak's. Either two people, or one person twice, travelling in the same direction as they were. Kwame and Mola, hopefully.

Colm kept moving, following Mak, ten paces back, as the ranger made his way up the slope out of the shallow valley. Mak slowed as he reached the top, raising his head cautiously over the ridge, then lowering it again, quickly. Another hand-signal. Halt. Then Mak pointed and beckoned. Tony. He wanted Tony up front with him. The other experienced ranger, though from a park fifteen hundred kilometres away. What was on the other side of that ridge?

Tony made his way past the others and then slowed to creep up the slope. He crawled the last metre or so. When he reached Mak, the Garamba ranger whispered to him. Tony nodded. As one, the two of them raised their heads over the lip of the ridge. Colm found he was holding his breath.

After what seemed like an age, but was probably no more than a few seconds, Mak and Tony lowered their heads and leaned towards each other, whispering. After a quick conversation, they pulled away. Mak eased up to look over the ridge again and Tony did something Colm did not expect at all. He tilted his head back and made a loud sound like the call of a bird. It was very clear, and very realistic, or so it seemed to Colm. It echoed around them, bouncing off the sides of the shallow valley, startling in the relative quiet. Colm found himself looking up and down the valley, half expecting to see birds flying in answer. Instead, he noticed not extra birds but fewer people. Jane was gone.

Colm went cold. He couldn't see her. Had she left? Been taken by something? He blinked, raised a hand to rub his eyes, then stopped. He'd seen her. She was just below the top of the opposite ridge, almost hidden in the long grass, facing back the way they had come, her rifle pressed against her shoulder, her eye against its sight.

Mak was still looking over the top of the ridge in front of them, with as little of his head protruding as possible. Tony, his hands tight on his gun, was watching Mak. After the sound of Tony's bird call had died away, everything seemed very quiet.

Then an answering cry came from somewhere ahead of them. Another bird call, but very different. Mak pushed himself off the ground a little. Colm caught a view of his face. Mak was smiling. He said something to Tony, not whispered this time. Colm heard it. 'When I get there, I'll signal, then bring them. Warn them.'

Mak stepped over the ridge and disappeared.

———

'On the other side of this ridge there is a dead elephant and at least two severely injured or dead men,' Tony said. Colm and Fatou exchanged a glance. 'Mola and possibly Kwame are watching them. I am going to go back to the ridge to wait for Mak to signal. When he does, we are all to go join them. Is that clear?'

Colm found himself nodding.

'Colm,' Tony went on, 'go and repeat what I have just said to Jane. Make sure she hears you coming.'

With that, Tony scrambled back up the ridge and looked over, awaiting Mak's signal.

Colm felt a tiny inner petulance at being asked to act as messenger boy, but he squashed it. He was excited. He was participating in a potentially dangerous situation. Potentially! There were dead people on the other side of that ridge! Everything was about to get real. Much more real than bear bones in a museum.

He set off to complete his allotted task. Jane was barely a hundred metres away. He passed Kennet, who patted him on the shoulder. He crossed the tiny stream in the ditch at the centre of the valley. He walked up the slope as obviously as he could. When within easy hearing distance, he said 'Jane.'

'What?' she said, without looking at him.

'I have a message from Tony.'

'Keep below the ridge,' she said, without moving. 'What is it?'

Instinctively, Colm crouched, facing Jane. She was lying just below the top of the ridge, her silhouette broken up with grass, some of which was growing there, some of which she had uprooted and covered herself with. She was in sharpshooter position, or at least, that was what Colm would have called it. The way snipers always seemed to lie in films, her rifle tight into her shoulder, her eye tight against the scope, her finger on the trigger.

'Tony says there's a dead elephant and two dead or injured men over the other ridge. Mola is watching them, and Mak has gone to meet Mola. When Mak signals, Tony is to lead us all down to them.'

'Roger that,' Jane said. 'Tell Tony and Mak I'll wait here to make sure no one is following us. I'll catch you up when you make camp.' She still hadn't moved or looked at him. 'Go. The others are moving.'

Colm looked behind him. Jane was right. Only Fatou and Kennet were still in the valley; Tony was already out of sight.

He looked at Jane one more time, then hurried after the others.

CHAPTER SIXTEEN

REALITY WAS WORSE THAN HE EXPECTED.

Colm followed Kennet over the ridge into a larger valley, parallel to the one they had just left. It was as steep, but deeper and broader, the stream in its middle older and angrier. And it was filled with death.

The elephant lay on its side. Colm approached from the back, saw its tail and its rear legs first. Colm had never been this close to an elephant before. He'd only seen elephants in real life once. On that occasion they were too far away to seem real. He remembered them the way he remembered cartoons, although he could still recall their smell. He knew they were large animals, but it wasn't until he was standing right next to one that he appreciated how large.

Colm walked around the great legs, keeping his distance, afraid to get too close. Fatou and Kennet were ahead of him. Fatou had taken out her phone, unwrapping it from its plastic bag protection, switching it on to use some of the precious battery. As she raised the phone to take a photo Colm turned his head and saw the true horror.

The animal's huge body was riddled with bullet holes, randomly, wildly. Dozens of them. Blood still dripped down the creases in its thick skin. Flies had gathered in clouds, already feeding, already breeding.

Tony was on the other side of Fatou, a few steps ahead of her. He held his rifle at shoulder height and was pointing it across the valley at the far ridge. He was alternating opening each eye, one looking through the sight on his rifle, the other at the foreground. His expression was frozen, his jaw clenched, but his legs were stiff, and his feet were moving, swinging his torso first one way then another. He was so wound-up Colm wouldn't have been surprised if he'd flown apart under his own pressure.

Colm walked until he was level with Tony. Then he realised what had made the ranger so angry.

'Double god,' he whispered.

The elephant's head had been destroyed. By dozens of bullet holes, more than dozens – hundreds. Colm stepped back, steadied himself, and the ground crunched under his feet. Gravel in the grass, but it sounded metallic. He looked down. Not gravel. Bullet casings. Hundreds. This close. Five metres from the elephant. They'd fired this close. The poor creature must have been already on the ground to let them get this close, mustn't it?

The visible eye socket was empty, the mouth open, the lower lip partially severed. The tusks were gone, sawed through by the looks of it. The trunk had been hacked off and pushed out of the way to make sawing through the second tusk easier.

Kennet suddenly filled Colm's view. A remarkable change had come over him. His perpetual distraction had been swept away. He walked right up to the massive ruin of the elephant's head and put his hand on the creature's brow, ignoring the blood and flies.

'One day, I hope to see such a sight for the last time,' Kennet said, quietly, as if he were talking only to the elephant. 'This should not have happened to you. This should never happen again.'

Fatou was crouching, picking up handfuls of empty bullet cases and letting them slide through her fingers. She looked up at Colm. They chose not to notice the tears in each other's eyes.

———

Kwame's voice broke through Colm's thoughts. Colm hadn't heard it since Mak had sent Kwame on ahead just before they stopped to eat, close to the waterbuck herd. It seemed like days ago, although it was no more than a few hours.

'These two are poachers,' he said.

Kwame was standing by two bodies, talking to Mak. The two bodies Mak had told them about when they'd been up on the ridge. Colm had barely registered them on his descent into the valley, the view dominated by the monstrous shape of the elephant. Now he noticed them properly, and they grabbed his full attention.

'That one got too close to the elephant,' Kwame continued.

Colm would have worked that out. The man was young, perhaps early twenties, perhaps younger. He was tall and slim. He wore a t-shirt and trousers, the t-shirt grey, the trousers brown, neither were military issue like everybody else seemed to wear around here. If he had been wearing boots, they were gone. His feet were bare. And his body was crushed. His arm was trapped behind him at an impossible angle, his chest was caved in, and one leg was snapped, the broken bone of its femur sticking into the air like a knife. Only his face seemed untouched, though his eyes were open, and his final expression one of fear. There was pink foam on his lips.

'And that one got too close to whoever did that,' Kwame said, tilting his head slightly towards the elephant.

The second poacher had been shot. He had almost as many bullets in him as the elephant.

'I think there were four of them,' Kwame went on. 'Looking for whatever they could find. Chancers, after bushmeat. They weren't tracking the elephant – it came from that direction, down the valley, and they came from this one, up it. The meeting was a coincidence. And they had a go. They tried to kill it. On their own, they would have failed.' Kwame reached into the grass beside the crushed poacher and pulled out a twisted piece of metal.

Colm realised it was a rifle. Not an automatic rifle like the ones Tony and the other rangers were carrying, but an old one. The words bolt-action, single-shot appeared in his brain from he didn't know where. This rifle wouldn't fire again. It was bent out of shape. As if an elephant had trodden on it.

'If the other three were similarly armed, all they would have done, unless they were extremely lucky, was irritate it. It would have killed them all if they hadn't found somewhere to hide. But they were extremely unlucky, because not only did they come across an elephant they couldn't kill, they also came across another group of more serious poachers. At least twenty. That group had been tracking the elephant. They shot at the first group, but there was an injured elephant between them, so two from the first group managed to run back the way they had come and escape, although at least one of them is injured. The newcomers did this to the elephant, then went that way.'

Kwame pointed in a direction about thirty degrees off the line the first group of poachers had taken.

Mak walked in the direction Kwame was pointing, examining the ground.

A thought occurred to Colm. 'We saw elephant tracks when

we first left the vehicles this morning. Is this the same animal?'

'Possibly,' Kwame said.

For a full minute, no one spoke. The loudest noise came from the flies.

Fatou broke the silence. Colm was strangely conscious of her Belgian accent for the first time today.

'How many groups of men with guns are there? We knew of three. Are these two of the three or are there now five?'

Kwame didn't answer. He looked at Mak, who was standing a little way off, binoculars to his eyes, scanning the land in the direction the large group had taken.

A large group of men carrying two large tusks, Colm thought.

Mak lowered the binoculars, took his gun in his hands, and came closer.

'This was almost certainly the gunfire Jane heard. It's in the right direction, and just at the edge of hearing for where we were. We saw nothing else. And these four may be the men who were in the poachers' motel last night.' He cleared his throat. 'I say there are still three groups, at most four, and one of those groups is now down to two men, one wounded, and they were poorly armed in the first place. What we know to our advantage is that they are all that way,' Mak swept his arm northwest through northeast, 'and we are heading that way,' he jabbed his finger southwest. 'We need to be a long way from this elephant before we make camp. The vultures and hyenas will be here soon, and there may be lion after nightfall, so let's go.'

Fatou stepped towards the dead men, as if she was about to say something, but Mak cut her off.

'There is nothing we can do. We haven't time. Leave them.' He shouldered his gun and walked quickly to where he had left his backpack. He reached down to it but stopped midway and stood up again.

'Where's Jane?' he said.

CHAPTER SEVENTEEN

'I —' Colm began. He had forgotten to pass on Jane's message. Death had driven all other thoughts from him. 'She told me to tell you, and Tony, that she was staying behind to make sure no one was following us. She said she'd catch up where we make camp.'

Mak swore.

'We need to go back for her. She doesn't know what's out there. They only have to change direction by—'

'By nearly a hundred and eighty degrees,' Tony interrupted. 'We'd see them first.'

Mak seemed to relax a little at that. 'Yes, true.' He looked back the way they had come from, as if he had forgotten. 'We still need to go back for her. It will be dark soon.'

Kennet was still by the elephant. He turned, his face glistening with tears.

'If Jane said she will find us, she will find us,' Kennet said, his voice clear, despite his distress. 'She does what she says.' He sniffed. 'It's annoying.'

Mak shook his head.

'It's too dangerous, Mr Haven. Kwame, go get her.'

Kwame nodded and set off back the way they had come.

Kennet looked back at the elephant. Reached for it one last time but didn't touch it. Nonetheless, a cloud of flies left the corpse and, for a moment, hovered round his head like a black halo.

'Where is Mola?' Colm asked.

'Following the trail of the large group. We need to know where they're headed so we can report back. Hannington will want to go after them.' Mak hoisted his pack onto his back. Kwame shouldered his own. Colm realised he hadn't taken his off. He had forgotten the weight of it. Thinking about it brought the weight back. He suddenly felt very tired.

'Alright,' Mak said, exhaling. 'Let's go.'

———

Mak led them in a new direction. He followed the tracks of the elephant and of the men who had been following it, leaving by the route they had taken to the kill site. He paused every so often, staring at the ground, concentrating hard as if deciphering an ancient text. On the third such pause Colm broke the ten-pace rule and caught up with him.

'What are you looking at?' he asked. Mak was on his haunches over what appeared to be nothing more than a patch of flattened grass. 'Was that done by the elephant?'

Mak shook his head.

'Men. Boots. Half a dozen different sizes. I see different markings on some of the same size, too. Kwame was right. At least twenty. More, I think,' he said. 'Soldiers, without great discipline.'

'Soldiers? I thought they were poachers?' Colm said.

'Soldiers are sometimes poachers. These are soldiers who

have been sent to be poachers, I think. The pattern fits. Professional poachers, the ones here for money, for greed, are disciplined. They wouldn't waste hundreds of bullets killing a single elephant. They'd shoot it once with an elephant gun. Or tranquilise it from a helicopter, cut off its tusks, and leave it to bleed to death. Professional poachers are single-minded and ruthless. The men who killed this elephant, and that boy who was shot, those men are not professionals.

'They are walking side by side, three, four, five abreast, crushing a lot of grass, leaving a trail so wide we could see it from a plane. Experienced soldiers walk single file, to leave as narrow a trail as they can. And the elephant...' Mak paused, rubbed some grass through his fingers. 'The way they killed the elephant was wild. Like it was a game. Uncontrolled. I have not seen a death worse, save when they haven't killed the animal. Inexperienced, ill-disciplined soldiers, on an ivory raid. The worst kind of visitors to Garamba.' He stood up, leaving Colm staring at the crushed grass, wondering how the ranger had read so much from it.

Colm heard something. A strange sound, just on the edge of his hearing. Like a – like yipping, like excitable puppies in the distance. He turned his head towards the noise. It was coming from behind them. He stood up, next to Mak. The elephant's carcass was still visible, perhaps a kilometre and a half back. Colm could see large birds spiralling over it. Vultures. They were landing. Some close to the elephant, some on top of it. The yipping reached a brief frenzy, then subsided a little.

'Dogs?' he said.

'Hyena,' Mak replied.

Colm took a last look at the dead elephant, its outline obscured by an increasing number of vultures jostling for a meal. He saw streaks of movement through the grass in the distance. They must be the hyena arriving. Hyena. The animal the young man on the plane —Jack, that was his name — the animal Jack had wanted to see over anything else. Colm wished he hadn't seen them himself. At least not like this. Perhaps closing in to eat an animal they had killed, or that a lion had killed, or that had died naturally. But not to a kill like this.

It wasn't that they were going to eat the elephant; that was what they did. Colm had no problem with that. It was that they were going to clear away the evidence. The crime would disappear. A part of Colm felt it should stay there, a monument to shame. A reminder. A wake-up call.

Within a minute, Mak had them on the move once more.

The march north in the morning had been leisurely. A little nerve-wracking in places, but not too strenuous overall. The return journey was a different matter. Mak kept them moving quickly, at perhaps twice the speed of before, which was tiring in itself. Colm thought of himself as fit, and whilst he was carrying his share of the food and water, he had no gun. He carried more of a burden than Kennet, less than the rangers, and less than Jane, though she was still somewhere out there in the last of the afternoon.

Mak followed the tracks of the elephant and its pursuers for another half hour before changing course again. Colm's sense of direction was thrown in this vast wilderness, but in his mind, they'd been walking back towards Nagero along the same straight line they'd followed on the way out until they'd reached the elephant. Then they'd turned left, walked for an hour or so, and now they were turning not quite right, heading back towards their original heading at an angle of perhaps forty-five degrees. A right-angled triangle.

He thought back to school, to his maths lessons with Miss McSweeney, and triangles. Pythagoras's Theorem. Anything to take his mind off the weight of the backpack. Pythagoras's Theorem said that, in a triangle where one of the angles was ninety degrees, the length of the side opposite the ninety-degree angle multiplied by itself was the same as the length of the other two sides multiplied by themselves and then added together.

If this triangle had one ninety-degree angle, and two forty-five-degree angles, then the other two sides were the same length. They'd walked one of those two sides. It had taken an hour at a reasonable pace. Four kilometres in the hour? So once they'd travelled the long side they'd be back on their original heading. Four times four was sixteen, two sixteens thirty-two. What did you have to multiply by itself to make thirty-two? He couldn't remember. His brain was starting to hurt.

'We'll camp here,' Mak said. Colm was grateful for that.

Though not for long. Mak insisted on a cold camp, which meant no fire, no hot food, and no hot drink. Despite the heat of the day, once the sun had gone, it cooled very rapidly.

They were still in the grasslands. The only trees they could see were short and young, their trunks no thicker than a wrist. 'They get eaten or knocked down before they get much taller, or at least they used to,' Kwame had told them. But because there were no trees to provide cover, Mak wouldn't let them put their tents up either, as they would be too easy to see as soon as it grew light. They lay sheets on the grass, and wrapped themselves in woven blankets, and talked quietly while they ate cold rations and drank water. Colm quickly decided he'd been more comfort-able walking with the heavy backpack.

But stopping moving allowed Colm some time to reflect. There were long silences. Mak was alert and on watch as long as there was light. Tony went to sleep almost immediately, before the sun set. Kennet sat cross-legged, head bowed, deep in thought. Fatou made notes. She had a small notebook and a pen that she unwrapped from a sealed plastic bag. She took it out, held the notebook in one hand and the pen in the other for some time, then started to write. Colm noticed her handwriting was quick and wild, her pen flicking across the paper in swift, long strokes, and what was left on the page was reminiscent of an assembly of spiders' legs. She paused occasionally, thinking.

'What was odd?' Colm asked, after watching her for some time.

'*Pardon?*' she said. 'I mean, what?'

'After we left that building, you said "Didn't you find it odd?" to me. I was wondering what.'

She looked at him. Her eyes flicked to her right. She said, 'Oh, I remember. It was not important. Perhaps we can discuss it when we return to the ranger station. For now, I want to write down all I saw today. I don't want to forget anything.'

Colm nodded. 'That's a good idea,' he said.

He dug into his backpack and found his own notebook.

When the sun set Colm was expecting it. From bright to night in minutes. They all had small torches, and Mak told them to keep the beams pointed at the ground, not to raise them at all. Colm arranged his in such a way that he could still see to write and kept writing. By now, he was drawing the triangles of their route changes that afternoon. What multiplied by itself was thirty-two?

'Five comma six five six eight four,' Mak said without turning his head. He was sat at the back of the camp looking the way they had come. He did not have a torch switched on, but the faint light from Fatou's torch just allowed Colm to pick out his shape.

'I'm sorry?' Colm said. He realised he'd asked the question out loud.

'The square root of thirty-two is four root two, which is approximately five comma six five six eight four,' Mak said, still otherwise motionless.

'Oh, thank you.'

'And tuck your trousers into your socks.'

'Sorry?'

'Less chance of insects or snakes using your trousers as a burrow.'

'Oh. Of course. Thank you.'

Mak didn't reply.

The first of their visitors that night arrived soon afterwards. Out of the darkness came the call of a bird. Similar to, if not the same as, the bird call that had answered Tony's cry on the ridge before they'd walked into the valley of death.

The call was answered with a similar cry. Colm couldn't see for sure, but it sounded like it came from Mak.

Within a few minutes, Mola walked into the camp.

'Nearly missed you,' he said, without ceremony, as he slipped his backpack to the ground close to where Mak was sitting. There was a click – Colm recognised the sound of the safety catch being set on a rifle – and then the sound of Mola sitting down. He exhaled heavily. After a few seconds there were more scrabbling sounds, a cap being unscrewed, and determined gulping. Another pause, another drink, the screwing of a cap.

Mak had still said nothing.

'At least twenty,' Mola said. 'Loud and young. Carrying the tusks. They followed the two poacher boys, but after two kilometres the poacher boys went west. The soldier boys sent five off after them, but the others turned east, very suddenly, as if it was part of a plan. I followed them another hour. Dead straight, still carrying the tusks. Couldn't move through country at all without leaving a path of destruction and shooting at anything they saw; it was as if they were wanting to be found. But had I followed them any further I wouldn't have found you by dark. Nearly didn't, as I had to go slow in case the other five came back.'

'Did they?' Mak asked.

'Didn't see them.'

Mak exhaled. 'Very good. Thank you, Mola. Go to sleep. I

will wake you when we can't stay awake any more. I'll get Kwame to call it in when he gets here.'

'Where is he?'

'Escorting the sister back. Should only be a few minutes.'

Mola didn't say anything else. Colm heard him shuffling, pulling things out of his pack. After a couple of minutes, he went quiet.

Colm realised Fatou had switched off her torch, and the only light was from his, illuminating his foot and his notebook. He put his notebook away and switched off the torch. He sat there in the dark, just listening.

The silence and the darkness that followed didn't last. Not because of new light and new noise, but because of absence of the torchlight and the sound of voices allowed his ears and his eyes to adjust to other sounds and lights that had been there all along. He could hear a distant squabbling and squawking, like turkeys in a pen, punctuated by the occasional yip and bark. The sounds were a long way off. He tried to pinpoint them in his mind, thinking of the triangle, and where they were on it now. If he was right, he was listening to the vultures and hyena as they tucked into the carcass of the elephant. And, he realised with a shudder, into the bodies of the two young poachers.

But the lights surprised him more. Slowly, the dark stopped being dark. He realised he could see the shape of Fatou, wrapped in a sheet, barely three metres away. He could see Kennet, still sitting, hunched, just where he had been. He could see Mak, watching the way they had come. He could see a shape lying in the grass close to Mak. Mola. How could he see them?

He looked up and gasped.

The sky was clear. No clouds, not one. He could tell this because there were more stars above him than he had ever seen in his life. Thousands. Tens of thousands. Millions. Beyond count. The sky was dusted with them. In the absence of all other light, they washed the grass sea with a soft white glow.

Colm turned. Behind him Mak was standing. He hadn't been standing the last time Colm had looked his way. Perhaps he had stood up to prevent himself falling asleep. Colm was looking up at him from maybe ten metres away. Mak was motionless, his rifle tucked under one arm, its barrel pointed at the earth. He was looking in the direction they had been travelling, towards Nagero and safety. Colm leaned forward, put his hands on the grass, and pushed himself to his feet.

Standing, the starlight showed him even more. The grass that had started to feel endless and all-consuming shimmered in the slight breeze. The sound of the vultures and the hyena four kilometres away, or thereabouts, waxed and waned with the intensity of their bloodlust and feasting. And the starlight played on the grass.

I am in Africa, Colm thought, looking up at the sky. In the middle of one of the lightest places on earth, where, even now, nature dwarfs man. Once upon a time Ireland was all forest, until man cut down the forests and killed the bears for jewellery. Then, men didn't know the impact of what they were doing. They were thinking of survival, though they made jewellery from the dead. But they didn't know, couldn't see the impact of what they did. Couldn't see there would soon be no more forests, no more bears, if they didn't change their behaviour. Here, some men knew, and some men had changed their behaviour, and were on the frontline preventing those who had not changed their behaviour in a desperate fight to save something of the natural world. Here, there was still a chance to save something, before the whole world became a city centre.

He thought of Niamh and their unborn child. Would their child outlive the last elephant? Or would Hannington, Mak, and all the determined men and women across Africa and Asia fighting to protect the elephants find a way to stop the slaughter?

Then he froze. A new sound. A roar. Not like the monkey call he'd thought was a lion back at Nagero what felt like a year ago, though it was only yesterday. A real roar. A lion, surely. A real lion this time. He could feel his rational mind shutting down. He needed to run. The sound was too close. He needed to run. He was panicking. He recognised he was panicking, and leaned forward, put his hands on his knees, forced himself to breathe, deeply, to take back control of himself, to stop himself doing something stupid, something without thinking. Breathe, breathe.

'That's it. Breathe,' said a voice. He felt a hand on his back. He breathed, he could do nothing else, but he saw, out of the corner of his eye, the barrel of a rifle next to him. He panicked more. But he stuck with it. He knew he had to breathe. And the barrel of the rifle was pointed at the ground, not at him. He breathed. His mind was reasserting itself. He didn't need to run. There had been a roar, and then there was a second, but they were both a long way away, where the vultures and the hyena were now in an even greater frenzy. He took one, two, three more huge breaths, then stood up. He clenched his fists, scrunched his eyes closed, then opened them.

The voice that had spoken. It was female. He turned to face her.

It was Jane. She was grey in the starlight, like a ghost. She was looking in the direction the roars had come from. She patted Colm on the shoulder.

Kwame had walked to Mak.

'No one is following us,' he said.

CHAPTER EIGHTEEN

THE VEHICLES WERE A MOST WELCOME SIGHT. THEY HAD BEEN moved since Colm and the others had left them yesterday, and now faced the other way, towards Nagero. The other four rangers who had journeyed out with them greeted Kwame and Mola as if it were just another day, not one fraught with danger and death. Mak, however, was visibly relieved to see them.

The night had been one of the most uncomfortable in Colm's memory. Worse, even, than when he'd gone camping with scouts as a kid. He'd felt too wet, too cold, too hot, and too uncomfortable all at once. The grass and earth, so soft when he first lay down on it, felt like concrete after a while. The sound of the wind in the grass had initially been soothing and relaxing, but a mixture of nobody else talking and his own imagination had transformed the same noise into a sinister cover that concealed the approach of all manner of nightly terrors. The light of the stars, the most amazing and beautiful thing he had ever seen only a few short minutes earlier, had become a spotlight cutting through his eyelids and disturbing his very soul. He'd been convinced he would never fall asleep.

When Mak woke him in the morning Colm discovered his body had become one great ache. He'd needed Kwame's help to lift his backpack, or he would never have got it on his back.

The four rangers waiting for them were full of energy. They helped everyone unburden themselves and stowed the bags in the vehicles. They spoke steadily to Mak in an African language. Mak nodded several times, and his face grew even more serious. Colm asked Kwame what the language was.

'Swahili. Deng is from Sudan, he doesn't speak Zande or Bangala.' Another difference for Colm. He spoke English, and had schoolboy memories of Gaelic and French, and some awareness of German, and he might possibly recognise Italian and Spanish if he heard them spoken. But here everyone spoke at least three languages without thinking. His world felt very small.

The two-and-a-half-hour drive back to Nagero was as uncomfortable as the journey out. Perhaps more so, because every jolt impacted on limbs and muscles already aching. But the drive meant they weren't walking, and they weren't carrying, and Colm was fine with that.

He was in the Land Rover. Mak was in the front with two of the rangers whose names Colm couldn't remember. Colm was in the back with Fatou, Kwame, and Mola.

Mak leaned back and addressed everyone in the back. 'Deng and Gasimba came across the tracks of many men. Perhaps the killers of the elephant. They found them earlier than we did, not long after they left us. The tracks came from the direction of the forest, due east. But they found the tracks of men splitting off from the main group, heading in different directions, south and southeast. There may have been more than twenty of them, at least to start with.'

'Who do you think they are?' Fatou asked.

'They could be any of more than a dozen organisations we've come across. Or they could be a new one. Their lack of discipline suggests they are new, or this is a squad of new recruits. The army will deal with them quickly.'

The Land Rover bounced along. Colm held onto the seat. Fatou stared over Colm's shoulder, eyes steady, as if she was staring at nothing. Somehow, Mola slept.

————

If the vehicles had been a welcome sight; the walls of the ranger station at Nagero were more so. The driver, Gasimba, slowed down as they approached the compound, stopping completely at the gate. The two rangers on guard both came to Mak's side of the Land Rover and spoke with him. Once the conversation was over, Mak motioned for Gasimba to drive on, and he took them through the gate and to a halt two metres from the veranda of the main building. Behind them, the two sentries closed the gates as soon as the second vehicle with the other two rangers, Kennet, Jane, and Tony, had passed through.

The compound was strangely quiet. The only vehicles in it were the ones they had just arrived in, and other than the two men on the gate there was no one else in sight. No one came out to greet them.

Mak opened the door and got out. Kwame shook Mola awake and jumped over the side. He exchanged a glance with Mak and ran back to the gate, calling to the two men on sentry duty as he ran. Mak walked quickly up the steps to the veranda and into the main building.

Colm and the others got out of the vehicles at a more leisurely pace. Colm felt himself relaxing, releasing a tension he hadn't realised ran so deep. The uncomfortable night, the threat from armed men in every direction, the uncertainty, the isolation had all combined to erode his confidence. Arriving within the ranger station's fence brought a feeling of safety he hadn't known he needed. He started to notice things he had hardly thought about since he was last within the compound. The heat. The humidity. The fact that it hadn't rained for perhaps twenty-four hours. Despite the heat, he found himself longing for a hot drink. He followed Mak onto the veranda, determined to hunt down some coffee.

As he reached the top step, he noticed Jane. She had jumped over the side of the other truck, the rifle she'd had with her throughout the trip clutched firmly in one hand. She looked in every direction. He could see her eyes moving over every surface, sweeping each centimetre of the compound and fence. Her expression didn't change, but she took the rifle in her left hand, removed the magazine, slung the rifle over her shoulder by its strap, flicked the bullets from the magazine one by one, then quickly slotted them back in. Colm counted seven. She slipped the rifle from her shoulder, slammed the magazine back in, and walked purposefully down the side of the main building and out of sight. For some reason, Colm felt less safe now.

Fatou followed Colm onto the veranda. Mak stepped out of the radio room as Colm reached the doorway.

'Hannington is still gone,' Mak said, 'and most of the men with him. Another two took Erik to the hospital at Dungu. The only people here are Agoyo in the medical hut, and Jean and Félix on the gate.'

'Why is Hannington still gone?' Colm asked. 'He was only chasing down five men, wasn't he?'

'I could not reach him. But we have seen enough in the last twenty-four hours to know he may have encountered more than five men.'

'What do we do?' Fatou said. Kennet joined them having taken his time getting out of the Land Rover.

'There are too many armed men wandering around the park. We will lock down until Hannington comes back. There are only eleven of us trained to shoot here. Twelve, counting your sister,' Mak said to Kennet. 'If twenty armed men appear at the gates, we will be ready. Would someone go and see how Agoyo is?'

Mak was already striding towards the gates, where Kwame was still talking to the sentries. Colm and Fatou exchanged a glance and started walking towards the medical hut together.

Once out of earshot of everyone else, Colm asked the question again.

'What was odd?'

Fatou didn't answer at first. Five metres from the medical hut she stopped walking. Colm stopped too.

'In that building. The one in the middle of nowhere. Did you see any sign that anyone had stayed there the night before?'

Colm shrugged.

'No, neither did I. Jane ushered us out of there before we'd seen anything. I should have insisted.' Fatou twisted her foot on the earth.

'But why is that odd?'

'Because it's part of the story, and it's a good part. The description of the men camping in the decaying ruins of a monument to colonial futility.'

Colm raised his eyebrows. 'Good line,' he said.

'They need the coverage; they need the sympathy. Why would they not want us to see what it was that told them men had spent the night there? Perhaps the remains of a fire, or marks in the dust, or discarded burger-wrappers, anything that would make it real.'

'Jane's not one of the rangers, is she? She's Kennet's sister.'

'Kennet's sister, the teacher, who looks more natural with a rifle against her shoulder than she does without one? That's another story. Something is odd.'

Colm looked back at the main building. Under the veranda a figure had just emerged from the radio room, a rifle slung across their back, two other guns over one shoulder, and a heavy-looking bag over the other. The figure dropped the bag onto the veranda table, sliding the two guns next to it. The figure turned and Colm could see their profile. It was Jane.

'I agree,' Colm said.

There was a thunk, followed by the metallic rattle of a chain. The gates were now locked.

'Let's see how Agoyo is,' he said, and opened the door to the medical hut.

CHAPTER NINETEEN

AGOYO WAS LYING IN THE SAME BED HE HAD BEEN PUT IN TWO nights earlier. The dressing on his leg had been changed, but otherwise he didn't look as if he'd moved. There was a chamber pot next to the bed, and the expected smells rose from it.

'Colm Reid, Irish Telegraph,' Agoyo said. 'And this lady was never introduced.'

'Fatou Ba,' Fatou said, shaking Agoyo's hand with a mosquito net between them.

'Of the Irish Telegraph?'

'*Le Post du Soir*,' she said.

'Is that in Kinshasa?'

'Brussels,' she said.

Agoyo raised his eyebrows. 'You are Belgian?'

'*Oui.*'

Agoyo pushed himself into a better position to look at them.

'Forgive me,' he said. 'I learned at school about Belgians, and in my mind, they are all white men in hats, and they smell like the devil.'

'The world changes,' she said. 'Though I do wear hats. And I haven't washed in some time.'

'I could see you in a hat,' he said.

'Let me empty that,' Colm said, picking up the chamber pot. As he lifted it, he caught Agoyo's eyes. Agoyo nodded.

'Now, *Mademoiselle Le Post du Soir*, tell me,' Colm heard Agoyo say to Fatou as he stepped out of the medical hut, 'what is going on out there? Everyone is too busy to come and see me. I even miss Erik's company, despite him being unconscious.'

Colm stepped out into the yard. He carried the chamber pot over to the latrine hut, balancing the contradictory tasks of avoiding spilling anything over the edge and not looking at the contents at all. He emptied it quickly. There was a tap outside the hut at knee height. The water was warm. Colm rinsed the pot and returned to the medical hut.

There was only one ranger on the gates now they were locked. Everyone else seemed to be standing round the veranda table. He could see ten people, including the two other rangers who had made the trip into the park with them, and the other gate guard. The only person missing was Jane. No, there she was, leaning against the wall of the building at the far end of the veranda, watching, listening. Colm thought he should be listening too. But so should Fatou. And the evidently bored Agoyo.

Colm went back into the medical hut. Fatou was laughing, and Agoyo had a big grin on his face. Colm replaced the now-empty chamber pot by the bed.

'How do you feel about an assisted hop?' he asked.

'A what?' said Agoyo.

———

Between them, Colm and Fatou helped Agoyo hop across the yard to the main building. One of the rangers saw them coming, and Mak stopped talking until they had settled Agoyo on a stool, his back to the building wall, his wounded leg on another stool.

'I had better repeat myself,' Mak said. 'A woman from Nagero village has come to the gate. She was gathering fruit in the forest east of here and saw a large group of soldiers. They had stopped to eat. She didn't let them see her, and she didn't wait around.'

'Did she see how many?' Fatou asked.

'She did not. She saw at least six, but heard more, and had a feeling there were a lot of them. What that means, I don't know.'

'Are they the same ones who killed the elephant?'

'Very unlikely. Those men were heading away from where these men were. They would have had to double back on themselves and cover forty kilometres of grassland faster on foot than we did on wheels. I am assuming these men are ones we've had no warning of until now. Whether or not they are affiliated with any of the others is a different question.'

'How far away?' Colm asked.

'Less than three kilometres. They could turn up at the gates at any moment. I've sent word into the village for everyone to get out and head for Wando, that's the next village along the R420. But if these men have a plan, it will be to attack here.'

'Shouldn't we get out too?' Fatou asked.

'We can't. We have to protect the armoury and the confiscated ivory. You, however, can. I can't spare any men, but you can take one of the vehicles and drive to Wando or Dungu and wait until it is safe to return. But if you do, you need to go now. The same goes for you,' Mak looked at Kennet, Jane, and Tony in turn. 'I'd welcome extra hands if there's going to be a firefight, but you are under no obligation to me or to Nagero. It is your choice, each of the five of you. I cannot guarantee your safety whatever you choose. Stay or go. Choose quickly.'

'I'm staying,' someone said. Colm was surprised to realise it had been himself. He hadn't needed to think. If he wasn't going to get to see rhinos, then he could write a story about the men defending an ivory store against the odds. He felt proud of himself. It was what a journalist would have said.

'I'll follow your lead, Mr Haven,' Tony said.

'I will stay,' Kennet said.

'We need better intelligence,' Jane said. 'If there are twenty of them armed with AKs then the walls and gates will give us the advantage. If there's fifty of them armed with anti-tank guns, then we should all go. You can always find them later and take back anything they steal.'

'I agree, but I can't risk sending anyone to scout. I've too few men as it is.'

'What about reinforcements? Hannington and the others?' she asked.

'The last radio contact with Hannington he was still chasing the men who shot Agoyo and Erik. I have not been able to speak to him since hearing the information from the woman who came to the gate. He is out of range.'

'I choose to go to Wando,' Jane said. 'Open the gates and let me out.'

'Jane, it will be safer in here,' Kennet said.

'Not if they have anti-tank weapons, or grenades, it won't. Even petrol would be a problem. The fence is wood, Ken. It'll stop a bullet and it's a useful obstacle, but it won't stop fire or high explosives. A couple of dozen Molotov cocktails and they could burn this place to the ground without firing a shot. I'm going to Wando. Are you coming?' The question was directed at Fatou, who hesitated for one, two, three seconds, and then shook her head.

Jane picked up a rucksack that was next to her feet and slipped it onto her back. She picked up the rifle she'd been carrying for the last day. She stepped off the veranda without another word and walked across the compound to the gate.

The remaining sentry at the gate looked at Mak for instructions. Mak hesitated for a moment, then shrugged, and signalled to open the gate. The sentry unlocked the padlock, pulling out the chain, and opening one side far enough to create a gap. Jane walked through it, and the guard closed the gate behind her.

'She didn't ask which direction Wando is in,' Fatou said.

'She already had a bag packed,' Agoyo said.

'Colm, Fatou, Kennet. If you are staying, you should take a gun. If these men get in here and we can't stop them they will kill all of us, you included, despite journalistic neutrality, despite anything. They have no concept of non-combatant status. If you have a gun, you might get lucky and die more quickly.'

Colm didn't know what to say.

'I don't want a gun,' Kennet said.

Colm looked at Fatou.

'Show me how to use one,' she said. 'I can decide if I use it later.'

Colm nodded. Mak seemed satisfied.

'Come on. We have a lot to do and, if those soldiers come sooner rather than later, very little time in which to do it. This is what I want,' Mak said, and he laid out his plan.

CHAPTER TWENTY

BUT THE SOLDIERS DID NOT COME SOONER. THE RANGERS, helped by Colm, Fatou, Tony & Kennet, prepared to enact Mak's plan. They were sent to bring extra guns and ammunition from the armoury and told to stash them in locations Mak made them memorise. 'If your own weapons jam, or you run out of ammunition, you must know where to go for more,' he said.

'I've never fired a gun,' Colm said, feeling the weight of the three he was carrying to one of the hiding places.

'You get used to it,' Kwame said, taking two of the weapons from Colm and placing one on the ground. He held the other demonstratively.

'Hold it like this. Always keep the barrel pointed at the ground or at least away from other people. Never point it at anyone you aren't prepared to kill. When you want to fire it, do this, see? Flick this switch to that position,' Kwame flicked it, but flicked it straight back again, 'then line these two sights up with who you want to kill and squeeze the trigger. Keep the butt against your shoulder or the recoil will bruise you. It's a semi-auto, which means it fires a single shot but automatically loads the next one. When the magazine is empty press this to release and push a new one in. I hope you don't have to use it.'

Kwame picked up the other rifle and handed the two back to Colm.

They filled every possible container with water and left them all around the perimeter. If someone set the fence on fire, they would at least have a chance of putting it out. Though, as Mak pointed out, the wood was so wet it would take a lot of fuel to ignite it. Colm found himself hoping for rain.

Mak and Kwame backed the two vehicles up to the gates. Mak put lookouts on the roofs of four buildings in the corners of the compound next to the fence. The roofs were slightly lower than the top of the fence, even without the razor wire, but the lookouts could see over it if they sat up. Mak sent two men to sleep. He had organised them into overlapping shifts. Three pairs of men, three hours rest, six hours sentry. That left five weapons-trained people in the compound. Four, really, as Agoyo, whilst able to shoot, wasn't particularly mobile. Mak, Kwame, Tony, Mola, and Agoyo stayed in the compound with Kennet, Fatou, and Colm. Kennet, Fatou, and Colm moved bedding into the main building from the dormitories.

Then they settled down to wait. When night fell, Mak sent everyone who wasn't in the sentry rota to get some sleep.

Colm could not sleep. After lying in the dark under a table in the radio room for two hours he got up again and went out onto the veranda. It was lit by the single weak bulb overhead. Earlier, they'd managed to turn the huge table on its side to act as an effective piece of cover. It had taken eight of them. It was a very heavy, very solid piece of wood. Now Agoyo was asleep on a mattress behind it.

How Agoyo was managing to sleep was a mystery to Colm. Not only were there armed men somewhere outside the fence perhaps planning their deaths, but there was the basic but ongoing problem that the night was loud. The ever-present background music of insects and frogs echoed through the compound in competition with the slow rumble of approaching thunder. Rain was coming again.

The insect noise was a ringing. Colm hadn't thought about it until now, but as soon as he thought of ringing, he could only hear ringing, like a muted version of his grandparents' hall phone when he was a child.

There was another rumble of thunder, deep, and rolling.

He heard the call of something. A tentative sound, as if whatever made it wasn't sure. It might have been a bird, or an animal, he didn't know. It was like nothing he'd heard before.

He stood on the edge of the veranda looking around the compound. It was difficult to see. There were lights on in some of the huts, but they were low wattage, like the bulb on the veranda, and showed little. The stars and the moon had disappeared, presumably behind clouds he could not see. There were no floodlights or security lighting. He knew that lookouts were on four of the roofs, and they had powerful torches, but they were switched off. He hoped the lookouts hadn't fallen asleep. Though if the rain started again, they'd have trouble seeing anything even with torches.

It was strange to see no one on guard at the compound gates. A chair the sentries sometimes used sat empty, someone's cap abandoned on it.

The ringing of the insects was joined by the buzzing of what sounded like a different type of insects, all at once, as if somewhere out there was a conductor orchestrating the natural music. There was another rumble of thunder. The air was packed with noise, and the pressure was building.

There was a heavy thump, and Colm jumped. It had come from the direction of the fence near the medical hut. The sound of movement behind him startled him further. He turned

quickly. It was Kwame. He had been sitting on a stool towards
the end of veranda, quite still, so still Colm had not noticed him.
When the thump came, Kwame stood up and walked quickly off
the veranda towards the source of the sound, a rifle against his
shoulder. He disappeared into the shadows by the side of a shed.

Another sound, this time like a clock ticking, either an insect
or a bird, Colm didn't know. Tick, tick, tick.

Colm watched the darkness where Kwame had disappeared.
There was no sign of him, no movement. More thunder, and
away to the north, a flash of lightning followed, after many
seconds, by more thunder. Still some way away.

Kwame stepped onto the veranda behind him causing Colm
to jump again.

'Just a snake,' Kwame said.

'A snake?'

'It came over the fence.'

'What was the noise?'

'The snake. Must have dropped the last metre.'

'It was loud.'

'Big snake,' Kwame said. 'Two metres. Egg-eater.'

'Did you kill it?' Colm asked.

'Why would I kill it? It was just a snake.'

Colm looked at his watch. It was only midnight. One o'clock
in this time zone.

'Still early,' he said.

'Let's hope it's a short night,' Kwame said.

Colm didn't know what he meant and didn't ask. He closed
his eyes and breathed in. He could hear the insects and the wind.
He could smell the approaching rain. He breathed out, opening
his eyes.

'Do you think she'll be alright?' Colm asked.

'Who?'

'Jane. Walking to – where was it?'

'Wando. She should be. They haven't reached here yet, so unless they went past us, she'll be fine. Better than we will, perhaps.'

Kwame wasn't looking at him. He was watching the fence, or at least the outline of it in the dark.

He set his rifle down gently, leaning it against the big table, and reached for something on his chest, raising it to his eyes. Colm realised it was binoculars. There was a click and a high-pitched whirring, and the faintest hint of a green glow ringed Kwame's eyes. He adjusted the binoculars with his other hand. He froze.

'Wake Mak and Mola,' he said. 'Wake everyone, but as quietly as you can.'

He lowered the binoculars and took two steps forward, reaching into his pocket to bring out a piece of cloth. He stood on a stump stool and reached for the lightbulb that lit the veranda, and, protecting his hand with the cloth, unscrewed it and stepped off the stool to the ground. The veranda was plunged into darkness.

'Now!' Kwame hissed.

Colm walked into the radio room, feeling his way in the dark. He heard Kwame waking Agoyo behind him. He found a foot and shook it gently.

'What is it?' said Fatou's sleepy voice.

'I think they're here,' Colm said.

Outside someone fired a gun.

CHAPTER TWENTY-ONE

IT WAS THE FIRST TIME COLM HAD HEARD A GUN FIRED, AND IT wasn't quite what he had expected. It sounded like someone banging a steel pan with a stick, but the pan was muffled and there was no reverberation. Perhaps the sound had been absorbed by the wood of the veranda and the building. He was surprised it didn't scare him. Nor did he expect it to smell like that. He had an image of his mother, a memory from when he was small, of her hands in plastic bags with rubber bands round the wrists, and her hair strangely sculpted by a paste with an eye-watering stench. This smell was the same. Ammonia. He had not heard of gunfire smelling of ammonia before.

After thinking it through he made the decision to crawl under the table where his bedding – and the gun he had been allocated – were. He would wait there to see if anyone fired back, before continuing to follow his instructions and find and wake Mak. He was pleased with his confidence under fire. Though there had only been one bullet and it hadn't been fired in his direction.

Colm didn't need to find and wake Mak. Mak, Mola, and

Tony rushed through the radio room to the veranda less than a minute after that first shot was fired. At least Colm assumed it was Mak, Mola, and Tony.

'Stay there, all of you,' Mak's voice came from the darkness as he ran by. *All of you.* Kennet was in the room. Colm had forgotten him.

'Kennet?' Colm said. There was no answer.

Colm lay down on the mattress under the table again. He heard Kwame whispering out on the veranda, then Mak, then Agoyo, then another shot from one of them.

'Miss left, height good,' Agoyo said quite distinctly. A third shot followed. 'Hit. Chest. Down.'

More shots rang out from elsewhere in the compound. The sentries on the roofs, hopefully. There were shouts too, but Colm couldn't tell if they came from the rangers or whoever was attacking them in the dark. And more shots, somewhat muted, perhaps beyond the fence, somewhere in the night. These were different. The shots inside the compound were individual, distinct. Someone was choosing to pull the trigger before each one was fired. The shots outside the compound were continuous. Automatic. They sounded uncontrolled and desperate. They reminded Colm of the elephant, riddled with hundreds of bullets.

More whispering followed, and someone – it was too dark to see who it was – entered the radio room from the veranda, passed through it, and disappeared deeper into the building. A moment later there came the sound of a door closing. It might have been the door that led from the kitchen to the rear of the compound.

More shots. Outside the fence again, but different from the previous ones. Individual. Louder. Three in rapid succession. Bang, bang, bang. More shouting, though from further away, followed by rapid fire, higher in pitch than the three bangs.

Another bang. Then – nothing. A silence that slowly filled with the sound of insects. Colm counted. One minute. Two minutes. Three.

'Stay here.' Kwame's voice came from the veranda, speaking to Tony or Mak, whoever was still with him. Colm guessed Tony. There was the sound of footsteps on the planking, then on mud, moving away.

'What's happening?' Fatou said. Her voice was tense.

'Don't know,' Colm said. 'Perhaps they've gone.'

More footsteps. 'Where's Kwame?' Mak's voice coming onto the veranda from the right, quiet and calm.

'Northwest sentry,' Agoyo said. 'Wait, he's coming back.'

For Agoyo to know Kwame was coming back, he must be able to see in the dark. Colm guessed he had Kwame's binoculars, and they were thermal or had night-vision, or something. Colm heard boots hit the veranda.

'They've gone into the park. We shot at least four, including the one that climbed over the gate. Jean counted at least a dozen more. Some had torches.' Kwame's voice.

'They didn't put up much of a fight.' Mak.

'Jean thought something spooked them. They were climbing the walls, trying to get over the wire, then suddenly they were running away from something outside, not us.'

'Alright.' Mak paused. 'Perhaps we got lucky. Give it fifteen more minutes, then everyone back to sleep.'

'Did you hear those three shots?' Tony's voice.

'Yes. Different calibre. Then a fourth.'

'Last one fired. What's the northeast sentry firing?'

'AR-15. Every one of us has an AR-15.'

'That wasn't an AR-15. Wasn't an AK either.'

'A different faction?'

'Could be. Kwame, see if you can raise Hannington, let him

know. If you can't, call the station at Faradje, make sure the warden knows everything.'

'Should we ask for help?'

'Yes. At the very least we need the ivory and confiscated guns collected.'

The rangers fell silent.

Men had died no more than a hundred metres away. Colm could still smell ammonia in the air.

Colm thought about death. Thought about his regular commute to work. Standing on a station platform as a train passed at a hundred kilometres an hour. Waiting at a crossing for the lights to change to stop the traffic that was, otherwise, travelling a perfectly lethal fifty kilometres an hour. The line between life and death was thin. He put his hand on the rifle Kwame had shown him how to use. It lay on the floor beside his mattress. When the shooting had started, Colm hadn't once thought of picking it up.

Kwame was standing over him, speaking into the radio.

'Nagero mobile one, this is Nagero station. Are you receiving, over?'

There was no answer, other than static.

After Kwame had repeated the call half a dozen times, Colm spoke.

'What about the men who were shot?' he asked.

'We leave them till daylight,' Kwame said. He repeated his call into the radio.

'What if they're wounded?'

'What if the men who ran away are hiding just out of sight waiting to see if we'll open the gates and find out?' There was an edge of exasperation in Kwame's voice that Colm hadn't heard before.

'Sorry, I hadn't thought.'

———

'Colm, wake!' Colm felt a hand on his shoulder and chest, pushing, shaking. Where was he? Who-?

Fatou. Her hand was warm through his shirt.

'They've come back. Mak told me to wake you and Kennet. Where's Kennet?'

'Where's Kennet? I thought he was in here with us.'

'He's not.'

'One of the other rooms, maybe?'

'SHHHH.' The sound was loud and came from the veranda. Agoyo or Mak.

It was still dark. Colm had been asleep, but he had no idea how long. Five minutes? Five hours?

Then he heard the voice, clear and mellifluent, floating through the night air.

'Rangers of Nagero,' it said. A man's voice, rich with life and reason. 'There is no need for you all to die this day.' Whoever he was, he was outside the compound, not too far from the other side of the gate.

'Rangers of Nagero. We only want the teeth of the elephant. That is nothing more than the milk of the cow. The eggs of the chicken. Let us in, let us take them, we will not harm you.' The voice put Colm in mind of a talk show host who hadn't been able to make it as a politician.

Colm rolled out from under the table and bumped into Fatou, still crouching close to him. He got to his feet and, feeling his way along the radio room wall, found the doorway to the veranda. He crouched down. Fatou crouched beside him, her hand touching his back for a moment.

'Go speak to Jean, find out how many he can see,' Mak was saying. 'This man was not in the first attack. This is something else. What can you see?'

Someone stepped off the veranda and ran across the compound.

'Nothing yet. No one, just Jean and Félix in position,' Agoyo said.

'Tony, would you mind finding Mola and asking him to check the back wall, make sure this isn't just a distraction? Fire two shots if you see anyone who shouldn't be there.'

There was no reply from Tony, but footsteps moved along the veranda and disappeared into the dark.

'We need some light,' Mak said, his voice tight, as if he was talking to himself.

'Rangers of Nagero,' the voice came again. 'I know you can hear me. My men are not boys with guns, like these others I have seen running around your park. My men are trained. They have discipline. They will not run away when the shooting starts. They will still be standing when the shooting stops.

'I have been watching you for days. I know your strength, and your weakness. I know you blocked your gates with trucks. I know that tonight you fought off an attack from the so-called Soldiers of God. I know you killed some and the rest ran away. But they were not soldiers. They do not know God. My men are soldiers, and they do not need God. They need money. To get money they need ivory. You have ivory. Much ivory, just waiting to be burned. You will give it to me. You will move those trucks and open the gates in five minutes, or I will destroy them. I am talking to you, Sergeant Mak Kibwana. As ranking officer, there are many lives in your hands. You have five minutes to save them.'

'Did he say, "Soldiers of God"?' said a voice behind Colm. Kennet. Colm hadn't heard his approach.

'Quiet,' instructed Mak with a hiss. 'How does he know so much?'

'What if he isn't bluffing about the gates?' Agoyo said.

More running footsteps, two sets, from the left and the right.

'Jean and Félix have seen at least twenty men out front. It could be more – they might have both seen the same twenty, or there could be forty out there.' Kwame's report was breathless. 'Movement to either side too.'

'Mola says both your men in the rear have seen soldiers behind the compound. They think they're still there, hiding in the grass. They move just often enough to be seen.' Tony's voice.

Mak exhaled.

'We are surrounded. And they have sufficient discipline to show us we're surrounded without attacking or getting close enough for us to shoot them. But if they don't have missiles, explosives, or fuel, they still won't be able to get over the fence without losing many men. That's why they want us to open the gates. And if we open the gates, they will kill us all.'

'We must delay until dawn,' Kwame said. 'Much easier to defend the walls when we can see them coming. We only have three pairs of thermal binoculars. Hannington took the night vision scopes.'

'Four minutes,' said the voice.

'They won't delay. If they know we were attacked earlier, and there are only few of us, they must have been watching for a couple of days. They will have seen Hannington and the others leave, they will want to move before they come back.'

'Why didn't they attack yesterday when the gates were open?' Kwame asked.

'Maybe they only had one person watching. That would make sense. It would be difficult to miss more than twenty men in daylight, however disciplined they are.'

'What do we do?'

'If we open the gates, they will kill us all,' Mak said again. 'We call Faradje again, tell them we are under attack, then we delay, we hold them off until help gets here. Kennet, Colm, Fatou – get the guns you were given, and all the ammunition in there, and get behind this table with Agoyo. He has thermal binoculars; he'll be able to tell you if anyone is coming towards you. Kwame, get on one of those roofs so you can cover the gate. If they're not bluffing – wait, no, you need to come with me first. Tony, you can get into the loft space above us, it runs across this building. There are gaps, you can see all four sides. Give what cover you can from there when the time comes, but don't give your location away. Fatou, Kennet, Colm. If they get over the walls or the gates fall, get in the loft with Tony, shut the hatch, and stay quiet. Kwame, come on.'

Mak had already started moving.

'Where are you going?' Colm called.

Mak didn't answer.

CHAPTER TWENTY-TWO

THE METAL OF THE GUN WAS UNEXPECTEDLY WARM. THE bullets surprisingly heavy. Flick that switch, pull that trigger, when it's empty, depress that, slap a new one in, point, and pull. Easy.

Colm held it as if it was a snake.

A wind was blowing, and a gap appeared in the clouds letting the light of the moon and stars shine through. After the darkness, the moon was like a floodlight. Colm could see Agoyo propped up on two tree-trunk stools, one for his injured leg, one for his backside, so he could see over the upturned table with the binoculars. A rifle leaned against his shoulder.

Colm crouched beside him and watched Mak and Kwame crossing the compound with slow, long strides, turning their torsos through ninety degrees as they walked so that between them, they were covering half the compound with their rifles. What was the expression? With their field of fire?

In the starlight, on two of the roofs of the outbuildings, Colm could see the front sentries, Jean and Félix, lying flat, rifles in front of them. The fence was only slightly taller than the top of the buildings. Colm guessed that, lying down, they couldn't be seen from the other side of the fence, but they wouldn't be able to shoot over it either. The gap in the clouds closed and the compound was plunged into darkness once more.

'Three minutes!' said the voice.

Colm heard Mak and Kwame climb into the two vehicles and start their engines, drive them away from the gates, turn them round, and back them up until they were either side of the main building. Their headlights illuminated half the compound, including the gates. The gates themselves were massive feats of carpentry, many trees worked together, each with a hole the size of a fist to feed through the chain that held them shut. And, in front if them, a body lay on the ground. Colm had forgotten about that. The man climbing over the gates who Kwame had shot in the dark with Agoyo directing him with the binoculars. The headlights also showed the fence, and the roofs, and Jean and Félix lying down. There was another rumble of thunder, and another flash of lightning. They were much closer together this time.

'That is good, rangers of Nagero. Now open the gates! You have less than two minutes!'

Mak and Kwame ran back quickly across the packed earth onto the veranda. Colm felt the vibrations through the wood from their heavy boots. Kwame passed him and went to the radio.

'Faradje station, Nagero station, *code inconnu*,' he said, repeating it a second, and then a third time.

'One minute! This is your last warning,' the voice said.

Mak raised his rifle to his shoulder and pointed it at the gates. Colm did the same, though Colm was crouched behind the table. Mak was standing. Agoyo had let the binoculars hang around his neck. He picked up his rifle and took aim too. Above them, Colm heard Tony moving in the loft.

The silence of the next few seconds felt louder than the earlier shouting. Though it wasn't silent, not really. The insects were still ringing, accompanied by the frogs. And he could hear the rain in the distance, though it hadn't reached them yet. There was another flash of lightning. A very brief pause. More thunder. Wind. More lightning, right on top of them this time. The thunder that followed arrived less than a second later, but in fraction of a second there was a different thunder. Gun shots. Many bursts from outside the compound, coming from the northwest of the gate, from deeper in the park. Colm heard men cry out, and one started screaming. Mak and Kwame lowered their guns and looked at each other in reflected light from the headlights. Mak looked in the direction of the roof Jean lay sentry on. Kwame nodded and set off at a run.

The rain had arrived. And this time, it was heavy.

———

Colm felt the gun in his hands. Ran his mind over what he had been told. Switch, trigger, ammunition. He stepped back, into the shadows. The deeper shadows. He needed to know if he would pull the trigger. If something, if someone, came through the gates, what would it take for him to pull it? Would they have to be firing? Or would they just have to come through it? Could he do it at all? He thought of Niamh. He didn't think he could do it.

He thought about the elephant. A living creature killed by hundreds of bullets. What would the equivalent be for a person? Something so small that a single injury was hardly noticeable, but hundreds of them would kill. Bee stings? Shaving cuts?

They had cut off its trunk. They had cut off its trunk to get to the other tusk. An elephant had a trunk. That was one of the things that made it an elephant. They'd stopped it being an elephant to satisfy their greed. That was worse than simply killing it.

Colm gripped the barrel more tightly and put his finger over the trigger. He remembered the safety switch, but he didn't turn it off.

Another flash of lightning. The thunder followed immediately. It was on top of them. The rain was pounding on the roof of the veranda, on the ground of the compound, on the two vehicles. Their headlights lit up a wall of water. The gates were difficult to see, though they were only fifty metres away.

He saw Kwame running back, saw Mak step round the table and into the rain to meet him, saw Kwame shouting into Mak's ear. He heard a thumping above him, a shouting.

'Mak, Mak, they're behind us!' Colm caught the words. He looked at Fatou, she'd heard them too. It was Tony, above them. Mak and Kwame hadn't heard, the rain was too loud. Agoyo had heard.

'Tell him!' Agoyo shouted.

Colm's legs seemed to move on their own. He was standing up, moving along the table and round, down the steps, to Mak, who was turning. Kwame was running away, following some order.

'WHAT?' Mak roared on seeing him. He roared to be heard, not out of emotion.

'TONY SAYS THEY'RE BEHIND US!' Colm shouted back.

Mak's reaction was instant.

'COME WITH ME, STAY BEHIND ME, KEEP YOUR FINGER ON THE TRIGGER!'

And Mak was running. Colm followed him, again on instinct. He caught sight of Fatou, watching him, her rifle half-raised. Agoyo was watching the gate, ignoring everything except his task.

Mak stopped dead at the edge of the side of the main build-ing. It wasn't that dark back there. Colm stopped just behind Mak. He could see light bulbs burning in three of the huts, the latrines, the barracks, the armoury. But they were weak lights, the same as the bulb had been on the veranda. They only hinted at shadows, and there was a wall of rain between Mak, Colm, and them.

A figure ran across the edge of one of the weak pools of light blurred by the rain. A shot sounded. The figure fell. A flash of lightning lit up the whole of the rear of the compound for the briefest of moments. The fallen figure was lying on the dirt, pummelled by rain. Colm looked up to the roofs of the two buildings he knew had sentries on. Gasimba and Deng at the last rotation. But he was too slow, the light from the lightning strike had gone, and he could see only rain.

He felt a hand on his shoulder. It was Mak, shaking him, speaking to him. He couldn't hear.

'WHAT?'

Mak spoke again. Colm still couldn't hear it all, but he did pick out 'BINOCULARS'. He understood. There was no light here. Agoyo had the thermal binoculars, and he didn't need them. The two trucks' headlights were showing what was happening.

Mak dragged Colm to the back door of the main building and pushed him through it.

The sound of the rain changed; he'd stepped out of it. He realised he was drenched. He didn't care. He looked around. He'd not been in here before. Three doors. Not the first. The second led to a corridor, a light on. He went in. Opened the first door off it, then the second. The radio room. He entered, catching sight of Kennet against the far wall, sitting quietly, a bottle of beer in his hand. Out the other door, onto the veranda, back into the real noise, to Agoyo.

'MAK NEEDS THE BINOCULARS!'

Agoyo didn't lower his gun, just slipped the binoculars from round his neck with his steadying hand, passed them to Colm, then resumed his aim.

Back through the radio room, out the door, and Colm felt something punch his cheek. He dropped to the ground, dropped his gun, dropped the binoculars. He scrabbled, found both, crawled to where Mak had last been.

He was still there, crouched on one knee in a firing position. Colm stumbled to his knees beside him.

'HERE!' Colm roared, pushing the binoculars towards Mak.

Mak took them, raised them, adjusted them. Colm could see a faint green light around Mak's eyes. Colm felt his cheek. What had hit him? He couldn't feel anything wrong. Had it just been rain?

Mak said something in one of the languages Colm didn't know. But he knew the tone. That was the tone Colm used when he said the word "shit".

Mak dropped the binoculars and fired, blindly, into the darkness.

Colm felt the binoculars hit the knuckles of his left hand. He reached and picked them up with his right. Raised them to his eyes.

He'd never seen anything like it. What had been darkness and thunder and rain punctuated by three feeble dots of light from the bulbs became – not day, it was nothing like day – but it was as easy to see as it was in daylight. Colm felt his heart stop. Or thought he did.

There were two figures lying in the dirt now. One was moving, but not in a coordinated way. A quick glance at the rooftops showed one of the sentry posts empty, and the other one was occupied, but by someone who was no longer part of the fight. He saw two men, one against the wall of the armoury, the other crouching in the doorway of the barracks, both in firing positions, both occasionally letting off shots, but both clearly blind in the dark, because they were shooting at nothing.

And then he saw the real problem. There were men on the roof of the barracks. Of the latrines. Of the armoury. Of the ivory shed. At least five. And more on the ground, coming towards them, threading through the rain. Another four. These men couldn't see any more than the rangers could. Probably couldn't hear, either. But there were too many of them. They'd got over the fence, got past the razor wire, and they were here.

'ON THE ROOF,' Colm shouted to Mak, and, lowering the binoculars, tried to show him with an arc of his arm. Mak raised his fire. Colm raised the binoculars again.

Mak couldn't see anyone. His shots were missing. No one else could see anything either. All fire was wild. One of the rangers was barely two metres from one of the intruders, but both were being so cautious that neither knew the other was there. It was chaos.

But then there was another flash of lightning, and everything changed.

The flash blinded Colm, turning the pale green world of the thermal binoculars into white hot light. A second later Colm was hit by something heavy that knocked him face down into the mud. He heard multiple thunks as bullets hit all around him, into the earth and the wood of the building. He heard more shooting, and screams.

Then he heard it again. Just as at the start of the night. Bang. Bang. Bang. A very different gun to the others, clearly audible over the rain. Bang. Bang. Bang. Then a shout. An African language, but unlike all the other shouts in languages he didn't know, this one had come in a female voice. A fizz. More shots, more normal shots, not the bang bangs. Then a hand on his back, dragging him. He found his feet, made them work, helped whoever was dragging him. Suddenly he was out of the rain and lying on wooden boards. He was back in the building.

'You hit?' Mak's voice. Colm shook his head. 'Hey. Can you see?'

'Lightning. Through the binoculars. It's getting darker. It's coming back.'

Colm was telling the truth. He could see again. A little. He pushed himself into a sitting position but felt a hand on his arm.

'Stay low.' Mak again. 'I don't know what just happened. I saw Gasimba shot. Then, I don't know.'

Colm heard footsteps inside the building, coming towards them. He reached for his gun, but realised it was still outside in the mud. Mak pushed him against the wall, knelt in front of him, raised his gun towards the doorway. All Colm could see was his silhouette.

'Colm!' Fatou said. The silhouette relaxed.

'We are here,' Mak said.

Fatou was in the doorway, carrying her gun.

'Agoyo says to tell you they have not breached. There is still a firefight out front. Jean does not think it's Hannington and the patrols returning because the fire is AKs. What happened to you?'

Fatou changed tone completely with the last sentence. Colm could see in monochrome now, but he didn't understand what she was talking about.

'It's raining,' he said. And tried to sit up a bit better.

Mak inhaled, and then exhaled, big, cleansing breaths. Then he stood up.

'Thank you. Both,' he said. 'Stay here.'

He stood by the doorway, looking out into the back of the compound, then stepped through and was gone.

The noise of the rain seemed to be lessening. Gunfire was audible over it, coming from some way off.

'What happened out there?' Fatou asked.

'I don't know,' Colm said. He pushed himself up, to his knees, to his feet. His sight was returning. 'They were all over us, then there was a lot of shooting, and it stopped. Mak said he saw Gasimba shot. There were nine men out there a minute ago, then the lightning. I just don't know.'

There was a window beside the door. Through it fell the faint light from the bulbs across the compound. Colm went to it, crouched, looked out. It took his eyes a while to get used to the darkness.

He sensed Fatou crouching next to him.

'*Mon dieu!*' she said.

Through the window Colm could see a figure standing in the rain. It was Mak. His rifle was at his side. His head was sweeping left and right. There were shadows of shapes on the ground all around his legs. Bodies.

'Gasimba? Deng? Justin? David?' Mak called. Someone replied, Colm was too far away to hear what the reply was. Mak walked towards it and out of their sight.

Colm ran his hand over his eyes, squeezing them shut.

'She told me it would be dangerous,' he said. He sat back on the ground, put his head in his hands.

'Who told you?'

'One of the journalists on my paper. Aileen O'Connor. She–'

'You know Aileen O'Connor?'

Fatou's question was so direct, and so familiar, it cut him short.

'Yes, she works at my paper.'

'She is my hero! She is why I became a journalist!' Amidst the rain, the thunder, and the lightning, amidst the gunfire and the screams of injured men, Fatou's tone of voice, of adoration, was the strangest contrast Colm could have imagined. In that moment he remembered that Aileen O'Connor was the reason he had become a journalist, too. Which annoyed him.

'Don't you start,' Colm muttered. 'Yes, I know her. She warned me. She – aaah, she resigned from the paper because they wanted to send her here without any security. They sent me instead.'

'She is my hero.'

'You repeating that doesn't help.' Colm massaged his face with his hands.

There was another flash of lightning. This time, the thunder was a little further away. The storm was moving off.

'How did you do that?' Fatou said.

Colm lowered his hands and opened his eyes. Fatou had not been talking to him.

Standing in the doorway, soaked to the skin and motionless as time, was Jane Haven.

CHAPTER TWENTY-THREE

'Where's Ken?' Jane asked.

'Radio room,' Colm said.

Jane walked straight past them and into the building. Her voice reached them less than a minute later.

'Ken, we need to go. Now.'

'We have to meet them.'

'Ken, we're not going to meet them. They have no power here.'

'They promised to take us to the rhinos.'

'Ken, snap out of it. We have to go. Now!'

The explosion cut the conversation short.

At the time Colm thought it was the loudest sound he had ever heard. Perhaps it was. It was certainly louder than the gunfire, which was continuing outside the compound. It was louder than the rain, which fell like a wall of noise. It was louder than the thunder had been at any point. It was a bang, like the biggest firework in the world. It hurt his ears. The world went quiet in its aftermath. The building shook.

Colm found himself running, with Fatou and, as it turned

out, following Jane, running through an eerie world where sounds only reached him through layers and layers of cotton wool, running through the radio room and out onto the veranda, a distance of only a few metres that stretched as if he was running towards it but moving backwards.

Agoyo was still there, seated on a stool cut from a piece of trunk, his leg on another, but his rifle was on the floor, and his head hung forwards. Colm knelt beside him and saw thick red blood in Agoyo's eyes.

The headlights of the two vehicles no longer illuminated the gates. The gates were no longer there. That was easy to see. They had been replaced by a ball of flame.

'Ken! On your feet!' Jane shouted.

'Too late,' said another voice. It was Mak. 'All of you, get into the loft with Tony. Don't make a sound. If someone opens the hatch, shoot them. Keep shooting until they or you are dead. Go. Now. NOW!'

Fatou looked at him, looked at Jane, looked at the ball of fire that was all that was left of the gate, and ran into the radio room. Colm almost followed her, but Jane and Kennet weren't moving, and he hesitated.

'Agoyo! Agoyo!' Mak knelt beside the wounded ranger, using a field dressing to wipe the blood from his eyes. Agoyo started and his head snapped up. Mak exhaled. 'Just a splinter,' he said, holding it up as evidence.

'The gates. They blew up–'

'We can see that,' Mak said, He turned his head, listening. Colm realised he was starting to hear other things again as well. Rain. The roar of flames. Shouting.

'They are already down the sides and round the back,' Mak said. 'There is no escape now.'

'They were round the back before,' Colm said.

'They were. They thought the back was an unlikely exit

route, so they only put a dozen of their men to guard it. They gave those men instructions to climb the fence when the shooting started. They didn't anticipate that the shooting would start outside the compound. They didn't anticipate that the shooting would be started by men who weren't them or us, and they attacked too soon, and we fought them off. There'll be more of them soon. Where on earth did you come from?'

Mak's last question was directed at Jane.

Colm was listening, but he was watching as well. The fire where the gates had been was highlighting the edge of shadows. There were now twenty or thirty men in the front of the compound. All armed. All pointing their guns at the veranda. Walking slowly, disciplined, in formation.

'Shouldn't someone be shooting?' he asked.

'Give them the ivory,' Jane said, ignoring Mak's question. 'And give them Ken and me.'

'They are not going to be asking what I want to give them, are they?' Mak said. 'We're in their hands now.'

Mak put his rifle on the ground and raised his hands.

————

'Rangers of Nagero. I am very disappointed in you,' said the voice. The voice Colm had heard from the other side of the fence without seeing a face. Now he saw the face.

It was young. Younger than he was. An intelligent, healthy face. The man it belonged to was slender, and not particularly tall. Perhaps one metre seventy, one seventy-two. He was wearing an army dress uniform, not fatigues or battle dress, as if he were on parade. It was immaculate, down to the medals over the breast, and the shine on his shoes. His ceremonial hat peaked and large. There was a pistol at his belt in a leather holster in polished brown. Another soldier, who was wearing jungle camouflage, was keeping the smart man dry by holding a large golf umbrella over him. The umbrella was an off-gold colour with a logo. Milanese fashion.

The strange pair stepped onto the veranda out of the rain. The officer moved his head slightly and the soldier took the umbrella away and collapsed it, standing at ease holding the umbrella as if it were a gun. Three quick hand signals from the officer sent a number of the other soldiers running in different directions, some into the building, others down the sides of the building, others out into the compound. Eight remained with their machine guns trained on Colm and the others.

The officer glanced down at his shoes, noticed something, and held his hand out to the soldier with the umbrella. The soldier took a clean white cloth from his pocket and handed it to the officer, who bent down, wiped something from his right shoe, and handed the cloth back.

'Which of you is Sergeant Mak Kibwana?' the officer said, staring at Mak and Agoyo.

The wound on Agoyo's forehead was still bleeding, and he was blinking, perhaps afraid to move his hands to wipe his eyes.

'I am Sergeant Kibwana,' Mak said.

The officer didn't react. He instead looked at Agoyo more closely, leaning forwards from the waist, his hands clasped behind his back. He inspected Agoyo's leg wound, then looked at the bleeding from Agoyo's forehead. He straightened up and turned to Mak.

'I am very disappointed in you, Sergeant Kibwana. You cost the lives of many men by not opening that gate when I instructed you to.'

'I am not permitted—'

'I HAVE NOT FINISHED TALKING,' the officer said, his face suddenly rigid with anger. Colm saw the soldier with the umbrella look away, just briefly, an instinctive movement. Mak said nothing, just stared ahead of him, looking over the officer's right shoulder at the smoke pouring off the burning fence either side of the remains of the gate.

As soon as it had arrived, the officer's anger was gone.

'But where are my manners?' he said. 'I have not introduced myself. I am Captain Rick, and these men, along with myself, have the honour, the distinct honour, of serving in the Brotherhood of Souls. I shall not introduce all of my men; it would take too much time. Under different circumstances, I would shake you by the hand. However, as I am disappointed in you, I shall not do that. Instead, if I may, I will express my sentiments in the following manner.'

And with that, Captain Rick took the pistol from his belt, flicked off the safety catch, and shot Agoyo through the head.

CHAPTER TWENTY-FOUR

COLM WAS NUMB. PERHAPS HIS HEARING HADN'T FULLY recovered from the explosion that destroyed the gates, but the bullet that killed Agoyo sounded weak, no more than the snap of a Christmas cracker. It entered the ranger's temple and exited below his ear, taking a large section of his jaw with it. Blood, bone, and brain matter hit Mak, hit Kennet, hit Colm on his trousers and shoes. The bullet hit the floor of the veranda and buried itself in the wood, spitting out a large splinter that pinwheeled off the end of the veranda and disappeared into the rain.

Mak called out, before the shot, in the split second he realised what the captain was about to do. He reached out, but stopped instantly as two of Captain Rick's soldiers jabbed the barrels of their machine guns towards him, fingers on their triggers.

Colm felt fear rising within him. He felt the urge to run. A desperate, overwhelming urge, an instinct. But, just as instinctively, he knew he couldn't. If he ran, he would be shot. So he breathed. Controlled his breathing as quietly as he could, taking

long, slow, deep breaths. And he hoped, he really hoped, that
Captain Rick wasn't about to shoot them all.

He wasn't. The captain smiled at Mak, flicked the safety back
on his handgun, slipped it neatly into its holster, and fastened the
catch.

'There,' Captain Rick said. 'You understand how disappointed I am. Don't disappoint me again, Sergeant Kibwana.
Where is the ivory?'

Mak didn't move. A bead of liquid was running from the
corner of his eye. Colm couldn't tell if it was a rain drop, sweat,
or a tear.

'In a locked hut behind this building,' Mak said, his tone
distant.

'Give me the keys.'

'The deputy warden has the keys.'

'The deputy warden, let me see,' Captain Rick took a small
notebook from his left jacket patch pocket and flicked through a
few pages. 'Ah, yes, Deputy Warden Hannington Banze. He led
reinforcements to deal with a group of ill-disciplined poachers
only yesterday morning. It's surprising how stubborn those
poachers turned out to be, though perhaps, when we have the
ivory safely away, those poachers will disappear of their own
accord.

'Sergeant Kibwana, I shall believe you. The absence of the
key is no issue for determined men such as mine. I refer you to
what recently happened to your gates.'

The captain waved a hand at one of his men, who snapped a
smart salute and ran off.

'Now, Sergeant Kibwana, onto our second item of business.
Why don't you introduce me to your friends? Two white men
and a white lady, no less. A white lady who has suffered recent
trauma, I see.' Captain Rick was studying Jane with an air of

curiosity, looking at the filthy bandage on her arm, and the scar tissue and bruising on her face. 'And you are?'

'Jane Haven. I am a ranger, from Kenya,' Jane said, her voice flat, as if she were a soldier addressing an officer.

'No. No, you are not. I have an ear, Jane Haven, and I hear no Kenya in your voice. You may be working or living in Kenya, but if that is so you have not long been there. I detect a touch of the Baltic Sea in your tones. Are you perhaps from Sweden?'

'Norway.'

'Ah, my apologies. And you, sir, are, what, twenty-five centimetres taller than this lady, and at least twice her weight, but there are similarities in your faces that lead me to guess you are related. Who might you be?'

'I am Kennet Haven. From Norway. I have a conservancy in Kenya. Jane is my sister.'

'Do you indeed? You have also spent a lot of time in South Africa, I hear. A ranger and a conservationist brother and sister visiting Nagero from Kenya. How very interesting. And you, sir. Who might you be?'

Despite knowing the question, or something like it, was imminent, Colm still clenched inside, as if a hand had squeezed his heart. *Don't shoot, I'm a journalist; don't shoot, I'm a journalist.*

'Colm Reid. I'm a journalist from the *Irish Telegraph*, in Dublin.'

'Indeed, you are. But born closer to Belfast, I think? I had the pleasure of spending some time in Dublin one summer. The mystery grows. Norwegian conservationists, Irish journalists, Congolese rangers, and the Soldiers of God. I wonder how all these things connect.'

'Who are the Soldiers of God?' Colm couldn't help himself. He regretted speaking the second the words had left his mouth.

Captain Rick's eyes flashed, but only for the briefest of moments, before he smiled.

'I am glad you asked me that, Colm Reid, from the Irish Telegraph. The Soldiers of God is one of the names used by an old organisation that has been hiding in the jungle for nearly fifteen years. They have some lofty ambition to rule Africa according to the Old Testament, though given that, in those fifteen years, they have committed every sin listed in the Old Testament, and a number of others those ancient scribes never even thought of, I have not taken that ambition too seriously.'

Captain Rick clasped his hands behind his back and started to pace a tight line, turning back on himself after every three steps.

'The Soldiers of God have survived by crossing the borders when it suited them. If the Ugandan army got too close, they'd disappear to Rwanda. If the Rwandan army got too close, within a few days they would be in South Sudan.

'They haven't been heard of much recently. Rumours said their leader, a colourful character by all accounts, died and the rest of them went home. This is not true, but they have not been very visible for several years, that much is certain.

'Until now. Suddenly, my scouts come across not one, but three squads of soldiers in the forests around Garamba who claim to be of the Soldiers of God. Ordinarily, this would be but background information for me, like being told that my scouts have seen some trees. Except for the fact that one of those squads attacked this station last evening and was driven off.

'That in itself still wouldn't have been of concern to me. They are not soldiers, just boys with guns. However, when that same group came back a few minutes ago and attacked my men, they drew my attention.

'Boys with guns still have guns, and the AK-47 was designed to be used by people who don't know how to use guns. They shot some of my men. But my men *do* know how to use guns and shot a lot of their men. Except for these three.'

Captain Rick stopped pacing and raised his right arm, beckoning to someone out of sight deeper in the compound. Four of his soldiers walked into position below the veranda. Three of them were each dragging another man. They threw their prisoners to the mud and stepped back, pointing their weapons at the prisoners' backs.

'I've had a little talk with these three. They have orders, would you believe? They also have initiative. As I said, they are not soldiers. Their initiative was to storm the ranger station at Nagero which they had been told is full of guns and ivory. This was contrary to their orders. Ill-disciplined! I would have disciplined them already, but I am short of porters for the journey back. We shall come to that. This was contrary to their orders; did you hear that? And what were their orders?' He was looking at Colm as he spoke. Colm had no idea what he was talking about.

'You don't know?' Captain Rick continued. 'Their orders were to find a white man and a white woman by the name of Haven and to escort them through the jungle to the leader of the Soldiers of God at a pre-arranged camp site. What do you think of that, Colm Reid of the Irish Telegraph?'

Mak half-turned in Kennet's direction, then checked himself and faced over Captain Rick's shoulder again. Colm didn't know what to think. He hadn't heard of the Soldiers of God, he'd not come across them in Aileen O'Connor's notes. But Captain Rick had said they went by other names, so perhaps he had read about them under a different name. The description Captain Rick had given applied to a dozen of the groups in Aileen's list – moving from one country to another to flee pursuit. But what the hell had Jane and Kennet been up to?

'Why, Mr Kennet Haven, had you agreed to meet with the Soldiers of God?'

Captain Rick looked Kennet in the eye. It was a strange

sight. The officer was tiny compared with Kennet. More than twenty centimetres shorter and half his weight. Kennet looked down at him and smiled.

'They said they could take me to the last northern white rhinos in the wild.'

Captain Rick tilted his head slightly.

'And why do you want to go to the last northern white rhinos in the wild?'

'To save them,' Kennet said, very simply.

Captain Rick looked at Kennet for a full minute without speaking. Then he bowed his head, clasped his hands behind his back, and resumed pacing.

Off the veranda the rain was lessening, and the sunrise was imminent. Captain Rick's soldiers had started filing past carrying tusks from the ivory store. Some they stacked on the ground in the middle of the compound. Others they carried out through the smoking gap where the gates had been. The three members of the Soldiers of God were dragged to their feet and forced to lift a large tusk each. Once they had shouldered their burdens they were marched through the gateway at gunpoint. The gateway stank of petrol.

As they were leaving, another prisoner was being brought forward. It was Kwame.

'You see, this is the problem with the Soldiers of God. They are terrorists. They extort and murder. They have kidnapped the children of whole villages in Uganda, making the boys carry guns and the girls carry babies in their bellies. They have no *principles*. Unlike the Brotherhood of Souls. We do not kill unless under threat of death. We do not steal unless the theft changes nothing. Like your ivory. Your ivory will be burned when it is handed to the government, and once it is burned it will no longer exist. When we have stolen it then, for you, it will no longer exist.

'The Soldiers of God will not take you to the last northern

white rhino because these rhino do not exist. There are no rhino, not any more. I have never seen one, and nor have most of my men. Some old ones, perhaps. Ha! You are lucky you encountered the Brotherhood of Souls, or you would have ended up dead at the hands of the Soldiers of God. Or worse.' Captain Rick looked Jane up and down. 'Now, you will carry ivory in place of my men who died. When we have taken it to safety, if I am not disappointed in you, then I may allow you to leave. Perhaps after someone has paid money to encourage me to allow you to leave. Make sure you do not disappoint me.'

Captain Rick patted the shoulder of Agoyo's body, then walked off the veranda towards the gate, his umbrella carrier hurrying after him to keep him dry.

CHAPTER TWENTY-FIVE

THE SOLDIERS WALKED WITH THE MINIMUM OF CONVERSATION. It was the first thing Colm fixated on. He was expecting chatter, banter, perhaps even a song. But they were almost silent. Was it discipline, or was it that most of them were carrying tusks that weighed up to twenty-five kilogrammes? About four stone in imperial weight. The equivalent of carrying an eight-year-old child. And that was on top of bags, guns, ammunition.

They walked fast, too. Faster than he was expecting. Captain Rick and his men had sauntered into the compound as if they were taking a stroll in a park. But once they were outside it, they moved. Steady. Constant. Single file. Colm remembered a line from Star Wars. "Single file, to hide their numbers". Mak had said something similar when they had seen the tracks of the men who had shot the elephant. Captain Rick's men were not like those men. Captain Rick's men were sensible. Silent, single file, quick,

Which suggested that the chance of being found and rescued was minimal.

The second thing he fixated on was the park. It was very

different when you were forced to walk through it at gunpoint. Instead of a thing of wonder it had become a thing of dread. But he concentrated on trying to remember the notes he would have taken under other circumstances. His notebook was back in the compound. At least, he assumed it was. He hoped he would find it when he got back.

When he got back.

He fixated on the park. Garamba National Park, the size of Donegal. Was green. Incredibly green. Pleasingly green. Like a giant feckin' shamrock. They walked through grass that rose to anywhere between their knees and over their heads. They avoided the trees; he couldn't work out why. They marched on through the grass.

Even when silent, a group that consisted of so many men – there must have been about fifty – could not avoid having a presence. Were they scaring away the wildlife? Colm saw nothing larger than an insect, although some of those were fairly big. He saw caterpillars the size of his fingers, and cricket-like things as big as his hand.

And he heard things. A constant twittering, a tweeting. Was that birds or insects?

He heard what he guessed were birds, but not close by. In the trees. Like something impersonating a small dog.

'Is that a parrot?' he said.

Kennet looked back at him, his eyes wide in warning. The soldier behind him looked at him without expression.

Colm gazed ahead again at the grass. But kept the image of the soldier in his mind. For all Captain Rick's polish, slickness, and talk of discipline, the soldier behind him was a little shabby. Army boots, old and worn, the sole coming away on one. Jungle camouflage, fatigues, but sewn in places, as if they had been taken from a dead man and the bullet holes repaired. A peaked cap. Not an officer's cap like Captain Rick wore, just a simple cloth skull cap with a peak, dark greens and greys, like his fatigues. It kept the rain from his face but made seeing his eyes difficult. And his skin. His skin was the darkest Colm had encountered. Mak was very dark. Agoyo had been dark. But this man was darker still.

Inexplicably, Colm decided he liked this man, this soldier of the Brotherhood of Souls who was marching behind him, a rifle pointed at his back. Colm decided that this was a good man in a bad place. Why he decided this, whether following an instinct, or trying to convince himself he wasn't in immediate danger of being shot dead, he could not work out.

He shook his head. Kept walking. Focused on Kennet's broad back. Marched.

––––––

It was three hours before they stopped. And that is all they did. Stop. The line stopped. The soldiers put down their burdens and sat. One or two smoked. All drank. Colm and Kennet were offered water from a tin flask. The water tasted metallic. The flask was dented, as if a rock had hit it. Or a bullet.

Fifteen minutes, and they were on the move again. Through the grass like a fifty-person long snake. Single file. Hides the numbers. Avoid the trees. Why avoid the trees? Colm still didn't understand that.

Bird song. Insects. Quiet. The swishing of legs through grass. The occasional ting of metal on metal as guns hit something, perhaps water flasks. Mutters from up and down the line. No sign of large animals. Nothing. There were elephants in the park. Giraffe. Where were they?

Was he imagining things, or had it got dark? It was hardly noon. He looked up.

Above them was grey, and the rain, which had reduced to a

drizzle over the preceding three hours, tumbled from it. To the east the sky was fresh blue, as if it had just come out of the washing machine. They'd been walking almost towards that for some time.

It was in the west the change had come. The sky had shifted from drizzle-grey to grimace dark. Bad news dark. He knew skies like that. Skies like that took the roof off the outhouse. Skies like that held rain so raw it would rip the clothes right off ye. The sky last night had probably looked like that, but he'd not been able to see it, because it was night. The weather hadn't finished with them yet.

Biggest river basin on the planet. More water fell in the Congo basin than anywhere else. It was big, sure. Eighty-odd times the size of, yeah, yeah. Lot of water, that.

His feet kept moving, one in front of the other. Kennet's feet kept moving, one in front of the other. The tusk they'd given Colm to carry was not one of the bigger ones. He rested it on his shoulder until it rubbed too much, then he switched shoulders. They'd not given him a bag to carry, and he didn't have a gun, so in relative terms he was light of burden. His legs felt fine, right. Two hours a day in the gym, running and weights. No real-world exercise in a decade, but artificial, all the time. His legs were fine. His feet hurt, as you didn't get uneven ground on a tread-mill. He wasn't used to it. But other than that, he was fine.

Kennet didn't look quite so fine. He was a big man, two metres tall, probably a hundred and thirty kilos, twenty stone, two hundred and eighty pounds. He was broad. But a lot of that weight was round his middle, not balanced well on his legs. And they had given him one of the heavier tusks. He was sweating a river. His shirt would have been soaked without the rain. How would he cope?

Kwame, Mak, and Jean were ahead of him, each carrying a heavy tusk, each with their own soldier guard. Colm hadn't seen any of the other rangers. Perhaps they were all dead, like Agoyo. He knew Gasimba had been shot. He hoped at least some of them had escaped. Mola, and Deng.

The three captured Soldiers of God were ahead of the rangers in similar circumstances, burdened and guarded.

Colm couldn't see Jane. She'd been much further ahead when they left Nagero, and he hadn't seen her since. Captain Rick had said she should stay close to him to make sure she came to no harm. Had he been serious? Was he making sure she came to no harm? Or was he...

Colm's thoughts trailed off. They were moving too quickly for anything like that to happen. Weren't they?

Before he knew it, it was three hours later, and they were stopping again. Two things had changed on that march. The rain had stopped, and his feet were really starting to hurt.

––––––

Maths. They were walking quickly, but through long grass. Five kilometres an hour, absolute tops. Perhaps less. But go with tops. Forty-five kilometres by the end of the third march. By then it was very dark. The black clouds now covered the sky, and the sun was giving up.

But it hadn't yet started raining again.

The third break was only five minutes, and then they were on their feet and moving faster. As if they needed to be somewhere in a hurry. Colm saw Kennet stumble. He reached out, but Kennet righted himself and kept going.

Single file, and occasionally the column snaked out in front of him when it passed across a larger, flatter, open space, lone trees further apart, grass not as tall. But even then, Colm couldn't see Jane anywhere ahead. And the light was going fast.

The dark-skinned soldier with the disintegrating boot was

always right behind him. Holding his gun as if it were part of him. As the darkness grew it became harder to see his face under the peak of his cap.

Then, suddenly, they were somewhere.

The column snaked into trees. A change. Trees that vanished into the night above them. The birds had gone quiet. Insects, irritants, squeaked and chirped and rubbed. Into the trees, creepers hanging from their branches. It was a relief on the feet not to be dragging through grass.

Colm realised he could see. He shouldn't be able to see. Under the canopy of the forest there should be no light. The trees overhead, always in leaf, ever green, should block it all. And they did. Yet he could still see. The forest was lit with a soft green light that came from the floor. It was luminous. Something on the ground had absorbed whatever light had penetrated the gloom during the day and was releasing it to the night. It was not much, but it was enough for him to see where he was going. He took a step towards one of the patches of green but heard the voice of his guard instantly.

'Stop!' There was a click of something on the gun. Colm stopped, moved back into the line.

'The light,' he said, by way of explanation. The soldier did not respond.

And then they were somewhere. A camp. Tents and lean-tos. Some lights, shaded. There were soldiers here who hadn't been on the march. Colm followed Kennet; Kennet was following a soldier ahead of him. They walked to a pile of tusks and were ordered to drop the ones they were carrying there. They were led to a tent, ushered in.

It was just four sheets of tarpaulin, one huge, hung over a low branch thicker than Colm's waist. Two smaller at either end. One on the ground.

'Sleep,' said the dark-skinned soldier, pointing at the ground with his gun.

Kennet needed no further instruction and fell to the ground, lying on his front, using his arms as a pillow. Within a couple of minutes, he was breathing deeply, asleep.

Colm sat, felt the soft, thick earth of the savannah under the tarpaulin. He was hungry.

He was determined not to sleep. He sat. His legs ached like he didn't remember them aching, and his feet were screaming at him. But he needed to experience this. He listened.

The dark-skinned soldier watched him for a moment, a minute.

'It was a pigeon, not a parrot,' he said. And left the tent.

Colm listened. Men moving, all around, in the dark. Very little noise. Occasional conversations were low, brief, barely audible at all. There was the knock of wood on wood. But he smelled no fire, heard no laughter, no suggestion of alcohol. This was an army in stealth mode, on the march through territory it was wary of, and it camped quietly. The insects shouted into the night.

He wasn't going to sleep. He was going to experience this.

PART TWO

CHAPTER TWENTY-SIX

FATOU INHALED INSTINCTIVELY. HER BODY WAS GIVING HER no choice. She was going to scream. She opened her mouth. Then she felt a hand clamp over it like a vice, and another hand take her chin and her throat. She heard the words, the gentlest hiss, quieter than the rain, much quieter. But they were right in her ear, and she heard them clearly.

'Make a sound, and we are both dead.'

She froze. The hands over her mouth and holding her jaw didn't move, but she froze, took control of herself, then let her breath out slowly, so slowly. She nodded her head, only slightly, but the hands that held her head felt it. Their grip relaxed.

'No sound,' Tony's voice whispered as he released her.

From below, cutting through the sound of the rain like a blade, came that voice.

'There,' the voice said. 'You understand how disappointed I am. Don't disappoint me again, Sergeant Kibwana. Where is the ivory?'

Fatou had seen the man who owned the voice through a slim

gap in the floorboards of the loft. She had only seen his cap from above, as the umbrella had gone down.

She had heard him talk, then seen him lean forward over Agoyo, and look him over. She had heard him talk some more, and then she had seen him shoot Agoyo in the head. That was why she had nearly screamed.

Agoyo. She'd spoken to Agoyo for only a few minutes while Colm was emptying the chamber pot. Agoyo had been funny. Flirtatious. A wounded man alone in a hospital bed, happy with her company, and responding to her as a man responds to a woman he finds attractive. It had been the first normality she'd experienced in days, and it had meant so much. And now he was dead. There was no doubt about that. His head had exploded as the bullet passed through it.

Once Tony had removed his hands from her mouth and neck, she knew she wasn't going to make another sound. She wasn't afraid. She was numb. Her whole body was rigid. But in her head a part of her was ignoring everything, was rising out of the physiological reaction she couldn't control and was thinking with clarity. Agoyo was dead. Funny, flirtatious Agoyo who she knew next to nothing about. And the uncontrollable numbness began to dissipate. She forced herself back into a state of alertness. She wasn't going to miss anything. This story had shifted from something to be endured to something personal.

Agoyo.

Fatou lowered her head, so slowly, and looked through the sliver of a gap in the boards. She watched the rest of the show on the veranda without making another sound.

————

'I think they are gone,' Tony said, nearly an hour later. Fatou had not moved beyond the occasional stretch. She had heard everything. Colm, Kennet, Jane, Mak, all of them had been taken by this man who called himself Captain Rick of the Brotherhood of Souls as porters for the stolen ivory and hostages for ransom. She was sure Nagero ranger station was stripped bare of guns, of ivory, of men. They had listened as Captain Rick's men had smashed everything in the radio room, and then marched out into the night. All that remained were her and Tony Kanagi, the ranger from Kenya.

Tony had moved. The loft space was low, no more than a metre and a half between the boards and the roof at any point. Tony had risen to a crouch and moved to the hatch.

'I think they are gone,' he said again.

She shook herself, got to her knees, and picked up the rifle she had yet to fire. She crawled after him to the hatch. He opened it and lowered the ladder. He climbed down. She followed.

The hatch was above a store closet. Captain Rick's soldiers had raided it. They hadn't taken much, though. It still held cans of Coca Cola, tins of food. All heavy things for men carrying tusks. But they had rifled all of it, and the floor was covered in tins and cans. Tony stepped through them carefully and she did the same. Only two steps to the door, which was open. The cupboard was very small, but the open door allowed in a weak light from a bulb in the kitchen. Tony was crouched by the door, waiting for her to reach him. She crouched beside him, held her gun the way he was holding his.

He waited, motionless. She did the same. He was listening. She could hear nothing over the rain. He stood up. So did she.

'Wait here,' he said.

She nodded, though he was already looking away from her, moving through the open door.

He'd been gone about a minute before she decided she didn't want to wait any more. She stepped through the open door after him.

He was nowhere in sight, and she couldn't hear him. She could only hear the rain.

The kitchen had been rifled too. Anything that could have been opened and emptied had been. The bulb hanging from the ceiling was still throwing out its weak light, but it was pulsing, gently, as if it might die at any minute. Fatou knew where she must go.

She took each step as if the floor beneath her feet could explode with too much pressure. She left the kitchen and entered the corridor, where there was one door that led to the back of the building that faced the armoury, the ivory store and the barracks, a second door that led to rooms she had not been in, and a third door that led into the radio room and, through that, to the veranda. That was where she must go.

The radio room looked as she had imagined it would look after hearing the noise that had reached them as they lay above it. Every piece of equipment, every whiteboard, every map, had been smashed beyond recognition. The mattresses beneath the tables that she, Colm, and Kennet had slept on that night had been pulled out and slashed. She ignored everything, but she moved slowly, as quietly as she could.

She stepped out onto the veranda. She still held the gun, but only in one hand, and only by the bit on the top she thought of as the handle. She looked around the compound. One of the two vehicles still had its headlights on, pointing towards the remains of the gates. That gave the only available light. But it was enough. Almost. She could see Agoyo's body, slumped back.

When Captain Rick shot him, Agoyo had been seated on a stool, with his wounded leg resting on another. He was still seated on the stool, and his leg was still on the other, but without the tension in his muscles, his torso had slumped back. The light from the headlights threw shadows, and Fatou couldn't see Agoyo's face, but she could see the shape of him in the shadows, she could see where his head was, the back of it touching the ground.

She crouched down next to him.

She wished she could see him clearly, and at the same time was glad she could not.

She reached for the top of his head. That was safe. She relived the moment Captain Rick had shot him. Gun to his temple, his head exploding to the left side. The top of his head should be still the top of his head.

It was. She felt his hair with her fingers. Close-cropped. Not shaven. She felt his skull beneath his hair. Cold.

She knew nothing about him. That was not right. This whole night was not right. She exhaled until her lungs were empty. She closed her eyes.

———

One week ago, Fatou had been in Brussels, living her life. It had been an ordinary day at the office. An ordinary day involved cranking out eight or ten small pieces that were factually impeccable and attractively repulsive about the European Parliament, the Belgian Government, and, occasionally, the City of Brussels. This ordinary day was even more ordinary than most. Half the news desk had been relieved of their ten-pieces-a-day burden due to the visit of a philanthropist. Or, as Fatou and some of her colleagues had dubbed her, a "philanthropist", their hands providing the quotes in the air. This woman had been invited by someone, no one knew who, to come and talk to them for a whole afternoon on the subject of the future of journalism in Europe. Fatou, and those of her colleagues who were still participating in the human race, had carried out background checks on the speaker. Some of those background checks had not got beyond a google. At the other extreme, some of those background checks had resulted in arrests. When Fatou and her colleagues had pooled the results of those background checks, they had reached the same conclusion.

The woman talking about the future of journalism knew no more about journalism than Fatou knew about Bolivian national dance.

Fatou wasn't entirely sure where Bolivia was. Her first guess was it was close to Bavaria. She'd looked it up and learned. The woman talking had not.

So what? Fatou and her colleagues were used to being patronised.

But after that patronising talk, Fatou had caught up on the articles she hadn't written due to the talk, but was still, actually, expected to write, and was walking to the station to get her train home, late, nine-ish, when she had passed an alley and heard what sounded like a gasp.

Her instinct had been to run. It could have been a mugging, or a rape. There might be danger in there. She should run. But she had trained herself to head towards danger. She was a journalist. There was nothing to write about if you were too busy running away.

She had taken out her phone, switched on the torch function, and stepped into the alley to investigate.

In the light of that beam Fatou learned several things. The first thing she learned was the identity of the person from the office who had invited that woman to speak. The second thing she learned was why. The answer to both questions was the managing editor, who, revealed by the light from Fatou's phone, had the woman's left buttock in his hand.

The following day Fatou had learned she was being sent to the DRC to chase down a story that was no story in a place so dangerous she might not come back.

———

She kept her eyes closed for some moments, feeling Agoyo's hair through her fingers. She felt tears welling, but she refused to let them fall.

CHAPTER TWENTY-SEVEN

DESPITE AN INITIAL DETERMINATION TO STAY AWAKE AND experience the night in the rebel camp in the forest, Colm had swiftly realised that was a ridiculous idea. He was exhausted from the walk and the heat, dehydrated as he had sweated out more than he had drunk, and the next day was bound to be as bad if not worse. He had changed his mind, and decided to get as much rest as he could.

But then he had been unable to get to sleep.

The night he had spent at the ranger station had been luxurious – a bed, a mattress, and a mosquito net. The first night he had spent in the park had been less luxurious, under the stars without tent or mattress. But it had been in the grasslands where, it turned out, there were far fewer insects than in the forest, and the insects on the grasslands mostly seemed to sleep at night. In the grasslands, he hadn't really missed the mosquito net, despite how wet it had been over the previous forty-eight hours.

In the forest, the insects worked in shifts to trouble you twenty-four seven. And it wasn't just the mosquitos. Though

Colm wasn't sure he could distinguish a mosquito from any other small flying creature. He'd been told a number of unhelpful things about them, such as that you could only hear the males and it was the females that bit you and gave you malaria. He was kept far too busy flapping away flying creatures of various sizes to start trying to identify particular species. There were hundreds of tiny flies, like midges from back home, but even smaller and lighter, that crawled across his skin like tiny pieces of feather, an almost pleasant sensation. There were larger flies, like bluebottles but bigger, with red eyes and wings that were partially black, camouflage for the shadows. They were annoying. Colm thought he would recognise a tsetse fly – he'd studied them in detail at school, looked at photographs of them blown up to the size of his head that had creeped him out – but didn't think he saw any, which was the only positive he'd been able to come up with as he was being crawled over and landed on.

And it wasn't just the flies. He saw a millipede as long as his forearm scuttle across the tarpaulin and disappear off it again. That prompted him to tuck his trousers into his socks as Mak had instructed him the first night they had camped in the park.

And that was the last thing he remembered. Perhaps whatever thought process that memory had prompted had been enough to help him drift off.

He had been dreaming that someone was stabbing him with a spear once, twice, but the blade didn't break the skin, just bruised him. He woke on the third thrust of what turned out not to be a spear, but rather a gun barrel. A part of his brain was working faster than his consciousness, and that part waved his arm to show he was awake.

'Up,' a voice said.

It was the dark-skinned soldier, holding a lantern in one hand, his gun in the other. Behind him, through the tent opening,

Colm could see only darkness, as the light from the lantern dazzled him.

'No chance of any breakfast, is there?' Colm said as he sat up, in what he hoped was a friendly tone.

The soldier motioned with the barrel. Next to Colm's hand was a leaf with some cooked meat on it.

Squinting, Colm looked at the soldier more closely, hoping his scrutiny was concealed by the squint. The soldier wasn't wearing his peaked cap, so Colm could see his head and face clearly for the first time. His hair was cut roughly, as if it had been shaved with a knife then allowed to grow. He looked young, very young, but around his eyes were the lines of an older man.

'Quick,' the soldier said. 'We move now.'

As he said that, the tarpaulin that formed the roof of the tent was whipped away, revealing the shadows of the forest above. Three soldiers were rolling the tarpaulin into a tight cylinder. When they had finished, two of them hoisted it onto their shoulders and set off walking. The third followed them, lighting their way with a lantern.

'You, carry them,' the dark-skinned soldier said, pointing at two elephant tusks lying outside on the leaf-mulch that formed the forest floor. Two. Colm had forgotten about Kennet.

Kennet was behind him, lying on his back. He was starting to sit up, evidently in some discomfort. But he reached for the meat and ate. He nodded.

'Good,' he said.

Colm picked up the little Kennet left. It was cold. Salted. But rich, like game. Like venison, but not venison. Different world.

He looked at the tusks. Like yesterday, one was bigger than the other. He looked at Kennet, drained and fading, and reached for the bigger one.

Jaysus, it was heavy.

He hoiked it onto his shoulder. He felt lop-sided. This was going to hurt after not very far at all.

The camp was disintegrating. Where there had been tents and lean-tos, there were only trees and the forest floor. The column was reforming, winding out, north or northeast, the direction they'd been marching all of yesterday. As Kennet and Colm fell into line with their respective guards, all evidence that fifty or more people had been here was being removed, carried away, buried. That the whole performance was lit by lanterns and torches added to the strangeness of it all, and that it was conducted almost entirely in silence completed the sense of otherworldliness.

Colm didn't know what time it was. He knew his phone was still in his pocket, switched off in a plastic bag. He'd not touched it since they were taken. No one had searched him, but he didn't want to reveal its presence. Then he remembered he was still wearing his watch. He raised his arm, scratched his head, glanced at his wrist as his arm went down.

Six thirty. In the morning. It was too dark for six thirty. Seven thirty in this time zone. Too dark. Not like yesterday morning. Yesterday had been clouded over and raining, but the sunrise had been obvious. Today the sun could already be up, and he wouldn't know it. Perhaps the trees blocked out all light. Perhaps there were clouds covering the sun. He couldn't tell.

Flies buzzed around him. Possibly they were ones that had been crawling over him all night. Possibly they were their cousins, come to get a taste of an Irishman. Perhaps he was the talk of the fly community. He tried to think of some way to weave a pun out of social media and the word "buzz", but his brain wasn't cooperative. Instead, he waved his left hand at them to bat them away, but with the weight of the tusk on his shoulder, the action threw him off balance. He concentrated on ignoring the flies, determinedly not thinking of the diseases they might be carrying, as one landed on his face and paddled in the sweat on his forehead. At seven thirty in the morning. The air was thick with moisture.

They were not under the trees for long. The column wound out into the grass again. And it was dark, even out from under the trees, thanks to the clouds. Thick and black, like the smoke from a Victorian chimney. Like a shroud.

'The rain will come soon,' said a voice. Colm looked behind him. The dark-skinned soldier. He was looking at the sky, but his gun was still pointed at Colm's back.

Colm hefted the tusk a little, trying to make it more comfortable.

'What's your name?' he asked the soldier.

The soldier said nothing.

Ahead of Colm, Kennet was struggling, even with the smaller tusk. Sweat poured from him. His clothes were soaked. And every so often he lost his footing in the grass.

The pace was faster than the day before, Colm was sure of it. Or was he? Was he just not used to this, so it felt faster as the effort, the heat, the lack of sleep all caught up with him? No. This wasn't strenuous. He wasn't being stretched. He was fitter than this. The tusk was heavy, but he'd carried heavier. The terrain was a little bumpy, but he'd walked mountain ranges. The pace was faster. They needed to be somewhere.

Or...

They needed to not be somewhere. These soldiers had assaulted a ranger compound, killed many men, kidnapped nine people, and stolen millions of euros worth of ivory. The army would be after them. Hannington would be after them.

One foot, the other foot. Colm was very pleased he had chosen shoes like these. Indestructible, incredibly comfortable, just what you need when on a forced march through Africa carrying a tusk. He had no problem with his shoes, even though his feet were bruised and rubbed to pieces inside them. He noticed the side of the left one was coming away from the sole.

Would they be rescued? Or would they be killed? Or would there be a rescue attempt, a brief moment of hope, and then they'd be killed in the rescue?

Aileen Bloody O'Connor. She'd know the answer.

Thinking of Aileen made him think of Fatou. Hopefully she and Tony in the loft had not been discovered. Hopefully they had been able to raise the alarm almost immediately, though Captain Rick's men had smashed the two vehicles and the radio. Hopefully they were OK, and help was on the way.

He thought of Niamh. He wondered if he would see her again, if he would ever see their child.

Don't be silly, of course he would. Captain Rick was going to release them when the ivory was somewhere safe.

'We do not kill unless under threat of death,' Captain Rick had said, but he had shot Agoyo for no reason, other than to prove he would kill them if he wanted to.

Onwards. The ground was uneven, and each step bounced the heavy tusk just a little against him. The shoulder with the tusk balanced on it swiftly became a tender bruise. He moved it to the other shoulder, and the same happened there. The combination of the damage done yesterday by the weight of the smaller tusk, and the increased weight of the larger, meant he was in considerable pain before they stopped for the first time. Halt, down, drink. They had stopped for perhaps ten minutes, but it felt like less than two before they were up and walking again.

Ahead of him he could see one of the soldiers carrying a large tusk. He had taken off his shirt, folded it into a pad, and placed that on his shoulder to cushion the tusk against his skin. Colm spend the next three hours imagining the relief he could take from that. When it came to the next halt he drank, then took off

his shirt, folded it in a similar way, and got ready for the next
phase of the march.

As soon as they were up, he set the pad on his shoulder and
rested the tusk on it. Much better.

For the next three hours he worried less about the pain in his
shoulders and more about how pasty and pale his torso must
seem in the dark of the grass. To predators he must appear luminous. He was sure his captors would be laughing at him. He'd
burn, surely, even through the clouds.

There was shouting in the line behind him. He looked back,
and saw the column breaking, moving sideways, back towards
the tree line. A single word was moving up the line, passed from
one soldier to the next like a parcel.

'What are they saying?' Colm asked, as he and Kennet were
urged by the guard who shadowed Colm's footsteps to follow suit
and run for the tree line.

'There is a plane coming,' the guard said. 'We must hide.'

Once they were in the trees they were forced to keep moving,
away from the edge of the forest. For five minutes they pushed
and crashed their way through the undergrowth before another
message brought the process to a halt.

Colm couldn't see much of the column because of the trees.
But everyone he could see was sitting down and listening. Some
were looking up, but there was very little visible sky through the
canopy. He laid the tusk down and started to sit. His guard
grabbed him by the arm and pulled him back up.

'Not there,' he said. He pointed.

There was a stream moving through the leaves. Not of water.
Of ants. It was ten centimetres across, and the ants that made it
up were packed together, moving in a straight line. Colm had
almost sat on it.

'Saifu. Very nasty bites.'

Colm, painfully aware of his bare torso, imagined himself

covered with biting ants. He shuddered, and moved as far from the jostling mass of insects as he could. He sat on a fallen branch.

After a minute he heard it. The drone of an aircraft engine. Not a large one. Not a jet.

It came from behind them and passed by not too far overhead. It turned, and in a minute flew over them again. It must have been following their trail. It must have seen where they had broken for the trees. Someone knew where they were. Colm felt hope.

But it didn't last. Five minutes after the sound of the plane's engine had died away, they were ordered back to their feet. He put his shirt on his shoulder, hoiked the tusk into place and fell in line again.

He spent the rest of that second day like that, worrying about things he could do nothing about. There was a third stop, a third drink, before they were up and walking again.

The sun was gone by the time they arrived at the second camp. The lamps had been brought out and the column wove into the trees like a line of fireflies. The only thing that distinguished it from the first night was this. Kennet lay snoring on his back, and Colm was slumped in a weary heap under the tarpaulin, aches running through every muscle and tendon in the body whose fitness he had been so sure of, he heard a voice.

'My name is Jomo,' the dark-skinned soldier said.

It was a jolt of humanity in an otherwise soulless new normal.

CHAPTER TWENTY-EIGHT

'I NEED YOUR HELP.'

Fatou opened her eyes. Blinked. There was a gun barrel a few centimetres from her eyes.

'I need your help,' Tony repeated, offering her his hand. She took it and used it to pull herself to her feet. 'You'll need that.' Tony touched the gun she'd been carrying with his foot. She'd laid it on the boards of the veranda when she'd knelt beside Agoyo.

'We have to move him. We can't leave him like this,' Fatou said.

'We will. But first we have to search the compound and all the buildings. Find out who else is dead. Make sure there's no one injured or left behind.'

Fatou's mind was numb. What Tony was saying made sense, in a coldly logical way. She found herself nodding. As she leaned over to pick up the gun, she had the oddest sensation of watching herself do it, as if she was still hiding in the loft looking down on them.

Tony talked her through how to fire the gun again. She'd had it explained before, but hearing it again helped. It was a series of instructions she could follow.

'I will go first,' he said, and led her into the rain and across the compound to the first hut. It was the medical hut. 'Watch the compound,' he said.

He pushed the door open with the barrel of his gun, shining a torch inside, sweeping quickly. Then he took two steps forward and the door shut behind him.

Fatou watched the compound. The gates had stopped burning. The rain had finally extinguished whatever fire Captain Rick's men had persuaded to burn under the deluge. But the gates still smoked and steamed.

She shivered. Not from cold, but because rain was running down her spine. She was already soaked to the skin, and she'd only been out in the rain for a minute. Or perhaps two.

What was taking Tony so long?

She went to the door and pushed it open a centimetre.

'Tony!' she whispered as loudly as she dared.

There was no reply. She shivered again, this time from fear. She looked around the compound, suddenly convinced that Captain Rick had left soldiers in every building and every shadow.

'Tony!' she said again, louder this time.

'Come in, come in,' he said from inside. 'It's clear.'

She pushed the door open and went into the hut.

'Sorry, I thought this would make things easier,' Tony said. He was using surgical tape to fix his torch to the barrel of his gun. Fatou nodded.

The torch was still on, and she could see about half of the room. The beds Colm and Agoyo had slept in. The bed they had helped Agoyo out of not much more than twelve hours earlier. The shape left by his body was still evident in the slim mattress. The floor around the beds was covered with boxes and tools from the shelves and cupboards. Colm's bag had been upended and the contents scattered across the floor. The soldiers didn't seem to have taken much, if anything, though amid all the mess, it was impossible to tell.

'That should do it,' Tony said. 'Come on. One down.'

Fatou followed him out into the rain. They walked right round the hut, then moved on to the next one. The latrines. They were empty. The building after that wasn't.

It was the shower block.

There was no door on the shower block. Fatou remembered there was almost nothing in the shower block – it had three shower heads in the ceiling, a light over the doorway, and a chair. She had not been looking forward to using it in a camp populated almost entirely by men.

Tony walked up to the entrance and stepped through, gun raised, torch taped to its barrel. Fatou watched the compound, but she could see him out of the corner of her eye standing side on, facing down the length of the block. He had frozen. Something was wrong. When he'd gone into the first two huts he had gone in quickly, keeping low. But he wasn't moving. Then he lowered his gun and stepped forward.

'Fatou!' he said.

She ran in after him.

There were six bodies on the floor. They had been laid out in a row, from one wall to the other.

'Do you recognise any of these men?' Tony said. He played the light of his torch on each face in turn. After each one Fatou shook her head. Then she realised Tony wouldn't be able to see her.

'No. I don't think they are rangers,' she said.

Tony crouched next to each man, checking for a pulse in the neck. He shook his head. He stood up and played the torch along the line again.

'They were all killed by the same person,' he said.

'How do you know that?'

'They're shot in the same way. Look. Single bullet through the chest. Powerful rifle. Reasonably close range. There will be large exit wounds in their backs.'

'It wasn't me,' said a voice from behind them.

Tony span round, raising his gun and pointing it in the direction of the sound.

There was a figure in the doorway, silhouetted against the rain. His hands were raised. The light of Tony's torch fell on his face.

It was Mola.

———

Tony lowered his gun. Mola turned on the light.

'I had assumed it was broken,' Tony said, and reached to switch off his torch.

Mola was soaked but looked unharmed. He picked up a rifle he had leaned against the door frame.

'What happened?' he asked.

'Someone calling himself Captain Rick, from a group he called the Brotherhood of Souls, blew up the gates, killed Agoyo, and took the ivory along with at least Mak, Colm, Kennet, and Jane. What did you see?'

'They came in over the fence. Before the explosion, when the shooting started out front. Maybe a dozen of them. Ladders in two places, shot Gasimba, cut the wire. They killed Justin and David.'

'What happened to them?' Tony tilted his head at the six dead men.

'Someone had one of the elephant guns. I didn't see who.

They killed maybe nine of them in a minute. It could only have been Deng. I haven't seen him.'

'How did you escape?'

'I climbed the fence and went over their ladders to see if there were more of them. That was when the explosion happened. I came back up the ladder but there were too many of them and no one else was shooting. It would have been suicide.'

'It would.' Tony switched off the light. 'Let's search the rest of the compound. Find Deng and the others.

Mola, silhouetted again, nodded.

————

Mola led the way. The next building was the ivory store. The body of a ranger lay crumpled against the log wall.

'Justin,' Mola said. 'I closed his eyes.'

Fatou looked at Justin's face. He was one of the men Mak had sent scouting when they had left the vehicles on their trip into the park. Rain splashed off his head. There were three bullet wounds in his chest.

The door to the ivory store was propped open by a log. The padlock that had secured it had been discarded on the ground. It was smoking.

'What did they do to that?' Tony said.

'They melted it. Some kind of acid,' Mola said. 'Don't touch!'

Fatou had been reaching for it. She hadn't been thinking. It was strange. Was this shock? She looked at Justin's body two metres away.

Tony, using his torch and gun, went into the store.

'Clear!' his voice came after only a few seconds. The light in the store came on. He reappeared.

'They didn't take it all,' he said.

Fatou had a look inside. Whilst the majority of the ivory was gone, all of the smallest, and the largest tusks, a good number of the medium-sized ones remained.

'I bet Captain Rick wasn't happy about leaving some behind,' Tony said.

'He might come back for it,' Fatou said.

'I don't think so. This place will be swarming with the army and other rangers soon. He sounded too cautious to risk it.' Tony turned and left. Fatou followed, joining with Mola as they crossed the ground to the armoury.

'Where are they?'

'Where are who?' Mola said.

'The army and the other rangers?'

'Hopefully on their way. The last time I spoke to Kwame he said they had left messages at the station in Faradje.'

'Messages? Was there no one there?'

'Not in the night, no. There should be, but perhaps they have had trouble too.'

'How far away is it?'

'Not far. Maybe fifteen kilometres.'

'So they should be here by now?'

Mola shrugged. 'They will get here before the army. And Kwame couldn't reach Hannington.'

The lock on the armoury had been burned as well. Tony went in as before and called 'clear' a few moments later.

'They took some ammunition, but none of the guns,' he said.

'Wouldn't be able to carry them and the ivory,' Mola said. 'The barracks.' He pointed to the building in front of them. 'David is in there. I dragged him in and pulled him onto one of the beds. I closed his eyes.'

It was at that moment that they heard a roaring sound and saw the lights. A vehicle had driven into the compound, on the other side of the main building.

CHAPTER TWENTY-NINE

DAY THREE WAS THE SAME AS DAY TWO. DAY FOUR WAS THE same as day three. Every day the same. Grass, trees at the end, tent assembled, sleep, woken to a breakfast stolen from the fauna in the park, move, carry, walk, don't talk.

But the end of day four was different. The camp was different. It was already there. It was more permanent. There were more people in it. All men, sure, but they'd arrived somewhere. No, not all men. He saw women. Two of them at least. Girls more than women. Carrying water in what looked like twenty-litre bottles. Jaysus, they'd be heavy. As heavy as a tusk.

For the first time since leaving the ranger compound Colm saw Captain Rick. He had swapped his uniform for jungle fatigues, and his cap for a light blue beret. He was saluting another man, this one a little fat, wearing a worn and dirty dress uniform with medals on the left side of the jacket. It was unbuttoned, and he wore nothing underneath it. His belly protruded as if he were pregnant. Captain Rick spoke at attention, back straight, staring ahead at nothing. The fat man listened lazily, swatting a hand at a fly.

Colm and Kennet passed them without earning a glance. They followed the guard assigned to Kennet, who had not told them his name, and were followed in turn by Jomo. They were led to a small clearing. A soldier told them to put the tusks they were carrying on a pile with the others. They did so. Colm felt as if he could float. The soldier checked the bottom of each tusk, and for the first time Colm noticed there was a number written on each of them. The soldier took out a pencil and a notebook and wrote something down. He was operating some sort of cataloguing system to make sure none of them went missing.

Kennet's guard led them out of the clearing and off the track a little, towards a structure that was part hut, part tent. Three walls were of bamboo-like stalks, bound together with creepers. The roof was canvas. And the front wall was of tarpaulin, though it was rolled to one side.

Jomo motioned for them to sit, in the shade under a tree next to the structure.

Kennet collapsed immediately. Kennet was a mess. In four days, he looked to have lost about ten kilos, most of it sweated out of him. His face was drawn and pale. His clothing stained and limp. Colm hoped he didn't look as bad. Then again, who was there to see him?

Colm sat with more dignity, but he didn't feel much different. Any fitness he had felt at the start of the march had been driven out of him by the weight of that tusk. His entire torso ached from carrying it. Putting it down at the end of each day had become the greatest pleasure he could remember experiencing. Sorry, Niamh.

The ground was thick, spongy earth. It had been cleared of leaves and other dead vegetation. This camp looked as if it had been here a while. A hundred kilometres from anything.

Colm watched as the incoming soldiers melted into the camp. There was an order to it. There was more discipline here.

The tents and huts weren't in regimented rows, but that was because the trees weren't. The trees were huge, their upper branches blocking out the sun completely. From the air the camp would be invisible. You would probably have to stumble straight into it to see it from the ground.

Which prompted Colm to think about something that had been bothering him. If the purpose of taking the three of them was for ransom, who were their captors intending to ransom them to, and how were they going to get in touch with those people?

'Ken?' Colm said.

The big man didn't answer.

'Ken?' Colm said again.

'Hmmm?' came the reply.

'Who are they going to ransom us to? How are they going to get in touch with them?'

'Oh. They'll get in touch with a government and let them work out who they need to be talking to. I've heard of that happening.'

'How? We're in the middle of nowhere.'

'Satellite phone, probably. Unless they send someone to a town that's connected.'

'You don't sound worried.'

'Takes too much energy.'

Jomo stood a little away from them, gun ready. He didn't seem to tire. Slept lightly, woke at any sound, instantly switching to a level of alertness Colm found impressive. And unnecessary. What could they do? Even if there were no soldiers guarding them where would they go? A hundred kilometres in any direction and they'd still be lost.

Jomo's expression changed, ever so slightly. He said something in a language Colm didn't recognise to someone behind him. Colm looked over his shoulder.

A second soldier was approaching, gun held casually in one hand. He responded to Jomo's greeting. Then he said another sentence. In front of him, walking with a calm that surprised Colm, was Jane. In four days, the wound on her face had faded considerably, so much so that it looked like there might not be a permanent scar. Colm nudged Kennet's leg with his foot. Kennet looked up at him. Colm pointed at Jane.

'Stay there,' Jomo said to her.

The second soldier said something else and walked away.

'Are you OK?' Kennet said, trying to get to his feet. He failed, and just sat there, breathing heavily.

'Are you?' she said.

Kennet nodded unconvincingly.

'Just like a stroll in the park,' he said.

'We're no longer in the park,' she said.

'How do you know that?' Colm said.

Jane looked at Jomo who was watching them, expressionless. She didn't answer. Instead, she sat down next to Kennet, took his face in her hands, and looked at it.

'You need medical attention,' she said.

'How have you been treated?' Kennet said.

'Fine so far.'

'How did you get here?' Colm said.

'Same way you did.'

'No, I mean, you left the compound, you were walking to somewhere, I can't remember—'

'Wando,' she said.

'Exactly, and then suddenly, there you were, in the camp again, when it was surrounded by armed men shooting at each other. How did you even get in without being seen or shot?'

'It's a long story,' Jane said, distractedly. She was prodding and poking Kennet, checking his pulse, lifting his eyelids, feeling his limbs, his bones.

'Stop fussing, *Jannika*,' Ken said.

'I think we have time to hear it,' Colm said, sitting down on the ground a metre or so away from Jane and Kennet.

Kennet, perhaps thinking this was a good a way as any to distract Jane from her determination to give him a physical, looked a little more attentive.

'I'd like to know,' he said.

Jane looked at Jomo and the other guard.

'Very well.' She pushed back from Kennet and sat down. She looked at them both in turn and then started talking.

'I was walking along the side of the road towards Wando, following some women with baskets, when I heard men in the trees, talking and laughing. The women heard them too. They dropped the baskets and ran. I hid.

'The men came out of the trees and crossed the road. They were soldiers. Perhaps twenty or twenty-five. They passed me. I followed them, thinking I could warn you all somehow.'

'You followed them? Wasn't that dangerous?' Colm said.

'My father used to take us hunting when we were growing up. Stalking an elk is far harder than following loud, careless soldiers. It was easy. But I didn't get chance to pass them. They were spread out, so it was not easy to get round them, and they were, for all their ill-discipline, moving quite quickly and in a straight line towards the ranger station, so any route I might have taken would have been longer and probably slower.

'They reached the walls and started shooting, a couple of them trying to climb them. One got onto the top of the gate and was shot. I think three or four more may have been hit, perhaps killed. The others ran off.

'I thought it would be too dangerous to try and get back into the camp – everyone would be nervous, and I might get shot. I decided to keep following the soldiers so I would be able to tell Mak where they had gone. I followed them through the grass, keeping low. It was harder in the dark, but I could follow them by sound. If they'd stopped talking it would have been much more difficult.

'They stopped running after only a couple of kilometres. Four or five of them had an argument. Eventually they seemed to agree on something. Several of them walked out into the grass, one coming very close to where I was hiding. I think they were looking for wood. They couldn't find whatever they were looking for, so they ate cold food, drank, then packed up and set off back the way they had come just a few hours earlier. Once they had all passed me, I followed them again.

'When they got back to the ranger station it was surrounded by Captain Rick's men. I was close enough to hear them talking. They were angry someone else was trying to get hold of what they saw as their guns and ivory, so they attacked.

'There was so much gunfire I was sure everyone would die whether they were aimed at or not. I ran away, towards the runway, and when I had gone far enough that I thought I was safe from stray bullets, I came round and followed the treeline that runs behind the compound. I thought if I could get to the back of the fence, I might be able to get someone's attention, get someone to throw over a rope or something.

'What I found was two ladders against the back fence, and no one was around, even though there was still shooting inside and out front. I climbed one of the ladders and got into the compound that way. There were dead men all over the ground.'

'You didn't see anyone?'

'Not living. Not until I found you in the kitchen with Mak.'

Colm looked at her. A very matter-of-fact tale, the unembellished, everyday story of a lone woman in an unfamiliar place choosing to follow a couple of dozen armed men into the dark of a wild grassland.

'You had a rifle. What did you do with your rifle?'

'I left it in a ditch. It was too big to move with when I was trying to hide.'

Colm found he was tapping the ground with his fingers. He forced himself to stop.

'It wasn't that long a story,' he said.

CHAPTER THIRTY

FATOU HEARD A SECOND ENGINE, AND SAW MORE HEADLIGHTS. Car doors slammed, and there were shouts. Tony and Mola laid their rifles on the ground and put their hands in the air.

'Put the gun down!' Mola said.

Fatou had forgotten she was holding it. She dropped it to the ground and put her hands up just as armed men came around both sides of the main building at the same time.

There were four of them, two from each side. They were silhouettes, the car headlights behind them. Overhead the clouds were still thick and the rain heavy. The new arrivals didn't seem to have spotted Fatou, Mola and Tony standing in front of the barracks, not at first. Then they did.

'Don't move!' called a voice. All of the newcomers turned towards them, guns raised. Then came a sigh, audible even over the rain. 'It's alright, it's Mola.'

They weren't men from the office at Faradje. Or from the army. They were from Nagero. The man who had spoken was Hannington.

———

After that, things moved quickly. Hannington had the rest of the Nagero rangers with him, and their other vehicles. He set up operations in the radio room, bringing one of the portable radios in and calling the main ranger station in Faradje and the army in Dungu, reporting the deaths and the kidnappings, and requesting assistance to pursue the Brotherhood of Souls into the park.

Hannington's men saw to their brothers in arms. The bodies of Félix, Gasimba, Justin, David, and Agoyo were lifted with care and taken on stretchers to the medical hut, which became a temporary morgue. The bodies of another six of Captain Rick's men were found inside the compound and carried into the shower block with the others, the second temporary morgue. But it was outside the ranger station that the real carnage had taken place.

Fatou was struck by their youth. Many of the Soldiers of God were barely teenagers. They should have been in school, not lying dead in the mud, twisted and torn apart. Some with less obvious wounds looked alive, even though they were not. She followed Tony through the rain, stepping through the shapes lying on the ground.

Three bodies had been moved and laid out beside one another in the partial shelter of the compound fence. But the others, and there were a lot of them, lay where they had fallen. She knelt beside them one by one and took photos of each until the battery of her phone ran out.

'These were executed. Look,' Tony said. He pointed at two boys with bullet wounds in their legs that had bled into the mud. Each had been shot in the head. 'And these...' he crouched down beside another body to look closer but didn't finish his sentence.

'How many are there?' Fatou said, trying to count them but continually losing her thread and having to start again.

One of the men Hannington had assigned to the burial detail heard the question.

'Three,' he pointed at the bodies that had been lain side by side, 'and twenty-two,' he swept his arm across the carnage, 'including that one.'

Fatou looked in the direction he was pointing. Back at the gateway, a black shape on the red mud. The man Kwame had shot during the first assault, the one who had been climbing over the gates. His body had been consumed by the fireball that destroyed them. From this angle, she could just make out the shape of his skull and chest, but he was now little more than the memory of the shape of a man. She'd walked right by him.

The others in the burial detail were at work. Using two stretchers, two pairs of rangers started to lift the bodies and carry them round the back of the compound. They were to dig a pit a quarter of a kilometre away and bury all the dead in it, except the five rangers.

'Three and twenty-two, and five rangers, and twelve more at the back. Forty-two dead in less than a day. Senseless,' Fatou said to herself.

'And another seven missing,' Tony said.

Fatou and Tony had seen Mak, Kennet, Colm, and Jane taken by Captain Rick. Hannington's men couldn't find Deng, Jean, or Kwame. They assumed they had been taken too.

Once the radio calls had been made, the bodies had been moved and the digging had begun, there was nothing to do but tidy up. Fatou found herself in the kitchen doing nothing more complicated than picking everything off the floor, putting anything that was irretrievably damaged in one pile, and everything else back in the cupboards or on the shelves.

It took some time, and she found it strangely calming. The

voices of the rangers outside also helped a vague feeling of
normality return, despite how wide the gap remained between
what was happening and what was normal.

She finished. She didn't know what time it was. She relied on
her phone to tell her the time. She needed to see about charging
it. There were power points in the radio room. The generator
was still running, and her charger was in her bag. At least she
assumed it was. Her bag should be in the medical hut where she
had left it. But now she remembered entering the place with
Tony and seeing how it had been ransacked. Perhaps they had
gone through her bag too.

And the dead rangers were in there now.

She left the main building by the back door to avoid seeing
anyone in the radio room or on the veranda. The rain had eased
considerably and was now little more than a light drizzle. The
clouds were lighter, and visibility was much better.

She swallowed and walked quickly to the medical hut.

She reached her hand through the doorway and found the
light switch. For some reason she didn't want to be in a room
with five dead bodies in the dark. It would be hard enough to see
them again in the light.

The bodies had been lain on the beds. There were only four
beds and five bodies, so Gasimba lay on a stretcher on the floor.
Whoever had brought them in had tidied the room. They had
moved all the beds to the far side, against the back wall, so the
five men lay in a row. The medical equipment that had been scattered over the floor had been put back on the shelves and in the
cabinet, though the cabinet door was broken off and was now
leaning against the wall. In the near corner, side by side, were her
and Colm's bags.

She didn't look for her charger straight away. Instead, she
went to the beds and looked at each man in turn. Agoyo's head
had been bandaged, so the ruin of the left side of his face wasn't

visible. A dressing covered the entry wound as well, but his right eye was uncovered, and closed. He looked peaceful.

She stared at him for another minute, then went to her bag.

It looked untouched. It had been under the bed, so perhaps they hadn't seen it in the dark. She found her charger quickly and put it in her pocket.

Colm's bag, though, had been touched. It had been next to his bed rather than under it, and his bed was the one nearest the door – the first thing anyone coming in would have seen. Whoever had tidied the room had shoved everything back into it at random. The top wasn't closed, and Fatou could see a pair of socks on top of a pile of papers. A name on the top sheet of paper caught her eye. Aileen O'Connor. She reached for the paper, took it out, and read it. Aileen O'Connor's notes on the Congolese rebel group, M23. The notes were very thorough. This wasn't the work of a couple of days before departure. This had been pulled together over years. She pulled out more paper. Notes on Raia Mutomboki. And more, notes on the LDF.

Fatou emptied Colm's bag, then put everything back into it that wasn't paper. She sorted the paper into the best order she could, settled with her back against the wall of the hut, and started to read.

————

By the time she was interrupted, Fatou had got a quarter of the way through Aileen's notes, with annotations in what she presumed was Colm's hand, his lettering squat and neat.

The interruption came in the form of the door being pushed open. It was Tony.

'Ah, good, Fatou. I was looking for you. Can we have a quiet word?'

Fatou stared at him and waited. He didn't say anything.

'O-kay,' she said, squeezing the expectation into the second syllable.

'Those things we heard, when we were in the loft. That Kennet had arranged to meet the Soldiers of God. I think it best we keep that to ourselves.'

Fatou stared at him. She had completely forgotten about that. Captain Rick had said it. Kennet had admitted it. Kennet had somehow got in touch with this terrorist group and arranged for them to take him to wherever the last rhinos had been seen, which Fatou knew from Aileen's notes was in South Sudan, a few kilometres over the border from Garamba. Captain Rick had listed the atrocities of the Soldiers of God. She remembered with a sudden clarity. And now they sounded very familiar. Because she'd just read a very similar list of atrocities in Aileen's notes.

'I know who the Soldiers of God are,' she said, waving the sheaf of paper and getting to her feet. 'They're not called that in here, but the description fits.'

'Even so, it is not relevant any more, is it? Those men do not hold Kennet and Jane, so it won't help to tell Hannington about it.'

Fatou looked at him. She didn't say anything.

CHAPTER THIRTY-ONE

COLM WOKE WITH A START. SOMETHING WAS WRONG, BUT HE didn't know what. Whatever trigger his subconscious had responded to wasn't continuous. He opened his eyes, but it was dark. There was no light in the tent, and nothing beyond the faintest glow from a lantern somewhere outside that allowed him to see the shapes of Jane and Kennet. He lay very still and listened.

The camp was quiet. The jungle was quiet. He was getting used to the noise of the insects, and there didn't seem to be as many birds or monkeys as he had heard around Nagero. Perhaps they had fled the soldiers. Perhaps the soldiers had killed them all.

The soldiers themselves were quiet. During the day, they walked quietly, talked quietly. And right now, whatever time of the night it was, Colm could hear no one talking or moving at all.

What had woken him?

Then he tensed. He'd felt something. A movement. Just the slightest thing, something brushing against the material of his trousers.

It took all of his self-control not to move. Because his first thought was: snake.

Conceptually, he wasn't afraid of snakes. He was afraid of them experientially. He'd seen one in a tank once, but most of his experience of snakes came from TV and film. And TV and film showed the snakes that were the largest, the fastest, the most venomous. The peaceful, vegetarian, charitable snakes who only did good and were doubtless in the majority didn't get as much press as the others. Rationally, to Colm, snakes were something he could deal with. Unless there was one next to him, at which point his fight or flight instinct kicked in, and his subconscious told him to run away, run away now, or die in venom-induced agony.

Rationally, he realised running away from a snake that was touching his trousers was a sure way to get bitten. And, on the off chance this wasn't one of the vegetarian, charitable ones, he figured the snake would probably be able to strike faster than he could get up and run. It took all of his self-control to stay rigid.

He would, at that point, have taken the time to be a little proud of himself for exercising such self-control. Unfortunately, he never got the chance, as at that moment the movement came again. More noticeable. Heavier, this time. Against his trousers.

From the inside.

Something was crawling up his leg. *Inside his trousers*. It felt big. Heavy. His self-control fled, and he jumped up, undoing his belt as fast as he could, trying to hop out of the trousers without taking his shoes off, tripping himself and falling, banging his head on Kennet's feet, causing Kennet to stir, and only half-succeeding in not screaming.

Colm heard a noise and whipped his head round to the entrance to the tent. The guard outside, who had replaced Jomo at sunset the night before, was pushing aside the tarpaulin over the entrance with the barrel of his gun and stepping into the tent holding a lantern. He looked angry and opened his mouth.

But when he saw Colm on the ground with his trousers round his ankles he broke into a grin, and then laughed. Colm looked down.

There was a grasshopper the size of a banana on his right thigh. It sprang off towards the tent entrance.

With a swift jab of the butt of his gun the guard crushed its head, killing it. He picked it up and tucked it in a pocket on his belt. Still laughing, he left.

Colm pulled his trousers back up. The feel of the grime and dried sweat on his skin depressed him more than almost every other aspect of the situation. He lifted his head to see Jane watching him, her face just visible by the faint light from the lantern on the other side of the tarpaulin.

'I know, I know,' Colm said. 'Trousers in socks.' He had forgotten. He'd remembered every other night.

He fastened his belt and sat back down, his heart still racing. He breathed, slowly and deeply, to calm himself.

'What was it?' Kennet's voice was weak.

'Looked like a giant grasshopper,' Colm said. 'Ugly and smug. Not sure it deserved to die, though.'

Everything was quiet for a while. But Colm's adrenaline was still flowing, and sleep was, for now, an impossibility. He could see Jane was still sitting up.

'How do you know we're no longer in the park?' he said, quietly.

'Captain Rick told me. We left the park the day before yesterday. We're now in South Sudan.'

'Is that why we've stopped?'

'One of the reasons. The Congolese army won't follow them here. International incident if they do.'

'Not even for the ivory?'

'No.'

Colm double-checked his trousers were tucked into his socks.

'What are the other reasons?'

'They are going to video us, load the videos onto a website, and see if they can get anyone to pay to get us back,' Jane said. 'I assume that this camp is close to somewhere they can upload the videos easily.'

'How do you know that?' Colm asked.

'I heard them discussing it,' she said.

'They let you overhear them?'

'They did.'

Colm thought for a moment. More than a moment. Jane had spent three days away from them.

'Were you with Captain Rick all the time?'

'Almost.'

'Why did he keep you with him?'

There was a pause before she answered, but he heard a sound, as if she had shrugged.

'As a trophy. He showed me to his Major. Boasted about how much money I would bring.'

'Who are they going to ask to pay to get us back?'

'They were undecided. They think the Congolese government won't want foreign nationals being kidnapped and killed. It might threaten their tourist revenues. They might try them.'

'Are they right?'

'Certainly not about the government as a whole. Some individuals might recognise the risk.'

'But they were undecided?'

'Captain Rick seemed to think someone else would pay more, but he didn't say who.'

'When will we know?'

'I don't know.'

Colm thought that over as he stared at the tarpaulin side of the tent as if it was made of bars and stone.

'You spent three days with Captain Rick. What's he like?'

'He's a psychopath.'

————

The guard came back after dawn to wake them, though Jane and Colm had not slept. The guard brought food and was laughing as he entered the tent. Kennet roused himself, sitting up.

The guard had strips of meat for Jane and Kennet. He presented Colm with what was evidently the grasshopper Colm had found in his trousers in the middle of the night. It had been cooked.

'Insects are eaten a lot here, aren't they?' Colm said, eying it warily.

Kennet bit into the meat.

'Yes,' he said. 'Good protein. Very healthy. Like eating shrimp.'

'Would you like to swap?' Colm said. The guard was still laughing.

Kennet shook his head and took another bite.

'I've seen this on TV,' Colm said, and bit into the insect. The guard's laughter bellowed.

It was surprisingly tasty. The closest thing Colm could compare it to was nuts. But it wasn't nuts. It was its own taste. He crunched on through the rest of it. He was surprised by how little it bothered him.

'Your loss,' he said to Kennet. The guard laughed even harder, then abruptly fell silent at a voice from outside. He left the tent, then came back and folded the tarpaulin all the way to the right, opening the inside to the out.

Captain Rick was outside the tent. He was still dressed in

jungle fatigues, but he'd rolled up his beret and tucked it under a shoulder strap. 'Lady and gentlemen. I hope you had a pleasant rest. Today we are going to make a film. You will say your name, your occupation, where you are from, and that is all. Is that clear?'

'Yes,' said Jane.

'Yes,' said Kennet, pulling himself to his feet with Jane's help. Colm nodded.

'I said, is that clear?' Captain Rick said, taking a step forward. Colm noticed the guard to the side had his eyes downcast.

'Yes,' said Colm.

'Very good. You first,' Captain Rick said, taking a phone from his trouser pocket, turning it on, loading the camera, and pointing it at Colm. Before he realised what he was doing Colm had reached up to smooth his hair. 'Talk.'

'Er… I am Colm Reid,' he said. 'I am a journalist for the *Irish Telegraph*. I'm from Northern Ireland. I work in Dublin.'

'Good,' Captain Rick said, pointing the camera at Kennet.

'I am Kennet, Kennet Haven,' Kennet said. 'I run the Bandari conservancy in Northern Kenya. I am from Bergen in Norway.'

Captain Rick pointed the camera at Jane.

'I am Jane Haven,' she said. 'I am a teacher in Norway. I am from Bergen in Norway.'

Without another word Captain Rick turned and left. He gave the guard a disapproving frown. The guard didn't look back at him.

'Is that it?' Colm said. Jane shrugged.

Kennet said something to Jane that Colm couldn't quite catch, but it sounded like "*enlarer*". It sounded like a question.

'Close enough,' Jane said. She was watching Captain Rick walking away from them through the camp.

'Have you seen Mak and the others?' Colm asked. Jane nodded.

'They are a hundred metres further up on the right, being held with the three Soldiers of God. Tied to posts.'

'Are they OK?'

'So far. Though if this is the main camp, the need to keep us all healthy to carry the ivory has ended.'

That was a chilling thought.

'What now?' Colm said. 'They send those videos to the government, and we wait to see if anyone cares?'

Jane sat down on the tarpaulin floor.

'If they send them to the government. We could get lucky – if they send them to Reuters, or CNN, or the BBC, the story will be across the world in minutes, and someone will have to care. If they send them to the wrong department of any government, nothing might happen.'

'What do we do?'

Jane looked out of the tent, up towards the sky that was concealed by leaves and branches.

'We wait,' she said.

CHAPTER THIRTY-TWO

'I AM COMING WITH YOU,' FATOU SAID.

'I am sorry, *Mademoiselle Ba*, but that is not possible,' Hannington said. 'This is a very dangerous situation. Forty-two men are already dead, and six more, and one woman, are in danger if they are not already dead. This is a rescue mission. The murderers have a day's head start. We will be moving quickly, and there could be an exchange of fire at any moment. I cannot spare someone to protect you. You must stay here.' Hannington had said this, or something like this, at least three times already, and he was beginning to sound irritated.

'You are taking Tony.'

'Mr Kanagi is a...'

'Mr Kanagi is what? A man?'

'I was going to say Mr Kanagi is trained in firearms.'

Yeah, right.

'I won't slow you down, I won't inconvenience anyone, and I have already indemnified you. If anything happens to me it will not be the fault of you or the rangers of Garamba or of the DRC,' Fatou said.

Hannington turned away, beckoning to one of the sergeants who had come with the squad from Faradje.

'Any word from Dungu?' Hannington said. The sergeant shook his head.

'I can help you. I can tell your story. I need to tell your story. Not the story of the lost rhinos, that was Kennet's dream. I need to tell the story of the rangers of Garamba. I need my country to know there are still wild places in the world, places that everyone needs to stay wild, that are battle grounds, protected by men such as yourself, such as Agoyo, men who have died doing what so many think should be done.

'I live in an apartment in a city. A city of more than a million people. If you leave my city by road or by train the next thing you come to is another city. In every direction. There are farms, and then there are more cities. Every square centimetre of land is people. The people who live there, most of them, they have no idea that this park, this park which would cover a sixth of my country, exists. They have no idea that you are here, fighting to keep it. It would amaze them to see the grass, the trees, the creatures you see every day. And it would move them to tears to hear of poaching, and of the cost in lives.'

Fatou caught herself, worked up and almost shouting. She exhaled and spoke more calmly.

'I am a journalist,' she said. 'And I am coming with you to tell your story.'

She turned on her heels and walked away. She desperately hoped Hannington was watching her. But if he wasn't, what did she have to lose? She couldn't help herself. She looked back. Hannington wasn't looking at her. He was talking to that sergeant and issuing orders, crisp and precise.

Fatou refolded her determination. She had one more card to play.

————

She found Tony in the barracks. Three rangers were there, two stealing some sleep, the other dressing after a shower. He wasn't remotely concerned by her arrival or embarrassed by his lack of clothing. He even smiled at her as he pulled on his trousers. She rolled her eyes.

Tony was cleaning his gun. It was disassembled and laid out neatly on a blanket on one of the beds.

'Can we talk?' Fatou asked.

'Of course,' Tony said. 'Give me one minute.'

He reassembled the gun in a series of smooth, practised movements. He slapped a magazine into it.

'Outside?' he said.

She nodded. She followed him out of the barracks and into the compound.

There were men everywhere. The remaining Nagero rangers who had returned with Hannington had, after a couple of hours, been reinforced by another twenty-five from Faradje.

'Do we need some privacy?' Tony said.

Fatou nodded.

'This way.'

Tony led her to the corner of the compound where Captain Rick's men had climbed the fence using ladders. The cut razor wire had not yet been replaced, and another ladder leaned on the inside. Hannington's burial detail had been using it as a short cut to avoid having to go all the way round the fence to the gateway between digging shifts. Tony slung his rifle across his back and climbed the ladder. Fatou followed him.

She paused when she reached the top of the fence. She hadn't seen behind the compound before. The trees started three hundred metres away. She could see the burial team digging not far from the tree line. Between the fence and the trees was mostly grass, the occasional bush. The ground was uneven, but there was a pattern to it. It was cut by water, and the water followed the contours of the land towards the west.

She climbed over the top of the fence and down one of the ladders. They weren't really ladders. They were tree trunks with footholds hacked out of them with axes. They were slippery.

Tony was walking away from the fence, towards the trees, but not straight towards the men digging. He stopped fifty metres into the grass and waited for Fatou to catch up.

'What would you like to talk about?'

'I need you to insist I come with you on the rescue mission. I need you to take responsibility for me so that Hannington doesn't have any excuse not to take me.'

Tony looked at her. She could see him weighing things up.

'Why do you want to go?' he said.

'I need to see it. I need to tell this story.'

Tony continued to look at her. She could see him thinking.

'And if I say no, you'll tell Hannington that Kennet had arranged to meet the Soldiers of God.'

'Why would you say no?'

Tony opened his mouth to answer, but turned his head suddenly, away from her, looking into the grass.

'I said—' she began to repeat herself, but he held up his hand to silence her. She took in a breath, ready to shout at him, but didn't. He had slipped the gun from his back, and started to move forward, not quite parallel to the fence, walking slowly, carefully. He paused after a few paces to listen.

Then she heard it. A sound. A groan. A voice?

Tony was walking again, slowly, rifle tucked into his shoulder, finger on the trigger.

She followed him, keeping two metres behind.

He stopped, listening. Then the sound came again, a guttural groan, like the last whimpers of a wounded animal. Tony changed direction slightly and walked, watching the ground ahead of him.

Then he stopped again, rifle pointed at something beneath him, concealed in the grass. He froze for maybe three seconds, then he lowered his rifle, and ran forward, dropping out of sight.

She heard his voice.

'Get help!' he shouted.

She ran after him. Found him in a second or two.

He was in a depression in the ground, a shallow ditch dug out by a rivulet of lively water. He was kneeling in the water, next to a body. A man. In ranger's fatigues. The man looked dead, like a corpse, lying straight, feet in the water, body on the slope of the ditch. His immobile arms were locked tight around a long, heavy gun, with a scope and a big barrel, unlike the AR-15s the rangers carried. Then one of his hands moved.

Tony's head whipped around, and he looked straight at her.

'It's Deng. Get help!' he roared.

Fatou reacted before she thought to react. She looked over at the men digging the mass grave. She could see them, at least two of them. They were two hundred metres away.

'*Secours! Maintenant!*' she yelled. '*Secours!*'

She saw one of them look around, trying to place the sound of her voice.

'*Secours!*' she screamed, and jumped up, waving her arms.

It worked. He saw her. She saw him and the others with him drop their spades and start to run towards her.

'They are coming,' she said to Tony, a little breathlessly.

Tony was opening Deng's jacket. Underneath it, Deng was not wearing a shirt. The reason for that soon became clear. He had been shot, and the shirt had been ripped up and used as a bandage.

'OK,' Tony said, without looking at her. 'I'll talk to Hannington.'

CHAPTER THIRTY-THREE

COLM MISSED HIS NOTEBOOK AND PEN. OR, RATHER, HE MISSED notebooks, and pens. He missed Niamh, of course, more than anything. But he wouldn't want Niamh here with him. As long as he was here, though, the one thing that might have made it more bearable would have been his notebooks.

It was the third day in the camp, almost all of which had been spent in the same tent except every few hours, when he was escorted to a latrine pit that had been dug a hundred metres deeper into the forest. The trips to the latrine had been a highlight, if only because they allowed him to stretch his aching limbs. Kennet was too exhausted and ill to talk much. Jane didn't talk much however she was feeling. And the guards wouldn't talk at all. Colm sat in a corner of the tent and watched the trees and the passing soldiers and thought about notebooks.

He didn't really remember his first notebook. For a few years, at university, he'd told people a story about his aunt giving him his first notebook when he was about six years old, a princely gift for a precocious child that had fired his interest in observing and noting things down. He told this story as part of the myth he'd

created in his own head about how he was destined to be a journalist. He had a theory, or at least a belief, or perhaps a hope, a
desperate hope, that the passion and romance of his story made
him sexy and would thus increase the chances of him having sex
with multiple beautiful women of his choice.

Only two things turned out to be wrong with that story. The
first was that no matter how passionately he told it, not a single
beautiful woman who he told it to wanted to have sex with him
as a result. In fact, it was only when he told it matter-of-factly,
without embellishment, with little other than unadulterated
honesty, that his sex life got off the ground. The second was that
a few years later he'd mentioned the story to his aunt, and she
had told him she'd given him a notebook for his birthday when
he was nine because every time she saw him he was writing in a
notebook. The origin myth of his notebook passion turned out
to be a genuine myth, lost in the myths of time.

So, he had asked the Oracle who knew all, namely his
mother. His mother told him there was no first gifted notebook
that had sparked his need to note things. Instead, there had been
the book in which she totted up the household spending with a
pencil, the way she she'd been taught to by her mother. When
Colm was about five, he'd started adding his own entries
detailing what he thought she'd missed. Ducks in the park, no
pounds. By the time he was seven and had learned some numbers
he'd increased his contributions to correcting her maths, and by
the time he was nine he'd stopped correcting her maths because
by then he had learned enough maths to realise her maths had
been right in the first place.

Whatever the truth of it, he had had notebooks as far back
as his reliable memory went, and he had scribbled in them all the
time. Until he'd got a computer, and a mobile phone, and other
ways of recording things electronically. Then he started to use
notebooks a little bit less. He had no problem with typing

things, and for work he usually preferred it because it saved him having to type it up again later. But even with that, he still liked a pen and a notebook when he was recording something, well, something emotional.

This was a story. He was a journalist. He didn't need to bring emotion into this, that was not why he'd brought a notebook. He'd brought a notebook to the DRC because he was expecting it to be difficult to charge his phone regularly. But his notebook was back in the ranger station at Nagero, and his phone was in his trouser pocket with perhaps fifty per cent charge.

He had in his mind the image of himself sitting outside the tent, notebook and pen in hand, recording the events of camp life. It was a romantic image. The sun would be shining, he would be in the shade. There'd be laughter, there'd be chatter. Perhaps a monkey would swing from one tree to another, perhaps a lizard would run across his foot.

A harsh shout interrupted his thoughts. The clearing in front of him, long and thin and with three soldiers visible in it, suddenly erupted. Captain Rick's soldiers, ordinarily quick, efficient, and disciplined, began to scurry about like ants whose nest had been broken into. The lieutenants and the sergeants, the ones Colm assumed were officers and NCOs because when they shouted, other soldiers did things, were running around as if the world was coming to an end, shouting at each other and every soldier they saw.

Colm checked he was tucked into the darkest shadow in the tent and watched.

Kennet was a metre away, lying on his back and alternating between groaning and snoring.

Jane was seated, cross-legged to the side of the tent entrance, watching everything that happened. Her good hand was lying on the bandage that still wrapped her injured arm. The bandage looked like it hadn't been changed in a week and was stained with sweat and mud. It did not look hygienic.

The shouting and the running continued. Colm could see the boots of the two guards assigned to them under the gap in the tarpaulin. Whatever else was going on, they were staying in their posts. The guard who had shadowed Kennet from the start was standing at the left corner, and Jomo was standing to the right. Jane didn't have her own shadow.

'What's happening?' Colm said. It had been an hour since any of them had said anything.

'I don't speak any of those languages,' Jane said.

'There's some Swahili,' Kennet said without opening his eyes. 'They think someone knows where they are.'

Colm felt a surge of excitement. 'Hannington? The army?'

Kennet coughed and didn't answer.

Outside someone Colm hadn't seen before stopped in front of the tent and spoke rapidly to Jomo and the other guard. Then he ran away. Jomo immediately turned into the tent.

'Follow him!' he said, motioning towards the other guard with the barrel of his gun.

Jane was on her feet before he'd finished speaking. Colm hesitated, then started to get up. Kennet didn't move.

'Get up!' Jomo shouted, jabbing towards Kennet with the barrel of his gun. Jane grabbed Kennet's arm and tried to pull him to his feet.

'Help me,' she said. Colm grabbed Kennet's other arm and pulled.

Even after nearly a week of poor food and more exercise than the man had probably had over the rest of his life put together, Kennet was still very heavy. It took a lot of effort, and what felt like an agonisingly long time, to get him up. By the time they'd managed it Jomo was clearly agitated. Colm hadn't seen him like this before.

'Move! Follow him!'

Jane dragged Kennet after the other guard, with Colm right behind them and Jomo so close behind him Colm could feel the barrel of Jomo's gun press into his back whenever Kennet stumbled or slowed.

They were led along the long clearing, passing the place where they had dropped off the ivory little more than forty-eight hours ago. The ivory was gone.

Colm could see Captain Rick, a hundred metres away and visibly angry. The men around him, many of whom were taller, and some bigger, were cringing as he raged and lunged.

'That way!' Jomo hissed. Colm realised he had stopped to stare, and in that moment the other guard had left the clearing into the trees. He was moving along a narrow trail. Colm followed, very conscious of Jomo's gun a few centimetres behind him. The trail was narrow and overgrown. Colm was whipped by low branches, mostly dead this far from the sunlight, and stumbled over roots half-buried by rotting leaves. The guard led them at a shuffling jog that was the fastest pace possible without falling every few metres. The effect of their speed, and the forest, and the branches reaching for him, was strangely disorientating for Colm.

Another fifty metres and the shouts from the camp were falling behind them. The trail curved and twisted, rising a little before cresting a shallow hill. Just below the brow of the hill was a group of men.

'Stop!' Jomo said.

Colm felt himself stop physically, but in his head it seemed as if everything was still whirring. It took a while for the forest to stop moving, before he could properly focus on the people in front of him.

They were all men. And he recognised some of them. The Nagero rangers, Mak, Kwame, and Jean; the three Soldiers of

God captured back at Nagero, and another four armed guards. The three rangers each had their hands tied, and they were tied together using the ropes that bound their hands. The Soldiers of God were bound in the same way.

Kennet, Colm, and Jane were evidently not seen as dangerous.

Nine prisoners, six men guarding them.

One of the other guards shouted something. He started moving, leading the three Soldiers of God. They were followed by two more guards, then the rangers, then two more guards including the one who had been with them at their tent, then Kennet, Colm, and Jane, and finally, in the rear, Jomo.

'Good to see you,' Mak said without looking back.

'You too,' Colm said. He assumed Mak had been talking to all of them. 'You alright?'

Mak looked back, just briefly. His face was bruised and swollen, one eye bloodshot. Colm shuddered.

'What's happening?' Colm said.

The guard in front of him shouted at him in an unfamiliar language, though the meaning was clear: be quiet.

Mak didn't answer. They were led deeper into the forest.

CHAPTER THIRTY-FOUR

'There isn't another country in the world with more bureaucracy,' Hannington said, balling his hands into fists as if he were about to punch someone.

Mola flinched. He was just the messenger.

Fatou smiled to herself. She was from Belgium. Bureaucracy was not unfamiliar to her.

'It's already been six hours. What are they waiting for? They won't even send a plane for reconnaissance.' Hannington muttered, kicking the ground. 'We're going to lose a night.'

The convoy of vehicles had been loaded and lined up ready to go since mid-afternoon.

'Could you follow them at night?' Tony asked.

Hannington shook his head. 'We can only go so far in the vehicles, as far as you went to yesterday. After that it's too dangerous to move on foot in the dark. Ground's too wet.'

'Do you have enough men without the army?'

'I do not know. I don't know how many of them survived. I don't know how well-trained they are. I don't know how well armed they are. And I don't know where they are going.'

'You sent scouts.'

'Not back yet.'

Hannington, Fatou, Tony and Mola were standing in the middle of the compound next to one of the vehicles in the convoy. Several of the other rangers, some from Nagero, some from the force from Faradje, were deliberately hanging around close enough to hear what was being said.

'They certainly had discipline, and firepower to blow the gates, and acid to burn through locks. Their weapons were mostly AKs from what we heard and from what you've found. Effective at short to medium range, pretty useless at long range,' Tony said.

Hannington looked at him.

'What do you mean?'

'You have an armoury full of long range, high-powered rifles. They could give you an edge.'

Hannington didn't move for a moment, then very slowly nodded. He beckoned to one of the Faradje sergeants, a weather-beaten, wiry man of perhaps forty, who was standing next to one of the trucks.

'François. How many of your men can fire an elephant gun and hit a man at more than three hundred metres?'

François's eyes flicked. Fatou could see him thinking.

'You want longer range than an AK?'

Hannington nodded.

François blinked a couple of times.

'Those guns are heavy,' he said.

'How many?'

'Four? Perhaps five?'

'That would give you an advantage, would it not?' Tony said. 'Four or five men who can drop them before they're close enough to even hit you? You could have fifteen of them down before your men were in danger.'

Hannington nodded.

'But,' he said. 'François is right, the guns are heavy. The men carrying them wouldn't be able to carry close range weapons as well, they couldn't take the weight.'

'The enemy would be carrying lighter weapons,' Tony said. 'If we need them, we take them from their dead.'

'Why are you asking this, Hannington?' François said.

Hannington sighed, his anger fading.

'The army still can't tell us when it will have authorisation to send us any troops. We either stay here as these terrorists get further away with our men, or we go after them by ourselves. We don't know how many there are or how well-trained they are, but they mostly used AKs. With five long range rifles we would have an advantage over AKs. But without knowing how many there are we don't know if that's enough.'

'We'd also have to catch them in the open,' François said. 'The rifles give less of an advantage in the forest.'

Fatou had a thought. Something she'd seen, something she'd been told.

'Give me two minutes,' she said.

She left them and ran. She wanted to look back, to see if they were watching her go, and if they were, to see what expressions they had on their faces. But she resisted. She ran towards the ivory store. She was there in thirty seconds.

No one had given the ivory store a thought. It was still broken open and unguarded. She ran inside, switched on the light, and looked at the tusks that had been left behind by Captain Rick and his raiders. She leaned down and lifted the end of one off the floor. She had remembered correctly. There was a number written on it.

She grabbed the smallest tusk she could see, made sure it also had a number written on it, and ran back to Hannington and the others.

———

In the two minutes she'd been gone another man had joined the group. One of the Nagero rangers, one who had been sent out to scout the direction Captain Rick had led his men. And their prisoners.

'-deliberately,' he was saying. 'They know we have vehicles; they are on foot, and they can only be followed on foot.'

'Map,' Hannington said, and walked towards the main building. The scout, Tony, François, and Mola, followed him. Fatou went after them, waiting for the right moment.

They stood in the radio room looking at the map of Garamba on the wall. At some point during the raid someone had put a knife through the location of the Nagero ranger station. The knife had been removed, but the station's location was now a gash.

The scout traced a route along the edge of the park that worked at ninety degrees to the contours of the valleys in the east.

'They've deliberately taken a route through here, where the valleys are at their steepest,' François said. 'Can't drive. We're a day's march behind. They'll be out of the country before we catch them.'

They all stared at the map.

'We can drive,' Mola said, after a minute. He pointed, then traced a route with his finger. It started in the opposite direction, almost, to the one the scout had indicated, following a marked road. After perhaps thirty twisty kilometres the road came to an end just after fording the Garamba River, fifty kilometres from where Fatou and the others had looked on its waters close to the poacher's motel two days before. Mola's finger then moved up the broad valley floor until he stopped almost on the path of Captain Rick's men's predicted route.

'That means we'll drive more than a hundred kilometres to make twenty,' François said, although even as he spoke, the tone of his voice changed. 'Wait. I see. How fast could we drive that way? Thirty, perhaps forty kilometres an hour? And they're walking at perhaps four or five? We'd cover five times the distance but at least six times as fast. We'd catch them up. A little, at least.' He nodded.

There was a pause. Everyone was looking at the map, working it out.

'We still don't know how many there are. We know they lost fifteen men, but there may still be fifty of them. I can't chase fifty with thirty. Even with the long-range guns.'

'You know exactly how many there are,' Fatou said. She placed the tusk she was carrying on the table next to the ruins of the radio.

Hannington looked at her.

'How?' he asked.

She pointed at the number written on the base of the tusk.

'You catalogue them. I presume you weigh them and you record the weight in your catalogue. They didn't take much from your ammunition store and they took none of your guns. Mola and Tony said it – they didn't take the guns because they were carrying the ivory.'

Hannington stared at her, then, slowly, smiled. Fatou continued.

'Tony and I heard Captain Rick say he was keeping the three captured Soldiers of God alive to carry ivory. We heard him make Colm, Kennet, Mak, and Jane pick up ivory too. Your catalogue will tell us how many tusks have been taken and how much they weigh, and–'

'And from that we can estimate how many of them there are,' Hannington finished, musing. 'Very good, Fatou Ba, very good.'

'The catalogue was taken,' Mola said. 'We don't have the record of what we had in the store.'

Fatou deflated. She had been so convinced she had helped.

'Are your seizure reports up to date?' François asked.

Hannington nodded. 'First thing we do,' he said. 'Send them straight over.'

'Then we have copies at Faradje. It will take an hour. We can call Faradje and work out what's missing.'

'Do it,' he said, nodding to Mola.

François and Mola left, Mola taking the tusk from Fatou as he went.

Fatou reflated, a little.

———

'Forty,' François said ninety minutes later. 'It would take at least forty men to carry that ivory.'

'There's one woman,' Fatou said.

'Alright. Forty people.'

'There could be more than forty,' Hannington said.

'But the ones not carrying ivory would have to be carrying something very important. They came for the ivory. There won't be more than a handful not carrying it. Say forty-five of them left here. And nine of those were prisoners,' François said.

'Thirty-six. Captain Rick and thirty-five others escorting nine prisoners,' Tony said.

Hannington was nodding.

'We have thirty men. With the elephant guns, I'll take those odds without the army. They have nine hours head start,' he said. 'Thirty-six kilometres. They will camp at night fall. They will start again at dawn. If we set off at dawn and use the vehicles, we'll be closer to them when we find their trail than we are now.

Get some sleep, lady and gentlemen. We leave an hour before sunrise.'

There was a sense of satisfaction on every face. A problem understood. But it wasn't a problem solved.

'Can we get going now? I know you said you couldn't follow them in the dark, but that was when you thought you'd be mostly following them on foot. Mola picked the easiest route, and the trucks have headlights,' Fatou said.

Hannington looked as if he couldn't decide whether to strangle her or to kiss her.

'We leave now,' he said.

CHAPTER THIRTY-FIVE

The forest was dark and dead. Not the trees. The trees were alive, but the life in the forest was thirty metres above them. On the ground, dead branches, rotting leaves, stunted bushes, clinging onto life for a moment before new growth in the branches above stole the sunlight and they died in turn.

The guards kept them moving with threats and growls, but the two groups of three, the rangers, and the Soldiers of God, were tied together and the vague path wasn't broad enough. They kept stumbling and falling, especially Kwame. He didn't seem to be able to walk well at all, and it took the combined efforts of Mak and Jean to keep him going straight. The guards barked at them, aggressive but muted, thrusting their guns in their direction, but it was futile. Progress could only be slow.

Slow as it was, they kept moving. Colm could no longer tell if they were following a specific route, or if they were simply moving blindly into the forest. There was no visible path created by the passage of many feet, be they animal or human. The undergrowth was sometimes quite thin, when the tree trunks were thickest and the canopy above them highest, and the forest at its darkest. But if the tree trunks were thinner and the trees above them didn't block out most of the light then the growth on the ground was thicker. The guards had machetes, and hacked a path when the undergrowth was too dense to pass through. Anyone following them would have an easy time, but speed seemed to be the priority.

Then, perhaps half an hour after the sounds of shouts from the camp had faded into the trees, they heard the first shots. Distant and muted, pops and cracks. But undeniably gunfire.

That changed things. The guards called a halt, conferred with each other, then gathered the prisoners together, pushed them into the undergrowth, for some way, thirty, forty metres through dead branches, working round them, trying to make sure they broke no branches, left no trail. Now, secrecy was the priority. After twenty minutes of this the guards seemed satisfied, and they made them all sit facing each other, in the V shape created by of the roots of two huge trees. The guards formed a ring around them.

Colm was next to Kennet. The big man was suffering. His breathing was ragged. Jane, on Kennet's other side, put her hand on his arm, and whispered something to him in what Colm assumed was Norwegian. Kennet shook his head, said something like "*ikkyenna*".

Colm got his first proper look at Mak and the others as they were pushed into the gap between the roots of the other tree, the rangers together with the Soldiers of God. Mak and Kwame's faces he knew well. Jean's was not as familiar. The three Soldiers of God were boys. Colm was shocked when he realised it. They were no older than fourteen. They looked terrified.

All six of them, Mak, Kwame, Jean, and the boys, had been beaten. There were bruises and swelling on their faces. Their wrists were raw from the ropes. The Soldiers of God were pushed behind a root and out of Colm's sight. The rangers were made to sit down more or less opposite him.

'What's going on?' Colm said quietly.

Mak looked at him but said nothing.

Kwame, who seemed to have grown a beard in the last twenty-four hours, though Colm realised this was an illusion caused by a combination of stubble and dried blood, coughed. One of the guards looked at him, and Kwame, needing to cough again, did his best to smother the sound. The guard stepped towards him. Kwame shrank back, raising his hands as best he could, yanking Mak and Jean's with him, in supplication.

The guard said something. Colm watched Mak and Kwame's faces but couldn't see a sign of understanding.

'Be very quiet,' Jomo said, his voice flat.

A translation, perhaps.

The nine prisoners stayed still. Stayed quiet. Listened.

Their guards melted into the trees. They picked shadows, vaguely dappled by the weak light filtering down from the canopy. They were all in jungle fatigues, and they used them well. If Colm hadn't known where they had moved to, he would not have known they were there at all.

Colm listened.

The gunfire continued. Pop pop. Crack crack crack. Pop pop. Was that Hannington? Jane had said the Congolese army wouldn't cross the border, but would the rangers?

The pops and the cracks grew quieter, as if they were moving further away. Colm looked at his watch.

It was broken. He must have hit it on something during the race through the forest. The face was shattered, the second-hand twitching, the hour and minute hands loose and out of place.

Kennet had his eyes closed. He might have been asleep. His skin looked grey.

Jane had her eyes open. She was watching the forest, like a hunter watching for elk.

Mak and Jean had their heads bowed, but there was something about the way they held them that told Colm they were alert. They seemed too tense.

Kwame had his head bowed, and that reflected his posture. He was slumped, his limbs loose.

The guards were unmoving, shadows in the shadows, guns ready.

The forest was creaking in the wind. Something bounced around in the branches far above. He heard a scuttle, a bump, a cry. None of the guards reacted, so he assumed those were just the sounds of the forest.

The pop pops and the crack crack cracks continued.

Colm thought about what he could do. His options were limited. He couldn't move, he could only think. The only thing he could think to think about was the time. He counted. Slowly. One, pause, two, pause, three. Trying to make each number equal a second. Each time he got to sixty, he raised a finger. When all his fingers were raised, he lowered them again and made a mark in the leaves with his foot.

He had made two marks with his foot, and had seven fingers raised, when he heard the last pop pop. He kept counting.

When he made the fourth mark with his foot, which by his reckoning was forty minutes since he'd started and thirteen minutes since the last gunshot, he stopped counting and sat up a little.

He could see three of the six guards. The other three had moved from where he'd last seen them. Without him noticing.

He looked at the others. The Soldiers of God were out of sight, concealed by the root of the great tree opposite. Kwame looked to be asleep. Mak and Jean had their heads up, watching in different directions. Colm noticed they were holding hands.

He started to smile. Love in the most dangerous of situations. Then he saw Mak's hand squeeze and Jean's head move, switch his gaze to a different direction. Colm wasn't watching a closeness, at least not in the way he'd initially assumed. They were talking to each other by touch.

Kennet hadn't moved. Colm would have felt it. But Jane was on her haunches. Her right hand was resting on her bandaged left arm. And she was staring over Colm's shoulder into the undergrowth.

Colm listened. He slowly turned his head to look at what Jane was looking at.

CHAPTER THIRTY-SIX

FATOU, TONY, AND MOLA WERE IN THE FOURTH OF SIX vehicles. She could see the headlights of the ones in front and the ones behind. The headlights of the one they were in showed grass. Nothing but grass, other than the rear of the vehicle in front, and the shadow where the grass ended on the bank of the river to the right. She could hear water flowing in the dark. They were moving at perhaps eight kilometres an hour. 'Why are we going so slowly?' Fatou asked.

'Quiet,' Mola whispered.

'Why?' she asked, though more quietly this time.

'*Viboko*. Hippo. We're following the Garamba River. Hippos will be grazing.'

'So?'

'Why did they send you here? Don't you know anything about Garamba?'

'I only know what I read on Wikipedia. I read there are hippos.'

'But not about hippos?'

'Big cows, right?'

'Two tonne cows that get really angry if something gets between them and their river.'

'We're in a Hilux.'

'A Hilux that, like a hippo, weighs about two tonnes. Unlike a hippo, a Hilux doesn't have an attitude. If a hippo charged us, we'd be in a Hilux coffin. Be quiet.'

Fatou stopped talking and watched the night slip past. Insects were occasionally picked out in the glow of the headlights, flashing silver or gold. And larger things, mysterious shadows until she realised they were bats hunting the insects.

Two hours from Nagero, slow and steady. Fatou was excited, trying to hold inside her the thought that she was part of the rescue party, that by convincing Hannington to set off tonight rather than waiting till the morning she'd made a difference, that they would intercept Captain Rick and his captives and his ivory train, and return the world to its natural state. But the nature of the world had its own ideas.

The rangers in the vehicle in front of them were gesturing. Mola gripped her arm and pointed. He raised his other hand to his mouth, finger on his lips, the universal sign to be silent. Then he raised his rifle and aimed into the night on the right-hand side of the truck.

'There,' Tony whispered. He pointed at a huge grey shape just on the edge of the cone of grass lit up by the headlights of the Hilux. No, not one shape, two. No, three. Tony also raised his rifle and pointed it at the shapes. In the vehicle ahead of them Fatou could see all the other rangers were doing the same thing.

Fatou had seen two hippos in a zoo. Between her and them had been a moat and a concrete wall. And she didn't remember them being that big. Between her and these three, no, four, was nothing other than the side of the truck and about thirty metres of grass. And they were enormous. Mola and Tony were clearly very nervous about them, and Fatou felt her confidence ebb. She gripped the side of the truck till her knuckles hurt. And there weren't four, there were at least six. The truck kept moving, slow and steady. The hippos ignored them, intent on grazing.

It was ten minutes before Mola and Tony lowered their rifles. 'Alright,' Mola said.

The convoy kept moving, slowly. They had to stop to make bridges across new streams, fresh tributaries to the Garamba River that had cut steep gashes out of the earth that couldn't simply be rolled over. They had to stop to dig tyres out of mud. But the night didn't stop them. And every kilometre they moved forward, Fatou felt they were closing in on her story.

———

They camped eventually, after eight hours slow driving. They camped on the riverbank opposite the poachers' motel Mak had taken them to on Fatou's first foray into the park. She only knew this because Mola told her; she couldn't see it in the dark. They camped quickly, pulling the vehicles up in a semi-circle, and, mostly, sleeping under them. Guard shifts were set, night-vision binoculars passed from sentry to sentry. Fatou, as a non-essential guest of Tony, got to sleep in whichever shift she chose.

She chose to sleep immediately. She was exhausted. She lay down on the flatbed of the Hilux. Hard metal and covered in mud from rangers' boots. But she thought it safer than the ground. She wrapped herself in a plastic sheet. She'd be too hot, but hopefully it would keep the insects away. She used her bag as a pillow.

Her bag contained food, water, soap, a toothbrush, and a pack of notebooks and pens. The last thought she had before she drifted away was that a corner of a notebook was digging into her cheek.

———

She was awake before she wanted to be. It was only just light. She guessed she'd slept for about four hours, though it felt like four minutes.

What had awakened her was a call. A bellow. An animal?

She had slept in her clothes, so that wasn't a problem. She slid out of the back of the truck.

The sun was rising. South and east, between the direction the convoy was taking, and the direction Captain Rick's men had taken, was something prehistoric, something ancient, nodding in the sunrise on the other side of the river.

It took her a moment to realise it was a giraffe. Even a quarter of a kilometre away she could tell it was huge. Five metres tall? Taller? She stared at it. It was the tallest living thing she had ever seen. It walked, and kept walking, passing through the grass at a leisurely stroll, though its legs were so long it covered the ground very quickly.

Around her, the rangers were mostly awake and preparing to move out. Blankets were being rolled up, water drunk, and Fatou could even smell coffee. But she kept watching the giraffe. It was walking towards the river. She estimated where it would reach the bank, seventy-five metres ahead of her. She walked slowly towards it.

It was much faster than she was, and it got to the bank first despite travelling twice as far in the same amount of time. She reached the bank opposite it a few moments later.

The animal was already drinking, its long legs splayed out to allow it to lower its head to the water. It turned its head minutely as she stopped walking, perhaps getting a better look at her. If so, it didn't see her as a threat, because it turned its head back and kept drinking.

She watched it, just the few short metres of the Garamba River between her and it. She wanted to wade across and stroke its neck, but she remembered what Kwame had told Colm about crocodiles, and instinctively took a step backwards, away from the bank.

That step brought Tony into her eyeline. He had followed her.

'She is magnificent,' Fatou said.

'She's a he,' Tony said, indicating the part of the giraffe that proved it.

Fatou felt herself blushing, not because of the sight of the animal's very obvious penis, but because she'd not noticed it in the first place.

Mola joined them.

'There are fewer than fifty left in the park,' he said.

'How many were they?' Fatou asked.

'Hundreds,' Mola said.

'What happened to the others? What can kill something that big?'

'Predators do take them sometimes. Crocodile, lion, even leopard. Usually only the calves, though. Even lion would have to be starving before they'd take on an adult giraffe. But they are mostly killed by same thing that kills the rhino and the elephant. *Bracconiers.*'

'Poachers? They don't have horns or tusks. What are they poached for?'

'For meat. They're big. More than quarter of a tonne. A kilo can be sold for about two months' wages. One animal is worth the equivalent of a lifetime of work for a man.'

The giraffe finished its drink and raised its head high into the air. Slightly awkwardly it pushed with its front legs until it was fully upright again. Then, with a twitch of its ears, it turned and walked sedately back the way it had come. Fatou watched it with a feeling of awe.

'We need to get going,' Mola said.

Fatou nodded and followed him and Tony back to the convoy. Every few metres she looked back over her shoulder at the retreating giraffe.

CHAPTER THIRTY-SEVEN

JANE SEEMED TO BE STARING AT A TREE. WHICH COULDN'T BE right. Colm looked back at her to check he was following her gaze, then looked again. She was looking in the direction of a tree, certainly. But beyond the tree he saw something move. At least he thought he saw something move. It was so slight, just a shift in the light. A shadow had flickered, perhaps. He relaxed his eyes, let his focus go, allowed himself to see the light, not the things the light was illuminating.

He had a sudden memory of a garden. When he was young his parents had taken him to visit a relative. A Great Aunt. He remembered being told they were going to visit his Great Aunt. He remembered never having heard the term "Great Aunt" before. He remembered thinking that "Great" meant "Big" and, as his Auntie Grace, his mother's elder sister, was very tall and very wide ('DO NOT call her WIDE!' his mother had said when he had made this observation) he assumed his Great Aunt would be enormous. But his Great Aunt had turned out to be very old and very tiny. She had been his father's mother's sister, and she had lived in Lancashire, in England, where she had had a large house in a large garden. The garden had been a wonderland for Colm, at the age of whatever age he had been. Eight? There had been a vegetable garden, and a fruit garden, which included an orchard with pear trees and apple trees. And there had been what his Great Aunt had called "the ornamental garden".

The ornamental garden had a wall around it, a wall that was much taller than Colm had been when he was eight. The only way through that wall was a wooden door, ancient and rotting and stuck open.

'He can't do any harm in there,' his Great Aunt had told his mother. 'I haven't been in there in years.'

Colm had stepped through the open door and been amazed. It was clear that no one had been through that door in years. Inside, it was overgrown like the wilds of a different planet. There were flagstone paths that could be followed, intersecting raised beds that had probably once held flowers and other beautiful plants. By the time he had walked into the ornamental garden the whole thing was filled with rhododendrons. They had conquered everything else in the garden, apart from the nettles, and they were ten feet tall, and thicker than custard.

Or so he had thought, until he had spied a gap and left the path and found yet another world. The inside of the rhododendrons. The glossy dark green leaves, and the purple flowers, faced outwards, towards the sun. They coveted the sun, spread to embrace it. Behind the leaves and the flowers, they left no room for light to get in. Inside the rhododendrons was a world of trunks and branches and, occasionally, when a little light found its way in, nettles.

Colm had stung himself almost immediately. But he'd kept quiet. He had learned, by that age, that running to tell his mother he had hurt himself just got him told off for doing something dangerous and banned from doing it again. He didn't want to leave this magical new world.

He'd explored. He'd climbed over, under, and up the thicker branches and trunks. He'd found birds' nests, but not touched them. He'd found a rabbit skull and bits of fur. He remembered the feel of the thick carpet of dead and dying leaves beneath his sandals. He remembered the smell, the sweet smell, of rotting vegetation and fresh rhododendron flowers turned towards the sun.

But the reason it came to mind now was because most of all he remembered the shadow through the branches that had scared him. Something large in the garden with him, just the dappled movement of light through leaves and branches. Something that had terrified him until it had spoken and turned into his dad.

He was certain someone was moving in the undergrowth, fifty, perhaps forty metres beyond the tree Jane was staring past. He assumed it was one of their three guards who had moved out of his line of sight. He checked the other three. They were still where they had been, motionless, guns raised, listening, heads turning, looking.

Colm looked at Mak and Jean. They were no longer holding hands, but they were still looking in opposite directions, their eyes sharp, their bodies pressed as close against the tree roots as possible. They were not looking in the same direction as Jane either. Colm couldn't look in the direction Mak was – tree roots blocked that line of sight. But he could follow Jean's gaze. He did the same thing again, let his focus go, allowed himself to see just the movement of the light, if there was any.

For a moment he saw nothing. For two moments. Three. Then it came. A shift in a shadow.

Colm turned his head, strained his neck a little to look behind him, over the wall of the root, in a direction Jane couldn't see and Mak and Jean weren't looking at. He did the same thing again, softened his focus and waited. He counted.

On thirty, he saw something move, again, just a shadow inter-rupting a patch of light for a moment, nothing more.

Jane had seen someone move, Mak had seen someone move, Jean had seen someone move, and Colm had seen someone move, all in different directions. It was possible two or more of those someones were the same someone. In which case they could be the three guards, circling a perimeter.

On the other hand, they could be surrounded.

He felt a hand on his arm. It was Jane. She had leaned across Kennet to get Colm's attention. She didn't say anything, she didn't visibly do anything beyond putting her hand on his arm. But she pressed down. It took him a moment. Slide lower. His head had been above the wall of the root. He nodded and slid lower. He looked across at Mak and Jean. They were also now lower, not looking about them, but making sure the thickest parts of the roots were between them and as much of the jungle as possible.

The rangers, and the teacher, were behaving as if they thought there was danger, not protection, moving in the shadows of the forest. Colm looked at his legs. The roots burrowed into the earth faster than he was long, and his feet and shins remained above the wall of wood that protected the rest of him. He breathed and listened. Then he started to move his legs, to bring them towards him so they weren't exposed.

Then he heard a snap. It sounded like a twig. For a moment he thought it was him, that he'd disturbed something as he was moving his legs. But then a thousand guns started firing and he had other things to worry about.

CHAPTER THIRTY-EIGHT

THE CONVOY CROSSED ANOTHER BROAD TRIBUTARY OF THE Garamba River a kilometre northeast from the poachers' motel. It was fast-flowing, but not enough to trouble the vehicles. Fatou watched the water as the Hilux drove through it, clear upstream, cloudy from riverbed disturbed by the wheels downstream. The truck bounced as it climbed the bank then settled as they turned northeast and continued towards the place where they expected to cross the trail of Captain Rick and the ivory thieves.

'How much further?' she said, although even as she spoke, she thought she remembered the answer. Two hours from the ford, someone had said.

'Two hours,' Mola said. 'Give or take.'

Fatou remembered Hannington had told them there were no large animals left north of the river. The poachers had killed them all. She saw nothing to suggest that wasn't true. Grass, just grass. But ahead, many kilometres ahead, she could see the trees. The forest that stretched for a thousand kilometres, north and south. The forest they were heading for.

Two hours. The Hilux bounced and bumped, following the

others, fourth in line. They stopped once to allow one of the
Land Rovers to change a wheel. It had run over a rusted trap, the
vicious jaws ripping the rubber to shreds. The trap was so badly
corroded it didn't spring. It had just been lying there in the grass,
forgotten and useless, unless someone drove over it.

Once the wheel had been changed, the old wheel and the
trap were strapped to the roof of the Land Rover. The rangers
left nothing behind, even on this mission.

The grass was monotonous, a rolling sea, waves of wind
blowing through it. But Fatou was not bored. She sat in the back
of the Hilux, uncomfortable in every way – too hot, too sweaty,
too jarred, too punched by the metal of the side and bed of the
truck every time it went over the slightest bump, which was
every minute. And she was enjoying herself. This was a real story.
This was life, this was a story about a journey into the heart of
life. Everything, every part of the history of the world, was still
being played out here. In a more complex and subtle way than
had ever happened before.

Colm had told her a story about a bear, native to his home
country of Ireland, wiped out by man thousands of years ago.
Belgium was the same. No bears, no wolves, no wild animals
bigger than a badger. Perhaps the odd deer. But the clash
between people and animals in Belgium had been over long
before her great-grandparents had moved there. From the
Congo. In Belgium, there was nothing she could do. Here,
though...

She looked at Mola, sitting opposite her, one hand on the
side of the truck, the other on his gun. He looked lost in his own
thoughts, distant.

'Why do you do it?' she asked him.

He didn't react. Either he hadn't heard her, or he didn't think
she was talking to him. She reached over and shook his knee. He
looked at her.

'Why do you do it?' she repeated.

'Do what?' he said.

'This. Be a ranger. Protect this park that so many other men will kill you for trying to protect.'

He smiled, without humour.

'I was thinking that. I was just thinking that. Gasimba and Agoyo are dead. Agoyo had no wife, no children. Gasimba had a wife, three children. They are both dead. Agoyo will have no children. Gasimba will not see his children become women and man. Why do I do this?'

He drifted off again, seeming to forget that she was there. But he hadn't.

'I do this because I can. I know how. This is my country. Not the whole of the Congo, this part of the park. My village is Wando. I grew up in this park, helping my father hunt kudu and crocodiles and monkeys. That is what we ate, how we survived. Then someone came from the government and told us it was illegal to kill them, and we had no way to survive. We killed them at night after that.

'Then someone came and told us we could get paid for protecting them. Because they were endangered, and special to the Congo, and people from other places would pay to see them if they were still here, and they would keep paying. Many payments to see one animal. Better than one meal from one animal. Much better.'

He drifted off again, staring out over the grass as the truck bounced and jerked. Fatou was waiting for him to come back, but it was Tony who spoke next.

'My father had a farm, back home in Kenya. A small farm next to a large farm. Next to a huge farm. Cattle ranch. The cattle ranch was owned by a British lord. In the sixties he sold it to a Kenyan conglomerate. When independence came a lot of the British left, and they sold cheap. The new owners were rich, like the British. They were just like the British. Wealthy and looking for more wealth. They changed the ranch into a hunting lodge. Brought the big animals back and advertised for hunters. British, American, French, German. They came and they killed, but the lodge was a farm. The man running it made sure they bred enough animals that the ones killed each season were replaced each season. I was very young then. I remember my father got extra work helping to pick up the carcasses, take them to the taxidermists, make sure the hunters got their trophies.

'But in Kenya the government banned hunting early. When I was seventeen. And the hunting lodges had to close. My father's extra income was gone with the passage of a single law. We thought the hunting lodge would close, and we would starve, because our farm couldn't compete with the huge ones.

'But someone bought the hunting lodge and turned it into a game park. A private one but funded well enough to pay wardens and rangers. I got a job there when I was eighteen, looking after the animals, keeping the poachers away. If I hadn't done that, if that park hadn't been bought by someone who wanted to see rhino, and lion, and elephant, and giraffe, and crocodile, and buffalo, I don't know what I would have done.'

Tony stopped talking.

The truck bounced and bucked. Fatou thought it was slowing.

'It's just a job?' she said.

'No,' Tony and Mola said at the same time. 'Not any more,' Mola added. 'This is what I do.'

Tony nodded.

The Hilux stopped.

Ahead of them, in the column, there was the sound of doors slamming and men calling.

'We're there,' Mola said, and vaulted over the side of the truck.

CHAPTER THIRTY-NINE

COLM PRESSED HIMSELF INTO THE GROUND AND INTO THE SIDE of the thick tree root as soon as the firing started. Instinctively he put his hands over his ears, expecting the noise to be deafening. But it wasn't. Irregular cracks and pops, like cheap fireworks. It was annoying more than anything. And there weren't a thousand guns firing. He guessed there were perhaps a dozen. Their six guards firing in one direction, and their unseen attackers firing back. The attackers seemed to be arranged in a quarter-circle, or at least the ones firing were. Smart enough not to encircle their prey and risk shooting each other.

The fire fight wasn't just annoying, it was boring. No one seemed to hit anything. Colm could still see three of their guards, including Jomo, each crouched behind a tree root, taking careful aim and firing bursts of shots toward the guns firing at them. Colm didn't dare raise his head high enough to see if he could see who was firing at them; all he knew about them was from the noise of their shots and the reaction of the guards. He could hear the bullets flying through the air. But, after the firing had been going on for a minute, he didn't think anyone had hit a tree, much less a person.

He could see who was going to win, though. The side that had brought the most bullets. The guard on the other side of Jomo changed the magazine on his AK-47 about five seconds after the shooting started. If each of them had twenty magazines, at that rate the battle would be over in under two minutes. And Colm doubted they'd carried that many. But Jomo and the other guard were not firing as wastefully, using three-shot bursts, making the magazines last a lot longer.

Finally, someone hit something. One of the attackers' bullets hit the tree root Jomo was crouching behind and Mak, who was lying in the V between that root and the next, was hit by a splinter thrown out by the impact. He brushed it away. A moment later Colm heard the whine of a second bullet very close to his own head, but it disappeared past the tree and into the undergrowth.

The rapid exchange of fire lasted only a couple of minutes, before everything dwindled to the occasional exchange of shots. All involved were now conserving ammunition, waiting for the other side to do something stupid.

'Who is shooting at us?' Colm whispered to Kennet. He just shrugged.

The sporadic exchange of fire continued for five more minutes until it stopped completely. The forest was quiet, but for the background noise of the insects which nothing could switch off.

Colm looked over at the three rangers. Mak and Jean were alert, ready for something. Perhaps they were planning to rush the guards if the shooters turned out to be from the Congolese army, or Hannington and the rangers.

Then a voice came out of the trees, and they found out who had been shooting at them.

Though not immediately, as the voice spoke a language Colm hadn't heard spoken before, not even in the last few days. He wasn't sure if Mak or Jean understood it. But Jomo evidently did, Colm could see it on his face. Jomo said nothing in response.

The voice came again, this time in English.

'Brotherhood of Souls. You have a zibb. It is time to extend. You are in our territory now. Pop down your guns and run or all will die today. Leave your prisoners. They are our prisoners now.'

Zibb? Colm thought.

Jomo and the other two guards Colm could see exchanged glances. Colm understood their dilemma. There might only be six men hiding in the trees, and they might be low on ammunition. In which case, it was a fair fight, and their best chance would be to keep fighting rather than voluntarily surrendering their weapons and turning around to make it easier for their assailants to shoot them in the back. Or there might be thirty men in the trees with a hundred thousand rounds, in which case not running would almost certainly mean death.

There was a single shot. It sounded louder, deeper, slower than the others had. It wasn't slower, though, because Colm only heard it after he'd seen the throat of the guard nearest him explode, and his body drop, blood spraying the ground, a tree root, and Jomo, as he fell. The guard furthest from Colm took one look at his newly dead colleague, turned, and ran, dropping his gun after three or four strides. Another burst of gunfire, and he fell, hit in the back. The shots had come from a different direction to the earlier shots. The attackers had been using the little ceasefire to move into better positions.

There were more running footsteps, more firing, behind the tree Colm, Jane, and Kennet were protected by. Shouts and shots followed, then more running. It sounded as though the other guards had not been instantly gunned down and had escaped.

The only one left was Jomo. He looked at the AK-47 he was

holding, then very carefully unfastened the strap, slipped it from his neck, placed the gun on the ground, and pushed it as far away from him as he could using his foot. Then he sat down with his back to the root until Colm could see only the top of his head. Jomo called out.

He called out in what sounded like the same language the unseen speaker had first used.

'What's he saying?' Colm whispered to Kennet.

'I don't know. I don't recognise the dialect.'

The unseen voice answered. Authoritative, arrogant.

Jomo responded.

The unseen voice answered again. Questioning.

A third voice joined in, high and nervous. It came from close by, just on the other side of the roots that protected the rangers. Colm realised it was one of the three Soldiers of God. Colm had forgotten about them.

Jomo was getting to his feet. He rummaged in his bag and pulled out a knife. A simple, clumsy looking blade and a handle wrapped in string. He took a deep breath and stepped out of the cover of the tree, walking round the roots and bending down. He was cutting the ropes that bound the three Soldiers of God. Within a few seconds the first, then the second and third of them were on their feet. They raced behind the tree to collect the discarded guns, Jomo's and the two dropped by his dead colleagues. The second they had the AK-47s in their hands, they were transformed from sullen, frightened teenagers to vicious animals, wild-eyed with bloodlust.

One of them started to go through the bags left by Jomo and his colleagues, idly throwing anything that didn't appeal to him to the forest floor, and shoving everything that did into one bag. He took food, knives, ammunition.

The second and third child-soldiers returned to Jomo, who had remained where he had been when he had freed them. One of them hit him in the stomach with the barrel of the gun. Jomo doubled over, and the other hit him on the back of the head with the butt of his gun. Jomo collapsed to the floor, flat on his face. One of them kicked him in the stomach, but he didn't react. The blow to the back of the head had either killed him or stunned him. The soldier who had delivered the first blow pointed his gun at Jomo's head and put his finger on the trigger.

Colm assumed this was it. They would kill Jomo, then they would kill the rangers, and then they would kill Kennet, Jane, and him. Niamh. Oh, Niamh.

A great voice shouted. 'STOP!' The child-soldier froze.

Another dozen armed men were walking out of the trees. Jungle fatigues, green t-shirts, army boots, AK-47s. The uniform of all the cool guerrilla groups. Two men stood out. One, the one who had shouted, was not wearing a camouflage jacket, but instead an officer's jacket with rank insignia Colm didn't recognise sewn to the shoulders. He wore gold jewellery, a thick bracelet that hung low on his wrist, and several rings. This man was the one who had done all the talking so far.

'I want him alive,' he said to the child-soldier who had been about to shoot Jomo. He turned his attention to the others without checking to see his order carried out.

'Who are they?' he asked, pointing to Mak, Jean, and Kwame.

'Nagero rangers,' one of the child-soldiers said. 'Brotherhood made them carry ivory.'

The officer turned to Kennet, Colm, and Jane.

'You are Kennet Haven. You are Jane Haven. You I do not know.' As he said each name, he jabbed a finger. The final jab was in Colm's direction. He raised his eyebrows. He was expecting a response.

'Colm Reid. Irish Telegraph,' Colm said, pushing himself to his feet and offering his hand to the officer, who was so surprised

he shook it. 'Thanks to you and your men for saving us. Er...
sorry, who are you?'

The officer was a little taken aback.

'Brigadier Okumu of the Soldiers of God,' he said. 'Kennet
Haven asked to meet the General. I am to take Mr Haven to
him.'

The Soldiers of God. From the hands of one outlawed group
to those of another.

The other man who stood out did so for different reasons.
He was the tallest of the twelve, taller than Colm, although not
as tall as Kennet. He was dressed like the other soldiers, but he
carried a very different gun. Not an AK-47, a long-barrelled rifle
with a scope, similar to the ones in the Nagero armoury, similar
to the one Jane had carried on their first foray into the park a
hundred years ago. A hunter's rifle. This was the man who had
shot the guard through the throat.

But the most unusual thing about him was neither his
weapon nor his height. It was his skin colour. He was white.

CHAPTER FORTY

THE TRAIL LEFT BY CAPTAIN RICK AND THE IVORY THIEVES was narrow. Single file. But forty or fifty pairs of boots had damaged the grass. The trail couldn't be missed. It wound up the hill and into the first of a series of steep ravines cut by young streams. There was no way the vehicles could take them any further.

'How far behind are we?' Hannington said.

Someone answered him. Fatou didn't catch it.

'What did he say?' she asked Tony. Tony shook his head. He had missed it too.

'A night and a bit,' Mola said. 'They were here yesterday.'

'But they will have stopped moving overnight,' Tony said. 'We drove for half of it, we must have gained.'

Mola nodded. 'If they camped from dusk till dawn, they will be four to six hours walking time ahead. And they are laden. We should move faster.'

Hannington was issuing orders. The rangers were out of the vehicles and forming into groups of five, each group including one man armed with a long-range hunting rifle. The only group that didn't have a hunting rifle was the one Fatou was part of with Tony, Mola, and François. It was also the only group that didn't have five people in it.

Fatou was surprised to see the two rear vehicles, a Land Rover and something unrecognisable that looked to have been created by welding the front half of a Jeep to the back half of a Volvo estate, turning and starting to drive back the way they had come.

'Are they not staying?' she asked.

Hannington, standing a little way off and looking at a map with one of the groups of five, heard her.

'They are all going back. Can't leave them here. We might not come back this way.'

He pointed at the map, pointed into the distance, said something Fatou didn't catch, and the group of five he'd been talking to nodded and set off at a quick pace following the trail of Captain Rick's column. Hannington looked at his watch.

'Where are they going?' Fatou said.

'This is going to be a very long walk if I have to explain everything to you, Fatou Ba.' He walked over to join her, Tony, Mola, and François. 'So just listen and don't ask questions.'

Hannington put two fingers in his mouth and let out a piercing silence. He tried again. Nothing that time either. He took his fingers out of his mouth, shook his head, and looked at Mola.

Mola grinned and raised a hand to his mouth as if he was about to make a similar attempt to whistle. But then his other hand emerged from his pocket holding a whistle, and he blew a shrill blast on that.

Hannington waved the other groups towards them; four, excluding Fatou's group and the one that had already set off.

He waved both arms in the direction of the trail.

'Five-minute intervals,' he said. 'Keep moving. They could be six hours ahead of us, perhaps a little less. If they keep on the same heading, we need to gain three hours a day to catch them before they reach the border. They will most likely be on the move twelve hours a day. That means we have to cover in nine hours the distance they cover in twelve. My man here,' Hannington put his hand on Mola's shoulder, 'saw them at Nagero. They are organised. They are disciplined. They are fit. They are trained soldiers, not poachers or have-a-go heroes. They will be moving as quickly as they can, and they are dangerous. They have already killed five of our men and stolen ivory that cost the lives of our friends and brothers, as well as our elephant. And Mak Kibwana, Kwame Ilunga, and Jean Kabila are their prisoners, along with our guests from Kenya and Ireland. We must catch them before they reach the border.

'Group two,' Hannington pointed to one of the groups of five and looked at his watch, 'One minute. I will tell you. Group four, five, six, seven,' he pointed to the other four groups in turn, 'you will set off in eleven, sixteen, twenty-one, and twenty-six minutes. Time yourselves. We will leave in six minutes.'

Fatou realised what that meant. Her, Tony, François, Mola and Hannington were group three. She smiled to herself. She was in the command group.

There were nods, back slaps, words of encouragement. Group two set off, moving quickly, following the trail.

She looked at her watch. Five minutes, and they would be on the move themselves.

She adjusted her backpack, checked the straps were tight, that it fit comfortably on her back. She had no gun, so was lighter than the others. But she was slighter too, and not used to this. Their first trip into the park had taught her a lot, but one of the things it had taught her was that she was nothing like as fit as she had thought she was. She went to a gym three times a week, didn't drink, didn't smoke, could run ten kilometres on a treadmill in just under an hour. But these men moved through this terrain every day of their lives, and it was nothing like a treadmill.

She realised Tony was watching her.

'Ready?' he said.

She nodded.

'Have you done this sort of thing before?' she said.

He shook his head.

'I've worked for Bandari, the conservancy Kennet runs, for more than ten years. It's in the heart of Kenya, a long way from the borders, and a long way from the wild. It is flat. You can drive across the entire thing. Sometimes I have chased poachers out of the conservancy, onto the Laikipia plateau. But the poachers I have dealt with are opportunists, amateurs. I have never hunted soldiers. My brother is a soldier. I would not want to hunt him on his own, and certainly not if he had forty men at his back.'

'Should I be afraid?'

'That would be sensible. But take heart from this: I have not hunted soldiers before, but Hannington has. Most of the men we are with have. These men are the equal of soldiers, and the better of many. If we can catch Captain Rick before he reaches the border, I do not fancy his chances.'

'What if we don't?'

'Then it's politics, and I have no head for that.'

Fatou nodded to herself, thinking.

'Now!' Hannington said.

Fatou looked at her watch. Their five minutes up. Hannington, Mola, and François were already moving. She adjusted her backpack one last time and followed. She heard Tony's footsteps in the grass behind her.

CHAPTER FORTY-ONE

BRIGADIER OKUMU AND HIS MEN LED COLM AND THE OTHERS back to the camp recently vacated by the Brotherhood of Souls. The Brigadier had the rangers' bonds cut, and allowed them, and Jomo, to walk with Colm, Kennet, and Jane. It seemed like a gesture of freedom, but the seven of them were ringed by armed soldiers, and the tall white guy with the hunting rifle stayed behind them, perhaps fifty metres, watching them with an expression of contempt.

It took a while to get back because there was no obvious track for much of the trip. Kennet tried to keep close to the Brigadier, and asked him about rhinos with the eagerness of a child. When had they last seen them? How far were they from here? When could they see them? The Brigadier's responses were non-committal at best.

'That will be up to the General,' was the gist of it, before the Brigadier marched ahead in irritation.

Colm's mind was on other things.

No obvious track. 'How did they find us?' Colm said, out loud, but to himself.

'I've been thinking the same thing,' Mak said, very quietly.

Jomo looked at them both sharply, but said nothing.

Mak looked at him.

'What's your story?' Mak said.

Jomo didn't answer.

'I don't know ru!ooro, but I recognise it. You spoke it to Okumu. How do you know it?'

Jomo still didn't answer.

'They're too far away to hear, and you're stuck with us now,' Mak said.

Jomo said nothing, but he gave Mak a look. It was almost pleading.

'That's not the question that's most in my mind,' Mak said. 'The question that is most in my mind, Kennet Haven, is what have you done? Back at Nagero Captain Rick said those three boys,' he motioned to the three former prisoners who were chatting and laughing and waving their machine guns like baseball bats, 'told Captain Rick that they were at Nagero because you had contacted them and asked them to escort you to find the last rhino. You admitted it. You contacted the Soldiers of God! Do you know who they are? What they have done? Did you see those three boys? Do you know how those three boys became Soldiers of God? The Soldiers of God have been raiding villages in Rwanda and Uganda for a decade. They kill the men, rape the women, and steal the children. The boys they get drunk and give guns and make them new Soldiers of God, and the girls are never seen again, unless one of them staggers out of the jungle ten years later with stories of rape and having children at thirteen, and more rape, and they get home to their families, what's left of them, who reject them because they are "spoiled". And you have treated with these people?'

Mak's voice had risen as he spoke, and Jean put a warning hand on his arm, his eyes on the nearest of their captors.

Mak exhaled.

'What have you done?' he hissed at Kennet.

'They know where the rhinos are,' Kennet said.

'There are no rhino, Kennet! There is no way this group of thieves and murderers would know where a live rhino was and not kill it and sell its horn. You have no idea what you're doing.' Mak said this with quiet anger, while keeping his expression as calm as he could. A couple of the escorting soldiers had glanced at them more than once, but they were keeping their distance, and Colm hoped they hadn't heard what Mak had said.

'I have to do anything I can,' Kennet said. 'If I can save them, I will.'

'You've killed us all, that's what you've done,' Mak said. 'There are no rhino. If they have promised to show you rhino, it can only mean they have another use for you. This is going to get very messy very quickly. If we're all alive in the morning I will be very surprised.'

Mak shut up.

Kwame was not well. He had suffered more at the hands of Captain Rick's men than Mak and Jean had. Whether he'd been subject to harsher treatment, or had not been well to start with, Colm didn't know. But Jean was keeping Kwame upright, and still Kwame threatened to fall over every few metres. Jomo had joined Jean and was helping him, but Mak pushed Jomo out of his way and looped Kwame's arm over his shoulders.

'I will look after my men,' Mak said. He walked on, holding Kwame up, and did not look back at Kennet.

Kennet looked at Jane.

She said something. Sounded like 'Hannah's red.'

Kennet shrugged.

———

When they reached the camp Colm was surprised to see it hadn't changed much. The tarpaulins were still in place, the hut-like structures still standing. There were half a dozen dead bodies piled part way along the main clearing, and the occasional bullet hole visible in the tree trunks, but other than that, all that had happened was that Captain Rick's men had moved out and the Soldiers of God had moved in.

Colm and the others were led to the small clearing where they'd dropped off the ivory when they had first arrived. They were told to sit on the ground. All seven of them did, but in three groups. The rangers sat together, as far from Kennet as they could. Jane sat with Kennet. Colm tried to strategically position himself between them. And Jomo sat next to Colm.

'When can we see the General?' Kennet said. 'I want to see the rhinos. I will help with the negotiations with the Ugandan government. This man is a journalist, he will tell the world the true story of the Soldiers of God, not the propaganda that has been distributed for years.'

There was something artificial about the way Kennet spoke, as if the words weren't his.

'Wait here,' the Brigadier said. 'You, come with me.' He pointed at one of the three soldiers who had been a prisoner of the Brotherhood of Souls. The boy looked scared, but crossed the clearing to stand beside the Brigadier, and followed as he left. The white guy with the hunting rifle went after them. The remaining soldiers stayed in a circle around Colm and the others.

'How did they find us?' Colm muttered to himself.

'I don't know,' Jomo said.

Colm looked at him.

'Your name is Jomo,' he said.

Jomo nodded.

'Where are you from?'

'Uganda. I was taken when I was ten.'

'Taken?'

'Like he said,' Jomo said, quietly. Only Colm could hear him. Jomo nodded at Mak. 'The Soldiers of God destroyed villages, killed the men, raped the women, stole the children. The Brotherhood of Souls did the same. I was taken when I was ten.'

'How old are you now?'

'I don't know.'

'It's twenty sixteen. When were you born?'

Jomo looked up at the trees. His eyes were moving, like he was working something out.

'I think I am twenty-eight,' Jomo said. His eyes seemed glassy, as if he were tearing up. If he was, the impression didn't last more than a moment.

'Eighteen years?'

Jomo shrugged.

'You haven't seen your family in eighteen years?'

'My family are dead,' Jomo said.

Colm shifted his position. He didn't know what else to do.

'Do you have a family?' Jomo asked.

Colm thought for a moment. He was sitting next to Jomo, a few centimetres from him. Jane and Kennet were to one side of them, the three rangers two metres to the other. The clearing was small. Four metres round. Their guards were looking less than attentive. The two child-soldiers were sitting down, chatting, laughing. The men were standing. Two were smoking, the smell of their cigarettes sharp and unpleasant in the otherwise clean air. Three were talking together, only occasionally looking at the prisoners. The others were silent, staring into nothing, their guns an extension of their arms. They looked bored.

'I have a wife. She is pregnant with our first child.'

'Where do you live?'

'In Ireland.'

'Where is that?'

The question threw Colm for a moment. No one had ever asked him that before, not even in India.

'It's an island off the coast of Britain. In Europe.'

Jomo nodded.

'Europe is north?'

'Have you seen a map of the world?'

'Once. When I was about eight. At school. I don't remember it well.'

Colm nodded, but in his head, he was reeling. That someone hadn't seen a map of the world more than once. That someone had been in the jungle with these monsters for eighteen years. And then he reeled again, because Jomo was one of those monsters. And yet he didn't seem to be a monster.

With sudden and absolute certainty, Colm realised the rhinos weren't the story here.

CHAPTER FORTY-TWO

FATOU, HANNINGTON AND THE OTHER THREE HAD BEEN walking for two hours before anything changed. The landscape was the same. They were climbing hills, dropping into valleys. They forded streams, some small enough to jump over, others that had to be waded across. They were in the grasslands of the park, the savannah. They were walking parallel to the forest, and from the vantage point of the hills she could see it stretched forever to their right, to the east, and rose ahead of them to the north. The savannah would end soon enough, whether the trail they were following turned into the trees, or simply ran into them.

Sure enough, before long the trail turned into the trees, but they didn't.

A ranger was waiting, where it turned. He was from the second group. He was on his own. They did not see him until they were a hundred metres from him, because he was hidden in the grass. He shouted, told them he was there, then stood up and made his report.

'They camped in the trees. Two hundred metres in,' the

ranger pointed. 'The first group found it and scouted the site. They say it was clear. If the trail hadn't led to it, they wouldn't have known it had been used as a camp site. Very disciplined. They moved out again in the morning, this morning. They joined their own trail a little further up. They are six hours ahead, we think. They are moving quickly.'

'They will expect to be followed. That many deaths, that much ivory. They will expect to be pursued quickly,' Hannington said. 'Very good. Thank you. Catch up with your group, go.'

Hannington called a halt and wrote a note. He found a stick and impaled the note on it. The note told the groups behind them not to follow the trail into the trees, but to keep moving. Then Hannington had them underway again.

Grass. The grass was endless. Fatou had never seen grass longer than a few centimetres before coming to the DRC. The grass they were walking through wasn't the elephant grass they'd pushed through on the first journey into the park, it was much shorter. But it was still up to her waist. Leopards, hyena, and lion could move through grass this high without fear of being seen. Despite Hannington and, on their first trip, Mak telling her that there were virtually no large animals left north of the Garamba River, she still mistrusted the grass. And there might still be snakes.

Captain Rick's men had flattened a trail, only fifty centimetres wide, but it made walking easy, following their path. Hannington picked up the pace, and Fatou found herself walking so quickly she was almost running.

Three hours later, with sunset approaching, everything changed. They climbed a steep hill and reached its crest. Below them the savannah eased out to the west, and the forest encroached from the east. But ranger groups one and two were both waiting for them at the foot of the hill. They were separate, four men two hundred metres ahead, four two hundred metres to the west, and two on the trail at the foot of the hill. The leader of each group. Hannington ran ahead, François at his heels. Fatou wanted to run too, but Tony held her back.

'Chain of command,' he said.

Hannington and François talked to the two group leaders, then beckoned Mola, Tony, and Fatou to join them.

'We have a problem,' Hannington said as soon as they were within earshot. 'Show them.'

One of the group leaders walked away into the grass. Fatou watched him. Tony followed him, and Hannington motioned for her to follow Tony.

The group leader stopped. Tony caught up with him. Fatou caught up with Tony. She saw it immediately. Another trail. A broader trail. Many feet had walked this trail. She followed it in both directions with her eyes. To the west, it disappeared into the grass. To the east, it joined the trail of Captain Rick's men.

'What does this mean?' Fatou said.

'It means we're not the only ones following these bastards and the other guys are ahead of us,' Tony said.

Mola nodded. 'Or worse,' he said.

'Worse?' Fatou said.

'They could be Captain Rick's men,' Mola said. 'In which case we are now heavily outnumbered.'

'I suspect they are not,' Hannington said. 'This trail is broad, different discipline.'

'Then who are they?' Fatou said. 'Soldiers of God?'

Hannington looked at her sharply. 'Why do you say that?' She was also conscious of Tony watching her.

'Captain Rick said there were three squads of the Soldiers of God in the park. He was surprised, he said, because he hadn't heard of them in years and, suddenly, they were everywhere. One of the squads attacked the compound before he did. He didn't say what happened to the other two.'

'Why did no one tell me this before?'

Fatou felt cold, the way she had felt at school when she realised she'd done something wrong but only after the teacher had caught her at it.

'Sorry, I–'

'It's my fault,' Tony said. 'I completely forgot. Everyone else who heard him say it was taken. I forgot Fatou and I were the only witnesses. And I also didn't really believe him. Completely slipped my mind.'

'*Merde*,' Hannington swore. 'Three squads? And the one at Nagero had twenty-five in it? Reasonable to assume the others were a similar size. These could be the tracks of one or both of them. Which means either there are fifty more armed men between us and Captain Rick, or there are twenty-five and another twenty-five out there somewhere we don't know. *Merde.* This is too dangerous. We have to wait for the army now.'

'They will cross the border before the army get here,' François said. 'We should turn back.'

'Not necessarily,' Tony appeared lost in thought as he spoke. 'Captain Rick said the Soldiers of God were after the ivory, just like him. And they fought each other. Most of the dead at Nagero were Soldiers of God killed by the Brotherhood. If they catch up with Captain Rick, there's going to be a battle. All we would need to do would be to wait for it to be over and then sweep up the mess.'

'What if we catch them before there's a battle?' François said. 'We don't want a fight with these guys, we want a fight with the other guys to get our men and the ivory back. If we catch up with the Soldiers of God, it is Captain Rick who will be sweeping up the mess.'

Tony kicked the ground.

Mola looked at Hannington.

Up the hill, the fourth group came into view. A member of the second group went to meet them.

'I think…' Hannington began. 'I think… this may help us.'

'How?' François said.

'With our friends in Dungu. They might not be too quick to respond to a report of kidnapping and stolen ivory, but they will be concerned that there's about to be a battle on DRC soil in which neither of the sides is the Congolese army.'

François looked sceptical. 'You think that will motivate them more than forty-two dead men?'

'Quite possibly. The Brotherhood of Souls I have never heard of, and neither had the army. But the Soldiers of God are wanted terrorists. And they are from Uganda. Mola, the radio.'

Mola unstrapped his backpack and took out the radio handset. He switched it on and handed it to Hannington.

Hannington took it and took a deep breath.

'Here goes,' he said.

CHAPTER FORTY-THREE

Brigadier Okumu came back an hour later, with the child-soldier he had taken with him.

Kennet started to get up, but the Brigadier waved him down.

'Where is the ivory?' the Brigadier barked at Jomo, reaching for him, pulling him to his feet.

'Wha— I don't know,' Jomo said. The Brigadier struck him. Hard, with the back of his hand, his rings cutting into Jomo's flesh so that his lip started bleeding.

'I don't know! I wasn't near it. I was guarding them! Captain Rick had it hidden. He is paranoid!' He had his hand to his face and the blood ran down his fingers.

The Brigadier hit him again, with a closed fist this time, hard. Jomo doubled over, his hands going instinctively to his stomach, blood flying freely from his face. He tried to keep his feet, but the Brigadier kicked him hard in the hip and he went over, landing on Colm.

'One man didn't hide half a tonne of ivory. Do you think I am an idiot? Where is it?' The Brigadier was snarling now.

Jomo groaned, his face twisted, his hands on his stomach, his eyes closed, tears mixing with blood.

'I don't know!' his very voice was an effort, an agony. 'I was on guard. I didn't see it after we dropped it here.'

'Here?'

'Here, in this clearing. They made us pile it here and then I was on guard, down there, I didn't see it again, I don't know what was done with it.'

The Brigadier had stopped listening and was talking with the child-soldier he had taken with him. Colm couldn't tell what they were saying as they were speaking in the language Mak had called ruTooro, but the Brigadier seemed to be as angry with his own soldier as he had been with Jomo. He pushed the soldier over, shouted at everyone, waved a hand at Kennet, and stormed off.

Jomo was pushing himself to his knees, breathing heavily.

'What are you doing?' Colm said. 'Lie still, get your breath back.'

Jomo shook his head.

'Look,' he said.

The circle of guards had all raised their guns and were aiming them at Colm and the others.

'The Brigadier said that if the ivory was here then the simplest thing would have been to bury it where it was. We all have to dig, or we are all going to be shot. And you,' he said to Kennet, 'he said that if you mention rhino again, they are to shoot you, it doesn't matter what you are worth as a hostage, he finds you too annoying.' He started scrabbling at the leaves with his hands. A moment later, Mak and Jane did the same.

'Dig, everyone,' Mak said. He was staring at Kennet with menace. His look was the loudest 'I told you so' Colm had ever seen.

Fortunately, the Brigadier had been right.

Mak got everyone organised. They used the largest branches they could find to sweep the clearing free of leaves and twigs, and then used the branches to loosen the earth, splitting into two teams, one on loosening duty, the other one earth removal. The ivory was in a shallow pit only covered by five centimetres of earth. They found it almost immediately.

There was a heated argument between the guards before one, the largest, left.

'What was that about?' Colm said to Jomo. Jomo had torn a strip from his shirt and was holding it over his mouth, trying to stop the bleeding.

'They were arguing over who got to tell the Brigadier. They were keen to carry good news to him. The one who went threatened to cut the balls off anyone who tried to get ahead of him.' Jomo's voice was muffled, but the agony in it after he had been punched and kicked had eased.

'Friendly bunch,' Colm said.

The soldier was back with the Brigadier, and the white guy with the hunting rifle, within a few minutes. The Brigadier had changed completely. He was smiling, as if all his birthdays were happening on the same day. He walked to the edge of the pit, crouched down, reached in and touched the top of one of the tusks.

'That is more like it, my friends. That is excellent work. This Captain Rick thinks like me. When we catch him, I will thank him before I kill him. This is excellent. We shall take this gift to the General. You shall all help carry it to him. That way he will be pleased with all of you. He might let you live. He might even talk to you about rhino.' This was directed at Kennet. 'Though he might not. He has been very temperamental lately. It is difficult to say. But you are big and strong, and if you carry ivory to him, he may look on you with favour.' He looked up at the sky.

'It is getting late. We shall camp here tonight and leave in the morning. Stay alert. This Captain Rick thinks like me. He will want this ivory. He will not be able to rest until he has tried to take it back. He will fail, but he will try. Lay your traps well.'

And with that he turned and walked away, the white hunter at his heel.

————

The rain came again that night. The guards had been expecting it, and had made a shelter between two trees, running a rope across and stretching a tarpaulin over it, holding one side out by attaching the corners to two sticks. Most of the guards had gone elsewhere in the camp, only two remained. They lit two lanterns just before sunset. Half an hour after sunset the rain came, and the guards sat in their shelter, barely looking at the prisoners.

One minute it wasn't raining, the next water was hitting the ground like stones. The trees absorbed much of the force of the downpour, but the water trickled down leaves and off branches and twigs and a secondary rain fell on the tarpaulin, making a regular drumming sound.

The guards didn't let Colm and the other prisoners leave the middle of the clearing, so they were swiftly soaked. The ivory in the pit, smeared with soil, was quickly cleaned, seeming to glow and sparkle in the lantern light as the raindrops bounced off it.

'Nice weather,' Colm said to one of the guards. The guard, who didn't seem to speak any English, didn't respond.

'*Tá an aimsir go maith*,' Colm added.

The guard moved. He stood up, as did his companion. It wasn't a response to what Colm had said. They were looking past him.

The Brigadier's white companion was walking towards them through the rain, four other soldiers behind him. He didn't have his rifle with him. It looked as if he was unarmed. He was seem-ingly oblivious to the rain.

He came straight to Jane and stood and stared at her. Two of the soldiers with him went to the shelter, evidently as replace-ments for the two already there, who looked unhappy as they walked out into the rain.

He stared at Jane for a whole minute, the raindrops bouncing off his head and shoulders. Then he nodded, and the other two soldiers who had come with him grabbed her by the arms and began to drag her, feet leaving grooves in the mud, back the way they had come. She didn't resist. Her face had gone blank, and Colm could read no emotion in her expression. The white man turned and started to follow. The two relieved guards fell in behind him.

'Hey!' Kennet said, standing up and lurching towards the men dragging his sister. He immediately slipped in the mud and went down on one knee. The white man turned back and kicked him, hard, and Kennet overbalanced and fell into the pit of ivory, now half-filled with rainwater. The white man resumed his walk.

Colm watched Jane being pulled away. Her eyes were moving quickly, in every direction, as if they were filming the camp. She said something, loudly, to make sure they could hear it over the rain. The only word Colm caught was "Ken".

After a few seconds, she was lost to sight.

'She looked frightened, yes?' said one of the guards from the shelter. Colm reached for Kennet and helped him squelch out of the pit. He looked at the new guard. There was an evil on the man's face.

'She is my sister,' Kennet said, breathlessly, on all fours on the edge of the pit, covered in mud and soaking wet. 'I have known her for her entire life.'

The soldier came out of the shelter and hit Kennet in the

back with the butt of his rifle. Kennet went flat in the mud but pushed himself up again. The idiot just wouldn't shut up.

'I know all of her expressions,' he said. 'All of them. And I have never seen her frightened. That wasn't fear.' Kennet looked up as the soldier in front of him raised the butt of the gun over his head. 'That was fury,' Kennet said, and the soldier brought the gun down on his nose. Colm heard a crunch and saw blood as Kennet slumped forward into the mud once more.

CHAPTER FORTY-FOUR

FATOU HEARD THE PLANE LONG BEFORE SHE SAW IT, A constant droning buzz. It flew out of grey clouds perhaps a kilo-metre behind them. Mola was talking to the pilot on the radio. As soon as he saw the plane he waved, though at that distance Fatou doubted if the pilot would see them.

As it grew closer, it flew lower. At first Fatou thought it was going to pass over their heads, but it was getting so low, and not in line with them, that she realised it was going to land. For a moment she worried. Was the grass too long, was the flat area of land before the next hill too short, would the plane hit them? Then she let it go. Trusted that the rangers, and the pilot, knew what they were doing.

The plane touched down and bounced along the ground, coming to a stop thirty metres away. It was a single propeller plane with six passenger seats, including the one next to the pilot. Only that one was occupied. The occupant slipped out of the plane before it had fully stopped. Hannington strode to meet him. They shook hands and exchanged words, though Fatou couldn't hear them over the noise of the engine.

The newcomer was not dressed like a ranger. He was in army uniform. He turned round and jogged back to the plane, opening the door, climbing back in. Hannington followed, then waved to François, Mola, Tony, and Fatou to join him. Fatou had not been expecting that.

———

The plane took a very bumpy ride across the thick grass. It turned and took off in the direction they had come from, not in the direction they needed to go, and the first thing it did was bank steeply. Fatou was glad of her seatbelt, and particularly glad of Tony's, as at that angle, without it, he would have slid out of his seat and onto her.

Below her she could see the rest of the rangers, already moving out in groups of five, five minutes apart, following the now much broader trail that obscured the narrow one created by Captain Rick and his men.

'This is Lieutenant Fall,' Hannington said. 'We have worked together before. He has been sent to perform reconnaissance for the army to allow the generals to make an informed decision.' Hannington said this with a straight face, but Fatou could see Lieutenant Fall suppressing a smile.

'Call me Mars,' the lieutenant said.

They had been seated and strapped in straight away to allow them to take off as quickly as possible. As the introductions were made the lieutenant reached across and shook everyone's hand, which took much learning and stretching. His shake was surprisingly light. Fatou found herself worrying she might have gripped him too hard, but he smiled warmly at her.

The plane levelled after its bank. Below them, Fatou could clearly see the trail in the grass. Since the newcomers had joined it and made it five metres wide it was easy to spot, even from this high in the air.

'We think the ones calling themselves the Brotherhood of Souls are about six hours ahead of us, so assume thirty kilometres at the outside. We estimate there are about forty of them with nine prisoners. The men following them, who we are currently assuming are the Soldiers of God, are three hours ahead, fifteen kilometres. We do not have an accurate estimate of their numbers. We believe there were three groups in the park, one of which was wiped out. That group numbered twenty-five. If the other two were the same size, then this is either one or both of those, which would make twenty-five or fifty. But from the tracks we only know there are at least a dozen and probably more.'

'If it is the Soldiers of God in those numbers, the brass will be very interested. There'd be a chance one of their leaders was with them. Kinshasa has wanted them for years.'

'What's our airspeed?' Hannington called to the pilot.

'A hundred knots,' came the reply, 'and I can't fly any slower without stalling.'

'A hundred and eighty kilometres an hour,' Hannington calculated. 'We should see the second group within twelve minutes, and the first within twelve minutes after that. Much quicker than walking. Wake me in ten.'

He sat back in his chair and closed his eyes.

Fatou checked her watch, memorised when twelve minutes would be up. Then she gazed out of the window. On the right-hand side of the plane, the side she was sitting on, she was looking roughly southeast. All she could see, as far as the horizon, was trees. The Congo rainforest stretched on forever. She remembered her notes. The forest was so large it made its own weather. She could see clouds forming above it as they flew, the shadow of their plane sliding over the tree tops below.

She looked down. The trail was still very visible, parallel to the edge of the forest.

'Why are they walking through the park?' Fatou said. 'If they were in the forest, we wouldn't be able to see them at all.'

'For speed,' Mola said. 'Much quicker through the grass. If they thought we were close enough to catch them they'd move into the forest, but until then they'll stay in the grass.'

Fatou looked across the plane past Tony, trying to see the grass on the other side of the aircraft. But because the plane's nose was slightly higher than its tail all she could see was sky.

They flew on. Fatou checked her watch. Four minutes gone. Below them the trail was still clear and easy to see, down one side of a valley, across a stream, a dirty streak of muddy footprints on the other side tapering out as the trail climbed the opposite bank.

The minutes ticked by.

It was halfway through the ninth minute that the pilot spoke.

'We have something,' he said, pointing down and to the right.

He was right. The plane's shadow bumped and skipped on the ground a little to the left of the trail below, and suddenly there were men.

'Count them!' Hannington said.

Mars pulled out a camera with a telephoto lens.

'Even better,' Hannington said.

Mars focused on the men.

'What's our altitude?' he asked.

'Three hundred metres, a little over. Why?' the pilot replied.

'You might want to go a little higher. I think they're shooting at us.'

'What with?'

'AKs.'

'They'd have to get very lucky.'

'Or we'd have to be very unlucky. My friend here has lost five of his men this week. He might be on a streak. Best to be safe.'

The pilot nodded, and the plane started to rise. Mars took photos.

Fatou looked down at the men on the ground. They had been quite small at three hundred metres, but by the time the pilot levelled off again they were tiny. Fatou couldn't count them. If they hadn't been so close together, she might not have noticed them at all. They were behind them and out of sight within a minute.

'How many?' Hannington asked.

Mars was staring at the screen of the camera. Fatou could see he had zoomed in close, to take the shot, and had zoomed in closer to examine it. The picture had become pixelated.

'Fifty, give or take. Two large tusks each carried between two men. Discarded by the Brotherhood, or from somewhere else? Oh, wow, will you look at this.' He handed Hannington the camera.

'What am I looking at?' Hannington asked.

'Unless I am very much mistaken, my friend, that face there looking straight up at us, is the face of Brigadier Josef Okumu, of the Soldiers of God. Wanted for war crimes here, in Uganda, and in Rwanda. The top brass are going to be very interested in this. Pass me the radio.'

The last instruction was to the pilot, who unclipped a handset and handed it back to Mars.

Fatou looked at her watch. Fifteen minutes had now passed since Hannington had calculated they were a maximum of twenty-four minutes from Captain Rick and his prisoners. She could no longer see the trail.

'We need to go lower again,' Hannington said. 'Can't see it from up here, not until those idiots catch up and make it as wide as a runway.'

The pilot nodded and tilted the control column forward. They began to descend.

After another minute they could see the trail again, threading like a silver wire through the grass almost perfectly parallel to the edge of the forest.

Fatou watched the time pass on her watch. Eighteen minutes, nineteen, twenty. The thread remained, but there was no one on it. Twenty-one, twenty-two, twenty-three. Still nothing. Fatou looked at the pilot, who would be the first to see anything. He was showing no sign of seeing anything different. Twenty-four, twenty-five, twenty-six.

'They're moving faster than we thought,' Hannington said.

Twenty-seven, twenty-eight.

'There,' the pilot said. Fatou saw it a moment later. The trail suddenly moved sideways, its narrow thread broadening all the way to the trees, and then it stopped completely.

Mars was clicking with his camera.

'Circle it,' Mars said.

'They're hiding in the trees,' Hannington said.

'Won't they shoot at us as well?'

'They might. But as hard as it would be to hit us with an AK at three hundred metres, it will be practically impossible to do it shooting through trees.'

'But they had the big gun. The one they used to blow up the gates at Nagero.'

Mars looked sharply at Hannington. But Tony intervened.

'They didn't use a gun for that. They used a bomb made out of a hand grenade and a tank of petrol. We saw nothing other than small arms.'

'Besides,' Hannington said. 'They've hidden themselves. The Soldiers of God might be happy to risk an international incident by shooting at a military plane just before crossing the border, but this Captain Rick doesn't seem to be. Very different.'

'Sounds like you admire him,' Mars said.

'He shot Albert Agoyo in the head,' Hannington replied, and held Mars's gaze. Mars nodded.

'Pass me the radio,' Mars said. He reported the finding of the second group, and its precise location.

Albert Agoyo. Fatou had thought Agoyo was his first name. She knew so little about him. She felt a sudden sadness wash over her.

CHAPTER FORTY-FIVE

COLM WAITED UNTIL THE GUARD HAD RETURNED TO THE shelter before edging through the mud to Kennet. He was out cold, face down in the mud, thick blood spreading from his submerged face. Colm tried to roll him onto his side to stop him suffocating or drowning or whatever would happen if he was left as he was. Jomo crawled over to help. Between them they managed it, propping his head up on his arm. Colm wiped Kennet's face as best he could, clearing off the mud and blood. The rain helped. But the blood kept coming. Colm was no first aider.

'What do we do?' he said.

'Keep pressure on it and hope,' Jomo said.

'Leave him,' Mak said. 'He deserves it.'

'But Jane?' Colm said.

'There's nothing we can do for her,' Mak said. 'He's killed us all.'

From somewhere in the camp there came a scream. Loud, and long, a scream of terror. It was abruptly cut off.

The soldier in his shelter laughed.

'Is that the sound of fury where you come from?' he shouted over the rain.

Kennet lay there in the mud, blood running out of his nose. Colm tried to tear a strip off Kennet's shirt to put pressure on the wound, but the fabric was too wet, and he couldn't do it.

He noticed Jomo's face. He was frowning.

'What's wrong?' Colm said.

'That scream didn't sound like fury,' Jomo said, very quietly, so only Colm could hear him. 'It sounded like agony. A man's agony.'

Jomo turned his head very quickly to look behind him, away from the direction of the scream.

He was alert. Like an animal. Colm could almost see his ears pricking up.

'What is it?' Colm said.

Jomo held up his hand as if he wanted somehow to silence the rain.

For a minute, perhaps longer, Colm heard nothing except that rain, that thunderous rain. Then he realised that some of the rain wasn't rain at all.

It was gunfire.

The guards had heard it too. They stood up, gripping their guns, pointing them at the six men sitting and lying in the mud. There were more shots, from the other direction now. Soldiers were running, seemingly at random, passing the clearing in both directions, shouting.

'Get down,' Jomo said as he slowly, non-threateningly, lowered himself to lie in the mud beside Kennet. Mak and Jean did the same, pulling Kwame down with them. Colm was the last of the six to do so.

The soldiers guarding them looked at them and, bizarrely, laughed, as if the sight of six men lying in the mud and the rain was the funniest thing in the world. A moment later, the sound of a stray round whizzed close enough for them all to hear it, and the soldiers dropped to one knee, guns up, looking for something to shoot at.

Men were running everywhere. Most were unarmed, racing for weapons, slipping and falling in the torrential rain. Some had torches, others had lanterns. And out of the trees on the far side came a rain of a different kind. Guns firing, many of them. The camp was under a determined attack. For all the Brigadier's talk of being ready for the return of Captain Rick's men, they very clearly weren't. Assuming this was Captain Rick's men.

More bullets came closer, some of them hitting the tarpaulin the guards were sheltering under and causing it to slide off the rope, exposing the guards to the rain.

Four soldiers ran to the edges of the pit and crouched, one at each corner, leaving Colm and the others between two of them. One of them shouted to the two guarding the prisoners. Jomo translated.

'They've been sent to protect the ivory,' he said.

Suddenly, over the gunfire, over the rain, lying in the mud beside a pool of water that held half a tonne of ivory, Colm heard a laughter very different from the mockery of the guards. This laughter was deep and rich. It was Kennet. He had come round lying on his back. His eyes were open, and he was laughing. His whole body shook.

'*En lærer*,' he said between laughs. 'A teacher!'

The soldier nearest Kennet shouted at him.

'He's telling you to shut up,' Jomo said.

But Kennet kept laughing.

'Do you know what she said?' Kennet said, staring straight up at the night clouds, blood still running from his nose and to be diluted by the rain. 'As they were dragging her away? She said "You've had your chance, Ken. My turn now. We're leaving in fifteen minutes."'

Colm looked at his watch. A reflex action. It was still broken. Time was still.

The soldier stood up. And shouted at Kennet again.

One of the guards, the one who had hit Kennet, crossed the clearing, his face twisted in rage. He raised his gun, pointed it at Kennet. His finger moved to the trigger. Colm looked at Kennet. He was still laughing. Mak had been right. Kennet would kill them all. Colm heard the shot and felt a spray of blood on his cheek.

Kennet was still laughing. The soldier who had been about to shoot him was dead, toppling sideways into the mud. The soldier next to him turned to see what had happened just as his chest exploded. The soldier who was next quickest to react had managed to get his gun to eye height by the time he died. Colm rolled to see what was happening.

Standing fifty metres away, as motionless as stone and with the white guy's hunting rifle in her hands, was Jane Haven. She fired twice more, killing two of the three remaining soldiers, then she threw the rifle to the ground, pulled a pistol out of her belt, and started to run towards the last soldier.

She was too far away. His gun was ready, she was well within range, and he fired. Just as Jomo barged him with his shoulder. Both men went into the ivory pool.

The soldier found his feet and turned his gun on Jomo. It was the last thing he did. Jane stopped running ten metres away, held the pistol with both hands, and shot him.

From the first shot to the last about fifteen seconds had passed.

———

For a moment there was nothing but rain. Nothing at all. No one spoke, no one moved. No squelching of boots in mud, no shouted orders. Not even any shots.

'That,' Mak said, 'was fury.'

'Pick up their guns and all the ammunition you can find. We need to go, NOW!' Jane said. 'On your feet, everyone!'

There was a burst of gunfire from deeper in the camp, followed by a shout, but both noises seemed a long way off.

Colm struggled to his feet. Jane turned off the lanterns the guards had been using in the shelter and picked up two of their guns. Just before it was switched off, the lantern light gave Colm his first clear look at her. She was covered in blood. More than Kennet, more than Jomo. She was drenched in it.

'Are you alright?' Colm said.

Jane looked at him as if it was the strangest question she'd ever heard. Then she looked down at herself.

'It's not mine,' she said. And held out an AK-47. 'Take it and get their ammunition. We need to move.'

Jane's voice seemed very loud. The rain had stopped. The quiet was broken almost immediately by gunshots further along the camp. Colm could hear the wind in the treetops. He took the gun. Jane checked the other one and test-fired a shot into the trees. As she did so, the clouds above the clearing parted and bathed the clearing in moonlight.

Jane saw Kennet's face for the first time.

'What happened to you?' she said. Kennet didn't reply, just smiled at her glassily.

'What happened to Ken?' Jane said to Colm, watching every-where. He saw her raise the gun in his direction and fire, crack, crack. He thought he felt the bullets fly past his ear. He turned in time to see another soldier falling fifty metres behind him.

'He told them you didn't look scared as they dragged you

away, that you looked furious,' Colm said. 'One of them hit him in the face with a rifle.'

But Jane had heard enough. She was looking past him, at Jomo.

'Thank you,' she said.

Jomo nodded.

———

A lantern came into view a hundred metres away in the dark. Crack, crack, crack. Three shots from Jane's AK and the lantern fell to the ground.

'We need to get out of the camp, leave a false trail, then loop round and join the trail back to the park. That will be the fastest way. Can you show us?' Jane said to Jomo.

Jomo nodded. He had an AK over one shoulder and still held a rag to his mouth. His lip had not stopped bleeding.

'This way,' he said, and started walking, Jane beside him, keeping to the edge of the trail. Colm couldn't help but notice Jomo was leading them in the direction most of the shooting was coming from.

Mak and Jean had both armed themselves and, keeping Kwame upright between them, followed. Kennet and Colm brought up the rear. Kennet had not picked up a gun.

Colm passed the last of the dead soldiers. He saw a magazine clip on the ground. He picked it up and stuffed it into a pocket.

They walked slowly. Kwame was barely able to stand, and Kennet was in a daze.

'That way,' Jomo said, pointing about twenty metres off to the left. There were two structures, with walls made from bamboo canes tied together, and roofs of branches and leaves. Between them was a path. Opposite the entrance to the path half a dozen Soldiers of God were firing into the forest at targets unseen, using trees as cover. There was no cover between them and the two bamboo huts other than the patches of shadow cast by the trees overhead.

Jomo stopped and whispered to Jane. Jane nodded. Jane spoke to Mak, and then came back to Colm.

'We need to get between those huts,' she said. 'We can't go behind them, with Kwame and Kennet we'd make too much noise. Jomo and I will provide cover. Mak and Jean will lead Kwame through, then you follow. Walk slowly to the path and turn down it, that's it. If they see you and start shooting, lie down immediately. Clear?'

Colm nodded. Mak and Jean were already moving, guiding Kwame between them. Jomo and Jane melted into the shadows. Colm gripped Kennet's arm in case he decided to move before it was time.

Mak and Jean reached the huts. The soldiers opposite continued to fire into the trees. Answering fire hit the far hut sending splinters of bamboo flickering into the air. One of the soldiers looked back and saw the three men. Mak, who was nearest to him, noticed and raised his gun in greeting. In the dark, the gesture was all the camouflage that was needed. The soldier must have mistaken Mak and Jean for comrades helping another wounded comrade. He raised his hand in return and turned back to his post. Mak and the other two disappeared down the path. Colm's turn.

He gripped Kennet's arm and pulled, steering him the way he wanted to go. He kept him to the shadows, splashing through puddles and squelching through mud. The firing to their right continued, sporadic shots, occasional three-shot bursts. Each step Colm took he expected to feel the sting of a bullet. Or maybe to stop feeling anything at all.

What he felt was Kennet starting to pull away from him. Not walking away, falling away. His entire two metre height fell straight forward, without raising his arms to protect himself. He splashed into a puddle like a falling tree.

The soldiers saw.

Whilst Mak and Kwame might have got away with looking like Soldiers of God helping a wounded comrade in the dark, that wouldn't work for Kennet and Colm. There were shouts. One of the soldiers stepped towards them, weapon up, pointing at Colm. Colm froze.

More shouting. This time, however, it was Jomo. He stepped into a patch of moonlight and shouted at the soldier, not aggressively, but informatively, just loud enough to be heard. The soldier lowered his gun and used it to motion to one of the sheds.

Jomo turned to Colm, spoke to him more quietly in English.

'I told him I was moving the prisoners and one has been shot. There is rope in that shed. Get it.'

'Why?'

'To drag him with.'

Drag him. Even with the weight he'd sweated off in the last week Kennet was still twice the size of Colm. Nevertheless, he slung the gun over his back and tried to get his hands under Kennet's arms. That was a mistake. Prisoners don't carry guns. The soldier realised that and raised his gun again.

Crack, crack.

The soldier fell to the ground. The others were in a panic. He had been shot, not from the path, which Colm had expected, as that was where Jane was, but from the trees behind them.

'Get the rope!' Jomo hissed.

Colm stooped to turn Kennet's head, to make sure he could breathe, then ran for the hut.

It was a storage shed, and it had already been looted. It was a mess. But Colm found a length of rope about three metres long and ran out again.

Jomo crouched by Kennet, watching the firefight only metres away on the other side of the track. He grabbed the rope from Colm and threaded it through the armpits under the big man's chest. He wrapped one end round his left arm and handed the other to Colm.

'Pull,' he said.

The mud helped and hindered. It helped as Kennet's hundred and twenty kilos slid over it with relative ease. It hindered as Colm and Jomo's feet did the same. Colm was moving with the grace of a new-born goat on a frozen lake. Jomo fared better, but not much. But they were moving, and slowly, metre by metre, they got him down the path between the huts.

Behind them Colm saw Jane move into the mouth of the path, firing at someone he couldn't see. After the last pair of shots Jane reloaded the gun so quickly Colm thought he'd imagined it. She followed them, walking backwards, keeping pace but not looking at them. Jane was moving with them, looking in every direction but at them.

After five long, slow, painful minutes Colm saw Mak ahead.

'What happened to him?'

'I don't know, he just went down.'

'Shot?'

'I don't know.'

'Alive?'

'I don't know.'

'Well check, you don't want to be dragging a dead body through this forest. Might as well shoot yourself.'

Colm was momentarily flummoxed, his mind a total blank. How did you check if someone was alive? But Jomo wasn't flummoxed and put two fingers to Kennet's neck.

'Alive. Strong,' Jomo said. 'Get him over, on his side.'

Colm and Mak helped turn Kennet. Jomo ran his hands across Kennet's clothing, looking for holes and blood.

'I don't think he's been shot,' Jomo said.

'Pity,' Mak said.

'What's wrong with him?'

'Could have just passed out again. He lost a lot of blood.'

Jane had stopped. 'Keep moving,' she said. 'Someone will come looking.'

'They'll never find us in the dark,' Colm said.

'They will,' Jane said, pointing at the ground.

Even in the near total blackness Colm could see it. The faintest of lights came through the canopy overhead, stars or moon poking through the clouds, and reflected off two slender silver tracks. The grooves Kennet's heels were making in the mud.

Jomo stood up. He and Colm gripped the ends of the rope. Mak walked back to Jean and Kwame, a hundred metres further into the forest. They set off. Even with Kwame unable to do much more than stumble they were still faster than Colm, Jomo, and Kennet.

―――――

It was an hour before Jane let them stop. They moved through the trees in as straight a line as they could, but also tried to move on the driest earth to minimise the trail they were leaving.

'It doesn't matter,' Jane said. 'We won't be able to hide from them.'

'Then why are we running?' Colm asked, stretching his back and his arms.

'To spread them out as much as possible.'

Colm waited for her to explain, but she didn't. He looked around and realised he couldn't see her. He could hardly see anything.

'How long till dawn?' he said.

She did not answer.

Colm stared in the direction he thought she'd been when she last spoke. Nothing. Just dark on dark.

He listened. He looked across at Jomo, but Jomo was no longer there either.

He heard a hissed whisper.

'Do not move.'

No other sound but water, still bouncing off the leaves forty metres overhead, trickling, falling, keeping him soaked to the skin long after the rain had stopped.

He turned his head to see if that changed the sound. It didn't.

He realised he hadn't heard anything else in a while either. No shouts or gunfire. The ever-on insect symphonies were still there, but that was it. No birds.

Then he did hear something. Something big. Not too far away. It sounded like a growl, or the start of a roar.

Colm turned to face the noise. A lion? They didn't live in the jungle, did they? He thought he'd been told that by someone, the fallacy of the black-and-white Tarzan movies, lions in the jungle. They lived on the plains, in the grass, where their dinner was.

But other cats lived here, didn't they? Leopards, invisible in the night. Anything would be invisible in this night.

The growl came again. It had moved a surprising distance, but not further away from him. Either it had moved or there were more than one of them.

Double god.

He froze. Deliberately. Best thing to do. If he ran, he couldn't take Kennet. But Jane and Jomo knew where he was. And they both had guns.

Unless the reason they'd disappeared was because, whatever that thing was, it had already got one of them. Was Jane dead? Being eaten by a hungry leopard? Had Jomo seen it and hidden? Why hadn't Colm heard anything?

Then he remembered he had a gun. Strapped over his back, forgotten for the hour or so he'd been dragging Kennet through the forest. He reached his hand up to the strap and started working the gun round from his back to his hands.

Then he smelt it. Strong, musky, not unpleasant. But definitely, definitely, a large animal.

The growl came again, and this time it was closer. The smell was stronger.

Slowly, so slowly, he eased into a crouch, tucked up against Kennet. He found the trigger with his finger. He thought of Niamh.

This time, the thought of her made him think he could pull the trigger, because if he didn't, he might never leave this spot.

There was a crack no more than six feet away. It was loud and sharp. Colm felt himself flinch, but otherwise managed to keep still. It was the sound of a branch snapping.

He heard an exhalation, and the low growl again, turning up towards the end into the start of a roar that ended before it got going.

Whatever it was, it was huge.

Then there was another sound, a crash, behind and to the right of the creature from where Colm crouched. If there were two, they didn't know about each other, as whatever it was that was in front of him turned and headed away with a vast blast of sound like a car horn in a crash. Feet hit the forest floor with a power that caused the ground to shake. There was another blast of the horn, the dying sounds of crashing through branches, then nothing. Slowly, the sound of the forest returned.

'About three hours,' Jane's voice came out of the dark from Colm's right.

'What was that?' Colm said.

'Bull forest elephant. You did well,' Jomo said from right beside him.

'How do you know it was a bull?'

'From the smell.'

Jane had crouched down too. Colm felt rather than saw her beside him, her hands moving on Kennet's neck.

'He's alright,' she said.

'How can you see anything?' Colm said.

'It's not that dark,' she said. 'We need to go.'

'Shouldn't we wait for him to come round? We'd go three times as fast.'

'Could be five minutes, could be five hours,' she said. She was on her feet. Colm felt for the rope.

———

They stopped once more before dawn, just to breathe. Kennet showed no sign of coming round. This time Mak had picked the place to stop, and they caught up with him and the others.

'Drink,' Jane said, handing round a water bottle.

'Where did you get that?'

'From the storage hut.'

Colm drank. He hadn't realised how thirsty he was.

'What happened to that white guy?' Mak asked Jane.

She didn't look at him.

'He touched me without asking,' she said.

'How did you get his rifle?'

'I touched him without asking.'

'With what?'

'With this.'

She pulled something out of her belt and held it up. It was about the size of a pencil, but it was solid metal slightly rounded at each end. She put it away again.

———

Dawn came while they were walking. The sun rose as fast as it set, and it felt like no more than ten minutes elapsed between no light and all the light they were going to get. The change seemed to make things harder.

What had felt like clear earth and mud in the dark turned out to be more complicated. A mass of shrubs, creepers, and vines, much of it flattened by the first flash of water, was now springing back like nature's snares as Colm and Jomo dragged Kennet's massive form along the ground.

Kennet's shoes were a mess. Well, the one he was still wearing was. The sole was hanging off, the heel worn through, blood spattered about it.

'We're leaving a trail of blood,' Colm said.

Jane looked at him. Nodded. Motioned him to stop.

'Bind his feet,' she said.

'What with?'

Jane shrugged and turned her back on him, pointing the gun back the way they had come.

Colm looked around. Looked at Kennet. Why was he such a big bastard. Weren't Norwegians supposed to be slight? Svelte. Fast on skis. Kennet was none of these things.

'Quickly,' Jane said.

Colm tried to rip a strip off Kennet's shirt. He still couldn't do it. The fabric was too wet. Jane handed him a knife.

'Where did you get that?'

'Borrowed it.'

He took it. The blade and handle were clean, but the bolster was sticky. Blood drying very slowly in the humidity. Colm cut the shirt. Then he took a few steps and grabbed a creeper growing up a tree trunk. It was thick, about a centimetre in diameter. He gave it a tug. Tough. He pulled, ripping it off the tree trunk, trying to snap it. Very tough.

He cut the creeper and made two lengths, each about two

feet long. He turned back to Kennet. Who was sitting up.

'How much did I drink?' Kennet said, holding his hands to his head.

He sat like that for some moments. Jane must have heard him, but was ignoring him, instead moving in an arc away from Colm and Kennet, an arc that seemed centred on a tree a hundred metres behind them. Jomo was doing the same but in the opposite direction.

Colm was starting to get used to their seemingly random movements, and ignored her in return, turning back to Kennet.

'Can you stand?' Colm asked.

Kennet's response was to hold out a hand. Colm put the cut lengths of creeper down and took Kennet's arm, trying to pull him up. It wasn't easy.

'Yer a big bastard,' Colm said.

Kennet made it to his feet.

'Ow,' he said, stooping to pull a thorn from his heel, nearly falling back down in the process. 'What happened to my shoes?' He looked up. 'Where's the camp? Where's everyone else?'

Jane was now motionless, squatting in a firing stance, fixed on a spot.

'How many did you kill?' Kennet called to her.

She was moving again, with remarkable speed, but not allowing her aim to waver. Further from them, into the under-growth, then she was out of sight.

'How many did she kill?' Kennet asked Colm.

Colm hadn't thought about it. Crack, crack. Crack, crack.

And the two soldiers who had dragged her away. And the big white guy. The blood on her face. On the knife.

He hadn't thought about it.

'At least nine,' Colm said. 'She said she is a teacher,' he added.

'She is,' Kennet said. 'She teaches other women how to kill. What did you do with my shoes?'

———

Colm was tying the strips of Kennet's shirt round Kennet's feet with the lengths of cut creeper when Jane and Jomo came back.

'They're coming,' she said, and jogged straight past them. Jomo stopped behind them and motioned for them to get a move on.

Colm tested the last knot one more time and stood up, patting Kennet on the arm.

'Good to go. She's not much for conversation, is she?' he said.

Kennet was already too out of breath to reply.

They followed her through the trees, moving quickly across the driest patches of ground, through the lowest growth, occasionally slowing and slipping through deeper growth, carefully, then speeding up again.

'Are you sure they're coming?' Kennet said on one of the occasions she'd let them catch up.

She said nothing.

They kept going, but at Kennet's pace, which wasn't much quicker than they'd managed when Colm had been dragging him. Unfit, uncoordinated, and without shoes, Kennet was no jungle gazelle. Colm was worried the big man would die of a heart attack before anyone had another chance to shoot.

Then he heard it. A shout. Words in a language he didn't speak, but the meaning was clear enough. This way. I have found them. This way.

In a moment Jane had moved from being ahead of them to being behind them, close to Jomo.

'Keep going. Follow Mak. That way. As straight as possible, whatever happens,' Jomo said.

'What's that way?'

'A valley. When you hit it, follow it southwest. It will take you back into Garamba.'

'Where are we?'

But he and Jane were gone.

Colm and Kennet started to run. Sort of. Kennet's running pace, in his current state, was still slower than his normal walking pace. Colm held the gun tightly to stop it banging against his chest.

They did not speak.

Soon they could hear the men hunting them. Their voices, and the sound of them pushing through the undergrowth.

'I can't,' Kennet said, his hand on his chest, slowing from a run the speed of a walk to a walk the speed of a crawl. Then he stopped completely, leaned on a tree, breathed heavily.

'At least get on the other side of it,' Colm said, raising the gun, pointing it in the direction they'd just come from.

He remembered the safety catch as soon as he lifted it. He lowered it again, checked the catch. It was off. Had been since he'd picked it up. Could have shot himself in the leg any time. What an amateur.

He raised it again.

Then he saw them. Coming through the trees, quickly, three men. Fanned out, guns raised, expressions expectant. They knew they were close. One of them shouted, pointed. Colm fired.

He'd read something about the difficulty of shooting accurately, that handguns were almost useless beyond three metres, that semi-automatics were pretty random beyond thirty. It had never made much sense to him until he emptied an entire magazine firing at the three men and couldn't even tell where his shots had gone. A leaf fell lazily from the canopy above.

The three soldiers didn't fire back. They kept walking.

Colm reached into his pockets for ammunition. He had dropped some overnight, but he still had three magazines. He fumbled with the empty one, dropped a full one, reached for a second, looked up.

The three men were ten metres away. Close enough to be accurate. Close enough not to miss. They raised their guns.

Jane Haven stepped out of a bush five metres behind them and shot them all twice in the head.

Time slowed for Colm. He saw Jane stand and fire. Crack, crack. Pivot a fraction. Crack, crack. Pivot again. Crack, crack. Each head exploded in turn, the bullets crushing the backs of their skulls and leaving through the front. The third to die was still raising his gun. He had no time to react to the death of his companions.

But as the second was dying Colm saw someone else. A fourth man, and a fifth, emerged from trees behind Jane, already aiming straight at her. They fired.

So slow. The third crack, crack from Jane's gun, before she dropped and turned. The muzzle-flash from the two new arrivals. A line of spits of mud flew up from the forest floor in front of her as the bullets got closer. They would reach her before she was facing them.

Then both men started to dance.

It was the strangest thing to watch. The two men were firing, guns held at waist height, pointed straight at Jane. And then dancing, on their toes, arms wild, shooting into the canopy. Then they fell to the ground, a red mist hanging in the air behind them.

Jane had finished her turn, was crouched, in firing position, a breath from firing again.

Rain and insects. Nothing else.

A beat.

Colm fumbled around, not taking his eyes off Jane, found the dropped magazine, fitted it, finger back on the trigger.

Jane didn't move.

'That's the second time today you have saved my life,' she said.

Colm was staring straight at him but hadn't seen him. Jomo moved, just a twist of his torso, and went from being not there to being there. He was standing in the shadows of some undergrowth, greens and blacks. His jungle camouflage, the colours of his gun, the colour of his skin, meant he was a chameleon, at one with his environment.

His gun was at shoulder height, just as Jane held hers. For a moment, many moments, they stared at each other.

'Will you two hurry up,' said a voice behind him. Colm jumped, his finger tugged the trigger, and he put three bullets into a tree to his right. The voice was Kennet's. The sound of Colm's shots caused both Jane and Jomo to turn, aim, and not fire. Two guns that had killed five people in the last five minutes were aimed at his head.

Very slowly Colm took his finger from the trigger and raised the other hand.

'Sorry,' he said.

Jane turned back to Jomo.

'Those were Captain Rick's men,' she said.

Jomo nodded.

'I am on your side now,' he said.

She nodded. Tilted her head towards Colm and Kennet. Waited for Jomo to move.

He closed the gap from where he was to where Colm was without seeming to cross the space in between. He used the shadows of the trees and the undergrowth.

'You're a ghost,' Colm said when Jomo was standing next to him.

'I hate the forest,' Jomo said.

Jane joined them a moment later, handing Colm some of the magazines she'd taken from the dead.

'Let's catch them up,' she said.

CHAPTER FORTY-SIX

DESPITE RECEIVING THE NEWS THAT ONE OF THE COUNTRY'S most high-profile terror targets had been spotted, the army still took its time. It was six hours after the spotter plane had flown away before Fatou heard the thump thump of helicopter rotors.

The rangers had kept moving, now knowing precisely how far their quarry was ahead of them. They closed the distance on the Soldiers of God, but calculated the Brotherhood of Souls would be getting further ahead. Even so, by the time the army reached them, they had stopped by the border.

'Is that the end of the park?' Fatou asked.

'That's the end of the DRC,' Hannington said. 'It is illegal for us to walk another step.'

They had left the grassland behind some time ago, and they were some way into the forest. Hannington sent out patrols, and then turned and led them back through the trees until they reached the grass once more. There, they settled down to wait. The sun rolled across the sky, and the minutes moved so slowly. The patrols came back with little to report. The minutes moved even more slowly. Until the thump thump told them that the army was finally here.

They appeared over the horizon, following the edge of the forest. There were five, no, six of them. When they saw the rangers they slowed, circled, and landed in the grass. Mars was the first man out of the first helicopter.

Five of the helicopters were large. Each carried about twenty men and a lot of equipment. The men emptied each helicopter in minutes, and then, as one, they rose into the sky once more. The sixth helicopter went first. It was a gunship. Their escort.

Once the sound of the rotors had died away Mars brought over an officer and introduced him to Hannington. A captain. Fatou didn't catch his name. At one point she caught the captain looking in her direction. She had the feeling they were discussing things they didn't want her to know about.

Whilst Hannington, Lieutenant Fall, and the captain were deep in conversation, the newly arrived soldiers built a small village. Large tents went up in minutes. Tables were set up, gas stoves were laid out, latrine pits were dug. Fatou watched the coordination of the exercise with fascination. Each man knew his allotted task, and the camp was up and running remarkably quickly.

Hannington was walking into the forest with Mars, the captain, and some of their men. Eight of them, well equipped with backpacks, guns, knives, helmets, even some sort of binoculars attached to their helmets. The men were small and quick, surprisingly small for the amount they were carrying. Fatou started after them, but Lieutenant Fall turned to her.

'I'm afraid this is now a military operation, Ms Ba. No press.'

Fatou stopped, disappointed.

She went to Tony, who was reassembling his gun on a blanket underneath a tree.

'What don't they want me to see?' she asked, bluntly.

Tony looked at the group Hannington was leading into the forest.

'My guess would be those guys are Congolese special forces and they are about to cross the border. They wouldn't want any witnesses to that.'

'There's only eight of them.'

'Special forces against those idiots who shot at a plane with AKs? Eight's too many.'

'But Captain Rick's men didn't shoot.'

'They're not after Captain Rick's men. They're after that Brigadier.'

'But what about Jane, and Colm, and Mak, and the others?'

Tony shrugged. 'Hannington will have a plan. He has to, those are his men.'

'Aren't you worried about Kennet and Jane and Colm?'

'About Kennet, yes. He's overweight, unfit, and dangerously naïve. If he doesn't drop dead of a heart attack, then he'll say something stupid, and someone will shoot him. About Colm, yes. He's fit enough, but it's rare anyone comes out of these forests after being kidnapped. Whole villages disappear and are never heard of again. Anything might happen to him. He might be bitten by a snake, left to die under a tree, his body consumed within a week. But am I worried about Jane? No, not really. Not if the stories are true.'

'No? She's a woman.'

Tony raised an eyebrow.

'I mean she's smaller than either of them, and she's been injured recently. Her face. Her arm. What stories?'

'The ones Kennet has told me about her. He has a big mouth.'

'What stories?'

'I don't have a big mouth.'

'You can't tell me there are stories and then not tell me the stories.'

'Oh, yes, I can.'

'But her arm. It's broken. I could see the splint under the bandage.'

'Her arm is not broken. There's no splint under that bandage. I saw her bandage that arm myself, back in Nanyuki. That thing that looks like a splint is called a Kubotan.'

'What's a Kubotan?'

'A small metal stick about the size of a pen. It's a weapon. Special forces use it when they run out of bullets.'

'Special forces?'

Tony nodded.

'Like those men?' Fatou waved in the direction Hannington, Mars, and the captain had led the eight.

Tony shrugged.

'I don't know those men.'

'Kennet arranged to meet the Soldiers of God to be led to the last rhinos in central Africa, and took his sister as a bodyguard?'

Tony looked about them, making sure no one was close enough to hear her. He beckoned her closer.

'Yes,' he said.

'Knowing the danger of it?'

'Yes,' he said.

Fatou frowned.

'That's crazy,' she said.

'That's what I said.'

————

Hannington, Lieutenant Fall, and the captain returned an hour later. It was after sunset by then, but the route into the forest had been marked with lights every ten metres, short white lights with spikes underneath to drive them into the earth.

Hannington left the officers to join Tony and Fatou.

'Well,' Tony said.

'Well, what?'

'How are you going to get your men back?'

'I'm working on it.'

'What does that mean?'

'It means I'm working on it. Rescuing my men, and the Norwegians and the journalist, would be a publicity coup for the army, but not as big a publicity coup as getting the ivory back or capturing Brigadier Okumu, dead or alive,' Hannington said.

'The hostages are with the ivory, or they were six hours ago.'

'We don't know that. We didn't see them.'

'We do know that. We didn't see any discarded ivory. Which means everyone is still carrying what they set out with. Which means everyone is still there.'

'The photos Mars took showed the Soldiers of God had two large tusks.' Hannington held up his hand. 'I know, I know. They could have come from the elephant we saw poached a few days ago. The evidence would support that – a large group of undisciplined men killing the elephant with AKs. But they might have picked them up after the Brotherhood left them behind.'

'If they had lost someone, we would have seen the body, or the vultures, or some sign.'

'I agree. But they've been over the border for six hours. There could have been more men waiting for them. The ivory could have been split up and in a dozen different consignments by now. These are not my arguments, you understand.'

Tony nodded.

'So how are you going to get your men back? How am I going to get my men back?' he asked. He looked at Fatou. 'And whilst we're at it, we'd best pick up the other journalist.'

'I am open to ideas.'

'If you knew where they were, would somebody be prepared to go and get them?'

Hannington gave Fatou a quick glance. She put her hands up.

'Don't look at me. I'd only report the truth, that they were rescued just before they crossed the border.'

'Possibly. But we'd have to know where they are. And the army would have to capture the Brigadier first. Once they have him, I think they'll go after the ivory.'

Tony nodded.

'When you need to know where it is, let me know,' he said.

CHAPTER FORTY-SEVEN

JANE AND JOMO ALTERNATED POSITIONS, FRONT AND REAR. Colm preferred it when Jane was ahead. She was easier to keep in view, though only just. Her clothes were lighter than Jomo's, but they were so sweat, mud, and blood-stained it hardly mattered. Her skin was lighter too, but she had darkened it with mud.

She told Colm and Kennet to do the same, rubbing handfuls of earth into her arms as she did so. Colm noticed her bandage was gone and there was no sign of an injury or a scar on that arm. Colm put his hands into the soil and smeared it on his forehead, his cheeks, his arm, the back of his other hand.

Jane's head snapped round. Colm listened. He could hear nothing beyond the insects and rain. Jane nodded at Jomo, and they were off again, Jomo in front, Jane in the rear. Kennet followed Jomo, and Colm followed Kennet, and Mak and Jean followed Colm, supporting Kwame between them.

Kennet seemed to have recovered from the blow to his head, but also from his fatigue of the march out. He remained a little dazed, and what he said didn't always make sense, but he was relatively bright.

Kwame, on the other hand, was deteriorating.

'It is something inside him,' Jean said. 'He coughs blood. They broke something inside him. We need medical help, a proper hospital.'

'We are four days' march from the nearest road,' Colm said.

Mak shook his head.

'The army have helicopters,' he said. We need a radio. They can get him out of here.'

Colm looked up at the trees.

'And a clearing,' Mak added. 'A radio and a clearing.'

They headed east through the day, moving as quickly and as quietly as they could, trying to avoid making any noise that fractured the background symphony of insects.

Occasionally birds would call out, startled warning cries. When they did, the seven walkers would stop, hold their breath, and listen for any sound that might suggest pursuit. Colm was sure Jomo and Jane could hear things he couldn't, but they said nothing.

———

It was late afternoon when they found the valley. In the lead, Jomo stopped walking. Kennet and then Colm caught him up and found themselves blinking in an unaccustomed brightness.

The ground dropped away sharply for several hundred feet below them. A river had cut through the rock like a knife-wound, and the roar of water drowned out the trill of the insects.

It was strange to be looking down on the tops of trees that must be as tall as the ones they'd been walking through. The river was invisible beneath them.

Jomo started down the valley side, but stopped almost immediately, dropping into a crouch.

A flight of birds had burst out of the tops of the trees below.

They were screeching in alarm, fleeing from a central point. Something had startled them.

Jane moved up to join them. She exchanged looks with Jomo. He turned, and continued into the valley, picking a trickier path on a line that didn't intersect with the point from which the birds had fled. Jane motioned for the others to stay put. Mak shook his head, pointed at Jane and one direction, then at himself, and another, then at Kwame and the ground. Jane nodded. Jane and Mak set off after Jomo but on a different line. Colm looked back, the way they had come. He realised they'd be silhouetted by the light behind and took a few steps into the valley before sitting down, back against a tree trunk that was ten times as thick as he was. Kennet helped Jean ease Kwame to sit beside Colm. Jean let him.

Colm knew there was danger. Ahead in the valley, behind in the trees. There had been nothing but danger for days. But suddenly all he could think of was how tired he was. He hadn't slept in more than twenty-four hours. He hadn't eaten since the grasshopper. There had been plenty of water to drink, but he must have sweated out litres more. He hadn't changed his clothes in five days. Or was it six? He worked out later that it was eight. They were sweat, soil, and blood-stained. They were permanently soaking. They were scratched and torn.

His skin was deliberately covered in mud and soil. His hair was accidentally caked with it. Somewhere he'd scratched his arm deeply enough to draw blood and the wound wasn't scabbing over. Kennet's nose was still bleeding every so often. Every time he managed to get it to stop, he'd slip and jerk his head and it would start again.

And every part of him ached. His shoulders and back were the worst, from dragging Kennet through the jungle, from the unfamiliar weight of the gun. But his legs weren't far behind. And his arms and neck. Even his eyes ached.

Wherever they were, they must be at least five days from Nagero. Without food. With an army following them. Possibly. Possibly two armies. The battle in the jungle wasn't necessarily over, and, even if it was, it might not have ended conclusively.

A strange noise interrupted his thoughts. Over the rain, and the insects, and the roar of the river, and the calling of a bird that sounded in a terrible hurry about something, there was another sound, like an electric saw cutting through thick cream. He sat up and turned.

It was Kennet. He had fallen asleep and was snoring.

There was a movement a few metres away. Colm was on his feet and pointing his gun at it before he could think, though not as quickly as Jean.

'Not bad,' said Jane from behind him. 'Your reactions are improving.'

The movement Colm had seen turned out to be Mak.

'What was it?'

'Mudslide took a tree down,' she said.

Jane kicked Kennet awake.

'You have to see this,' she said.

———

Jean stayed with Kwame. Mak led them down the valley side, so steep in places they needed to hold on with both hands to avoid tumbling. Closer to the bottom the slope eased. The trees were huge, ancient, and the canopy above them boxed in the noise of the river. It was almost deafening.

Mak led them across a clear space where nothing grew because sunlight couldn't reach it. Then into a gash in the earth at the bottom of which they could see the anger of the water.

'Be careful,' he shouted as he climbed.

The gash was sheer, old earth covering ancient rock. It looked new, fresh cut. Exposed roots, some torn.

At the bottom of the gash lay a huge tree, fresh-fallen. The river had eaten away at the soil under its roots until there was nothing left to hold it up and it had come down, tearing the earth as it went.

'We must be quick,' Mak shouted. Colm could see why. The tree-trunk had dammed the river and a huge pool was forming behind it. Soon the water would be over the top.

But until that point, the riverbed downstream lay drained and naked.

Then he saw it.

A great head. Once. Now just smooth, bleached bone. Eye sockets vacant, dull, where life had once sparkled.

'Rhino,' Mak shouted.

The skull lay on its side on the riverbed. There were other bones nearby.

Kennet stepped into the riverbed, crouched beside it.

'There's no damage,' he said, running his hand over the plate between its eyes. 'Its horn is still here. It must have died naturally.'

Mak shrugged.

It was a photo moment, Kennet's great form, one hand on the skull. Pity he didn't have a camera.

Then Colm remembered his phone was still in his pocket, switched off, in a plastic bag.

'Don't move,' he said, taking it out, switching it on.

'We need to go now,' Mak said, starting to climb back up the gash left by the tree. Water was starting to flow through the great branches at the tree's crown, bubbling through the rocks, finding its way back into its bed. Kennet's battered feet were starting to get wet.

'Give me one minute,' Colm said, watching the water as his phone booted up. The water was rising alarmingly quickly.

'Take your time,' said Kennet, staring at the rhino skull, seemingly oblivious to the danger. 'How old do you think it is? How long do you think it has been here?' Mak didn't answer him.

'The water is almost at the top; you need to get out of there now!'

'Just one more second,' Colm said.

The phone was on. For a frustrating moment Colm realised he couldn't remember his pin number, but then muscle memory kicked in and he was in. It worked. He took a string of pictures.

'Get out of there NOW!' Mak shouted. Water was coming over the top of the log in a foaming wave. Colm and Kennet ran.

CHAPTER FORTY-EIGHT

'ANY WORD?' FATOU ASKED MARS.

The lieutenant shook his head.

'I don't know what you are talking about, Ms Ba,' he said.

He'd started this game the first time she had asked him. In case his captain was listening, she guessed. She wasn't supposed to know that eight Congolese army special forces men had crossed the border to look for the Brigadier. Mars's headshake was the real answer to the question.

It had been a day. Nothing had happened. Well, nothing had happened other than that another five helicopter-loads of troops had been dropped off. This time they had been accompanied by two gunships, and this time one of the gunships and one of the transport helicopters had stayed on the ground. The other five flew back the way they had come.

More men went into the woods, to the place where the two rebel armies had crossed the border. Fatou asked Mars again. He shook his head again.

'Are you named after the month or the planet?' she asked him one of those times.

'The month.'

'Were you born in March?'

'No, September.'

'So why Mars?'

'To defeat Captain Janvier. My father is a patriot.'

'I don't think I understand that.'

'It doesn't matter. As a name, it is not so bad. How about Fatou? That means generosity. Are you generous?'

'I don't know. I have never really thought about it. Sometimes, I guess.'

'Very good, Fatou. I shall think of another question to ask you when you return in half an hour.'

Fatou found Tony sitting in a collapsible camping chair brought by the army. His eyes were closed, and his gun lay on the grass next to his feet.

'You're still not going to tell me?' she said.

'No,' he said, without opening his eyes.

'I can't stand this waiting. They could be anywhere by now. We need to do something.'

'There is nothing we can do. We can't go after them; the army won't let us. The army can't go after them, the government won't let them. We know the army have gone after them, but not the ivory or the hostages, just the Brigadier. When the army catch the Brigadier then they will turn their attention to the ivory. At that point, something new will happen. Until then, nothing is going to happen. I told you this last night. I told you this again this morning. Shall I write it down, so I don't have to tell you it again this afternoon?'

'Stop patronising me. Tell me why you are so relaxed. Tell me what you meant when you told Hannington to ask you when the army want to know where the ivory is.'

Something about the tone of her voice caused Tony to open

his eyes. She stood over him, the afternoon sun at her back so he had to squint at her.

'You are a journalist,' he said.

'Tell me what you know,' she said.

Tony opened his mouth, but it was someone else who spoke.

'He knows the Congolese special forces will be back in two days with the Brigadier, four at the most. That is why he is so relaxed, because until then, there is nothing to be done, so why worry about it?' It was Mola. He had approached them from the forest. His gait was leisurely; he, too, seemed relaxed.

'How do you know that?'

'Because of their equipment. Did you see what they had on their helmets?'

Fatou thought back.

'Some sort of binoculars?'

'Night vision goggles. From dusk till dawn this forest is pitch black. Using lights can tell the world where you are for kilometres in every direction. The safest thing to do is to set a small camp, post some sentries, and give them torches. If they hear anything, they switch on the torches and shoot. But from dusk till dawn is twelve hours. In the forest you can only keep moving for twelve hours a day. Using night vision goggles...' Mola left the sentence unfinished.

'They can keep moving for longer?' Fatou hazarded.

Mola nodded. 'We were three hours behind the Soldiers of God, the army turned up six hours later, so assuming the Soldiers kept moving in a straight line and at a constant speed, and assuming the army does the same, the army will catch up with them in two nights at the outside.'

'Eight against fifty.'

'Special forces in the dark? No contest.'

'What do we do until then?'

'We wait,' Tony said.

'Though I don't know why Tony thinks he knows where the ivory is. Your guess is as good as mine there.'

Fatou looked at Tony. Tilted her head to one side.

'I think he's about to tell us,' she said, with a bright smile.

Tony frowned a little. Then he realised what she meant. She was threatening to share the secret about Kennet.

He inhaled and exhaled heavily.

'Fine,' he said. 'No real reason not to tell you, other than for dramatic effect. Nothing anyone can do about it until they have the Brigadier, but here.'

He pulled a small black electronic device out of his pocket and handed it to Mola.

'What's this?'

'It's a tracker. It's tracking a device of Jane's.'

Mola stared at it, looked around him, presumably for Hannington.

'You've had this all this time?'

'I forgot I had it until we were nearly here.'

'Why do you have it?'

'Jane gave it to me. In case something like this happened.'

'She won't still have it. They will have searched her and destroyed it.'

Tony shook his head.

'It wasn't on her. It was in one of the tusks. One of them has been carrying it, and it's still transmitting. They're still moving. Twenty-one kilometres north-northeast of here.'

'You are mad. You have had this and you didn't–'

Mola abruptly stopped talking and strode off, the device in his hand.

'I really did forget I had it,' Tony said.

'But at some point, you remembered,' she said. She followed Mola.

———

Mola found Hannington. Hannington found Mars. Mars found the captain. It turned out Tony was right. Knowing where the ivory was would make no difference to the army until the Brigadier was taken. The plan remained the same.

They didn't talk about it when Fatou could hear, but Mola told her later.

By the time the sun set Fatou knew two things. The first was where the ivory was, and, by implication, where the hostages were, and, by implication, where the Brigadier was heading. An army private entered the coordinates shown on Tony's satellite tracker into a laptop, and they were displayed on a map. Every thirty minutes he updated the coordinates, and they watched the progress of the ivory through the forest. It stopped moving at sunset, which fit with what Mola had told her. In the forest it wasn't safe to move after dark.

The second thing she knew was that the army were not going to do anything with the information. Not yet. Not today. Mission one was the Brigadier. The plan was to wait until they had him. Plans could not be changed.

———

She slept terribly that night. She could not switch her mind off. She could process the logic. The ivory was on foreign soil. The army couldn't go on foreign soil. So close, but so far. She could also convince herself that nothing had changed. They had known where the ivory and the hostages were all along. They were at the other end of the trail they were following. After the reconnaissance by plane, they'd known exactly how far ahead the end of the trail was. And now they knew exactly where the end of the trail was, but there was nothing they could do, just as there had been nothing they could do before Tony pulled the satellite tracker from his pocket.

Shortly after sunrise, the ivory was on the move again. Fatou adjusted her walk. Every hour she would ask Lieutenant Fall if there had been any news before moving to the laptop and watching the movement of the dot on the screen.

That was all that happened that day. Twelve times she asked her questions. Twelve times Lieutenant Fall shook his head. Twelve times she saw the dot move on the screen.

That night, the second in the army camp, she slept worse.

————

The third day in the camp finally brought changes.

She lay on her bunk staring at the mosquito net for hours. She was sure she had got some sleep, but it felt as though she hadn't. She heard a helicopter starting its engines, which meant the sun was rising. As soon as it was up Fatou went to see Mars.

His tent was only fifty metres away. She tapped on the frame. A corporal stuck his head out. He knew immediately that she was there for Mars. The corporal pulled the flap back and pointed.

Mars was having no trouble sleeping. He was still asleep. Which meant no one had woken him with news, which meant there was no news. She went to find the private with the laptop.

He was awake.

He saw her coming and held out her phone. He had charged it for her overnight. He had a portable charger that would last the laptop a week, he said, with plenty to spare for phones, and they would helicopter in fully charged ones every three days. She thanked him by taking a selfie with him. He had a very serious face, and he was oddly nervous for a soldier, but his smile when it came was infectious.

'Nothing has changed,' he said.

'You mean...?'

'The tracker is still there. It did not move at sunrise.'

'What does that mean?'

'I can only see the facts. The tracker is still transmitting, and it has not moved. It might be because the ivory it is in is still in the same place. It might be because they found it and threw it away without destroying it. Speculation is not my speciality. But the technology gives us two facts. It is still transmitting, and it's been in the same place for more than twelve hours.'

'Thank you, private.'

'Call me Pierre,' he said.

'Thank you, Pierre. Call me Fatou.'

She left him and went to find Tony.

———

On the way she came across Mola, and another seven rangers, packing their backpacks with water and food, checking their weapons, testing a radio.

'What's happened?' Fatou asked.

'Army transport helicopter on the way out this morning saw five men ten kilometres back. Probably poachers. Rangers' job,' Mola said. 'We are bored just waiting. And besides, they have offered us a ride.' He grinned and nodded at the helicopter gunship whose rotors were starting to turn.

Fatou had an urge to go with them. To fly in a helicopter. To see them at work. She was bored too.

But the transmitter hadn't moved. That was a change. She had to stay here. The story was here. She wished Mola luck and continued looking for Tony.

———

He was on his own, sitting in the camping chair outside a tent. He had been on his own since Hannington and Mola had learned about the tracker. 'It gives them something to be mad at, something they can do,' Tony had said.

'They didn't move at sunrise,' she said without greeting. 'The transmitter is still in the same place and still transmitting.'

'Could just be a late start,' Tony said, but the tone of his voice was a little brighter, as if he suspected, or hoped, it wasn't a late start.

Behind them the gunship throbbed into the sky, hovered a hundred metres above the grass, sending it whipping away in a spiral beneath it, turned to face southeast, and moved off.

The captain and Lieutenant Fall were walking towards them. The captain said nothing, didn't even seem to notice them. The lieutenant also ignored them until the captain was past them. Then he turned his head towards Fatou and shook it.

Still no news.

Perhaps today wasn't going to be any different. Fatou lay down in the grass.

CHAPTER FORTY-NINE

'WE REALLY DID NOT THINK THIS THROUGH,' COLM SAID, looking at Mak, Jane, and Jomo on the other side of the once again fast-flowing stream.

The water was angry. The channel was only three or four metres across, but too wide to jump, too deep to ford, and too fast to swim. If they jumped in, they would be swept downstream and smashed against the rocks.

Though it had, in truth, been Kennet who had run the wrong way. Colm had simply followed him without looking up until he'd heard Mak's cry over the water noise.

'THIS WAY!'

But it was too late by then.

Jane was gesturing downstream. Follow the bank, was Colm's guess.

Mak and Jomo were already running back up the side of the valley, to collect Jean and Kwame.

Colm waved at Jane and pointed in the direction she'd indicated to make it clear he had understood.

He patted his gun, hoping it would give him some comfort.

'Let's go,' he said to Kennet.

———

They followed the valley southwest, tracking the stream from a hundred metres into the forest. Closer to the river the trees were younger and the undergrowth thicker, so going was slower.

'Was that the last one?' Kennet said.

'I'm sorry, what? Was what the last one?'

'That rhino. Was it the last rhino to live in the wild in central Africa? No one else seems to think there are any more. Can they really all be gone?'

'We can't know, I presume,' Colm said. 'That skeleton could have been there decades.'

Every couple of hundred metres they went back to the bank of the stream, to keep visual contact with the others, and to see if there was a place shallow enough or narrow enough or slow enough for them to cross. In one place there was a tree with a branch that stretched across the stream. But it was five metres off the ground, and neither Kwame in one direction nor Kennet in the other would have had a chance of hauling themselves along it.

Despite everything, Colm and Kennet made reasonable time. Mak and Jean were slower on the other bank because of Kwame.

They stopped at sundown. Colm and Kennet slept on soft earth beneath a great mahogany tree. Jean, Jane, Mak, and Jomo took it in turns to keep watch from the opposite bank, but it was so dark they would only have seen something if it stepped on them.

Colm was awake before the sun rose, and he watched the light flow down the valley. It was beautiful. Niamh would have loved this.

Jomo was the one on watch, standing next to a young tree.

'I'd kill for a bacon sandwich,' Colm called across the stream by way of greeting.

Jomo looked worried. Colm wondered if Jomo had understood him. Eighteen years in the forest, would he know what a bacon sandwich was?

'Five minutes,' Jomo called back, and disappeared into the trees.

He was gone longer than five minutes, but not much. He returned and started pulling things from his pockets, tossing them over the stream. Colm caught three thrown to him one at a time. He passed two to Kennet.

They were round fruit, similar to oranges. Across the bank, Jomo broke into one with his thumb, pushed the white flesh to his mouth and ate.

Colm did the same. The flesh of the fruit was soft, with a texture of pulp. It was slightly acidic, but after an eternity without food it tasted like nectar.

They set off again, two parallel paths separated by the narrow strip of unpassable water. The valley was unfriendly, alternating between too steep and too overgrown, with the endless presence of the river threatening to swallow them.

An hour of the morning was gone when Colm and Kennet reached a cliff. Their way forward was blocked completely. Colm could see no route up – at least, none he wasn't certain would end with him falling off into the river. Here it was raging over rocks so loudly they couldn't hear the shouted directions from Jomo on the other side of the water. In the end he directed them back the way they had come using hand signals and tried to get them to do something else using different hand signals, but Colm couldn't work out what they meant.

Jomo had a brief discussion with Jane, and then started following Colm and Kennet. As they made their way back up the valley, he shadowed them. Jane and the others were soon lost to sight.

It was half an hour before Colm found what Jomo had been trying to describe to him. A gentle slope that led up the valley side to the ridge above. Colm gave Jomo an exaggerated thumbs up and started up the slope with Kennet on his heels.

As he approached the top of the rise he turned to look back at Jomo. Jomo was holding his hand flat and lowering it. Colm understood.

'Jomo's telling us to get down, not to stand on the skyline,' he said to Kennet. Colm crouched, scrambled the last few metres to the top, laid the gun beside him, and looked over the top.

Colm had been expecting the top of the slope to be the top of a ridge, to be looking down into another valley. But he wasn't, he was looking along the forest floor. The stream had cut the valley from a relatively flat piece of earth, at least as far as Colm could see through the trees.

He relaxed. It was just more forest. He turned back, intending to wave a thumbs up to Jomo, and froze. He'd seen something out of the corner of his eye. Something pale, in a beam of light falling through the canopy. Had it been a bird? He looked more carefully.

There it was again. In the same place, in the forest, on his side of the river. A light thing passing through a beam of light. Too quick to identify.

He stared, eyes as wide as possible, trying to work out what he was looking at.

He saw it a third time. And this time he knew what he was looking at.

The light thing was a tusk. A tusk on a man's shoulder. No more than fifty metres back in the trees. There was a column of men carrying ivory in the forest, heading parallel to the valley they were following. In the same direction. And all the rangers and murderous Norwegians were on the wrong side of the river.

CHAPTER FIFTY

Fatou watched the helicopter gunship return. It landed on the grass, rotors thumping, and Mola and two of his rangers climbed out. What had happened to the other five?

The three men ran across the grass with their backs bent, instinctively avoiding the rotors despite there being more than a metre of space above the head of the tallest of them.

Mola stopped running when he was clear of the machine. He raised a hand in greeting to Fatou.

'Any news?' he shouted.

'Where are the rest of your men?' she shouted back, whilst simultaneously shaking her head. Another day almost done, and nothing else had changed. The tracker was still functioning and still in the same place, but other than that, no news.

'Not everyone could fit in the chopper. The others are walking the prisoners back to the pick-up point.'

'Everyone OK?'

Mola nodded. 'Ivory poachers from over the border. Nothing to do with anything else that is going on. They threw their guns down as soon as they saw the helicopter. We should borrow it more often. What's going on?' he said, looking over her shoulder.

Behind her Fatou could see running soldiers, hear things being shouted. Men were doing up their uniforms, grabbing their guns, grabbing packs.

'Someone's moving out,' he said.

'Something's changed,' she said.

She looked around for the lieutenant. She spotted him over by the laptop tent, standing next to the captain and Hannington, looking over Pierre's shoulder at the screen and reading something from a notebook.

'I can't go over there,' Fatou said. 'The captain doesn't want me to know what's happening.' She added just a hint of "Poor little me" to her tone. She hoped it wasn't too obvious.

'I'll find out,' Mola said. He dropped his backpack to the ground and jogged over to the group of officers.

———

Fatou picked up Mola's backpack. It was incredibly heavy. With difficulty, she dragged it onto her back and carried it to the tents. It pulled at her shoulders and pressed into her back. At the ranger's tent she tried to slip it off again, but it was so heavy she couldn't get her arm through. She felt herself getting frustrated. Then the weight lightened, and the backpack came off. Tony was behind her, helping her with it.

'What's going on?' he asked.

'I don't know,' she said.

She looked over at the laptop tent. Mola was jogging towards them.

'Hannington wants to see you,' Mola said.

'Me?' Fatou said.

'Him,' Mola said.

Tony nodded. He left them.

Mola looked at his backpack on the ground.

'Thank you,' he said.

'What's happened?'

'They've had radio contact from the team in the forest. They caught up with the Soldiers of God early this morning. They're half a kilometre from them. They're going to attack after dark.'

'Good,' Fatou said.

'That's not all. The tracker has stopped transmitting. It didn't move. Its last location was the same one it's been transmitting from for the last twenty-two hours, but now it's not sending out a signal.'

'What does that mean?'

'Could mean many things. That's what Hannington wants Tony for. To ask if it could be the battery. But that's not all.'

'What else?'

'The team confirmed their location. They're half a kilometre from the Soldiers of God, and three quarters of a kilometre from the tracker's last location. And that is still not all.'

Fatou waited, impatiently.

'What?' she said.

'The Soldiers of God didn't wait until dark. The army team say there has been a battle in the forest. Their guess is that the tracker was in the Brotherhood's camp, and the Soldiers of God attacked the camp. The outcome of the attack is uncertain.'

'What happens now?'

'The army team will go in after dark and find Brigadier Okumu, alive or dead.'

'And then what?'

Mola shrugged.

'We will find out. It is going to be a long night.'

———

Fatou looked at Hannington. Hannington was looking at Tony. The captain was looking at Tony. Lieutenant Fall was looking at Tony. François was looking tired. Mola had gone to bed.

The six of them sat in a circle in collapsible chairs.

The captain, who had not given anyone permission to call him anything else, had turned out to be something of a weasel and a bureaucrat. But he was evidently very intelligent. He listened to Hannington, and to his lieutenant. He had allowed Fatou to join their council because he "wanted to show Congolese goodwill to the international press". Fatou had heard those words and interpreted them as meaning that she had finally convinced him she wasn't going to report anything about the Congolese army straying over the South Sudanese border. More importantly, though, he thought he was about to capture a terrorist wanted for war crimes in three countries, recover half a tonne of stolen ivory, and rescue six hostages, and he wanted to make sure she got his good side in the victory photograph.

It was four in the morning. They had had two reports from the army team out there in the forest, both tapped in Morse code, stilted and perfunctory, but translated and embellished.

The first report said that after the Soldiers of God had attacked the Brotherhood's camp in the afternoon, the Brotherhood had scattered. The Soldiers of God had captured the hostages and brought them back to the Brotherhood's camp where they had found the ivory, buried in a pit. Based on the timing, as soon as the ivory had been uncovered the tracker signal started to transmit again.

There was nothing uncertain about that. A report by professionals, clear and precise, dealing with facts based on what men in an observation post had seen, and that observation post that must, given the clarity and detail of its intelligence, have been practically inside the camp.

The second report was the one that had led to this council.

'I shall read it again,' the captain said, holding up a piece of paper, and addressing Tony. '"Rain. White woman kill six, free hostages, took forest. Have Brigadier, rendez-vous two, ten hundred." Who is this woman called Jane Haven? This woman!'

Tony looked sideways at Fatou. He shifted in his seat. The captain kept talking.

'For this report to come from this team it means they saw her kill six men. They would not report that otherwise. Do not leave anything out. Do not conceal anything from me again. You should have told me about the tracker days ago. This is your last chance. If you don't tell me everything you know right now—' The captain checked himself, gave Fatou a sideways glance, then licked his lips. 'Jane Haven. Who is she?' he finished.

Tony looked at the captain, who returned his gaze with cold eyes. Fatou fancied that Tony was weighing up the nature of the unspoken threat, and the likelihood of it being carried out. Fatou's personal assessment was "Potentially Fatal" and "Very High".

Tony took a deep breath. And then he answered.

'I don't really know, sir. I work for her brother in the Bandari conservancy in Nanyuki in Kenya. I've worked for the conservancy for fifteen years. Her brother became chief executive five years ago. He is obsessed with northern white rhino. The last three animals of that species in the world are in the Bandari conservancy. He read that the last northern whites known in the wild were seen in Southern Sudan in 2006. He became fixated by the idea that they were still out there somewhere. He contacted the South Sudanese government. They stonewalled for a year. Then he found a way to contact the Soldiers of God.'

That shook them up. Every man there sat forward. Fatou didn't move. She knew this part of the story.

'He agreed to meet them. In exchange for them showing him the last northern white rhino in the wild, he agreed to tell their side of their story.'

'Those men can't be trusted. The man is mad,' the captain said.

'I told him he was crazy. That if he did this, he would die. He told me not if he took his sister.'

There was a silence. Hannington broke it.

'He came to Garamba to get into South Sudan?'

'Yes. He agreed to meet the Soldiers of God in the park, for them to take him, and his sister, to South Sudan.'

'But he didn't meet them in the park.'

'He didn't. His sister did. They left a message at the poachers' motel. She met them on the road when she said she was leaving for Wando. But she didn't like them and didn't trust them. She followed them. When they attacked Nagero she drove them off. Then the Brotherhood attacked. She broke their attack on the rear fence. Killed half a dozen.'

'That was Deng. You found him with the rifle that killed them.'

Tony shook his head.

'I found Deng with the rifle that killed them. I also found him bandaged. She found him shot, dressed his wound, left the rifle with him, then came back into the compound to ensure she was captured with Kennet.'

Hannington sat back.

'Unbelievable,' he said.

'She killed six,' the captain said. 'My men reported it. I believe that. And if that is true, the rest is plausible. But how?'

Tony shook his head.

'I do not know. All I know is, Kennet thinks she is invincible.

Kennet is very naïve. He looks at the world through, what do they say, rose-tinted spectacles. He sees good in everything even if it is not there. It takes a lot to convince him it isn't. But in the five years I have known him he has consistently talked about his sister in terms of invulnerability. Her and her friends.'

'She told you she killed all those men at Nagero?'

Tony shook his head.

'That's my deduction. I heard the rifle. A Remington. Very distinctive sound. She left with it, she returned without it, I found it with Deng.'

'Unbelievable,' Hannington said again. Fatou thought he was right.

————

For two nights, Fatou had wanted to sleep, but hadn't been able to. This night, she needed to stay awake, but kept falling asleep.

She was woken by a hand on her shoulder. She was still in the chair she'd sat in for the council. She must have fallen asleep while they were still talking. She cursed in her head. The hand belonged to the captain. Everyone else had gone. It was daylight. How long had she been asleep?

'Fatou Ba, reassure me of our understanding.'

She ran her hand over her face to wake herself up.

'No Congolese troops crossed the border,' she said.

'Reassure me,' he said again. 'You are Belgian,' he added, as if this explained everything.

She thought for a moment.

'I have a DRC passport,' she said. 'My grandparents emigrated to Belgium in nineteen fifty-six. I am a journalist, but I am Congolese first, Belgian second, a journalist third.'

The captain gave her a long, slow look.

'You are lying. You are a journalist first. But that is enough.

You want the best story. I have the best story. Come with me.'
He offered her his hand. She took it, and he pulled her to her
feet.

'This way,' he said. He clasped his hands behind his back.

There were not many soldiers around. Fatou could see no
rangers at all.

'Tell me, Fatou Ba. How many countries have you visited in
your life?'

Fatou had to think.

'Maybe thirty?'

The captain nodded.

'There are one hundred and ninety-five countries in the
world today. The youngest of them all is South Sudan. You have
visited a little under a sixth of the countries in the world.'

Fatou nodded.

'In those thirty countries, how did you find the people you
met? Were those in one country angry, those in another smelly,
those in a third crazy?'

Fatou frowned at him, uncertain as to where he was leading
the conversation. But she answered.

'Individuals have been. I have never seen a trait applicable to
an entire people. Not one. Not habit, not skin colour, nothing.'

The captain nodded, evidently pleased.

'I have never left the DRC. This is my home. I am from
Kinshasa, which is three thousand kilometres away. Between
Kinshasa and Garamba are hundreds of languages, thousands of
tribes. And in my limited experience of all that variety, I have
never encountered a single trait that is applicable to an entire
village, let alone a tribe, let alone a people.'

Fatou nodded, though she was still not sure where he was
taking the conversation. He was leading her to the laptop tent
and Pierre, however.

Pierre heard them coming.

'Captain,' he said. Then, 'Fatou.'

Fatou said 'Pierre.'

The captain raised an eyebrow.

'I didn't realise you knew each other. It doesn't matter. I am,' he paused, thought, then continued, 'I am watching the endgame of this little dalliance with extreme interest. It is a chess game. Show her the tracker ping, private.'

Pierre flicked to a satellite view of a forest, which was little more than a screen of varying shades of dark green. Then a little purple dot appeared close to the bottom of it.

'And the team pings.'

Pierre clicked and tapped, and two groups of green dots appeared very close to the purple dot.

'You see,' the captain said. 'Whilst you were sleeping the tracker started moving again. Southwest, outside our border, but parallel to it, heading for Uganda. A team of my men went into the camp. They counted the bodies. They found half of the ivory left behind in a pit. We have sent men for that. But the other half is moving. We are closing in on it. The green dots are my teams. We will have everything back within a day.'

'What about the hostages?'

'For all the talk of this indestructible miracle woman we had earlier, I take confidence in the fact that three of those hostages are trained rangers with decades of experience between them. If they got out of that camp alive, they will find us, soon enough.'

Fatou stared at the map. Watched the dots moving.

'They counted the bodies?'

'They did. The Soldiers of God that Lieutenant Fall photographed numbered fifty-nine, and the estimates of the numbers of the Brotherhood were about forty. We have the Brigadier and six others alive. We have found thirty others dead. We don't know how many are from one side or the other, but to carry two hundred kilos of ivory that are still missing, we must assume there are many members of the Brotherhood still alive. Twenty-five at least. I was angry, when I learned that Tony Kanagi had concealed that tracker from us. But now I am happy we have it. We know where they are, and we know where they are going to die.'

Fatou stared at the map on the screen.

CHAPTER FIFTY-ONE

COLM WAS SCARED. HE WAS TERRIFIED. HE IGNORED KENNET and scrabbled back down the bank to looked for Jomo. His recent jailor, and now a man he trusted with his life. Jomo was there. Colm waved his arms, tried to communicate that there were soldiers in the forest. He made signals like guns, mimed carrying ivory. Across the water he saw Jomo react. Saw him understand. Saw him mime walking slowly. Saw him make a gesture, his arms coming together, that Colm interpreted as 'I will find you'. Then Jomo was gone.

Colm climbed back up to Kennet, who hadn't moved. He was still lying just below the ridge.

'I think Jomo said we need to wait for them to pass, then follow them,' Colm said. 'I think that's what he said. We should go the other way, back the way we came, away from them.'

Kennet raised his head. Then he lowered his head. He blew out. Then he inhaled.

'I like Jomo,' he said.

Such a simple thing to say. Colm turned over and lay on his back, looked at the sky. He thought.

'Alright,' he said.

He crawled back up to the ridge and peered over it. Looked for the place in the trees where the light had shown him the men passing by. He found it. He watched it. He watched it for a minute. For three. For five. For ten. Nothing.

'Kennet,' he said. 'Let's go.'

He left the gun and the spare ammunition in the mud at the top of the ridge. He didn't think he could use it. And if he did meet someone who might shoot him, he figured they'd be more likely to do so if he was carrying a gun.

Kennet lolloped behind him. The man was not right. He was still bleeding from his nose, and he walked stooped, his arms loose by his side. Colm found himself occasionally touching Kennet's arm, to remind him he was there.

They followed the ridge, but ten metres back, inside the trees. Colm walked slowly, kept Kennet slow, wanting to ensure they were falling behind the men carrying the ivory.

Colm looked at the sky. The night would come soon. They would have to find somewhere to sleep. To hide.

He thought about the distance they'd walked. Thought about where the cliff had been. Was sure they had passed it a long time ago. Berated himself for not thinking of that earlier. Jane and the others might have found a place to cross, and they'd have missed them. He steered Kennet back towards the ridge.

'My sister will find us,' Kennet said.

'How?' Colm said, and climbed a few metres, and looked down into the valley again.

It was a gorge now. The waters roared fifty metres below. Colm couldn't see any way to cross, up or down river.

The sun was setting. They kept walking, following the valley. Colm made sure he was always in front. He didn't trust Kennet. Not emotionally, just reactively. If Colm saw someone with a gun, he'd hide. He suspected Kennet, in the same situation, might say "Well hello, there!"

They reached the top of an escarpment. Colm could see the drop twenty metres before he reached it. The tree canopy just disappeared, fell away. He grabbed Kennet and pulled him to the ground.

'Me first,' he said.

Kennet nodded, as if he understood. Colm crawled forward, then looked back. Kennet hadn't moved. OK.

Colm looked down. Thirty metres down an almost sheer slope. There was something of a clearing. It looked like a quarry he knew back home, but it wasn't a quarry. It was cut by water. Something prevented trees growing there, leaving a broad, flat space.

With a camp in it. Shelters and tents in rows, men moving about. And in the middle of the camp, a stack of curved white objects. Tusks.

The light was almost gone, but in the last of it he saw one other thing to the left of the camp. The space opened into the valley he and Kennet had been following the whole day and the river ran past, no longer fast and angry. There it was broad and calm. It was fordable. They could cross it.

Colm slid back behind the top of the escarpment. Kennet still had not moved.

'We can cross the river there. When they move on in the morning, we can cross the river and join Jane and the others.'

Kennet smiled, and immediately fell asleep.

Colm crawled back up the slope and looked over. The light was gone now, and the camp was dark. He could see nothing.

He kept watching in the dark. For a long time. Clouds were blocking the moon, and whilst he was soon able to make out the shapes of nearby trees in the light of the visible stars, the camp at the bottom of the slope was swallowed in darkness.

After more than an hour he saw something strange. Small dots of greenish light, coming out of the forest, entering the space below, moving towards the camp from the west. They were not very bright, like fireflies at several hundred metres. But because there was no other light down there, the pale dots of greenish light stood out. Then he heard the first trurp.

That was the sound. Trurp. Three individual sounds taking place so close together they became one. Like the triple shots from the AKs, but faster, and quieter. Trurp. One, two, three, four, five, seven, ten, fifteen trurps. The green lights moved, and the trurps followed them. Colm watched, fascinated.

He could hear other sounds now as well, now. Closer than the camp at the bottom of the escarpment. In the trees, coming towards them. Someone trying to move stealthily but struggling to do so in the dark.

Colm lay as flat as he could and as still as he could. The sounds moved closer. There was more than one set of sounds. Whatever creature was making them, there was more than one of them. They were really close now, no more than ten metres away, perhaps less.

Then came a different sound. The last sound Colm wanted to hear. As he heard it, he felt his heart sink. In that moment, he knew for certain he was about to die.

'Hello? Who's there?' Kennet's voice said from behind Colm.

The noise in the trees stopped. The thin beam of a pencil torch whipped towards them. Colm lay flat and it missed him. It didn't matter. Behind him, all one metre ninety-eight of Kennet Haven was standing up and the weak beam picked him out as easily as if it had been a search light.

The torch moved towards them, keeping Kennet in its beam. A second torch came on, brighter than the first. Pointed at the ground, it swept back and forth until, inevitably, it found Colm.

The light stayed on him. He looked towards it, and it temporarily blinded him. He closed his eyes tightly.

Don't shoot, I'm a journalist. Don't shoot, I'm a journalist. Colm swallowed the courage to say it out loud.

He heard a voice. He didn't think it was the voice of someone who held either torch; it came from somewhere between the lights. It was distorted, a snarl.

'Oh, its them. Cut their throats and throw them in the ravine. Be quick about it.'

Colm recognised Captain Rick's voice. They weren't going to shoot. Triple god. He had to run. He had to run, but he could not move.

'Get up,' a different voice said, as one of the lights moved towards him.

'Stay down!' a third voice said, half a second before Colm heard the now very familiar sound of an AK-47 in rapid fire mode discharging its contents.

The torch light shining in Colm's face moved away with a jerk. He heard the click, click, slap of a magazine being ejected, and a new one slammed in to replace it. He heard footsteps, careful, cautious.

Slowly Colm's sight returned. He could see both torches were still on. The brighter one was fifteen metres away, pointing down the hill. The other one was in someone's hand.

It flicked at a shape on the floor. A fallen soldier. Then at a second. Then at a third.

At the third shape it stopped.

The third shape spoke.

'Who are you?' it said. It was Captain Rick. There was pain in his voice. He had been hit.

For a moment, nothing happened. Then, slowly, the torch beam changed direction until it lit up a face that hung there, disembodied in the dark.

'I am Jomo,' the face said. Two sounds followed his words. The sound of three rounds leaving a gun, and the sound of three bullets hitting Captain Rick.

CHAPTER FIFTY-TWO

COLM REID, IRISH TELEGRAPH, WALKED OUT OF THE TREES and into the army and ranger camp in the top northeast corner of Garamba National Park. He walked with Mak and Jean either side of him. As they emerged from the trees the three of them were surrounded by the soldiers and rangers who had been waiting for them to arrive for two days.

Fatou knew they had been escorted through the forest by members of the Congolese army, but also knew, from her promises, that no members of the Congolese army had crossed the border, and consequently, or so her story would have to tell it, the two rangers and Colm had made the journey unaided.

Hannington and Mola reached the three men before she did. Not by much. She kept back a couple of paces, to watch their reunion. Lieutenant Fall waited closer to the camp, but still watching them all.

Mak saluted. Hannington laughed.

'It is very good to see you, sergeant,' Hannington said.

'Very good to be seen, sir,' Mak said. 'How is Kwame?'

'He is alive, the helicopter got him to the hospital still

breathing, though the words the hospital sends are not yet positive.'

'And everyone else?'

'We lost Félix, Gasimba, Justin, David, and Agoyo. Everyone else is fine. Erik will make a full recovery.'

Mak nodded.

'It could have been a lot worse,' he said.

'It could. The army is content. They have Brigadier Okumu in custody along with eight others of the Soldiers of God. They have thirteen of the Brotherhood of Souls, Captain Rick is dead, and they recovered the ivory. A more senior officer in the Brotherhood was spotted, but he escaped. Nonetheless, the DRC was insulted, and the army responded to that insult. Without crossing the border.'

'I am personally very grateful for their swift and decisive action,' Mak said.

Hannington nodded. 'You are very well trained, Sergeant.'

———

'You look terrible,' Fatou said.

'I've felt better,' Colm said. 'Is that hot food I smell?'

'Haven't you eaten?'

'Not in living memory.'

———

Colm ate everything they brought him. Fatou watched. Eventually, he sat back and looked at the sky.

'I need to talk to my wife,' he said.

'No personal comms out here. I've tried,' she said.

'Does she know anything?'

'She will know nothing more than the last thing you told her.'

'They took videos of us, said they were going to post our messages online, hold us for ransom.'

Fatou shook her head. 'If they did, the army don't know about it.'

'I need to tell her I'm ok. Is there a way?'

'There is no way to communicate with anyone you can't see. Unless you are army. Or a ranger and the person you want to communicate with has a shortwave radio. Or you are from the *Post du Soir* and happen to know Private Pierre.'

Colm looked at her.

'Do you know Private Pierre?' he asked.

———

Colm clicked send and stood up. At least now Niamh would know he was alright. She had not heard from him for nearly a fortnight.

'Thank you, Pierre,' Colm said.

Pierre looked uncomfortable.

'Pierre did nothing he needs to be thanked for,' Fatou explained.

'Ah. In that case, my apologies, Pierre, I misunderstood.'

Fatou kicked Colm's ankle.

'Oh, and, Pierre, if there's any way I can make up for my misunderstanding, please let me know. My email address is–'

———

'What happens now?' Colm said.

'We will be flown back to Nagero in the morning,' Fatou said.

Colm leaned back in the chair and looked up at the sky.

'What story are you going to tell?' he asked.

'What happened?' she said. 'Out there, in the forest? How did you survive?'

Colm closed his eyes.

'By a series of miracles. My life was saved at least four times. Twice by Jane, twice by Jomo.'

'Jomo?' Fatou sat up and sat forward. Colm's eyes were still closed. 'Who is Jomo?'

Colm leaned forward again and opened his eyes.

'Jomo was one of the Brotherhood. Assigned to guard me. He did his job. He saved my life twice, but both times from the Brotherhood. He guarded me from the people who set him to guard me. He was the one who killed Captain Rick. Captain Rick told his men to cut my throat and throw me in a river. Jomo killed him. I didn't even get the chance to thank him.'

'He killed Captain Rick?'

Colm nodded.

'Why did he do that?'

'He didn't want to be one of them. He was kidnapped from his village when he was ten. He'd been a coerced soldier for eighteen years. He saw a chance to be free and he took it.'

'What happened to him?'

'The Congolese army put us under guard overnight. Kennet, myself, Jomo. I fell asleep. I woke up and Mak, Jean, and Kwame were in the enclosure with me. Kennet and Jomo were gone.'

'Jane Haven,' Fatou said, nodding.

Colm looked at her.

'How did you know?'

———

The other four rangers who had died had families. Their bodies had been taken back to their villages. But Agoyo had no family, other than the rangers, and they lowered him into the ground in a corner of the cemetery of the church in the village of Nagero, not far from the ranger station.

'Death will not stop us. Every tear will be wiped away. This pain will not last. We will not mourn forever. We celebrate our brother.' Hannington threw the first shovel of earth on the simple coffin in the grave. The other rangers took their turns. Colm, Tony and Fatou did too.

———

The next day, they said their goodbyes to the rangers of Nagero, other than Hannington who had decided he had better take them to the airport himself to 'make sure they got on the plane'. They made one stop on the way.

Dungu hospital was surprisingly large. There were army trucks amongst the cars in the car park.

Hannington led them into the building. They passed a sign for '*Réception*' and followed it through double doors into a blissfully air-conditioned hall.

There was a large waiting area bustling with people. Hannington went to the reception desk and addressed the man behind it.

'Where can I find Kwame Ilunga?'

Before the man had chance to reply a different voice interrupted them.

'Colm? Colm Reid the journalist?'

The new voice was loud and caused a brief dip in the level of murmur in the waiting room.

It was Jack Luckwood, the missionary from the plane. He had a steaming cup in his hand. He held it up. 'Just getting coffee. It's my break.' Jack was wearing blue scrubs, like an orderly. 'The coffee's really good,' he said. 'It's from Kivu. That's south of here, near Kigali. And I remember you from the plane from Kinshasa, but I never knew your name,' Jack added, swivelling to look at Fatou and sending a splash of coffee out of his cup.

'Fatou Ba,' she said.

'Pleased to meet you, Fatou Ba. I'm Jack. Jack Luckwood.'

'What are you doing, here, Jack? Why are you in scrubs? I thought you were here to be a teacher,' Colm said.

'I was, but they needed people to carry stretchers and push trolleys this week. There's been some trouble close to the border. We've had quite a few gunshot wounds through in the last few days.'

'I know,' Colm said. 'We're here to see Kwame Ilunga.'

'Kwame! I carried him in two days ago. I can show you. Follow me!'

Jack led them out of the waiting area and through a maze of corridors. Colm walked beside him, with Fatou, Tony and Hannington behind them.

'You've changed,' Colm said.

'Have I?' Jack said. 'Perhaps I have. It's been a long time.'

'Thirteen days,' Fatou said.

'Has it only been thirteen days?' Jack said. 'The lady on the plane was right. This is a war zone. I had never seen a bullet wound before. Now I've seen dozens. I was squeamish at the sight of blood. Now I don't notice it. I used to need ten hours sleep a night. I've not slept ten hours in total since I got here. I thought I knew some things, but I have learned how little I know.'

'You have changed,' Colm said. 'And those thirteen days have been very long.'

They walked in silence down another corridor.

'I saw hyena,' Colm said.

'Really? Where were they?'

'In Garamba, about two hundred kilometres from here.'

'Do you think I could go see them sometime?'

'You could ask the assistant warden if he would show you around. He might. You've helped his men, after all,' Colm said.

'I would like that,' Jack said. 'Do you know the assistant warden? Could you ask him for me?'

'I am the assistant warden,' Hannington said, making Jack jump.

———

Kwame was awake. He was sitting up in bed in a paper gown. He had bandages around his head and arms. He greeted then slowly.

'How are you, Kwame?' Fatou asked.

'Alive,' he said. 'And bored. I want to get back to work.'

———

'I enjoyed our chess games, Colm Reid. Though should you visit us again, I hope it will be less eventful,' Hannington said. Colm smiled and shook his hand.

'Fatou Ba, I hope you find a story for your audience.' She shook his hand.

'And Tony Kanagi, it has been most entertaining having you as a guest, but please, if you see Kennet Haven again, which I am sure you will, explain to him that the next time he gets a crazy idea, Garamba is unavailable. The only reason the army is letting you go and not hunting him down is that it was the Brotherhood of Souls that did all the damage and killed my men. The Soldiers of God did nothing but turn up to be scattered and killed. He was lucky. Very lucky.'

Tony nodded. He offered Hannington his hand. Hannington hesitated, then shook it.

They watched Hannington walk back to the Land Rover, the

same one in which he had picked Colm and Fatou up in nearly a
fortnight before. They watched as he drove away.

———

Tony's flight from Kinshasa left two hours before Colm and
Fatou's flight to Paris. They said goodbye at the gate.

'Where do you think Jane, Jomo and Kennet went?' Colm
said.

'Kenya. They might beat me back.'

'Why didn't they want to be rescued by the army? Kennet
was in a state.'

'I don't know. Perhaps because of Jomo. You say he saved
Jane's life twice, as well as Kennet's. But he was one of the Brotherhood. He would be wanted for theft, kidnapping, accessory to
five murders. Perhaps Jane didn't want to risk the DRC justice
system not being merciful.'

None of them said anything for a few moments. The noise of
the airport filled the space between them.

'Good to meet you, Tony, but like Hannington said, the next
time Kennet has an idea, please lose my number,' Colm said.

Tony nodded. He shook hands with both of them.

———

Colm and Fatou found a café and bought coffees.

'What angle will you take?' Colm asked her.

'With the story? I've been thinking about that. I see three
stories.'

Colm nodded.

'There's the story of the rhinos. Wiped out while the world
wasn't watching. There's the story of the last two weeks, of auda-

cious raids by terrorist groups, of theft, kidnapping, and heroic rescue and recovery by the Congolese army,' she went on.

'And there's the story of three men,' Colm finished.

'And there's the story of three men,' Fatou echoed. 'Agoyo, I mean Albert, Captain Rick – did you ever learn if Rick was his first name or his last name? No? – and Jomo. Same question about Jomo's name. Captain Rick was educated, wasn't he? You could hear it in his voice. And he'd travelled. Said he'd been to Ireland, recognised Kenya, South Africa, Scandinavia. And Agoyo and Jomo grew up in villages.' She took a drink. 'Do you remember, on the first day, something Kwame said, when you asked him why he did his job when so many were out to kill him?'

Colm nodded.

'It's going to be quite a story,' Fatou said.

'I'll send you mine if you send me yours,' Colm said.

'It's a deal.'

They finished their coffees in silence.

Eventually, their flight was called. They queued, standard class. They boarded. They were sitting many rows apart.

When the plane landed in Paris Fatou looked for Colm in the queue of more than three hundred, but she didn't see him again.

CHAPTER FIFTY-THREE

COLM LOOKED FOR FATOU AS THEY DISEMBARKED IN PARIS, but he didn't see her. He didn't look too hard, though, because he was distracted. Because, for the first time in fifteen days he had mobile signal. Niamh answered on the second ring.

'Where are ye?' she said without even a greeting.

'Charles de Gaulle. Paris.'

'I know where Charles de Gaulle is. Are you hurt?'

'No, my love, I am grand. Even lost some weight.'

Colm heard her exhale a thousand kilometres away.

'You coming home soon?' she said.

'As fast as I can.'

'Did you get my reply to your email?'

'Not yet – I rang you as soon as I had signal, I've not checked.'

Colm held the phone away from his ear and looked at it. There was a thin, keening sound coming from it.

'What's that?' he said.

'I have to go. Check your email,' she said, and hung up.

She phoned him back less than a second later.

'Hello?' he said.

'I've missed you,' she said. And hung up again.

He checked his email.

There were about twenty billion messages. He found the latest from Niamh.

It began, 'Our son was born...'

Colm stood in the queue, reeling. People walked round him. He stepped out of the queue and leaned against a wall as he read. His son had been born when he was in the forest, on the evening Jane Haven had appeared out of the rain and executed their captors. His son had a name. Cillian. 'Because it's a good Irish name, and he can't not have a name,' Niamh had written. Nothing, Colm was sure, to do with Niamh's crush on a certain actor.

'I have a son,' he said. No one heard him.

He joined the queue again.

Once through customs he found the gate for his flight to Dublin and settled to wait. He found a power socket, plugged in his charger, and started to write, his thumbs clumsy on the tiny keyboard. 'I had never heard of Garamba National Park three weeks ago,' he began. 'Perhaps many of you haven't either. It is a symbol. An example. A beacon. And the men who guard it lay down their lives to protect things that should be precious to all of us.' He kept writing, swearing occasionally as typos and auto-correct fought to turn his heart-felt words into a comic romp.

He paused when the flight was called. He joined another queue. On the plane he found his seat, switched the phone to flight mode, and kept writing. He wrote for the whole flight.

He came through customs in Dublin without a problem. In his mind he had expected there would be a sea of cards with names written on them, one of them reading "Reid". There wasn't. The only people waiting were an old couple, looking expectant. He didn't see who they were waiting for.

There was no queue at the taxi rank. There were no taxis either. He waited.

He read what he had written. He thought about Niamh and his son. He appreciated just how cool and pleasant and dry the air was.

'Where you going?' a voice said.

A taxi.

'Home,' Colm said.

————

Five hours later Colm lay in the most comfortable bed in the world, with the most beautiful woman in the world fast asleep next to him. He was exhausted as well, but his brain wasn't ready to stop, not yet.

In the corner of the room in his cot was Cillian. He had thick dark hair, and an angry red face. "Just like his da." Thanks, Niamh. But he smiled as he thought it.

He picked up his phone from the nightstand and opened the notes app where he'd written the story. He read it again. He made some changes. He selected the text, copied it, and opened the email app.

One of his twenty billion emails had been from the new editor. Ruadhán something. Good Irish name, Niamh had said. Ruadhán had wanted to know where he was, what he was doing, why he hadn't been into work for a fortnight, and what he had for morning copy.

Colm replied to the email and pasted the story into it. That was it. No commentary.

He searched the internet for Fatou Ba at *Le Post du Soir*. Found an email address. Pasted the story into an email and sent it to that address.

He put his phone back on the nightstand. He turned his head

to look at Niamh. Her face looked like she was free, in another world.

There was a chuntering from across the room. Colm slipped out of bed, walked to the cot. He looked inside. Two bright eyes were looking back at him.

'Wake me when he needs feeding,' Niamh had said. But she had also told him how to prepare the milk she'd expressed and left in the fridge.

Colm reached down and picked up the owner of the bright eyes. Holding Cillian to his chest, he slipped out of the bedroom and shut the door behind him with his foot as quietly as he could.

'I'm sorry I wasn't here when you arrived,' Colm said. 'But I will make up for it. I will feed you when you need feeding.'

Cillian twisted his face and clenched his whole body, his little fists tight. Colm started to get worried, but after a few seconds Cillian relaxed, keeping his eyes closed, and looking as if he'd fallen asleep again. A few seconds after that, Colm noticed the smell. Right now, feeding hadn't been Cillian's primary concern.

Niamh hadn't explained nappies. Feck it, she shouldn't have to. Colm had survived kidnap by not one but two terrorist organisations, he was afraid of nothing. And he had Google. He carried his son downstairs.

———

'I thought you were on paternity leave?' Bron said.

Colm looked up momentarily confused. He'd been trying to read an article in *Le Post du Soir*, which was difficult as it was written in French, and he had looked up eight words out of the first ten. It was Fatou's article. She'd beaten him to print by a day.

'I am. Ruadhàn asked me to come in.'

'Is that how you pronounce it?' Bron said. 'I just call him shiny suit. It's not your day for the desk. Get out of my chair.'

Colm smiled.

'Reid!' the voice came from the editor's office. It was the editor's assistant. A five-year-old called Tony. Well, probably closer to thirty in years, if not in temperament. 'He wants you now.'

I'll bet he does, Colm thought. He stood up and walked across the open plan. It was less than half full. It was early, and there had been cuts.

'Come in, come in,' Ruadhàn said. 'Sit down. Would you like a drink? There is coffee in the flask.'

Colm fancied a coffee. He was as exhausted as a man who had spent two weeks sleeping rough in a rain forest only to return to a home with a newborn baby in charge. He picked up a cup, held it under the nozzle of the flask and pressed the button. Nothing happened.

'Oh. Maybe it hasn't been filled yet. Never mind,' Ruadhàn said. 'Well done on this.' He waved a thin stack of A4 pages. 'I was against it when I heard about it, but you were already in the field. And I was wrong. Such writing. This is real journalism. This is global stuff. I'm running it front page tomorrow and giving it a lot more space in the Sunday supplement. I'm going to submit it for an Irish Press Award, and for a Daykin Award. It's just what we need, Reid. Though obviously we can't be sending you to Africa for a two-week holiday all the time, so you need to do the follow-up a bit more home-based, is that clear?'

Colm heard the words, and just smiled.

'Great. I will see you tomorrow, then!' Ruadhàn said.

'Actually, I am on paternity leave. I will be back next week.'

'Very good, very good.'

Ruadhàn was already looking at something on his computer screen. He'd forgotten Colm.

Colm left Ruadhàn's office and walked out onto the main floor.

Bron was at their shared desk. No point in going back there.

Colm headed for the lifts.

He was almost there when he heard his name called again.

'Reid? Spare me a minute?'

He looked back. Aileen O'Connor was standing in the doorway of one of the conference rooms, her arm out in invitation.

Colm accepted it and entered the room. He took a chair. Aileen shut the door behind her then sat opposite him. The table seated twenty. He felt like he was in a job interview. Excited and terrified at the same time.

'This is excellent, Reid. You have heart.' Aileen held up a copy of his story.

'Where did you get that?' he said. He'd only sent it to the editor and to Fatou.

Aileen waved her hand as if it was a stupid question.

'But this is better,' she said. She held up a copy of *Le Post du Soir*, the one with the article by Fatou in it. 'She has *detail*. Specifics. She is one to watch.'

Colm looked at the newspaper in Aileen's hand.

'You speak French?' he said.

'I'm a journalist, Reid, of course I speak French.'

Colm smiled.

'Would you mind if I took your photo?' he said. 'I know a fan of yours who would appreciate it.'

CHAPTER FIFTY-FOUR

FATOU WALKED INTO WORK A LITTLE LATE. WAITING FOR HER in her inbox was an email from Colm Reid at the Irish Telegraph. The subject was "Two things". There was no text, just two attachments.

The first was a photograph of award-winning journalist Aileen O'Connor, holding the copy of *Le Post du Soir* in which the first of Fatou's articles on the conflict in the centre of Africa had been published. Aileen was smiling and had her thumb up.

The second was the photo of a very new baby with thick dark hair and a screwed-up red face. The second photo had a caption.

'My dad wanted to name me Agoyo Jomo Reid. My mum thinks he's an eejit. My name is Cillian Reid.'

Fatou grinned.

ABOUT THE AUTHOR

Antony was born in Bradford and grew up in West Yorkshire, variously in Cleckheaton, Scholes, Moorend, and Ilkley. Grim and dour and wild. But also, magnificent and open and kind. Landscape, literature and a hint of mayhem rolled together from the start.

He later lived in York, Leeds, and Stevenage, the latter a town with no small literary association. Edward Bulwer-Lytton ("The pen is mightier than the sword") entertained Dickens at Knebworth House there, and E.M. Forster wrote Howards End in Rooks Nest, a house in the town. It was there that Antony wrote his first novel, *Hunted*. Sort of. He wrote quite a bit of it in Norwich. And quite a bit more of it in a hotel room in Bristol one sunny CrimeFest. And even more of it in the hour before work in East London. But he pulled it together in Stevenage, and that's what counts. Stevenage and Ilkley.

Once *Hunted* was published, in January 2021, he didn't hesitate – he got down to procrastinating the very next day. He wrote a sequel (*Endangered*) and a sequel to that (*Extinct*) and so it was obvious that the next novel he would publish was the prequel. He'll finish the edits on the other two any day now, he promises.

Antony now lives in Ilkley and can often be found walking the moors and making notes for another novel that he will not start before *Endangered* is finished. He won't, honestly.

www.antonydunford.com

www.twitter.com/antony_dunford

ACKNOWLEDGMENTS

The inspiration for this novel came from two real life attempts to find the last northern white rhinos in the wild. The first, in 2006, was by conservationist Lawrence Anthony, described in his book *The Last Rhinos*. The second, in 2009, was by presenter Stephen Fry, biologist Mark Carwadine and the BBC camera crew of the television series *Last Chance to See*. Lawrence reached Garamba but saw no rhinos. The BBC team were unable to travel to the region due to the ongoing conflict and reported that the rhinos were believed extinct in the wild, instead travelling to Ol Pejeta conservancy in Kenya where the last captive northern white rhinos were. In 2009 there were four of them. In 2016, the year when *Born the Same* is set, there were three. Today, in 2023, there are two. Najin, and her daughter, Fatu.

The descriptions of Garamba and Nagero were loosely taken from *Garamba: Conservation in Peace & War* an encyclopaedic work edited by Kes Hillman Smith and José Kalpers with Luis Arranz and Nuria Ortega. The book is out of print, so my thanks to Cathy Dean and Sam Lucock at *Save the Rhino* for helping me find a (signed!) copy that has been invaluable for research. The version of Garamba and Nagero presented in *Born the Same* is very much fiction, and all variations from reality are mine – *Born the Same* is not a travel guide.

I first wrote the story as a novella to present some of Jane and Kennet Haven's backstory as a teaser for the release of my first novel, *Hunted*. Unfortunately, whilst I created the character of Colm Reid to give the reader a pair of eyes unfamiliar with the region, the novella didn't really work as a taster for Jane and Kennet. It was very much Colm's story. I rewrote it as Jane's story, but it was not as good. It was forgotten about for some time until, towards the end of the summer of 2022 when I had been wrestling with getting the sequel to *Hunted* right for more than a year, I brought *Born the Same* out of its metaphorical drawer and blew the metaphorical dust off.

I used to work with a gentleman by the name of Colm Reid. When I left that place of employment he said, 'if you ever need a slightly grumpy Irishman for one of your stories, put me in!' The Colm Reid of *Born the Same* has a few similarities with the real one, but not many. The main similarity is the name. Any others you will have to ask him about. My thanks to him for making the challenge – the fictional him has been a joy to work with. I hope the non-fictional him wasn't joking when he offered himself as a character.

I would also like to thank a number of people for their time so freely given to read through and feedback and help protect the world from typos: Wendy Turbin, Judi Daykin and Bridget Walsh especially for reading the first full-length draft of this novel very quickly when the publication schedule was first laid down, and for not complaining at all when I rewrote the ending twice whilst they were reading it. Karen Taylor, Louise Mangos, Jayne Farnworth, Natasha Hutcheson, Elizabeth Saccente and Blu Tirohl for their comments and insights on the earlier versions. And special thanks to Joanna Brown, who not only read and shared thoughts on an earlier version of the story, but has also been a tireless promoter of *Hunted*, having personally given copies of it to her entire family and having convinced most of the population of rural Essex to buy it.

A special thank you to Louise Parker, generous and welcoming co-host of the writing retreat at which I did most of my final edits for *Born the Same*, and whose family in Western

Australia helped get *Hunted* one of its two Amazon bestseller flags.

Continuing in the selfless promotion vein, my thanks to Louise Slow for promoting *Hunted* on social media, and to John Blackburn for the same. John, if you read this far whilst on holiday, hello, and I hope you enjoyed this one too.

Thanks as well to Adrian and Rebecca of Hobeck Books who have patiently waited for this novel to arrive – the first draft I delivered in October 2021 was for a completely different novel (*Endangered*, the sequel to *Hunted*) that I have yet to finish. I'll be onto that next.

And thanks to the incredibly talented Jayne Mapp who designed another wonderful cover.

And finally, but most importantly, thanks to my Clare, for reading the first version of this two-and-a-half years ago when it rolled out of my head, and who has been instrumental in getting the full-length version finished by locking me in a room for nights on end and not letting me out till I'd finished it. And hello to Zach and Zoe, though I hope they don't read this till the summer as they both should be revising.

Antony
  Yorkshire, March 2023

HOBECK BOOKS - THE HOME OF GREAT STORIES

This book is the prequel to the Jane Haven series, Antony is currently (still) working on the second book. We hope there will be many more to follow after that.

If you've enjoyed this book, please sign up to **www.antony dunford.com** to read about Antony's inspirations, writing life and for news about his forthcoming writing projects.

Also please visit the Hobeck Books website **www.hobeck .net** for free downloads of short stories and novellas by a number of our authors. If you would like to get in touch, we would love to hear from you.

Hobeck Books also presents a weekly podcast, the Hobcast, where founders Adrian Hobart and Rebecca Collins discuss all things book related, key issues from each week, including the ups and downs of running a creative business. Each episode includes an interview with one of the people who make Hobeck possible: the editors, the authors, the cover designers. These are the people who help Hobeck bring great stories to life. Without them, Hobeck wouldn't exist. The Hobcast can be listened to from all the usual platforms but it can also be found on the Hobeck website: **www.hobeck.net/hobcast**.

Finally, if you enjoyed this book, please also leave a review on the site you bought it from and spread the word. Reviews are hugely important to writers and they help other readers also.

HUNTED

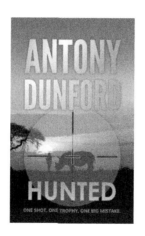

**Longlisted for a Crime Writers' Association John
Creasey (New Blood) Dagger 2022
Winner of a Chill With A Book Premier Readers' Award
Winner of a Chill With A Book Book of the Month Award
Longlisted for the 2020 Grindstone Literary Novel Prize
Shortlisted for the 2019 UEA Crime Writing Prize**

Once a member of the world's first all-female special forces unit, the Norwegian Hunter Troop, Jane Haven is now helping her brother Kennet protect some of the world's most endangered animals at his Kenyan Wildlife Conservancy.

Drawn away from her vigil protecting Douglas, the world's last remaining male Northern White rhino, Jane returns to find a scene of devastation and murder.

Everything and everyone Jane cares for is affected. But before she can track down the killers, Jane finds that

she's the one being hunted...

PRAISE FOR HUNTED

One target. One shot. One big mistake …
'In the Kenyan Savannah, Norwegian special forces veteran Jane Haven is one badass ranger you don't want to cross.' Jack Leavers, author of *Appetite for Risk*

'Hunted was incredible, really hard to put down.'
Colm Reid

'...a brilliantly crafted action adventure crime story, well paced and driven throughout' Freya Fowles ★★★★★

'Outstanding, the writing transported me to another world. It builds beautifully and gathers pace as it develops. I couldn't put it down and finished it in one sitting. More please!' James Leay
★★★★★

'This page turner is a winner on many fronts... The prose is stylish and descriptive. This is full throttle action crime fiction.' K. Taylor ★★★★★

'This is a terrific story in an evocative setting. It's extremely well written with lots of great dialogue and narrative.' Shona Inglis ★★★★★

'A real page turner.' Ian Donald ★★★★★

Printed in Great Britain
by Amazon

CW00517097

Pop-Up City

City-Making in a Fluid World

BIS Publishers
Building Het Sieraad
Postjesweg 1
1057 DT Amsterdam
the Netherlands
T +31 (0)20 515 02 30
F +31 (0)20 515 02 39
bis@bispublishers.nl
www.bispublishers.nl

ISBN 978 90 6369 354 1

Copyright © 2014 Jeroen Beekmans, Joop de Boer,
and BIS Publishers
Design by Vruchtvlees | vruchtvlees.com

Pop-Up City

City-Making in a Fluid World

Jeroen Beekmans

Joop de Boer

BIS

Preface

After covering temporary urbanism at Pop-Up City for six years, we knew that the time was right to reflect on how far pop-up thinking has travelled over the years and the manifold ways in which pop-up is revamping cities the world over. The chapters that follow are not just a collection of cool concepts and interesting initiatives; they are proof of a paradigm shift in how city-making happens, leading to changes in how cities are conceived, designed, and built.

On an ordinary weekday in April 2008, we spent at least fifteen minutes in front of a shop window in Berlin, taking photos of it from all sorts of angles. We were fascinated by the thick black letters in the window: 'Temporary Showroom.' The previous day, we had decided to start a small blog at popupcity.net about flexible, volatile, and temporary forms of architecture and urbanism, and we were eager to find any expressions of pop-up culture. Pop-up urbanism was not as pervasive in 2008 as it is today, and Pop-Up City was not the international platform with thousands of daily readers that it is today. At the time that we began writing on popupcity.net, urban planning and architecture were still the sole domains of the almighty architects and planners. The reason we started blogging in the first place was that we refused to think of cities as the product of master plans and fixed frameworks any longer. From the very beginning, we wanted to highlight the softer elements of city-making; the elements that have seen citizen-led initiatives provide small-scale improvements to

the city they live in. Starchitects play a role in transforming the concrete jungle into a cohesive city skyline, but they do not make cities — food truck owners, street artists, app makers, and rooftop farmers are the real city-makers. Even without knowing it, these city-makers eat, sleep, and breathe flexibility more than any brick and mortar structure ever could, and they are better able to cope with an environment of permanent change.

Our passion for the theme moved us to experiment with temporary city-making at Golfstromen, our creative agency. Pop-Up City's first headquarters was located in an empty building in the centre of Amsterdam that we transformed into a hyper-temporary art gallery and co-working space for three months over the summer. Our second office was a self-made, inflatable plastic bubble. In that same period, we turned an empty house into a psychedelic pop-up hotel, and we built the world's first one-person cinema inside of a cupboard in a residential building. Moreover, we have travelled extensively to cover events and uncover secrets in cities both near and far to see how people everywhere are doing pop-up city-making while meeting amazing individuals in the process. All of these efforts have resulted in a valuable collection of over 1,700 articles about the ideas that make the city of today and tomorrow, ranging from houses on wheels and playful urban space hacks to next-generation retail concepts and plug-in restaurants.

Our blog's content is as volatile as the themes that we write about; articles are easily lost in the ever-growing stack of blog posts and, although the subjects covered could appear to have a timeless quality, the Web remains hype-oriented. For this reason, we began to consider presenting Pop-Up City in more durable and memorable ways. In 2013, we were approached by Museon, a Dutch museum located in The Hague, to co-curate an exhibition on future urbanism, and translate Pop-Up City into a tangible physical format that you could walk around, touch, and explore in a way that digital publishing cannot offer. In that same year, we were given the chance to host a live urbanist variety show in a theatre in Amsterdam that brought the blog's content to life on stage with interviews, panel discussions, and even some delicious live cooking. After having manifested Pop-Up City in the form of events, it became time to explore other platforms with a longer shelf life. The next logical step in metamorphosing Pop-Up City was to write a book. For us, writing the Pop-Up City book was a way to reflect upon years of hard work, to get inspired once more by the greatest ideas we have showcased in the past, and to distill useful strategies for flexibility-oriented urban development in a fluid world.

There are numerous people worthy of our gratitude for this process. First of all, we have to spend some words on Chad Smith, a New York-based architect and blogger who has played a crucial role in Pop-Up City's existence. The funny thing is that he (probably) has no idea. In December 2008, we thought about ending our little blogging project, considering it to be a failed experiment with little regular readership. That month, Smith published a brief article about our design agency, Golfstromen, and our fresh blog on Yanko Design,

a popular international design platform. There, our work was described as "refreshingly free of any slickness, recognisable form, or even coherence." While our look may be somewhat slicker than before and we like to think of ourselves as coherent individuals, Yanko Design's glowing review of Pop-Up City in its infancy gave us a second wind and a renewed confidence in why we wanted to cover the temporary elements of the modern city. The visitor explosion that resulted from Smith's post made us realise that blogging is not only about choosing the right angle — it is also about keeping yourself motivated and inspired to write.

Many people have contributed, directly or indirectly, to this book. The articles written by us and our contributors over the past years have formed the basis for everything that is in the following chapters. In addition, there are plenty of wonderful people who have expressed their faith in the project during our crowdfunding campaign on Kickstarter, which helped us turn this ambition into a reality. Without this support, the book simply would not exist.

We would like to mention here in particular the names of the people who have supported us over the past year to make this book happen. First of all, we would like to thank our editor Adam Nowek for writing this book together with us, and helping us take its content to a higher level. His extensive knowledge of city-making (and ice hockey), the English language, and great sense of humour have made the process of making this book a true pleasure. Hannah Cook, Rebekka Keuss, and Melody Moon have done a great job collecting photo material as well as writing and editing the texts of the numerous inspiring examples showcased throughout the book. Without Stijn Hupkes and Rebekka, there would have been no Kickstarter campaign. Stijn created the amazing project video, and Rebekka's great sense of copywriting has helped us a lot in launching the project online. We also owe graphic design studio Vruchtvlees our gratitude. Without their immense talents, the book would not have looked this great.

Finally, we want to thank the people we started this journey for in the first place: our readers. We thank you for coming back each and every day, for reading our articles, and for sharing your inspiration with us. You keep us going!

Jeroen Beekmans and Joop de Boer
Amsterdam
April 2014

1

An
Introduction

~~~~~~~~~~~~~~~~

2

Living in the
Pop-Up City

~~~~~~~~~~~~~~~~

3

Work Life in the
Pop-Up City

~~~~~~~~~~~~~~~~

4

Food in the
Pop-Up City

~~~~~~~~~~~~~~~~

Urban Hack-tivism and the Facebook Generation

Shop 'til You Pop!

Marketing the City with Chocolate Bars

New Strategies for New Urbanscapes

Flexible Cities with Fluid Citizens

Flexible Cities with Fluid Citizens

An Introduction

Our cities are growing and changing faster and more drastically than at any other point in human history. Cities are gaining more influence over their internal affairs, allowing them to be major players in global societal, cultural, technological, and economic transformation processes. In order to better weather the winds of change, cities must be adaptable to unexpected needs, a state that the majority of cities have yet to achieve. Under the gleaming surface of urban planning rhetoric, an entire culture of inspiring and refreshing bottom-up initiatives and pop-up design projects are helping urbanites change the way they use and make the city of tomorrow.

The Crisis Years

Few could have imagined that 2008 would be a watershed year in the trajectory of the world's cities and their inhabitants, but here we are. A highly complex and undoubtedly corrupt economic system began to show the weaknesses in its armour and, whether unconsciously or not, prompted world citizens to behave in a different way. At the same time, a growing sense of mistrust between governments, citizens, and the private sector has emerged, due largely to a host of troubling developments such as terrorist activity, natural disaster mismanagement, and general dissent within the polity. Governments began to be seen as obstacles to progress, rather than the forces that prompt positive change. As

less willingness to contribute funds for urban regeneration. Complicating things even further is the looming threat of peak oil, forcing the creators of our built environments to rethink the energy sources for our architecture and our infrastructure. Creative solutions to continue building liveable cities had to be sought for. Urban planning, a field formerly known for wholesale neighbourhood development, suddenly began using a new vocabulary awash with buzzwords: placemakers interested in the DNA of the city applied urban acupuncture to solve new problems. Empty lots and vacant buildings became the breeding grounds for the creative class, giving place to shipping container villages for temporary housing, urban farms and trendy pop-up nightclubs. People started doing

We view Pop-Up City as an inspiring series of snapshots showing innovation and passion from individuals in cities across the globe

an alternative, citizens had to start thinking and doing in new ways, taking ideas from bottom-up governance strategies. New structures for decision-making, financing, governing, managing, and producing had to be thought of in order to prevent western society as a whole from driving over the edge of a cliff.

The way that cities were built and managed was also changing. Buildings, whichever type, could no longer be constructed with the same ease and levels of investment as before, with governments and other institutions showing

it themselves, crowdfunding their 3-D printed projects with aplomb. New money had to be found and companies and wealthy philanthropists were interested in stepping in.

Almost purely by chance, we joined the search for alternative ways to make the contemporary city by featuring them on our blog, Pop-Up City. In that sense, Pop-Up City could be considered a crisis blog, finding unique strategies in an era of widespread uncertainty. You can, if you prefer, read this book as a guide to crisis urbanism, but that glosses over a significant part of the story. Pop-Up City was already around before the crisis, so it would be somewhat reductive to say that we are only focussed on cataclysmic urban initiatives. We prefer to view the extensive archives of Pop-Up City as an inspiring series of snapshots showing innovation and passion from individuals in cities across the globe, regardless of whatever obstacles may be present.

The Internet of Cities

This new perspective of city life, one not based upon being in a fixed space but based upon a psychogeographical perspective that 'the city' consists of a worldwide network of disparate yet connected urban centres, comes from a very real sense of hyper-connectivity. One only needs to look at a network map for a reasonably sized airline or the traffic analytics reports for a website with impressive global reach to get a sense of how no stone remains unturned in the Internet age. We can be anywhere we want at any time (or, at the very least, a relatively short amount of time), a thought that barely crosses our minds when we board a Delhi-bound flight in Los Angeles. The city is no longer in isolation, but rather is part of an interconnected matrix that transcends space and time.

This connectivity has entrenched itself as a natural element in our lives. It feels normal, even natural, for us to have access to a world of information in our pocket. Cisco, the American networking technology corporation, estimated in 2013 that there are over 10 billion 'things'

connected to the Internet, be they laptops, smartphones, alarm clocks, cars, cows, televisions, or our own bodies. 39% of the world's population in 2013 is able to use the Internet, and in the world's highly developed countries that proportion sits at 77%. On the surface this is a victory for efficiency: perpetual connectivity offers us the opportunity to better organise a busy schedule or perform tasks that were once using slower methods involving now-antiquated technologies (paper, for instance). The mobile phones of yesteryear have evolved from simplistic communication devices into the productivity-oriented smart devices of today and beyond.

A connected world is a socially enhanced world as well. While we might bemoan the person that just cannot put their phone down at the dinner table, it is easier than ever before to interact with people in faraway places, both in social and productive ways, as large swathes of the population invest more time interacting with their online contacts rather than those that they can engage in a face-to-face conversation with. Setting up a date for a group dinner or a protest can happen through a few flicks of the thumb. Digital connectivity fanned the flames of massive movements such as the Arab Spring, Euromaidan, and Occupy Wall Street, transforming them from small-scale demonstrations to globally connected movements using Facebook events and Twitter hashtags to relay important information and even inspire satellite events in faraway places. At the governmental level, militaries are using unmanned aerial vehicles as security agencies battle attacks from activist groups or foreign agents, even shifting how we conceive of something extremely physical such as warfare. Once incredibly complex tasks are reduced to basic commands on a handheld digital device.

These technological developments have led to changes in the way we think, behave, and interact with spaces. It is difficult to imagine, but humanity is changing at a fundamental level as you read this. Children are now growing up having never experienced a world without touchscreen devices, resulting in a visually-oriented society. A population thinking and doing with a completely realigned perception requires a new kind of city-making.

Building for Adaptability

The way contemporary cities are made no longer fits the dynamic of the age. Why does a society in which people become exponentially more flexible and mobile by the minute fail to make cities more adaptable to change? Cities are intense sites of activity and innovation, and yet most urban planning departments appear to be stuck in a postwar mode that fails to address the needs of new activities and new users.

Modern cities are a mixture of ego-driven architecture, profit-oriented pursuits, and long-term master plans. Office developments are designed for the first entity to use them, leaving inflexible spaces for future tenants once the original tenant packs their bags for greener pastures in the next fashionable building. Every city is littered to varying degrees with vacant buildings designed for perpetuity in an age of uncertainty, though this is not merely a result of tough economic times. At a fundamental level, there is a mismatch between the built environment and the actual use patterns of the city. Spaces, be they public or private, are being used in less predictable ways, muddling the role of planners and architects. A reformed kind of urbanism recognises the need for multifunctional spaces and places that can adapt to unexpected uses.

A healthy and successful metropolis must be aware of its surroundings, its assets, and its competitors in order to develop itself in a constructive manner, allowing space for impermanence. In the coming chapters, we present a diverse collection of temporary initiatives and projects that we have found in cities all over the world. These instances of pop-up urbanism give us an indication on how today's urbanite, as a new stakeholder in urban design, can positively transform his or her surroundings.

Whether it is a more efficient way of shopping for groceries or a tiny urban hack that offers convenience for commuters waiting at a bus stop, we see Pop-Up City as the city of the not-too-distant future: it is a city where existing urban planning frameworks and architectural landscapes do not hinder spontaneous human activity, but rather serve as an encouraging platform for innovative and inspirational activities to flourish. Chapter Two looks at how living spaces are becoming increasingly temporary, more easily transportable, and more fused with urban amenities and professional activities.

Chapter Three moves on to working life and the innovations that are inspiring contempo-

we have found that the Pop-Up City is everywhere: citizens in all urban areas are becom-

Spaces, be they public or private, are being used in less predictable ways, muddling the role of planners and architects

rary employees and freelancers to work from almost anywhere in the urban realm. By the time we reach Chapter Four, we find ourselves a bit hungry for information on food production and consumption in the modern city centre. Chapter Five investigates the way we shop and how this is affected by technological advancements that are easily installed onto a smartphone. Chapter Six examines public spaces and how interventions of all sizes are making them more inclusive and enjoyable for all. Finally, Chapter Seven looks at how pop-up urbanism is affecting and refreshing processes of urban development in cities across the globe. All of the projects presented on these pages are helping us change the way we think about building better, more resilient urban areas: urban areas teeming with temporary pop-up initiatives are prompting cities themselves to become more responsive and more adaptable to the needs and desires of locals and visitors alike.

All of the initiatives and trends featured on the following pages contribute in their own small way to a conversation of how we are beginning to re-conceptualise the city through the efforts of creative individuals with limited resources. After years of relentless digital globetrotting,

ing less reliant on inflexible urban governments and becoming more so on their immediate social and professional networks in order to make positive changes to their urban landscapes.

Plastic Cocoons, Container homes, and Lofts With Legs

Container Homes, Plastic Cocoons, and Lofts with Legs

Living in the Pop-Up City

Nowadays, we move to more places more often and we travel further distances than ever before. Humanity is loosening itself from a fixed relationship with place. The option to be a part of anything, from a social movement to a company, anywhere in the world, offers us incredible freedom, but can also lead to restlessness and the feeling of missing out on being involved in a community. In the past, the workplace was a massive determining factor of where to live, ensuring that your daily commute would not consume hours each day. What happens, though, when work has turned fluid and spreads everywhere and nowhere? Never before in history have we ever had access to more international contacts in order to make ends meet. Even interpersonal relations are becoming more flexible, with divorce rates at their highest in human history. Home ownership is declining amongst younger generations, due to the barriers to entry into the housing market as well as a fear of spatial commitment. Despite all of this flexibility, houses remain static physical objects - beacons of peace and rest in a fluid world - but, at the same time, it is dragging us down.

The Urban Nomad in a Globalising World

The mortgage: a word that literally means death pledge, it often requires a contractual obligation of thirty years, demanding steady, long-term employment. As a consequence of increasingly flexible lifestyles, many people around the world are unwittingly tied to an environment that no longer suits their needs or even their lifestyles. The average expected stay of a first-time buyer of a single-family house in the United States has already declined from sixteen to eleven years. Renting is increasingly becoming the preferred mode of living stretching beyond the wild and carefree days of youth. Rental homes now house families, seniors, and single professionals with greater frequency. Almost all aspects of life have become less binding. In extreme cases of lifetime renting, people become modern nomads, defined by the eminent Urban Dictionary as "anyone who has not lived in one place more than three years in the last decade of their life and has no idea when or where they will ever settle down for good."

The traditional arrangement of the living environment prevents many of us from committing to the lifestyle that has been made possible by new technologies. Although these flexible lifestyles are not suitable or accessible to the majority, we see more and more social groups incorporating flexibility into the way they live. As a result of globalisation, two travelling classes are created: one on the higher rungs of the societal ladder that is able to enjoy the benefits of international air travel and convenience-based technologies, and one in the lower sector that selectively acquires particular benefits to a flexible world due to cost or time restraints. As a result, both groups are increasingly reliant on temporary, adaptable living arrangements to varying degrees. While their nomadic lifestyles differ enormously, mobility and flexibility are characteristics that are shared by all.

The term *urban nomad* refers to those in the upper echelon of society, with lifestyles that bear similarities to those of Bedouin nomads. However, these social groups do not travel through the desert from one oasis to another at great risk to personal safety and health, but instead

Many people around the world are unwittingly tied to an environment that no longer suits their requirements or even their lifestyles

Moreover, they "cannot call themselves 'locals' anywhere, because they have not been there long enough and probably will not be."

roam the international cityscape searching for a place to work and earn a living. The urban nomad is not wrapped in a linen robe to protect him from the scorching desert sun, but is dressed in a tailored business suit that helps open the proverbial doors to the world. It is not a camel that carries his possessions, but a stylish four-wheeled suitcase, preferably small enough to take as a carry-on for international flights.

For resting and sleeping, the urban nomad depends on ephemeral residential concepts, which are traditionally facilitated by hotels. 40% of the hotel bookings in the United States are business-related, while over 65% of the guests stay for only one or two nights. When staying for more than a week or less than a day, new concepts aim to fill the gap to increase living efficiency and convenience. Japanese capsule hotels offer micro-chambers to those in desperate need for a quiet place to rest for a few hours. Tired workers finding themselves too far from home to go back for a nap and do not want to be caught falling asleep at work can rent a hotel room for a quiet place to rest for a few hours. One example of this is Nap Cafe Corne, a micro-hotel and bar specifically for women that offers a place of solitude to recharge for the remainder of the workday. Sleepbox is another concept of small hotel pods that can be installed anywhere, creating an instant hotel room wherever and whenever necessary, such as hospitals, shopping malls, office buildings, or airports. Sleepboxes have been installed at Moscow's Sheremetyevo International Airport, providing globetrotters with a place to get a bit of rest before that transcontinental flight to Narita.

Shared and Parasite Houses

In many global cities, the number of expatriates is growing exponentially. Cities with considerable expatriate communities, such as Singapore and Hong Kong, are home to neighbourhoods that primarily host foreigners. The arrival of airplanes full of foreigners seeking work has resulted in an influx of people with little knowledge of the local language or social mores. According to a 2012 article in *The Guardian*, there is a growing discontent amongst Berliners who are actively protesting against the presence of expatriates temporarily settling in the city to live the Berlin dream, which, in their opinion, compromises the 'authentic' atmosphere of neighbourhoods such as Friedrichshain and Neukölln, and increases the rents for locals.

While some locals in cities across the globe are taking a critical stance against the influx of guest workers from other parts of the world, other cities look for new concepts to allocate this nomadic workforce. Online peer-to-peer platforms such as Airbnb and Wimdu offer marketplaces for empty apartments and rooms, providing a useful service for urban nomads to find quick and easy accommodation with a home-like atmosphere. Conversely, it is often flexible workers that rent out their rooms while abroad temporarily. In fact, the flexible class tends to share their houses. Airbnb offers a popular short-stay housing solution that fills a niche market between a hotel and an apartment. With rooms in 34,000 cities in

▷ CONTINUED ON PAGE 27

PACO: A Second Skin from Tokyo
–

Japanese architects Jo Nagasaka and Schemata Architects have designed PACO, a complete house in the form of a three-by-three metre cube. It is intended as a second home, with the minimal equipment required for living, including a hammock, shower, desk, and sink. The architects created PACO as a conceptual model to investigate a new, flexible lifestyle.

POPUPCITY.NET/1429

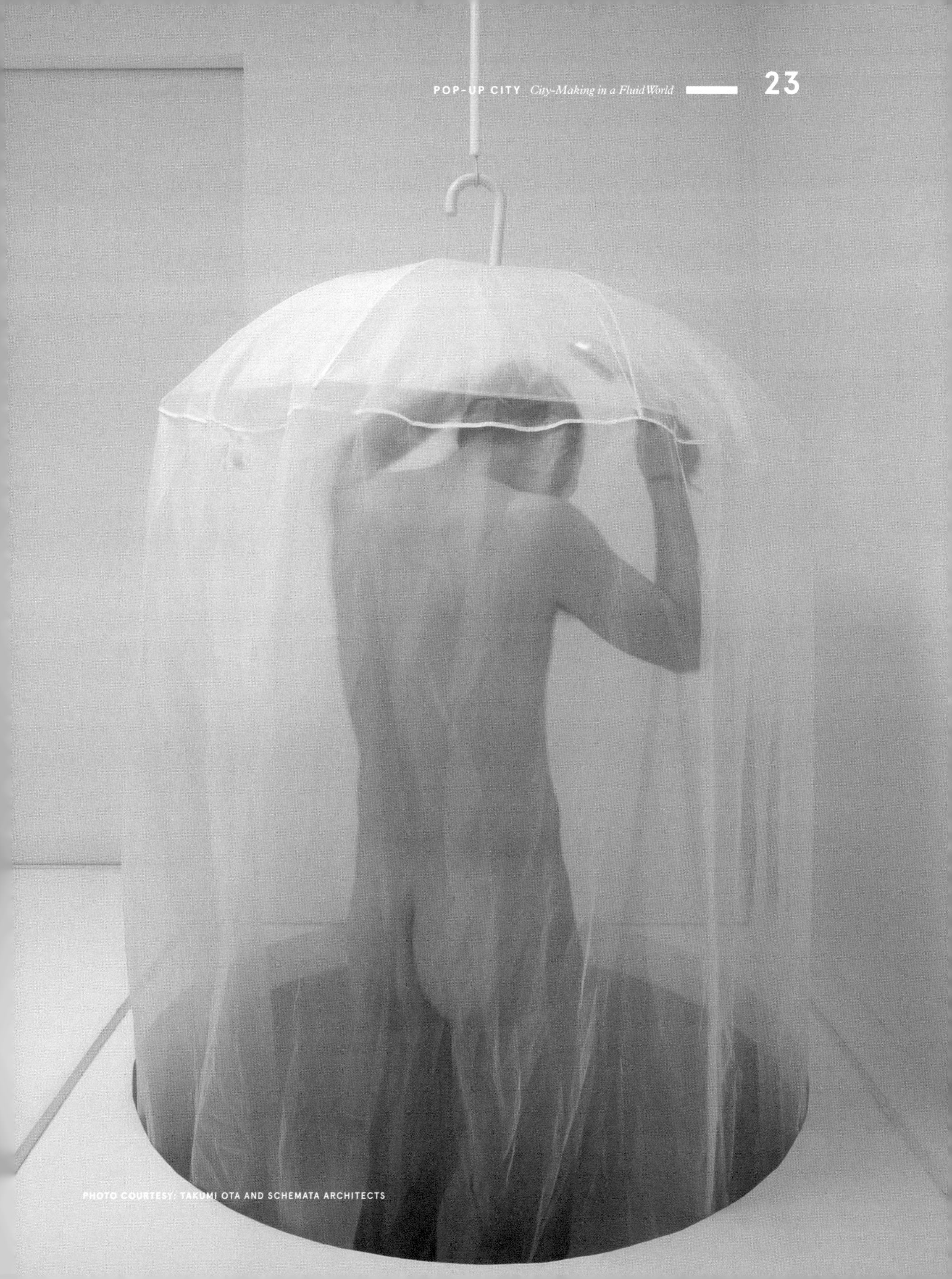

PHOTO COURTESY: TAKUMI OTA AND SCHEMATA ARCHITECTS

It's a Nap in a Box!

—

Design office Arch Group has developed the Sleepbox, capsules designed to give people the opportunity to take a nap inside of busy urban environments such as airports, train stations, and shopping malls. The capsules have also proven capable of regenerating derelict buildings. The four-storey Sleepbox Hotel in Moscow contains 46 sleeping units for up to two people on the second and third floor, and ten single-person boxes on the top floor.

POPUPCITY.NET/26555

PHOTO COURTESY: ARCH GROUP

Tiny Pop-Up Modules for Students

Swedish architecture firm Tengbom has put together a sustainable, innovative, compact yet exciting response to the growing problem of student housing. Twenty-two pop-up modules are planned to appear on Lund University's Campus offering a small home suitable for one student and comprising of a sleeping loft, kitchen, bathroom, and small garden patio. With an efficient and ecologically friendly design, the project challenges the prototypical designs for student accommodation that needs to be increasingly flexible for the different needs of a globalised student base.

POPUPCITY.NET/30134

PHOTO COURTESY: TENGBOM

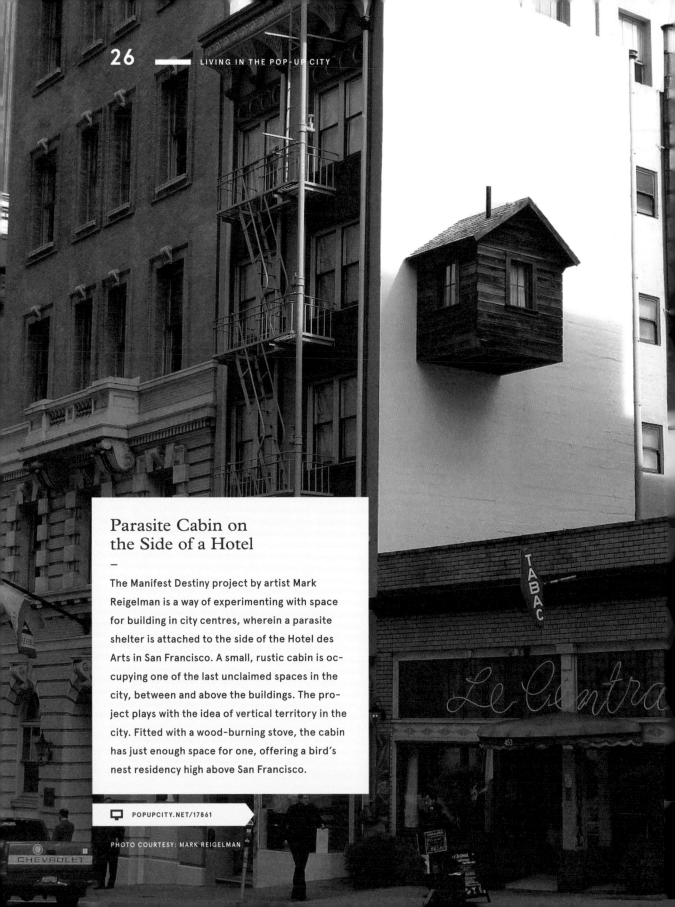

Parasite Cabin on the Side of a Hotel

–

The Manifest Destiny project by artist Mark Reigelman is a way of experimenting with space for building in city centres, wherein a parasite shelter is attached to the side of the Hotel des Arts in San Francisco. A small, rustic cabin is occupying one of the last unclaimed spaces in the city, between and above the buildings. The project plays with the idea of vertical territory in the city. Fitted with a wood-burning stove, the cabin has just enough space for one, offering a bird's nest residency high above San Francisco.

POPUPCITY.NET/17861

PHOTO COURTESY: MARK REIGELMAN

192 countries, Airbnb has swiftly become the worldwide leader in accommodation. Trust and credibility are the main drivers of this massive success, pushing other types of conventional hospitality and accommodation in an unprecedented manner. Thanks to online developments, a reliable system of mutual trust and credential payments has been created with the potential to change the way people find lodging. Civic governments around the world generally have no policy framework to respond to the peer-to-peer accommodation trend, with many cities such as Amsterdam and New York unsure of the legal positioning of those renting out a room.

Another option to live a flexible life without spending time in hotels alone is the mobile apartment block. One example comes from German designer Werner Aisslinger. Aisslinger's twenty square metre parasite apartment

all of the eccentric and unnecessary parts of architecture are stripped away in a manner that it can be placed just about anywhere, offering the intimacy of a private home in an efficient and minimal design. Ideas such as these provide the flexible urbanite with a living space that need not be spatially fixed.

The Dark Side of Flexible Housing

Not everyone in the world can afford a life in hotels, Airbnb flats, and parasite apartments transported by helicopter. As attractive as a more flexible lifestyle is to many individuals, it can be a costly endeavour that many are simply forced into. Those that cannot afford a more adaptive lifestyle, often migrant workers or refugees, depend on flexible shelters, illegal

> Hong Kong's informal housing market is a very real manifestation of the downside to living in a highly globalised alpha world city

known as The Loft Cube can be lifted by helicopter and lowered onto an existing building, enabling affluent urban nomads to combine a flexible lifestyle with the domesticity of home ownership in a unique location that is impermanent. A similarly minimalist living concept comes from Japanese architects Jo Nagasaka and Schemata Architecture Office. The concept, called PACO, is a box for living wherein

subletting, or squatting. These social groups come up with rather creative solutions to their acute housing issues, though often at great cost to personal safety, hygiene, and well-being.

Hong Kong is an apt example of the dark side of living flexibility. The city's high-rises are awash with informal rooftop communities built by migrants with questionable legality.

▷ CONTINUED ON PAGE 31

Billboard Turned into an Artist Residency

Mexican paper company Scribe has devised a way of combining advertising and public art by launching Scribe Billboard, a temporary residency for artists located inside of a billboard. The residences offer a kitchen, bathroom, and desk space, all accessed through a hidden door on the face of the billboard. During the artist's stay, they produce a mural on the blank billboard space. The Scribe Billboard is one of numerous public exposure projects that promote both the artist and the company.

POPUPCITY.NET/27710

PHOTO COURTESY: SCRIBE MEXICO

Belgian Artist Transforms Billboards into Homes

—

Given that billboards can be as large as small apartments, it seems only natural that Belgian artist Karl Philips combined living and advertising in his project The Good, the Bad, and the Ugly. The project transforms billboards into parasite apartments, allowing inhabitants to make a living out of a structure that was generally not seen as a liveable structure. These mobile, live-in advertisements make for inconspicuous living spaces, appearing as regular billboards to passers-by. Philips's project is an ideal option for the nomadic city-dweller that may be short on rent money but in excess of living space.

 POPUPCITY.NET/29258

PHOTO COURTESY: KRISTOF VRANCKEN

IKEA Launches Flat-Pack Modular Refugee Shelter

With plenty of experience in manufacturing prefab designs, IKEA has teamed up with the Office of the United Nations High Commissioner for Refugees (UNHCR) to launch a modular refugee shelter that can be set up in four hours, accommodating up to five individuals. The structure's lightweight construction is composed of a steel frame with lightweight polymer panels, all of which come collapsed in a cardboard box. IKEA's temporary housing is more flexible, easier to transport, and simpler to assemble than the poorly designed canvas ridge or hoop tents that generally house refugees. This low-cost temporary housing represents a new outpost of flexible architecture in humanitarian efforts.

 POPUPCITY.NET/29419

PHOTO COURTESY: IKEA FOUNDATION

Emergency Housing in Five Hours

Pieter Stoutjesdijk, a graduate of the Delft University of Technology, has designed an emergency shelter that can be set up within an astonishing five hours. Challenged to design an emergency shelter after the disaster of the Haitian earthquake in 2010 that could be quickly made and distributed to those in need, Stoutjesdijk used a CNC milling machine that laser cuts the 2,484 fiberboard pieces required to construct the shelter. This quick-fit shelter is suited to the tropical climate of places such as Haiti and can receive a special coating to ensure waterproofing and at least a fifteen-year lifespan. Furthermore, the design of the house allows for steam, electricity and drinking water for those inhabiting it.

 POPUPCITY.NET/30351

PHOTO COURTESY: PIETER STOUTJESDIJK

Hong Kong is a city with an extremely limited proportion of developable land, resulting in housing that is small, unaffordable, or both. As a result, communities of migrant workers illegally settle on the roofs of buildings, where they build new micro-villages. Cage homes are also an informal solution to housing price issues in Hong Kong. These homes, located in decrepit tenement structures, are characterised by dormitory-style bunk beds that are surrounded by cage wire to keep one's belongings safe from theft. These accommodations are not designed with families in mind, but rather to maximise space use for living, if one can call it that. Hong Kong's informal housing market is a very real manifestation of the downside to living in a highly globalised alpha world city: despite Hong Kong's placement at the pinnacle of The Economist's spatially-adjusted liveability index in 2012, housing typologies such as these indicate that there is room for civic governments to intervene and provide housing options with a similar flexibility in mind but with more humane conditions at a lower price point. Adequate housing is, after all, a human right, especially in a high-density urban environment.

The most extreme examples of flexible housing typologies are found in the world's temporary 'cities': refugee camps constructed at the fringes of the world's geopolitical hotspots. Temporary shelters in these places that seemingly pop up out of nowhere are often used for a much longer period of time than initially designed for. This is precisely why more and more designers and architects are creating new concepts for this impermanent way of living. Swedish furniture retailer IKEA has teamed up with the United Nations to create a flat-pack house that can be set up within a few hours. Similar to their entire line of furniture, IKEA's flat-pack house comes in a plain cardboard box with the typical IKEA instruction booklet, nuts, and bolts. Once assembled, the shelter provides accommodation for one family and generates its own electricity with solar panels embedded in the rooftop. While IKEA's emergency flat-pack house can only be shipped to people in need of an emergency shelter, one Dutch designer need only e-mail the necessary files. The plans for Pieter Stoutjesdijk's do-it-yourself emergency house can be downloaded from the Internet and laser-cut by the nearest local laser cutter. Within an astonishing five hours only, Stoutjesdijk's shelter, which consists of 2,484 parts, can be assembled without tools or any additional materials due to a friction fit design.

Applied designs such as easy-to-assemble emergency shelters and more spontaneous designs such as cage homes are signs of humanity's ability to adapt to circumstances. As flexible solutions tend to be oriented towards a more upmarket clientele, these developments are a testament to how flexibility in living situations is having an effect on all socio-economic levels of the world's societies.

Pop-Up Residences for the Poor

Housing designs in this category are not only necessary for the world's most troubled regions, but also for those languishing in highly-devel-

▷ CONTINUED ON PAGE 34

Parasites Harvest the City's Spoiled Energy

—

Michael Rakowitz explores the concept of energy parasitism in his project ParaSITES, in which sleeping bags and igloo-like structures are attached to wasted hot air sources, transforming them into sleeping places for homeless people or tourists. Rakowitz's innovative urban activism experiments with the possibility of reusing wasted energy in urban areas.

🖵 POPUPCITY.NET/24846

PHOTO COURTESY: MICHAEL RAKOWITZ

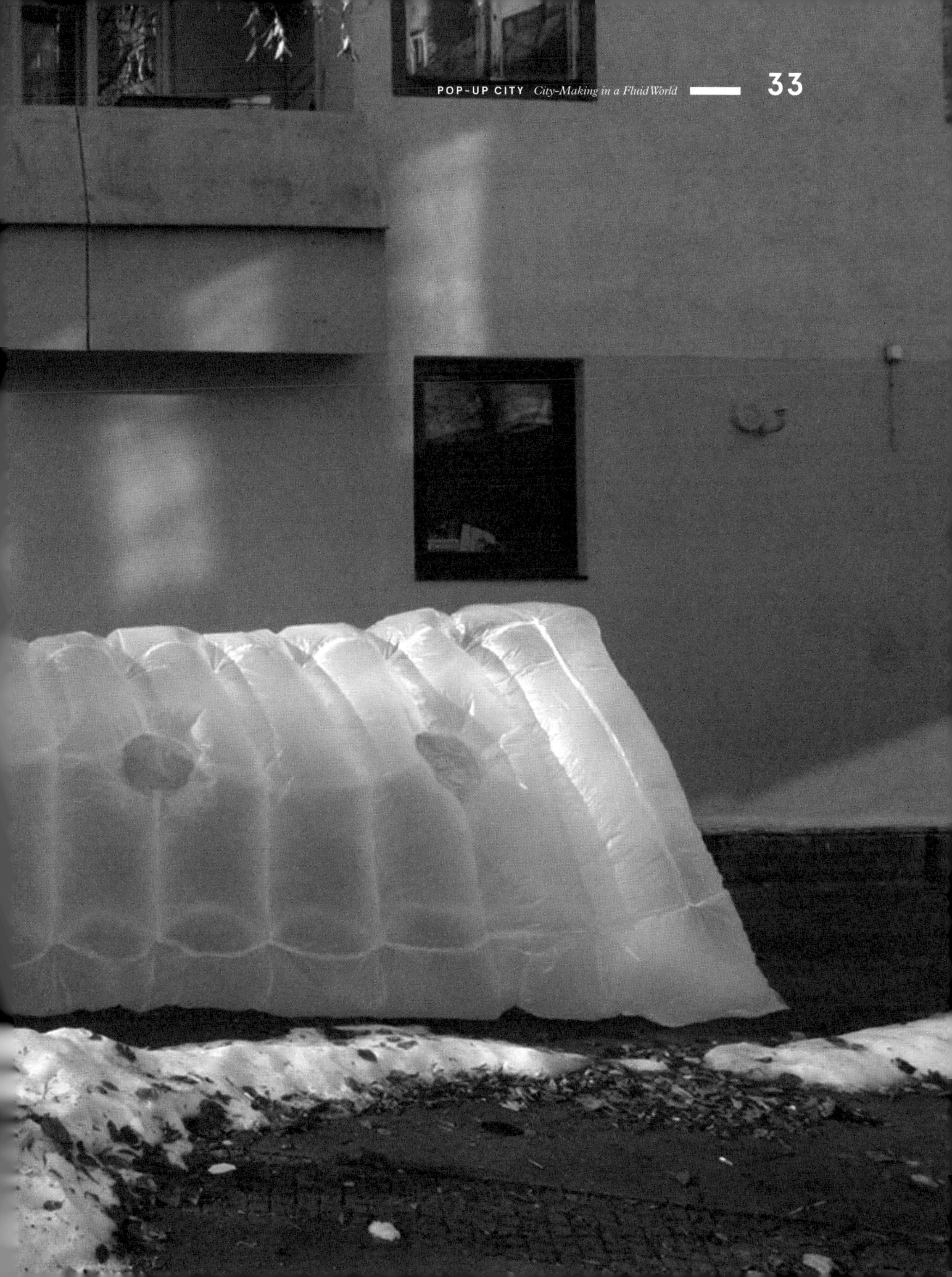

oped urban areas. In recent years, many designers have worked to develop solutions for these cities. They form a group of the smallest urban housing solutions, although you could ask yourself whether they provide serious accommodation. Artist Michael Rakovitz has constructed a series of portable inflatable shelters to be used by homeless individuals in colder cities.

continue to face unprecedented inflows of job-seekers from the country's rural areas who generally cannot afford to buy or rent a house when they arrive in the huge, expensive, and over-populated metropolis. Design studio People's Architecture Office (PAO) came up with a solution in the form of a mobile Tricycle House that can be taken anywhere by means of pedals.

Real freedom begins when our material burden is minimised

His ParaSITE shelters harvest the energy that escapes from buildings by attaching one end of the shelter to a hot air ventilation shaft of an adjacent building to warm the home. Another artist, Winfried Baumann, established the Urban Nomad series, which produces instant shelters, kitchens, and medical stations geared both towards the homeless and the more affluent. Many of the shelters, which fall somewhere between art and product design, appear focussed on the tech-savvy urbanite, some featuring docking stations for a laptop so that owners can look at their screens on-the-go. A slightly more luxurious option is the micro-house, a home designed for people seeking non-rental accommodation but cannot quite afford an expensive apartment. Micro-houses are small, mobile, and flexible, but complete with all the necessities for a home, including a bed, dining table, kitchen, water tank, bathtub, and stove, all neatly and precisely stacked on top of a footprint of only four to five square metres.

Internal migration in many countries is also causing cities to swell in population numbers to the point where residents experience housing shortages. Many Chinese cities, for instance,

The Tricycle House is a fully equipped modular house that can be extended to a bigger size thanks to its accordion-like construction. Several Tricycle Houses can be combined in order to form one large modular house or even an entire village. Although the concept is rather utopian and not necessarily affordable for those who cannot afford conventional housing, design concepts such as the Tricycle House mark a development in thinking about hyper-flexible housing at an affordable price point in the world's fastest growing cities. Increasing rental costs in Beijing inspired architecture graduate Dai Haifei in 2010 to make a small one-person home for himself in the shape of an egg. At under €750, Dai's pop-up apartment enabled him to spend his nights close to the company where he interns. The City Egg is made of impressively simple materials, including sack bags, bamboo, wood chippings, and grass seeds. The seeds will grow naturally and will create an isolating wall. Two small wheels enable the City Egg to move wherever the owner chooses.

▷ CONTINUED ON PAGE 48

A Mini-Camper for Bicycle Riders

—

Artist Kevin Cyr has designed a camper specifically meant for cyclists. The piece is part of a greater project called Home in the Weeds, described by Cyr as "examin[ing] the idea of shelter as a safe haven for a future worst-case scenario as well as more optimistic notions of home and self-preservation." The micro-caravan emulates a full-sized camper, complete with power outlets and reflectors, perfect for the mobile urban dweller.

POPUPCITY.NET/13963

PHOTO COURTESY: KEVIN CYR

Swedish Concept Hotel Offers Homeless Experience

—

Faktum Hotels in Gothenburg, Sweden has foregone the traditional route of traditional rooms for places that the city's homeless might use. Meant to raise awareness of the homeless living in the area, visitors book rough 'bedrooms' in ten locations where homeless people are known to stay. Revenues are used to support the charity work of Faktum Magazine.

 POPUPCITY.NET/26069

Modular Accordion House on Three Wheels

—

Chinese cities are bursting at the seams with migrants from all directions, resulting in housing shortages, with surpluses only occurring in districts far away from the workplace. People's Architecture Office, a Chinese design studio, has come up with the Tricycle House, a housing unit attached to a tricycle. The structure is made of translucent, foldable plastic with integrated facilities including a sink, bathtub, stove, and a bed that doubles as a dining table. The modular design allows for expansion and interconnection between units, encouraging organised, hyper-flexible housing.

POPUPCITY.NET/26115

PHOTO COURTESY: PEOPLE'S ARCHITECTURE OFFICE AND PEOPLE'S INDUSTRIAL DESIGN OFFICE

Vertical Campsites for the Homeless
–

As cities endlessly debate how best to ensure that all urbanites have a roof over their head, some architects are taking matters into their own hands by building shelters for those with immediate needs. French architecture firm Malka Architecture have installed 23 vertically-secured units on to the side of a railway viaduct in Marseille, fully equipped with an isothermal blanket to keep the user warm. While it is not a permanent solution to homelessness in Marseille, the project is a small stopgap for those who would otherwise be sleeping exposed to the elements.

Collapsible Shelters

Chat Travieso, a Brooklyn-based artist and architect, has produced a series of simple shelters that can be affixed to the side of a building as a parasite shelter or transported from place to place as a basic roof to put over your head. The lightweight structures are sturdy and well-designed in a tactical way that provokes how we conceive of the provision of private spaces and shelters.

POPUPCITY.NET/29168

PHOTO COURTESY: CHAT TRAVIESO

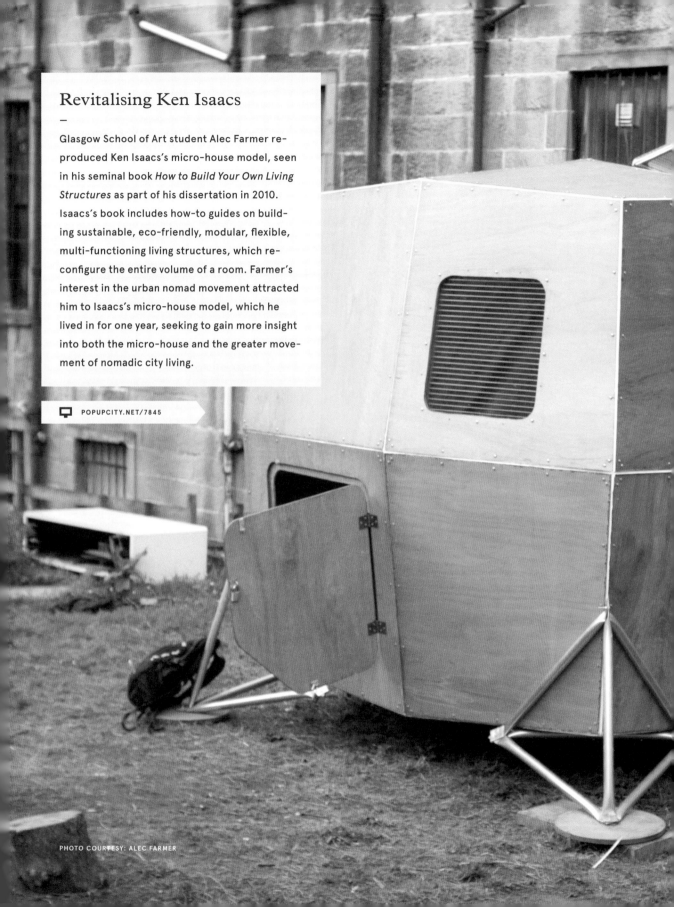

Revitalising Ken Isaacs

—

Glasgow School of Art student Alec Farmer re-
produced Ken Isaacs's micro-house model, seen
in his seminal book *How to Build Your Own Living
Structures* as part of his dissertation in 2010.
Isaacs's book includes how-to guides on building sustainable, eco-friendly, modular, flexible,
multi-functioning living structures, which re-
configure the entire volume of a room. Farmer's
interest in the urban nomad movement attracted
him to Isaacs's micro-house model, which he
lived in for one year, seeking to gain more insight
into both the micro-house and the greater movement of nomadic city living.

POPUPCITY.NET/7845

Electric Plywood House on Wheels

DIY Nomadic Living

Jeff and Arlene's first home is smaller than most, with no mortgage payment and an entirely sustainable infrastructure. The newlyweds decided to build the house themselves, resulting in a small cottage on wheels, about 2.5 metres wide and 7 metres long. Complete sustainability creates low living costs for the couple as well as the peace of mind that their lifestyle will produce minimal negative environmental impact. Jeff and Arlene's tiny cottage is a single example of a greater movement towards modular neighbourhoods as well as consolidated and sustainable living spaces.

Designer Jay Nelson has created an electric camper that he calls The Golden Gate. Designed for one person, the house can drive up to sixteen kilometres on a charge, at speeds of up to 32 km/h. The Golden Gate consists of a kitchen with a sink, stove, as well as a toilet and a bed, making the vehicle great for travelling within an urban region outfitted with power outlets.

POPUPCITY.NET/5272

POPUPCITY.NET/17746

Living in a City Egg

–

As an answer to the exorbitant housing costs in
Beijing, recent graduate and architect Dai Haifei
has hatched a unique, mobile living space. His
design, which he calls the City Egg, peaks at two
metres in height, made of sack bags, bamboo splints, wood chippings, and grass seeds,
complete with wheels for mobility. He parks his
one-person home in front of his office, where
he works long hours, eliminating the need for a
working space in his home. The City Egg is an experiment not only in materials and construction,
but also a new urban lifestyle based on individual
mobility and minimisation of expenditures.

🖥 POPUPCITY.NET/10168 ▷

PHOTO COURTESY: DAI HAIFEI

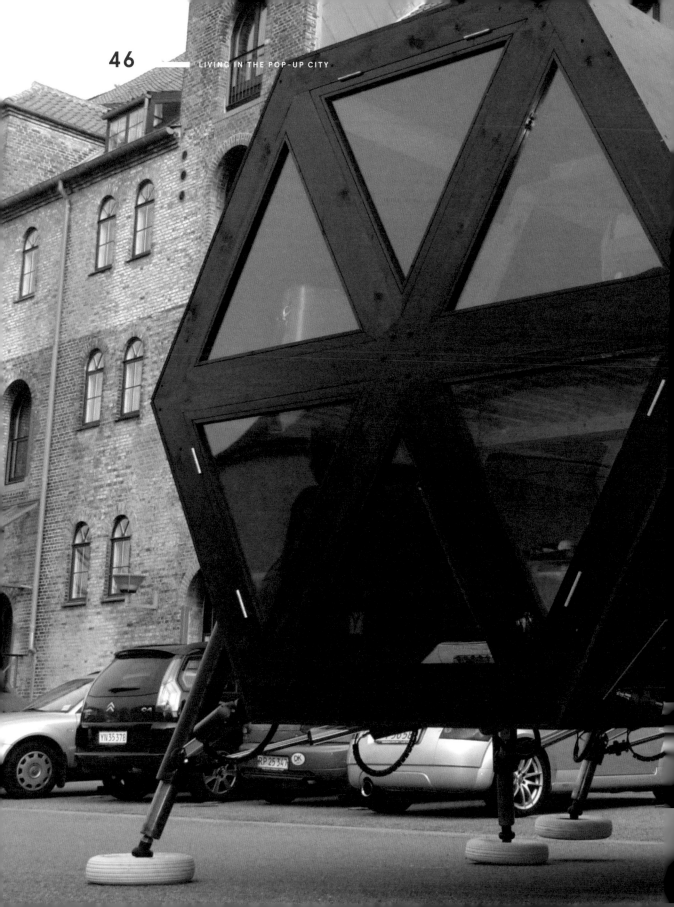

A House with Legs

—

Copenhagen-based design platform N55 has created a sustainable house that can walk. The four-person home can move its legs by collecting energy through solar cells and small windmills. The Walking House allows for a fluid, cosmopolitan lifestyle: perfect for flexible people who can live and work anywhere and everywhere.

POPUPCITY.NET/592

PHOTO COURTESY: N55 (ION SØRVIN, ØIVIND ALEXANDER SLAATTO, SAM KRONICK)

The Tiny House Movement

Some city dwellers explore the possibilities of living in smaller spaces from a more idealistic point of view. The proponents of the Tiny House Movement, for instance, live in buildings with small footprints on purpose and share

Mobiators look at the Dutch capital in a different light, and have successfully found spaces to temporarily inhabit and infiltrate. The Walking House by Copenhagen-based collective N55 is a similar mobile construction that facilitates a nomadic lifestyle in an environmentally friendly way. The Walking House stimulates fantasies about fluid urban neighbourhoods comprised entirely of walking houses and unharnessed

Anyone can be a producer and consumer at the same time

their lives with the rest of the world on blogs such as The Tiny Life. They consider downsizing the space that they live in as a part of their lifestyle. "Focussing on smaller spaces and simplified living, people are joining this movement for many reasons," writes Ryan Mitchell, the founder of The Tiny Life. "Environmental concerns, financial concerns and seeking more time and freedom." Most people in the world collect so much stuff in their life that they require bigger homes with a larger footprint. The Tiny House movement questions this lifestyle by stating that real freedom begins when our material burden is minimised.

In Amsterdam, the Mobiators, a pair of nomadic urbanites, have put the nomadic lifestyle into practice in a European city. Over the past few years, they have been temporarily setting up their self-built, foldable, completely transportable, and utterly uncategorisable home, the Mobi-01, in playgrounds, parks, music festivals, and lakeside communities around the city. The

mobility. In some ways, it is reminiscent of Archigram's famous Walking City concept from the 1970s. In Scotland, designer Alec Farmer looks at lifestyle experiments from the past decades in order to create a new perspective on living based upon Ken Isaacs's classic DIY book, *How to Build Your Own Living Structures*. Alec Farmer has built and lives in a replica of Isaacs's micro-house in the centre of Glasgow. The main objective for Farmer was to find out how to build sustainable, eco-friendly, modular, flexible, and multi-functional living structures.

Plug-In Living Environments

Mobile living does not have to be focussed on a freely accessible public domain. Unoccupied indoor spaces also provide great opportunities for flexible living concepts. In some areas, huge vacancies have arisen as a result of a disastrous

▷ CONTINUED ON PAGE 54

The Hyper-Flexible Living Mat

As individuals become more flexible in their lives, so too should their living spaces. Landpeel is a modular flooring system that contains pieces that can fold upwards to create furniture that can be pulled out and folded away with ease by the user. Shin Yamashita's design can be folded into a variety of small table structures, sofas, and chairs. Landpeel provides ideal interior furnishing that reduces the amount of furniture required by the seemingly mobile individual.

Robotic Furnishings

Imagine if your furniture built itself. Anyone who has ever built their own knock-down furniture can attest that this would be a fabulous development, but it may be closer than we think. Roombots are a series of robotic modules that can be automatically transformed on command into various pieces of furniture such as desks, sofas, tables, or chairs. The oddly-human robots are shaped not unlike an L-shaped tetromino and are being developed to be configured by the user through tactile interaction and web interfaces.

⌨ POPUPCITY.NET/12635

PHOTO COURTESY: SHIN YAMASHITA

⌨ POPUPCITY.NET/11877

PHOTO COURTESY: BIOROBOTICS LABORATORY, EPFL, AND MASSIMO VESPIGNANI

Design, Download, and Print Your House with WikiHouse

The next revolution in architecture comes without the architect. WikiHouse is the first open-source platform for home design. It allows anyone, including non-professionals, to design, print, and build houses using Google SketchUp, a free three-dimensional modelling program.

WikiHouse aims to make it possible for anyone, regardless of formal skill, to build their own custom-made homes. This concept brings into question the relationships between designers and clients, offering affordable housing suited to personal needs.

POPUPCITY.NET/14213

Don't Forget to Fold Inn Your Room!

The Fold Inn by Dutch designers Lieke Jildou de Jong and Alei Verspoor, is a collapsible bedroom that provides the user with walls and a bed within a space similar in size to that of an elevator. This project offers a unique alternative to a hotel, sleeping at work, or festival accommodation: the Fold Inn is a temporary room within a larger vacant space that challenges the conventions of how a home is built and where it is placed.

POPUPCITY.NET/30595

PHOTO COURTESY: LIEKE JILDOU DE JONG AND ALEI VERSPOOR

Portable and Printable Architecture

—

In Amsterdam, architecture office DUS has created the world's first moveable 3-D print pavilion,
which they call the KamerMaker (literally, room
builder in Dutch). While it has the appearance
of a rather large metal tower, the KamerMaker
allows architects to print small rooms using PLA,
a corn-based bio-plastic. The printer can create small interiors of up to 2 metres in width, 2
metres in length, and 3.5 meters in height. The
KamerMaker raises greater discussion concern-
ing similar architectural techniques of the future,
including the use of additive manufacturing technology and biodegradable plastics in on-demand
architecture.

POPUPCITY.NET/22879

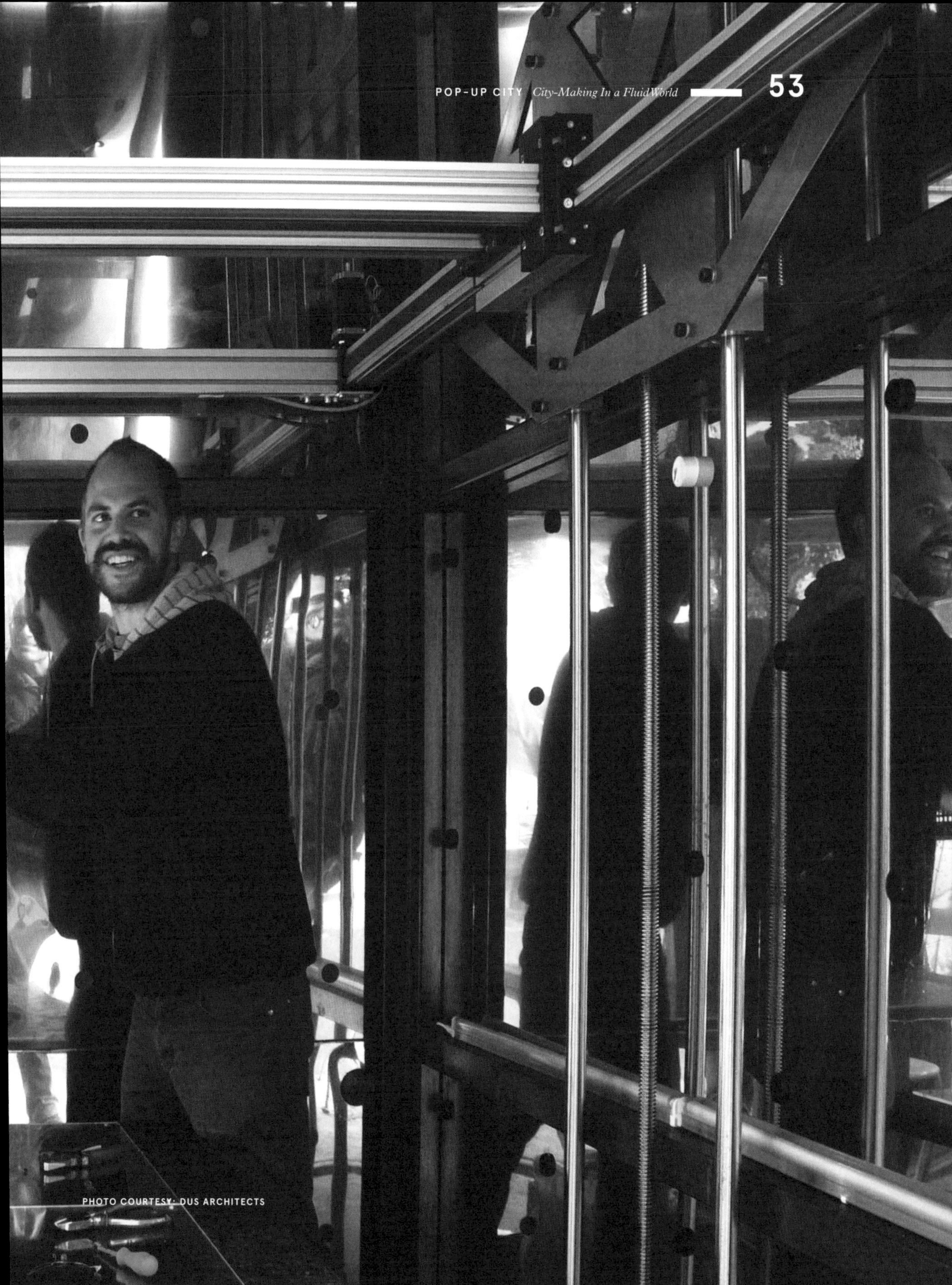

PHOTO COURTESY: DUS ARCHITECTS

mismatch between planned building production and actual demand for space. This, however, provides the opportunity for great and unconventional indoor spaces to be used as living quarters, such as office towers and public buildings, as made strikingly clear by the Dutch office Rietveld Landscape in the exhibition Vacant NL during the 2010 Architecture Biennale in Venice, which showed, to scale, every single vacant public building in the Netherlands at the time. In many cases, transforming these spaces into houses is more complicated than it seems at first glance, due in part to legislative and financial hurdles. Building your own house in a vacant office might not yet be possible in

The End of Architecture?

Looking at all of the attempts that are made to make living more flexible, the question might arise as to whether or not we will still be building houses in the future. At this point, however, the concepts and projects mentioned remain niche phenomena. But the position of architects in the design process may very well change a great deal, taking into account the emerging open design communities that share their expertise and designs online. This makes good design available to many. It is no

As 3-D printing becomes more accessible, the house could emerge as a new type of factory

most cities, but there are many lightweight alternatives, such as small living pods, which give a sense of security amidst the raw nature of temporary vacancy. Other lightweight, easy-to-assemble products offer instant living solutions within the solid walls of the vacant office property. The Fold Inn by Dutch designers Lieke Jildou de Jong and Alei Verspoor, is a bedroom on wheels with a box that unfolds into a flexible sleeping place. When expanded, this unique alternative to a hotel room covers about the size of a conventional elevator. The box comes complete with the standard necessities and can be arranged into a room with wooden walls.

longer the autocratic architect, wielding their knowledge-based power over residential design. Instead, everyone can be part of a design and building process. One of the first experimental open-source housing design projects is the WikiHouse. Starting with ten primary design principles in mind, an online community designs the house collectively while building upon each others' knowledge and solutions. Anyone interested in building the sustainable and adaptable WikiHouse can download the design, which is modelled in Google SketchUp, from the project's website and assemble it with minimal formal training in construction.

The client is back in charge when it comes to architecture. Platforms such as WikiHouse are the start of a shift in the way houses are designed, built, and financed. In the future, architectural designs will be freely available on the Internet and can be produced using local laser cutters or 3-D printers. Additive manufacturing is emerging as a new way of construction in the built environment. For now, a limited number of architecture offices worldwide are attempting to print a house, but technological advancements are gradually making house printing a more realistic endeavour. Ready-to-print design concepts are serving to democratise a sector of city-making that once had high knowledge barriers to entry.

The question here is who will lose their vaunted position in the world of domestic architecture: the architect, the construction company, or the property developer? In any case, it will not be the person with the printer. In order to develop a way of also producing architecture besides only designing it, Amsterdam-based architecture firm DUS have built their own 3-D printer, dubbed the KamerMaker. This giant version of an UltiMaker 3-D printer is able to print entire rooms and other large-scale constructions. Predominantly using plastic as a building material, DUS are printing a canal house in Amsterdam. While building a house is not yet as simple as hitting the print button on your keyboard and the technology remains underdeveloped, 3-D printing could offer architects and would-be homeowners a quicker and easier way to build the house of the client's dreams.

The Next House
Is a Hybrid

Urban nomads and tiny house dwellers are not the only ones living increasingly flexible lives with new architectural forms. What with working from home, planning leisurely activities at work, and being online on holiday, the lives of many urbanites have become fluid. The traditional segregation of duties between work and leisure is evaporating quickly. The house becomes a new kind of place with a new set of purposes: it is not only for eating, sleeping, and watching television anymore, but also for many other activities that were predominantly organised elsewhere in the city during the reign of a modernist planning and architectural ethos. The twenty-first century house is a hybrid house that accommodates multiple functions. First of all, work shifts to the house. This is not just work behind computer screens, but also production and manufacturing by craftspeople. Additive manufacturing makes producing complex objects more accessible for anyone with access to the technology. Plastic, metal, and glass items such as toys or household necessities can be manufactured at home. As 3-D printing becomes more accessible, the house could emerge as a new type of factory.

Houses have the opportunity to function not only as small factories, but also as restaurants, hotels, and print shops. The house is potentially a place where people not only spend their income, but earn their income as well. The hybrid household demands a new perspective for

▷ CONTINUED ON PAGE 60

This Stool Rocks the Future of Furniture Design

This Stool Rocks is a project by London-based designer and Assmbly founder James McBennett, proposing a revolutionary reinvention of the production chain of furniture. Assmbly, upon receiving a customer order, sends a digital file to the closest producer in a network of local manufacturers to produce the furniture using 3-D printing technology. Upon arrival, the customer can assemble the furniture in less than a minute, resulting in a final product that combines both the assemble-at-home concept with new technology in production. The concept redistributes and decentralises the assembly process, bringing clients and producers together in a unique style.

~~~~~~~~~~~~

Local 3-D Printing

The Amsterdam-based company 3D Hubs believes that anyone and everyone should be allowed access to 3-D printing technology. They have accomplished this by connecting 3-D printer owners to people who want to print through an online registration form and interactive global map of 3-D printer locations. The site incentivises 3-D printer owners by offering financial remuneration for print jobs, allowing those without access to printers to see their ideas come to fruition. This community-based sharing service advocates communal use of a relatively rare commodity, thereby saving money and encouraging local cooperation.

POPUPCITY.NET/27317

PHOTO COURTESY: JAMES MCBENNETT

PHOTO COURTESY: 3D HUBS

Tokyo's House in a Shop

More and more houses are being designed with multi-functionality in mind, but this design from Tokyo goes well beyond a simple open concept. Meet FIKA, the house that doubles as a storefront. Five days a week, the building is simply the owner's home, but on the weekend, it transforms into a lovely little store. Fika is a word that means coffee break in Swedish, and FIKA's owner puts Scandinavian designed goods for the home on display in this innovative home-shop.

A Model for a Future Suburbia

–

Dutch design group Droog and architecture firm Diller Scofidio & Renfro have collaborated to breathe new life into American suburbs by teaming up with suburban residents to encourage entrepreneurship through home business. Design teams match local skills and interests to produce Open House prototypes, such as domestic museums or block pantries, bringing commercial activity and creative power to formerly drab areas. The Open House model most importantly recognises the power of people, communities, and creativity as solutions to over-consumption and economic crisis plaguing American suburbs.

🖥 POPUPCITY.NET/12915

domestic architecture, one that should implement a more open concept in order to accommodate the wide range of potential functions. 3D Hubs, an Amsterdam-based start-up, is building a peer-to-peer network that connects the suppliers with the demanders of 3-D printers throughout a whole host of cities across the globe, whether they are in offices or homes. Users can list and geotag their printer, making it

goods can be rented out through peer-to-peer marketplaces, but services as well. EatWith, for instance, provides a platform for anyone in the world to rent out their living room as a temporary restaurant. Visitors can come and sit at your dining table to eat what you cook in your own kitchen. Other comparable online platforms allow home cooks to sell their leftovers on peer-to-peer take-away websites.

Users can list and geotag their printer, making it accessible for others who need to use one

accessible for others who need to use one. With the ability to turn a house into a small print shop for three-dimensional objects, 3D Hubs illustrates a broader development in which not only production becomes embedded in living environments, but also in retail.

3D Hubs is an example of a peer-to-peer service that combines supply and demand without a formalised intermediary retailer. Since it is becoming possible to rent out things via safe and secure digital environments, the dividing line between producer and consumer is removed. Anyone can be a producer and consumer at the same time. A car can be rented out for good profit through Snappcar, an unused room turns into a short-stay apartment with Airbnb, and an empty garage space becomes a parking spot with Park Circa. Bikes, tools, luxury goods, and even gardens can be rented out on dedicated peer-to-peer platforms. The sharing economy is growing larger and more influential, opening up the home for new functions. Not only

One good example of a hybrid house is a shop-meets-house located in Tokyo. The building, known as FIKA, functions as the shop owner's residence on weekdays, and during weekends the building turns into a store where a collection of Scandinavian antiques and household items is sold. FIKA was designed by ON Design Partners to specifically serve as a building that the owners can use seven days a week. Their main job when designing the house was to maximise the use of a tiny 32 square metre plot in a quiet neighbourhood. Another project created in the context of Droog Design's Open House project, a 2011 design competition to reconceptualise monotonous American suburbs, designers Janette Kim, Erik Carver, and Gabriel Fries-Briggs developed an extension that can be installed on the façade of a house in order to give it an instant showroom or space for alternative functions. In general, there is a growing interest in craftsmanship and homemade production, and design thinking is catching up. While the neighbourhood is traditionally thought of as the restful cocoon hidden away from the bustling city, new concepts for multi-functional homes are blending the living environment with the working environment, thereby enhancing the flexible lives of owners, tenants, and neighbours alike.

Co-Working in a Nightclub

Work Life in the Pop-Up City

Two hundred years ago, much of mankind worked in the fields; one hundred years ago, the majority of labour took place in dusky factories; and fifty years ago, people worked in office buildings. Now, people work everywhere. Only hunter-gatherer societies were more flexible in their working lives than the contemporary urbanite. Ever since the rise of agriculture thousands of years ago, however, people have tended to stick to their place — a place that required them to plough the land, to operate machinery, and to answer the landline phone. But those days are coming to a close as agriculture and heavy industry become self-operating and our communication devices shrink. People now change their job as easily as they replace their toothbrush, while business people travel the world to find new clients and employees, and cities adapt to more flexible work styles.

The Birth of the Nomadic Worker

In 2008, *The Economist* dedicated an entire issue to the emerging phenomenon of urban nomads. A series of articles describes an emergent tribe, roaming the world's cities, looking for a table to work at, outlets to recharge laptop and smartphone batteries, and social places to connect with other professionals. Sitting behind her laptop in a coffee bar, the Wi-Fi-hunting urban nomad is a new type of person on the streets of the global metropolis in the early twenty-first century, a person that provokes us to think of work less as a series of tasks requiring completion and more as a process of creating something useful or interesting. This new approach to work habits results in a highly flexible work style, putting its mark on many aspects of urban life. Work is perceived in a completely new way, and, more importantly, it asserts a new position in urban space, leading to new urban functions and forms.

Nobody could have missed the impressive renaissance of the coffee bar over the past decade. Coffee bars have gradually become the new office for young urban professionals; individuals who not only want to escape the confines of the cubicle, but also wish to make their flexible working habits an important part of their increasingly nomadic lifestyle. The swift rise in appreciation of high-quality coffee in that sense could be a direct result of this drastic change in work styles: these workers want there to be perks for being at work, and an enjoyable cup of coffee can be one of them. For many urbanites, working means hanging out and showing off, besides earning a living in a footloose economy. The restraining environment of the office is being replaced by inspiring new public urban arenas and living rooms. These can be classified as *third places*, a term coined by urban sociologist Ray Oldenburg to define the social places that are separate from the conventional environments of home and work. Third places are multifunctional and offer an attractive option for the flexible individual, regardless of whether or not she is looking to relax or finish that project. These types of spaces are not competing to be the place of a specific function, but, rather, on their coolness, even prompting the world's most prominent Internet startups to turn a massive campus-style headquarters into a playground. In each of these places, work blends with lifestyle.

The third places that are popular among flexible workers are hybrids between coffee bars and offices. While offices increasingly tend to look like bars with high-top tables and designer chairs, more and more bars tend to look like offices with shareable tables and ubiquitous power outlets. Co-working spaces are the most prevalent new concept that suit the needs of the urban nomads seeking these multifunctional spaces. Some co-working chains, such as NextSpace, The Hub, and Urban Station, have expanded to multiple cities, while others, such as Betahaus in Berlin, are focussed on serving the needs of their own communities. By designing places that have a hybrid form, co-working spaces provide an alternative working area that is both formal and casual, allowing users to create high-quality work within a constantly changing workplace with a loose professional network. These spaces minimise overhead costs for workers and place individuals from a wide variety of disciplines at the same table.

Jobs in the Cloud

The decline of the traditional office and the lively appreciation of the public sphere to work is a consequence of technological developments that unfolded during the past few decades. Over the past twenty years, the Internet has transformed itself from a parallel world into a system that is embedded into our daily

jobs in the cloud.

Cloud-based data storage removes the need for physical presence at the office, leading to new types of entrepreneurship, based on online connections as well as an immense expansion of international travel networks. CEOs of world-leading companies are now not the only ones travelling the globe to increase their business reach — millions of other workers, from rank-and-file employees to entrepreneurial freelancers, are expanding their professional foraging area in their hunt for knowledge, networks, and income. Technological advancements have resulted in the compartmentalisation of work, creating the microjob. Microjobs are where a project's tasks are broken down into the small-

Offices increasingly tend to look like bars and more and more bars tend to look like offices

lives. Not only have personal communication devices become crucial tools for productivity and social interaction, they are more mobile and powerful than ever before. Laptops are no longer expensive, state-of-the art innovations and the rise of high-capacity mobile Internet networks, smartphones, and tablets have made it possible to work anywhere. In 2005, laptops outsold desktop computers for the first time in the United States. Work could subsequently be siphoned from the office tower, resulting not only in many workers performing their tasks from a different location than the typical office space but also in radically new ways of delegating tasks, paving the way for all kinds of new

est possible components and distributed to a considerable number of workers. In a sense, microwork is part of a virtual assembly line for knowledge-based work that requires human intelligence as opposed to well-oiled machinery.

More workers and employers are turning towards flexible employment arrangements, as they have become more attractive in various fields of work. As an example, 39% of people between the ages of 15 and 24 in the Netherlands had a flexible labour contract in 2012, compared to 25% in 2002. In this case, flexible contracts have begun to unseat the traditional dominance of permanent contracts. The

▷ CONTINUED ON PAGE 71

C to the Office

—

Located in Berlin's Kreuzberg neighbourhood, Betahaus is a mixture between a 'regular' co-working space and a social community. The place is a hybrid form, somewhere between a Viennese coffee bar and a library that is open to every-body, providing for the needs of hardcore writ-ers, but also for those who enjoy a social working environment. Members can rent a flexible desk or become a more structural part of the concept and join collaborative projects. The basic phi-losophy of Betahaus is that workers benefit from using an ever-changing workplace.

POPUPCITY.NET/11833

PHOTO COURTESY: STEFANO BORGHI

It's Not a Bar, It's Not an Office: It's an Urban Station
—

One innovative new workspace popping up in a country near you is Urban Station. Operating franchises in five different countries, Urban Stations are warmly-designed member's clubs for mobile workers. The spaces offer workers flexibility in that they need not permanently rent a desk or office but only purchase the ability to access the bright, homey space. Urban Station makes mobile work more casual.

POPUPCITY.NET/11112

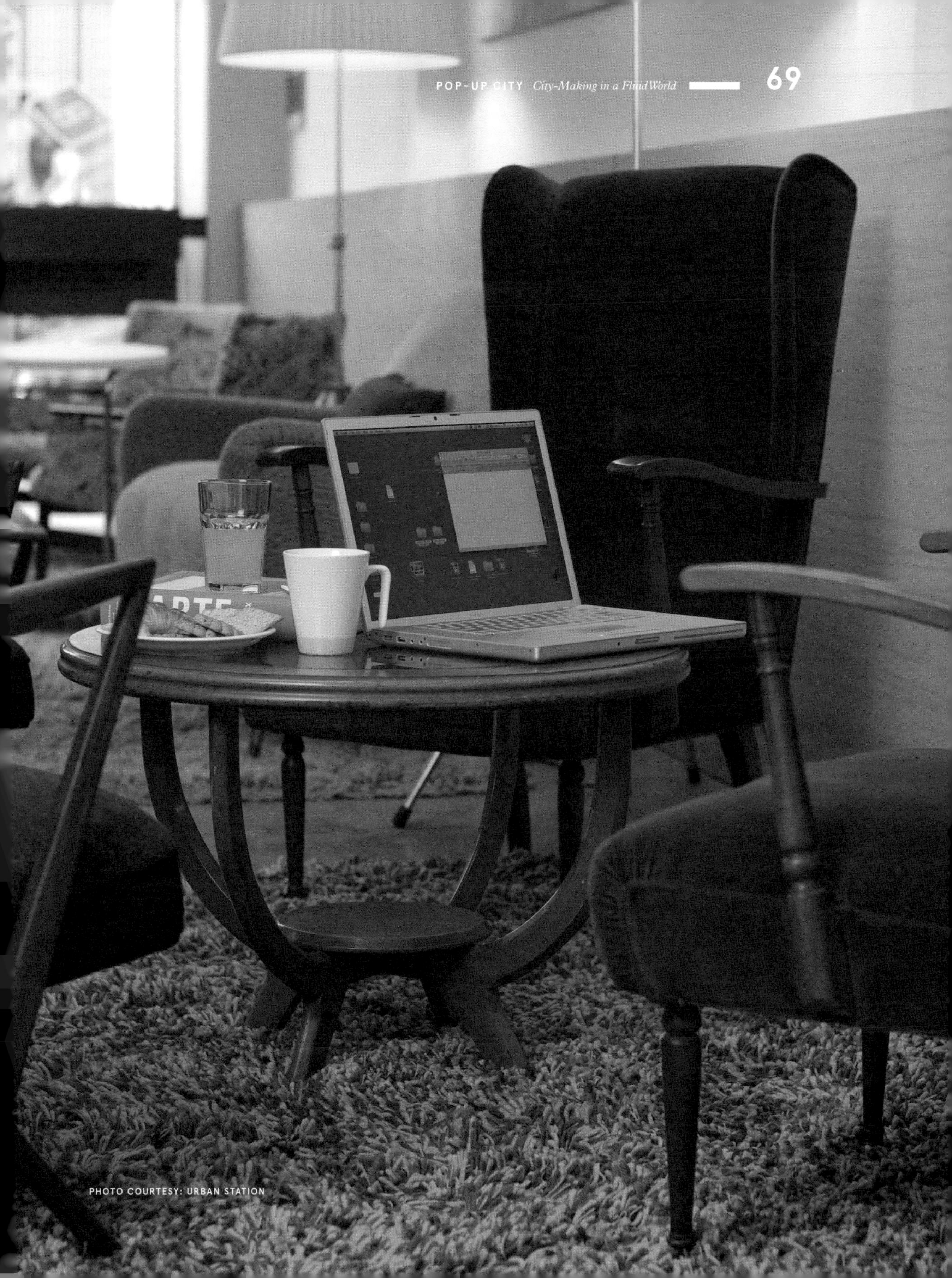

PHOTO COURTESY: URBAN STATION

Co-Working in a Nightclub

In case you think that Sweden just isn't dark enough, Stockholm Nightowls provided an interesting service between 2010 and 2012: a space to work late into the evening. Stockholm Nightowls offered an open space late at night in order to encourage *nattuglor* (literally, night owls) to hunch their shoulders over their laptops and get some work done while the city sleeps.

Think-Tank for Modern Office Solutions

PROOFF is a platform created by Dutch designer Jurgen Bey which does not merely come up with better solutions for current workplace environments but also poses new questions. By actively observing and researching contemporary working habits, PROOFF, which is short for Progressive Office, explores what can be improved, and — thanks to a large repertoire of designers — immediately turns their new insights into useful interior designs.

POPUPCITY.NET/7750

POPUPCITY.NET/2813

PHOTO COURTESY: JOHAN HEDBERG AND PIA HOGBERG

PHOTO COURTESY: PROOFF

proportion of freelance workers has grown dramatically over the past decade, and it will continue to grow even further, writes urbanist Anthony Flint in an article on *The Atlantic Cities*: "A study by Intuit predicted that the number of 'contingent' or freelance workers — those hired more on the consultant model for two days a week, for example, and who work for multiple masters — will rise from 20 million to 40 million [in the United States] by 2020." Freelance workers are completely free in their choice for a place to work. Many work from home, where they have no colleagues and thus limited possibilities for networking and collaborating. Their desperate search for some company and a professional network brings them to public or semi-public places to work.

The City Is an Office

While the first generation of mobile workers is aware of the convenience of working in a café, many are still discovering it as a new frontier of working in a relaxing, convivial atmosphere. Despite the unpleasant noise in many cafés and the awkward choice between drinking too much coffee or the embarrassment of consuming too little in the eyes of the baristas, working from this traditionally social space is nonetheless quite popular. The 'café' where patrons simply pay an entrance fee for the right to enjoy bottomless cups of coffee in an attractive setting such as London's Ziferblat is only one of many workplace typologies that provides a social space for visitors.

Other, more public spaces are quickly becoming potential offices as well, in part due to the strengthening of mobile phone networks. Cities are technologising public parks, making them an attractive option for sitting on a bench in the sun and typing up that invoice, either because of fast 4G connections or publicly-accessible wireless Internet. Athens, for instance, was one of the first cities to equip a park with wireless Internet in 2009. But what was once a novelty has become business as usual. New York City has equipped sixty public parks with Wi-Fi as of 2013 through a public-private partnership, while Mexico City used an innovative campaign that provides complimentary wireless when you deposit your pet's waste in the rubbish bin. In the private sector, a handful of multinational chains, including McDonald's and Barclays, offer free Wi-Fi in their branches, while airports and libraries have gained new functions as oases for urban nomads, not merely to catch a flight or borrow a book but also to increase the productivity of patrons. As a result, the next generation of urban nomads has an even more fragmented working relation with the city. They work from home, the park, the bus, a public bench, the coffee bar, and the launderette. At all places, they use multiple devices that are connected to a single cloud-based profile. The new office is in the cloud and the desk is scattered throughout the city.

Apart from bringing Wi-Fi to public spaces, cities have not yet fully adapted to the transforming labour market and flexible public working arenas. *The Economist*'s special urban-themed issue noted a considerable drop in demand

▷ CONTINUED ON PAGE 80

SPARESPACE by
Nieuwe Garde
PHOTO COURTESY: SABINA THEIJS

Mobile Offices for the Masses

Designers everywhere are striving
to create unique new concepts
for working spaces that are more
adaptable and more transportable
than the office furniture of the past.
BEEBOX is a collapsible office that
has acoustic wall panels to create
a private workspace for a busy
bee working at it. SPARESPACE is a
high-tech foldable working space
complete with walls that can be

turned into touchscreen displays.
Koloro Desk is geared towards
creating an aesthetically pleasing
working environment that is green
and organised. All of these concepts
are proof that not only are working
styles becoming ever more flexible
but that they are boosting demand for
furniture typologies that respond to
these needs.

BEEBOX by Buro Beehive and Fiction Factory

PHOTO COURTESY: THOMAS BORN

Koloro Desk by Torafu Architects

PHOTO COURTESY: TORAFU ARCHITECTS AND AKIHIRO ITO

Office in Disguise

Kruikantoor, a wordplay of wheelbarrow and office in Dutch, is an ingenious little unit that consists of two chairs, a work desk, lighting, electricity, and ample storage space so that the user can have everything they need at their own desk that collapses with incredible simplicity.

PHOTO COURTESY: TIM VINKE

Coffee On-The-Go for Commuters

—

As part of Zürich's plans for inspiring a modal shift towards more sustainable transport, designers and civic authorities have teamed up to produce a coffee drive-thru for commuters who travel by bike. The Velokafi features a wooden table designed to allow patrons to enjoy their drinks while perched on their bikes, cutting out the process of searching for a parking place, locking up the bicycle, and worrying about theft.

POPUPCITY.NET/28616

PHOTO COURTESY: PER KASCH

Please Inflate Your Office Here

–

Hong Kong-based artist Huong Ngô has designed the Pop-Up Studio, a mobile workspace for two. Unique in this category of portable studios, the Pop-Up Studio is inflatable and comes in the rough shape of a cube. In order to find an adequate place for the studio, Ngô places classified advertisements online, to which anyone can respond and have a blow-up office.

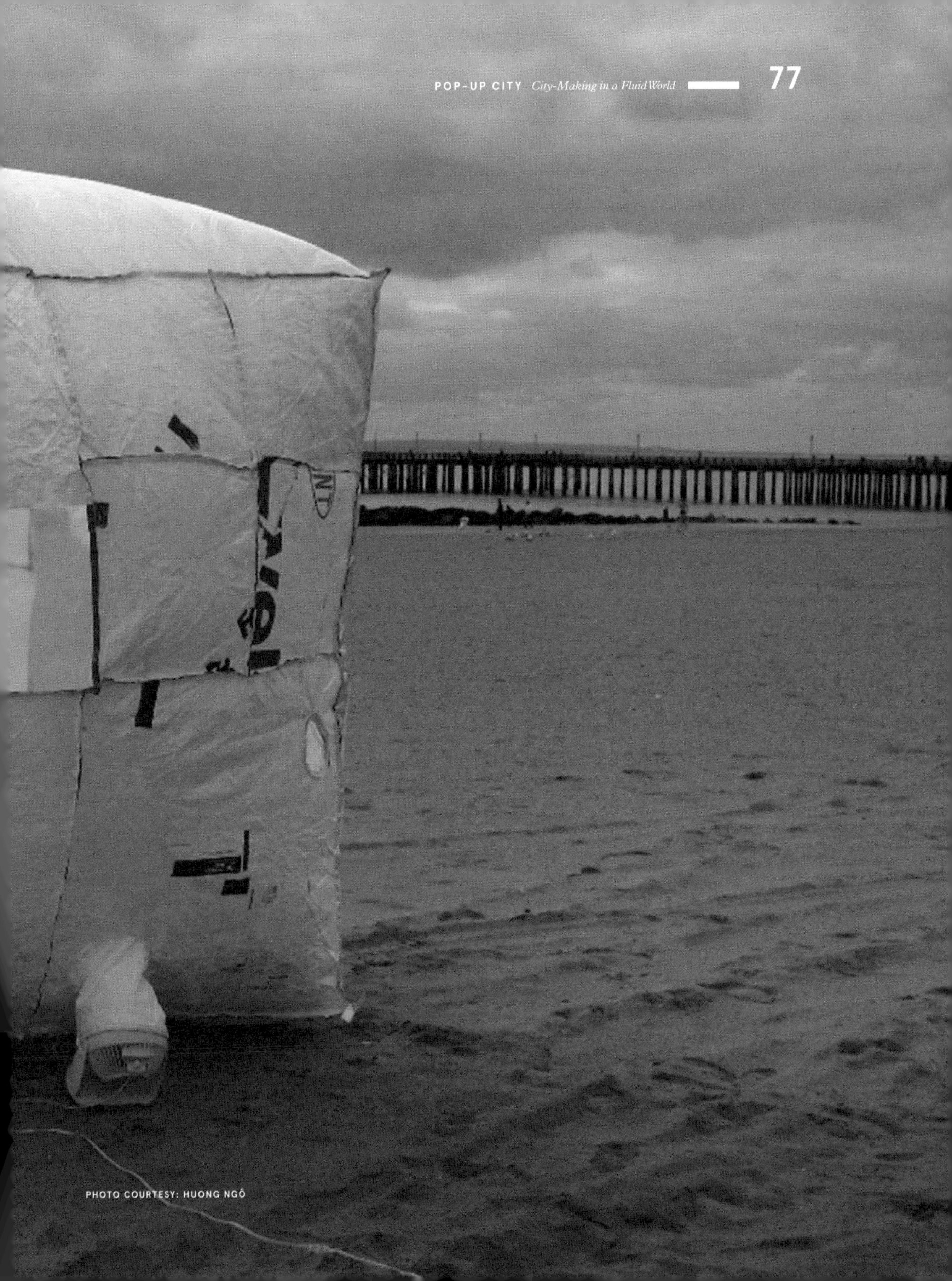

PHOTO COURTESY: HUONG NGÔ

A True Pop-Up Office

Remember those pop-up books from your childhood, where every turn of the page resulted in part of the page bursting out in a three-dimensional way? Imagine this concept applied to a mobile office design. The result is a life-sized structure that easily folds up, just like its book-sized siblings.

Designed by Liddy Scheffknecht and Armin B. Wagner, the pop-up office is constructed entirely of cardboard and tape. Your mobile office appears whenever the cardboard panel is opened, appearing magically before your eyes.

POPUPCITY.NET/4580

PHOTO COURTESY: LIDDY SCHEFFKNECHT AND ARMIN B. WAGNER

Micro-Jobs in the Smartphone Era

An Online Marketplace for Architecture

The Amsterdam-made app Roamler eliminates the need for recruiters that hire new talent by encouraging app users to explore the city in a new way. The idea is simple: companies that require some kind of support outsource their simple tasks that can be undertaken by any Roamler user who wishes to help in exchange for a small monetary reward. Other applications, including Easyshift, Gigwalk, and Scoopshot, use a similar concept of distributing workloads to willing users in need of a quick buck.

For many prospective homebuilders, finding the right person to design a house is a daunting task that scares off many, resulting in architects that have difficulties connecting with their potential client base. With CoContest, architects and clients can connect more easily using a web platform. The platform envisions itself as an online marketplace for interior design, where prospective clients can shop around for the styles and the prices that best suit their needs.

POPUPCITY.NET/14241

PHOTO COURTESY: ROAMLER

POPUPCITY.NET/28786

PHOTO COURTESY: COCONTEST SRL

for traditional enclosed working spaces, since people are no longer tied to specific spots for their work. At the same time, there is a rise in demand for semi-public spaces that can be informally appropriated to ad hoc workspaces. Flexible workplaces hold great potential as a strategy for temporarily revitalising an under-

scts by Cisco, *The Atlantic Cities* reports that "sixty percent of assigned desks or offices sit empty during the day. The average square feet required per employee has dropped from 250 twenty years ago to 150 today. It's 100 square feet in some corporate offices." Tighter economic budgets have slowed office space devel-

The new comprehensive 'office' for the urban professional is not yet planned by city planners

used neighbourhood. There is a significant need for cities to be able to repurpose the vacant left-overs of the cubicle era. By and large, however, cities do not yet seem to have a suitable answer to this demand for informal, flexible working spaces or even see the potential in neighbourhood reactivation through temporary reuse of vacant business districts. The new comprehensive 'office' for the urban professional is not yet planned by city planners, due to the difficult nature of creating a space that is appropriate both for work and social activity, as well as the rigidity of existing urban planning frameworks. In the meantime, pop-up citizens are creating these spaces for themselves.

Empty Desks and Vacant Offices

Even office workers from large firms no longer stick to their place. They spend more and more time on the go rather than behind their desks. Reflecting on a study of corporate as-

opments and even trimmed company payrolls to the extent where many cities have a significant surplus of office space.

Peer-to-peer desk and office rental services have created a market for renting out temporarily unused desks, rooms, and equipment. By enabling users to rent a fully-equipped desk for a few hours, a day, or sometimes even longer, firms such as LiquidSpace, ShareDesk, Coworkify, and Desktime are ensuring that companies are efficiently using their office space while allowing urban nomads to have the freedom to reserve a workplace at their own convenience. Companies have changed the way they distribute their own workforce, contributing to the peer-to-peer desk rental services. Consulting firm Accenture, for instance, no longer maintains a central office, but has moved its entire workforce to ad hoc desk renting facilities, meaning that all employees book their own desks for their own personal needs. By encouraging a workforce to disperse throughout the city, large firms such as Accenture are helping their employees to associate with other workers

▷ CONTINUED ON PAGE 86

Time Is Money at Ziferblat

Ziferblat is the first pay-per-minute co-working space to emerge in London's East End. Based on a Russian chain, where "everything is free, except the time you spend drinking your cup o' tea." This new concept has been enthusiastically welcomed in the trendy borough of Shoreditch. Ziferblat, meaning 'clock face' in Russian, allows guests to consume as much as they want, as long as they pay three pence per minute whilst inside. As customers enter the space, they are expected to use one of the clocks provided in order to keep track of the amount of time they have spent inside and therefore how much they owe. With no minimum time, guests are encouraged to help themselves to snacks and beverages, prepare their own food, and even play the piano.

POPUPCITY.NET/32072

PHOTO COURTESY: ZIFERBLAT

Doing Office in Public

—

Studio Shelf, a Cape Town–based design agency, is taking to their city's vibrant streets in order to confront the stereotype of the office worker that is confined to the cubicle. Their initiative, Shelf Public Office, relocates their studio one day per month into a public space so that they can better socially interact with clients, passers-by, and each other. Studio Shelf's day out on the streets occupies a sidewalk space that would otherwise be full of commuters rushing by, encouraging a greater interaction between the design world and the locals of Cape Town.

POPUPCITY.NET/30250

A Parasite Office Inside of an IKEA

Fifty artists and designers from Hamburg organised a parasite office inside of IKEA's Hamburg-Moorfleet location. The parasite office was meant as a protest against their expulsion from their office space in the Frappant Building, inside of which IKEA was planning to open up a store. While the intervention received great media attention, it did not result in a public provocation of IKEA: the Swedish giant appeared benevolent, offering the activists a fresh cup of coffee.

POPUPCITY.NET/5772

PHOTO COURTESY: MIGUEL FERRAZ

Public Benches for the 21st Century

Where there is a seat, there is something to place our stuff upon. We eat at a dining table and work at a desk, so why do public benches lack a smooth surface apart from the one we sit on? Torino-based design studio Adriano Design has created outdoor seating that fits the twenty-first century lifestyle. Wi-Fi is designed with a two-tiered structure that offers the would-be sitter either a small table or a place for someone else to join for a quick sit.

▭ POPUPCITY.NET/1145

PHOTO COURTESY: ADRIANO DESIGN

that they might not otherwise develop a professional relationship with.

Starting a Design Office in the Facebook Age

As the core of the knowledge-based office is transferred to the cloud, new types of firms emerge. Young entrepreneurs start a design office today in a very different way than even twenty years ago. Most stunning are the new offices that are built with a global focus. A few fresh graduates might open an agency while living in different cities around the world. One of them lives in London, the others in Berlin or New York, giving the office a global flair and the ability to connect with potential clients on a personal level in each of these cities. One good example is the Office of Subversive Architecture, with team members located in eight European cities, but they are far from the only example. When one partner gets a new project, the entire team works together in a decentralised way. Only when absolutely necessary do they meet together in person to do team-based tasks. Increasing numbers of new-style design agencies do not rent a full office space, but only single desks in other offices with underused desks. This way, they all have access to typical office equipment and still benefit from the advantages of shifting between different offices. All in all, a great symbiosis between the old-fashioned office in decline and the new parasite office in the cloud exists.

As city dwellers change the way they work, as well as the locations they work at, there is a transforming role for the city as we know it. Increasing flexibility in large firms means that anti-urban campus-style headquarters or conventional central business districts that are devoid of life on the weekends such as those found in Canary Wharf and La Défense, respectively, are becoming antiquated. The result of this is that cities will be less focussed on planning conventional office towers with a single anchor tenant and more focussed on reactivating underused buildings and neighbourhoods designed for smaller businesses and freelancers. In addition to this need to plan for neighbourhood reactivation, cities are beginning to recognise that flexible working spaces are *cool*: they are used by young, forward-thinking people with fresh ideas and a desire to make their neighbourhoods thrive, making them attractive places for people to live, work, and play in. As a result, cities are becoming highly competitive marketplaces, where urban labourers frantically seek out unique workplaces and property owners scramble to enter the ad hoc workplace environment.

The Carry-On Office

OPENAIRE by Nick Trincia is a hybrid laptop bag that can be quickly transformed into a lightweight but sturdy chair and a desk suitable for outdoor use, taking flexible working to a new level. Though it does not provide electricity or Wi-Fi to the user, it does give the user the ability to turn nearly any space into an office.

A New Space Dating Service

If you are looking for a mobile application that hooks you up with a private space to work in, then Breather is the app for you. Breather connects the user to unique private working spaces across their city. Similar to other services such as Uber and Sold, Breather makes sure that the user does not have to worry about any practical details, so long as the customer treats their space date well.

829 Bloor st. West
3 rooms available

LOCATIONS   RESERVATIONS   SETTINGS

POPUPCITY.NET/29009

POPUPCITY.NET/11820

Your Living Room, My Office

The convertible living rooms of the marketplace Huiskamerkantoor (literally, living room office) can be found since their 2013 establishment in Amsterdam, where people live, work, and share in other people's living rooms. Essentially the professional extension of the online travel community Couchsurfing, the co-working spaces of Huiskamerkantoor rely on the principle of sharing your own spaces with others to transform it into a more communal space.

POPUPCITY.NET/29568

PHOTO COURTESY: MISHA VELTHUIS

Fast and Flexible Creativity

New media platforms have pushed the advertising sector to engage in unconventional thinking in order to make an impact. One creative team with a fabulous name, The Pop Up Agency, took their show on the road, visiting fifteen countries in 2013 for only 48 hours in order to rapidly develop campaigns. By placing a time limit on the creative process and taking the process directly to the client, the studio of the twenty-first century proves that it need not have a fixed address.

POPUPCITY.NET/27122

PHOTO COURTESY: MARIE KJELLANDER

Swedish Design Hits the Highway

–

One inventive young art and design graduate from Sweden has fused his desire to go on an inspirational road trip with diving head first into the world of freelancing. Erik Olovsson repurposed a camper van into the Designbuss, a mobile design studio that allows Olovsson to travel throughout Sweden in search of new commissions that he completes by exchanging tasks, as opposed to cash, with his clients. The attractive wheeled office is a promotional tool, a design studio, a means of transportation, and a social space all at once.

POPUPCITY.NET/25770

A Mobile Design Agency for Beijing

—

Amsterdam-based design firm Lava took their office to the streets of Beijing's Dashilan district. The Mobile Design Agency, which is installed inside of a small diàndòng sânlúnchê (literally, electric tricycle in Mandarin, which is usually small and tin-roofed), tooted around the city, stopping to design fresh new logos for small businesses, completely free of charge. Lava has plans to take the concept on the road to visit other cities across the world.

POPUPCITY.NET/30912

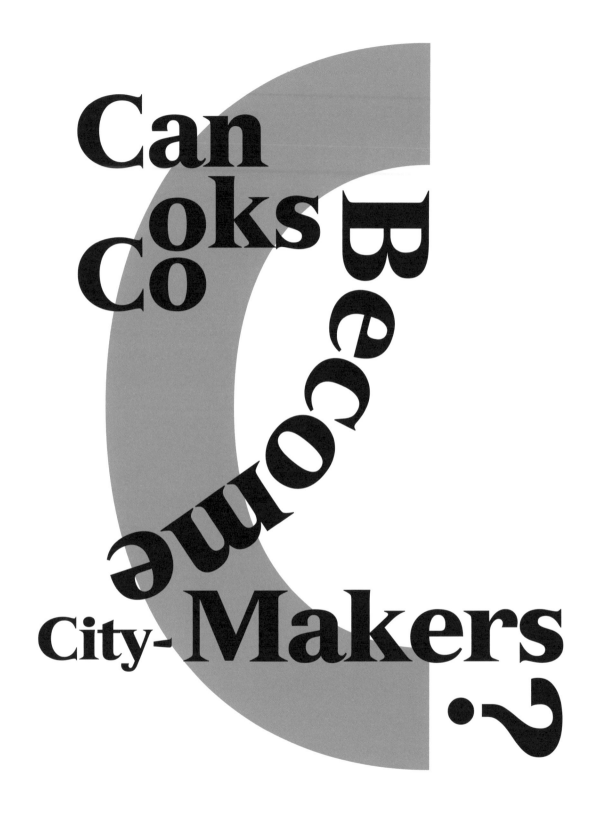

Can Cooks Co Become City-Makers?

Can Cooks Become City-Makers?

Food in the Pop-Up City

Food is far more than a collection of nutrients that sustains life. It is a powerful element in our lives that is capable of getting people talking, bringing strangers together, and ending conflicts of any size. Pop-up urbanism takes culinary culture to an entirely new dimension, where food trucks are the new take-aways, cooks are the new city-makers, and ordinary citizens are the new restaurateurs. The urbanite's hectic life affects the ways in which food is produced, sold, and consumed in urban areas, with hyper-temporary restaurants, food-tracking smartphone applications, farms on wheels, and massive public pop-up lunches reinvigorating culinary experiences in the city for those on the go. Civic governments around the world are now viewing food production and consumption as an essential element of urban planning.

Bringing Agriculture to the City

How has food production acquired such importance in the urban setting in recent years? As it stands, a small handful of multinational companies control the majority of the food distribution networks, inspiring more people to enquire into where exactly their food comes from, how it is produced, and how far it has travelled before it ends up on their dinner plate.

In an attempt to bring food production closer to consumers, urban agriculture has earned itself a pivotal position in the city, being widely acknowledged by civic governments and urban planners across the globe. When it comes to urban farming, Detroit has been setting the pace over the past decade, even despite doomsday scenarios for the city's financial stature. With the tremendous loss of jobs in the automotive industry estimated at totalling 435,000 in Detroit alone between 2000 and 2010, a ma-

cant land into farms of all shapes and sizes, producing everything from lettuce and tomatoes to eggs and honey. Urban agriculture adds value beyond making food more accessible to city dwellers, with research showing that urban farms encourage community engagement, a sense of belonging, and knowledge dissemination, all within a space that can fuse labour with leisure. Over the past decade, urban agriculture has spread to all corners of the Earth, with cities such as Detroit providing inspiration for all urban farmers, regardless of their location.

Urban agriculture is certainly not a new phenomenon: it has existed throughout history but is undergoing a major reconceptualisation with regards to how and by whom these initiatives are started and run. Ancient Egypt and wartime Europe witnessed in-city food production in order to lower logistical strains due to climate and warfare, respectively. The practice has been common during many times of strain or even crisis: in the Netherlands, urban agriculture was rather popular during the economi-

The popularity of urban farming bears a strong correlation with living in times of crisis

jor outflow of inhabitants and the city's official bankruptcy in the summer of 2013 have left Detroit with 360 square kilometres of underused property, amounting to 150,000 vacant properties equalling the size of the Manhattan peninsula. In an attempt to revitalise the local economy and promote a self-sustaining future for Detroit, people have started to convert va-

cally miserable 1980s, while shortages in both food and fuel inspired thousands in Havana to grow their own food supply. Analysing the peaks in popularity of urban farming over history, one could conclude that it bears a strong correlation with living in times of crisis. What makes urban farming appealing today is that it encompasses a wide range of functions that

▷ CONTINUED ON PAGE 102

The Green Thumb of Motown
–

Few cities have experienced the decline from being the global centre of a single industry to the site of extreme urban decay in the same way as Detroit. While much ink has been spilled on Detroit's decline, the city is reformulating itself as a paragon of urban agriculture. A vast collection of vacant lots and disused buildings are leaving a large canvas for farmers to paint on, prompting significant growth in the industry's employment numbers as well as in the availability of fresh produce.

PHOTO COURTESY: MERCEDESFROMTHEEIGHTIES (FLICKR)

Urban Green on New York Rooftops

—

Thought to be the world's largest urban rooftop farm, Brooklyn Grange has two acres of land in Brooklyn and Queens that cultivates produce for residents across The Big Apple. Not content with simply being a farm, Brooklyn Grange is a one-stop shop for everything agricultural as they also keep egg-laying chickens and an apiary, in addition to operating a consultation and installation service for building owners who want to make their rooftop a little bit greener.

POPUPCITY.NET/24430

PHOTO COURTESY: KRISTINE PAULUS (KPAULUS ON FLICKR)

From Factories to Food in Kwun Tong

—

While many of the world's alpha cities have been enthusiastic in developing rooftop agriculture, Hong Kong has lagged behind its peers, with many of the city's supertall towers housing illegal rooftop settlements. One initiative is working hard to change the status quo in Hong Kong. HK Farm, located in the rapidly transforming Kwun Tong district, is an agricultural plot perched on a factory rooftop in a neighbourhood witnessing a transition from industry to commerce. Interestingly, HK Farm is led not by agricultural experts but by enthusiasts from the design sector, maintaining a relationship with HK Honey as well as a community-oriented art and design platform at Shanghai Street Studios.

POPUPCITY.NET/24430

PHOTO COURTESY: GLENN EUGEN ELLINGSEN

do not solely lie in the realm of agriculture. It brings food production closer to the place of consumption, lowering transportation costs and air pollution output, and offering those less well-off in urban areas to build a self-sufficient and nutritional future. Moreover, urban agriculture, especially organised in cooperative ways, has proven to be an instrument that can rebuild entire communities, not only through food production but also through education and social networking.

Food: A Plug-In Strategy

Urban agriculture is more than a merely idealistic hobby. It is a useful tool for temporary revitalisation of unoccupied spaces. Not only are vacant lots temporarily revitalised by urban farms, but the urban farming trend also extends to empty office towers and building rooftops. Food is inextricably linked to our quotidian existence but our experience with it is always temporary. Some civic governments are beginning to realise both the importance of food to humanity and how the temporality of food can improve city living. Amsterdam's municipal government has opened an urban farming desk that helps proactive citizens convert vacant property into community farms, while the City of Helsinki has hired a municipal food strategist in order to improve the image of the city's culinary culture and its status as a hub for high-quality food.

In Tokyo, a former bank vault underneath an office building in the Otemachi business district accommodates PASONA 02, a high-tech, one square kilometre urban farm that, aside from growing agricultural and horticultural standards, provides agricultural training to young people who experience difficulties finding work as well as middle-aged people in search of a new career. Meanwhile in Dublin, a former chocolate factory has been converted into a hub for creative enterprises, while the building's roof hosts a modular urban agriculture initiative. Projects such as these are an indicator of how urban farming can be used not simply to bring food production closer to those who consume it; rather, the infusion of urban agriculture can serve as a launching point, prompting other interesting projects to pop-up in the vicinity.

Harvesting the Sidewalks

While one group of citizens starts a neighbourhood farm, the other considers the city's green spaces as one massive decentralised urban farm. Increasing numbers of urban dwellers are discovering urban foraging or sidewalk harvesting as an appealing way to obtain wild herbs, fruits, vegetables, and even meat without having to visit a supermarket. Urban foraging is a world with its own ruleset. It is generally not permitted, not to mention mildly disrespectful, to pick edibles from a privately-owned property, to pick more than necessary, or to sell the edibles that you might have found. In an attempt to add a digital component to urban foraging, the Amsterdam-based foragers at the Urban Edibles collective have developed Boskoi, a smartphone app for citizens to explore the edible species in the urban landscape and tag their location so that other urban foragers can also locate them. A similar initiative is Falling Fruit, an open-source platform for urbanites to map the location of edible plants in order to "facilitate intimate connections between people, food, and the natural organisms growing in our neighbourhoods." By using smartphone applications that are inherently social, cities can enable locals not only with the practical knowledge on *how* to forage for food in urban areas but also *why* it can be beneficial to their overall nutrition.

Civic authorities are also discovering urban foraging as a spatial development strategy. Seattle, for instance, is bringing food culture to a new

all be there for locals to care for and enjoy. All of this will be available for free plucking to anyone taking a stroll through the forest.

Farming the Kitchen

Agriculture is not only on the rise on tower rooftops and in public forests, but inside of homes as well. The rising popularity of aquaponics as an agricultural method is playing an important role within the urban agricultural landscape. Aquaponics is a self-organising system with an elegant water loop that grows vegetables, herbs, and fish simultaneously. Fish waste provides nutrients for the plants, while the plant roots filter water for the fish. Plants are fertilised organically and the need for disposing of fish waste is eliminated. Aquaponics reuses water effectively and efficiently, resulting in a lower environmental footprint compared to

Amsterdam has opened an urban farming desk at its city hall, while Helsinki has hired a municipal food strategist

level by means of a self-sustaining food forest from which every resident is allowed to harvest fruits and vegetables, free of charge. Authorities have decided to turn a seven-acre plot of land in Beacon Hill into an enormous food forest. The forest will contain many varieties of edibles, from apples to herbs and walnut trees. Even the more exotic offerings will not be excluded: be they pineapples or guavas, they will

other harvesting methods. It is ideal for areas with water scarcity issues and concerns over pollutants in plant cultivation. The scale of aquaponic systems can range from commercial to home use, making aquaponics a viable option for urban farmers. Dutch electronics firm Philips developed their concept for the five-layer Biotower, an aquaponics-based kitchen installation that would allow owners to grow food

▷ CONTINUED ON PAGE 107

A Transparent Urban Farm

Many urban farms tend to be tucked away from the public eye, sitting on rooftops or in enclosed spaces. ON Design Partners have created a more visible farm in Tokyo's vibrant Roppongi district. The farm is a collection of glass-sided boxes that maximise light and visibility, while providing a small farm plot used by the adjacent restaurant.

POPUPCITY.NET/14150

PHOTO COURTESY: ON DESIGN

Hydroponics in a Tube Tunnel

One problem for prospective urban farmers is that it can be difficult to locate sufficient space in a relatively central location in the city. Zero Carbon Food has tracked down a unique space to grow vegetables: in an abandoned London Underground tunnel. Using a hydroponic lighting system, Zero Carbon Food benefits from a consistently warm temperature in the tunnel in order to cultivate food close to consumers and restaurants.

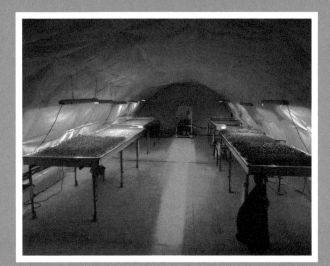

PHOTO COURTESY: ZERO CARBON FOOD ZCF

Amsterdam's Sandwich Factory (Ketchup Included)

Redeveloping former industrial districts usually leads to some interesting land uses, and Tostifabriek is no exception. Located outside of a former factory occupied by cultural institution Mediamatic, the Tostifabriek, which translates from Dutch as the toasted sandwich factory, was a temporary farm that cultivated all elements of the tosti, a Dutch café staple. Wheat was grown to make bread, pigs were raised for ham, cows were in the barn to make cheese, and, most importantly, the tomatoes were nearby for the ketchup. The project demonstrates how cultural staple foods can be produced in the heart of the city.

POPUPCITY.NET/25923

PHOTO COURTESY: DE TOSTIFABRIEK

in a closed system that is designed to house vegetables, algae, fish, and organic waste. Systems aimed towards more commercial operations are also popping up on Berlin and Tokyo rooftops for vegetable and rice production, respectively. These initiatives greatly expand the possibilities for crop diversification within the built environment at a personally manageable scale.

Urban Agriculture Becomes Serious Business

Urban agriculture has two faces. One side of the culture is primarily concerned with the social goals of urban farming initiatives. These projects have seemingly existed since time immemorial, as many city dwellers have always wanted to enjoy the fruits of agricultural and horticultural cultivation. The other side of urban agriculture is taking the farming aspect seriously by intensifying cultivation methods in the city, turning it into a lucrative business venture that contributes to the reinvention of food production. The new-found abundance of urban farming supply stores point to an increasingly professional attitude amongst the current generation of urban farmers. In Rotterdam, Uit Je Eigen Stad combines a large-scale urban farm on a derelict lot with a restaurant and shop to make a cohesive and profitable business model. The farm's business model includes a marketing team and even a creative director, and the food pro-

duced at Uit Je Eigen Stad reaches a wide market, securing an income for the farmers.

Urban residents and agricultural enthusiasts are not the only ones beginning to take farming in the city seriously; civic governments consider urban agriculture an economic accelerator. A 2009 study by economist Michael Schuman puts Detroit's urban agricultural workforce at over 4,700, while New York City's municipal government invested $600,000 in Brooklyn Grange, one of the largest urban rooftop farms on the planet. As a result of these collective efforts, urban agriculture is metamorphosing from a weekend hobby into a legitimate business sector that is able to generate considerable economic activity and serve as a city-making tactic.

The urban agriculture scene extends beyond the city's vacant lots, with farming initiatives and shops appearing all over the landscape of the world's cities, especially in the United States. These shops offer products that meet the needs of the urban farmer, varying from seeds and soils to rainwater harvesting barrels, drip irrigation systems, and even little roosters. In 2011, New York welcomed a truly stylish urban farming shop in Haysees's Big City Farm Supply Store, while Portland also established its own Urban Farmers Store. In the middle of the country, St. Paul's Egg Plant Urban Farm Supply is Minnesota's source for supplies and inspiration for your backyard homestead. Not to be outdone, the Seattle Farm Supply is the ideal place to start your organic rooftop poultry farm. The urban farming niche is large enough in some cities to enable people to make a living

▷ CONTINUED ON PAGE 116

Green Curry with a Side of Algae

Ever had a dollop of algae with your dinner? The next time you happen to be in Bangkok, we have a recommen- dation for you. EnerGaia are installing algae farms on Bangkok's rooftops and harvesting them for interested locals and restaurateurs alike. Otherwise empty rooftops are jam-packed with dozens of barrels containing the green goo, which is harvested three times per week, spun dry, and hand-filled in neatly designed jars. The next time you need a healthy side dish, think of algae!

POPUPCITY.NET/30170

PHOTO COURTESY: ENERGAIA CO. LTD.

Cargotecture Meets Aquaponics

Damien Chivialle's Urban Farm Units, or UFU for short, take this concept and apply it to a small space: namely, an ISO-standard intermodal shipping container. Each UFU contains a fish pond and a cleaning tank inside of the container itself with a greenhouse placed on the top. Rather than marketing and selling the units, Chivialle made the project open-source, allowing anyone with the technical know-how the chance to convert a disused shipping container into a productive farm with a small ecological footprint. Urban Farm Units are currently operating in Belgium, Germany, and Switzerland, with others planned for France and Portugal.

A Take-Away Biosphere

Dutch technology manufacturer Philips has been toying over the years with new concepts that are not merely about selling products but designing products that are efficient and convenient. The Biotower is a non-spherical biosphere housing a self-contained domestic farm, with the capacity to cultivate plants, algae, and fish in five different internal levels. The system is designed to cascade nutrients from the top level down to the bottom, reducing food waste and air pollution, as well as inspiring awe from your friends at your next dinner party.

POPUPCITY.NET/20857

PHOTO COURTESY: DAMIEN CHIVIALLE

POPUPCITY.NET/4950

PHOTO COURTESY: PHILIPS

Doubling Factory Production with Potatoes

–

One of the largest urban farms in Canada, Montréal's Lufa Farms is a 31,000 square foot greenhouse installed on the roof of a two-storey industrial building. Over forty different crops are produced throughout the year at this massive operation that uses the irrigation system of the factory below. The model Lufa Farms offers is attractive to many cities with vast low-density industrial districts that could double the productivity of any given factory.

🖥 POPUPCITY.NET/24430 ➤

PHOTO COURTESY: LUFA FARMS

Food Made-in-Transit

By the time most foodstuffs are loaded onto a truck, they are already starting their process of decay. Canadian designer Agata Jaworska proposes a new concept to reformulate the food production process as well as the transportation process. Jaworska's food packaging is designed to permit food maturation inside of it, resulting in foods arriving at the grocery store at the peak of their freshness.

In-Shop High-Tech Farming

While the rise of urban agriculture has sprouted primarily on rooftops and in community gardens, one storefront in London's Hackney neighbourhood is literally putting the farm in a shop. The aptly named FARM:shop is a volunteer-run farm, workspace, café, and exhibition space that pushes the envelope on food production in the city by experimenting with innovative techniques and offering their products for sale in their shop. FARM:shop is a hybrid space that links farming with social activity and urban culinary culture.

POPUPCITY.NET/24972

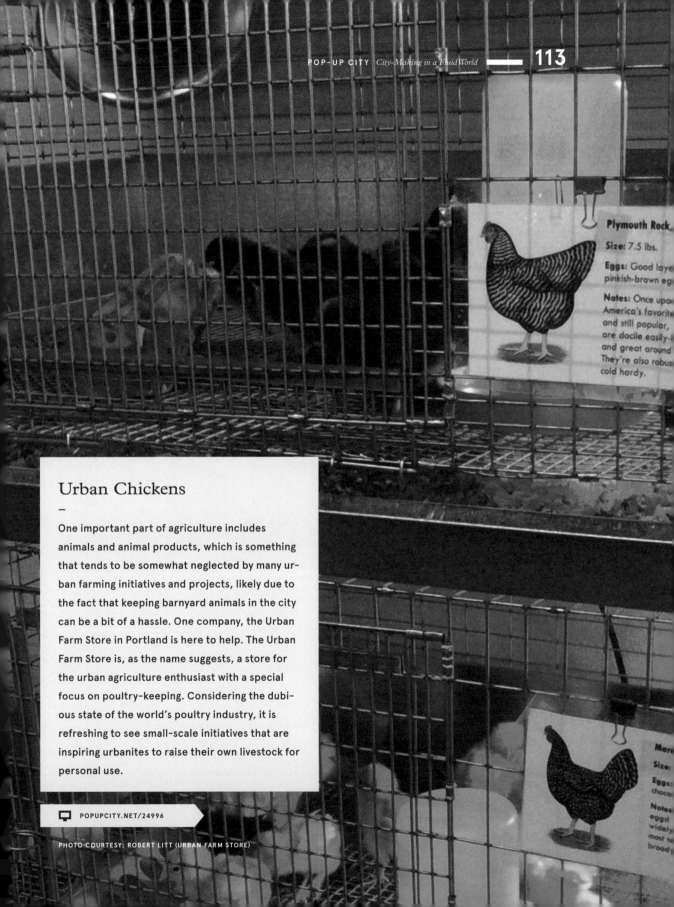

Plymouth Rock,

Size: 7.5 lbs.

Eggs: Good layer
pinkish-brown eg

Notes: Once upo
America's favorite
and still popular,
are docile easily-
and great around
They're also robus
cold hardy.

Urban Chickens

–

One important part of agriculture includes animals and animal products, which is something that tends to be somewhat neglected by many urban farming initiatives and projects, likely due to the fact that keeping barnyard animals in the city can be a bit of a hassle. One company, the Urban Farm Store in Portland is here to help. The Urban Farm Store is, as the name suggests, a store for the urban agriculture enthusiast with a special focus on poultry-keeping. Considering the dubious state of the world's poultry industry, it is refreshing to see small-scale initiatives that are inspiring urbanites to raise their own livestock for personal use.

POPUPCITY.NET/24996

PHOTO COURTESY: ROBERT LITT (URBAN FARM STORE)

Mar
Size:
Eggs
choco

Note
eggs
widely
most
broody

Sharing Seeds for a Greener City

Hawaii-based Eating in Public has created a design prototype for Seed-Sharing Stations, which offer urban farmers the opportunity to exchange fruit and vegetable seeds at no cost. The Seed-Sharing Stations, which are constructed using scrap metal, are a platform for knowledge exchange on all things agriculture. The prototype for building a Seed-Sharing Station is straightforward and freely accessible from the Eating in Public website, meaning that any agricultural enthusiast can build either a temporary installation or a more permanent place for sharing.

POPUPCITY.NET/26129

PHOTO COURTESY: EATING IN PUBLIC

A Marketplace for Backyard Farmers

Locafora is a Dutch digital marketplace for exchanging homegrown produce that you grow in your backyard. The service aims to stimulate good eating habits as well as lessen the amount of wasted backyard produce by letting producers set up a virtual store that lists their agricultural offerings. Locafora is one initiative trying to inspire slow food principles and urban agricultural know-how in a country full of cities that are rarely intimately connected with the food production process.

A Salad for Your Vending Machine?

In an attempt to change the way Chicagoans think about fast food and vending machine offerings, Farmer's Fridge offers up leafy greens in a jar. The vending machine, which looks similar to conventional vending machines, is filled with glass jars that are lovingly filled by hand each morning with fresh salads from local farms. Jars are returned to the machine so that they can be washed and reused.

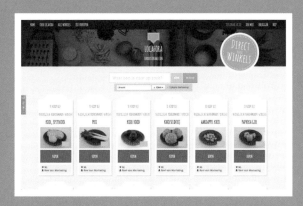

💻 POPUPCITY.NET/32254

PHOTO COURTESY: AFDELING BUITENGEWONE ZAKEN   PHOTO COURTESY: FARMER'S FRIDGE

from selling equipment. Over in London, an urban farming meeting hub called Farm:shop can be found in the streets of Hackney. Farm:shop is a workspace, café, and venue, all combined in a compact urban farm.

On the note of large-scale city farming, Lufa Farms in Montréal is an interesting case. The farm has a 31,000 square foot greenhouse perched on top of a two-storey building. Over forty different crops are produced year-round in the innovative greenhouse that shields crops from the harsh Canadian winter weather outside. The model that Lufa Farms provides is interesting and could be attractive for cities aiming to create added value for structures that were once assumed to only have a single use.

New Food Marketplaces

The marketplace is the historical *raison d'être* of the city. Gradually, the role of the market was primarily taken over by grocery shops and, ultimately, supermarkets, a place where no bartering in a chaotic setting was ever required. Nevertheless, in times where increasing numbers of urbanites want to reconnect with the products that they consume, the farmer's market is gaining a renewed position in urban living. What may be even more interesting is the emergence of online marketplaces where private urban farmers sell their home-grown produce. Launched in 2009, Veggie Trader was one of the first online platforms for buying and selling produce cultivated in the backyard. Users can post a listing describing their excess produce and specify what it is that they would like to re-

ceive in return in terms of other food products or simply cash. Veggie Trader also enables users to locate food available nearby and list their food-based needs in a Wanted section. Sadly, Veggie Trader ceased operations in 2011, but other similar digital initiatives such as Backyard Produce, Locafora, and The Farmer's Garden have picked up the slack.

Sometimes the focus on new ways of distributing food products comes from an unexpected source. One real estate developer in New York City saw a new business opportunity in exclusive farm-to-table food deliveries for locals. In 2010, The Albanese Organisation launched a new service for the residents of three apartment buildings located in Battery Park City. After residents sign up for the Community Supported Agriculture membership, they receive weekly deliveries of fresh, almost-locally-grown produce from Holton Farms from neighbouring Vermont.

Mobile Eats in Public Spaces

The local food culture is vital to the health of any community, and pop-up thinking is certainly making an impact on the patterns of how food is prepared and consumed. Street cuisine is omnipresent in urban areas, generally offering affordable nourishment of an occasionally questionable quality. As individuals begin to lead more fluid lives, the importance of street food availability grows exponentially, leading to the reinvention of a once soulless sector of cuisine or even the establishment of such a culture in a city that once had no street food culture to speak of. A general relaxation of permit restrictions on street food vendors as well as the prevalence of social media means that there are more options for eating on-the-go than ever before.

The food truck is also playing a central role in the rebirth of eating on the streets. The origin of the food truck stems from the latter half of the nineteenth century, when Texan cattle herder Charles Goodnight transformed an old United States Army wagon into a kitchen on wheels, allowing him to cook proper meals during his cattle drives. During the late 1900s, night lunch wagons popped up on the streets of New York in order to serve meals to those work-

places where street life can thrive," claims Petra Barran, the founder of London-based mobile food collective KERB, in an interview with *The Guardian* in the summer of 2013. California's two largest urban regions, Los Angeles and San Francisco, both boast vibrant mobile cuisine cultures that serve as a source of inspiration for the next generation of mobile caterers in other cities across the world. "LA and San Francisco are interesting to look at as these cities have special food truck courts and city-operated maps that show you where the food trucks are located," says Tio Tikka, a young mobile crêperie owner in Helsinki in an interview with Pop-Up City. "It would be interesting if my city, Helsinki, would sell licenses to food truck entrepreneurs for, say, €50 a month if they meet hygiene standards, and let them go wherever

Food trucks are the new frontier of urban food culture

ing the graveyard shift. Although the food truck has been on American city streets for generations, their popularity is rising in many places in the world, both in urban and rural regions. Food trucks are the new frontier of urban food culture. Increasing numbers of entrepreneurs open food trucks instead of restaurants, food truck festivals and gatherings take place in more and more cities, and the popularity of food on wheels leads to new associations that support and protect the rights of food truck purveyors. Mobile food has proven to be a useful strategy for neighbourhood regeneration, bringing new life to dead spaces such as vacant lots or underused car parks. "Creating more places where street food can thrive in cities creates more

they want to go."

Events such as San Francisco's Off the Grid provide a glimpse of how street food can become a pop-up strategy for neighbourhood revitalisation, and how cooks become city-makers. As of 2013, Off the Grid operates 23 weekly street food markets throughout the Bay Area. The markets are set up in fairly central areas on plots of undeveloped land to keep costs low and local vendors are invited to peddle their wares. Offerings range from fusion tacos to delectable cupcakes. Hungry visitors can expect to see many of the more well-known food trucks, as well as lesser-known startups, and even chefs of famous local pop-up dinners. Other coun-

▷ CONTINUED ON PAGE 131

We Need Tacos, Stat!

Need a street taco? Media designer Eric Lo did, quite badly. So badly, in fact, that he developed FoodCarts, a prototype iOS application that allows users to track down any food truck in San Francisco in real time. The application provides all of the necessary information: opening times, menus, prices, and reviews are all a part of the service. Other similar applications, such as Roaming Hunger, strEATS, and Street Food App are appearing in every city where the food trucks roam. These apps foster a more interactive experience between the hungry city dweller and the food vendor, turning the search for food into, in the words of taco-loving Eric Lo, a bit of "a social experience [and] an adventure." These applications are not just an easy way to provide real-time information, but also to promote the burgeoning food truck culture.

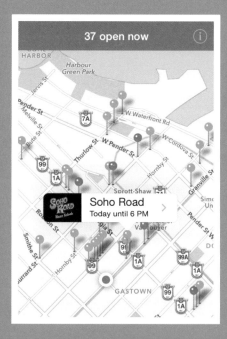

POPUPCITY.NET/12331

PHOTO COURTESY: STREET FOOD APP

Korean-Mexican Food on Wheels

Mobile food purveyors need to come up with creative new methods for building a clientele, and one effective strategy is to maintain a close relationship with hungry fans via social media platforms. One wheeled version in Los Angeles is Kogi, a Korean-meets-Mexican food truck. The party for your tastebuds that is a Korean taco has an extremely strong following on Twitter, allowing the cooks to keep in close contact with their patrons, building a more personal relationship with their fans. Order up!

Architecture Meets Ice Cream

Talk about a unique concept: Coolhaus is a purveyor of "architecturally-inspired" ice cream based out of trucks all over the United States. Wittily named if you mispronounce the name of a certain Dutch starchitect, Coolhaus applies the principles of the Bauhaus movement and Rem Koolhaas's iconic style into gourmet desserts constructed with love inside of a food cart, resulting in innovative flavour combinations by thinking of food as a piece of architecture. Coolhaus has expanded over the years into a series of storefronts in major American cities in addition to its fleet of trucks.

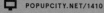 POPUPCITY.NET/1410

PHOTO COURTESY: ERIC J. SHIN

POPUPCITY.NET/6975

PHOTO COURTESY: ANDREW ECHEVERRIA

Travelling Food Truck Market

The only thing better than a food truck is a huge collection of food trucks. While some cities have semi-permanent food truck courts located in parking lots, one initiative in San Francisco is making these gatherings something of a special event. Off the Grid hosts over twenty weekly street food markets that roam across the Bay Area, seven days a week. Markets are set up on vacant plots of land to lower costs and feature both local favourites and up-and-coming food truck chefs.

〰〰〰〰

POPUPCITY.NET/22262

PHOTO COURTESY: BEGGYBERRY (FLICKR), SW77 (FLICKR)

**Government Services: Boston City Hall
to Go (Boston, United States)**

**Pet Grooming: Mobile Grooming Salon
(Amsterdam, the Netherlands)**

Fashion: Nike Ice Cream Truck (New York, United States)

Food Trucks without Food

Food truck principles are spreading all over the place to a wide variety of sectors, including fashion, government services, and pet grooming. The sportswear giants at Nike toured an ice cream truck around New York's five boroughs during two consecutive summers that served up both icy treats and sporting clothes. Boston's government recognises that municipal offices may not be in accessible locations with convenient opening hours for all local residents, so they opened up a truck that roams the city while offering essential government services to constituents in every corner of Boston. One entrepreneur in Amsterdam has taken her business, a pet grooming salon, and placed it inside of a truck so that she can visit clients whose puppies need a trim, regardless of their location.

POPUPCITY.NET/13647

PHOTO COURTESY: NIKE, INC.

Restaurants for All

Started originally as an annual event on the streets of Helsinki, Restaurant Day began as an opportunity for anyone to open up their own restaurant in any place for one day only. Frustrated by a rigid, non-spontaneous street food culture, Helsinkians of all ages and backgrounds ran take-away sandwich bars out of third-storey windows, build-your-own pizzas in a stone oven, and a soup kitchen promoting sustainable eating habits. Restaurant Day has since grown into a quarterly event that happens in over 200 cities all over the world.

 POPUPCITY.NET/20146

PHOTO COURTESY: TUOMAS SARPARANTA, HULDA SIF ÁSMUNDSDÓTTIR, HEIDI UUTELA, ROY BÄCKSTRÖM

Lunch on the L Train

In recent years, pop-up restaurants have appeared in the most unlikely of spaces, but this one probably takes the cake as the unlikeliest. New York's subway system, that grand labyrinth of public transportation that pumps the blood through the veins of New York City, was home to a theatrical one-day dining experience organised by A Razor, a Shiny Knife. The restaurant transformed an L-line train car into a choreographed flashmob-cum-bistro, providing a six-course meal to a dozen lucky passengers. The restaurant was a love letter to slow food placed in a very fast location, with new dishes strategically arriving from the station platforms. Even if only for a one-way subway ride, the restaurant was a way to breathe new life into an all-too-familiar place for New Yorkers.

POPUPCITY.NET/12992

PHOTO COURTESY: STEPH GORALNICK

Cheers to Eating Alone

—

Dining alone is generally not the most enjoyable task in the world. We must eat and we frequently do not dine with others, but a social stigma still remains when you take yourself out to that Vietnamese restaurant that you have been dying to visit. Eenmaal in Amsterdam is a pop-up project trying to change that with tables that accommodate only one person at a time. While Eenmaal's claim to be the world's first restaurant designed for people eating alone is far-fetched, the concept is an experiment in changing the perceptions of enjoying the city all by yourself. Eenmaal was only open for two days, leaving a legacy for those lucky enough to have tried it.

 POPUPCITY.NET/29372

PHOTO COURTESY: JAAP SCHEEREN

The Joys of Eating Together

The Atlanta-based producers of the sugary black gold otherwise known as Coca-Cola have been known over the years for their memorable marketing campaigns. One such example popped up on a cozy little square in the Italian city of Naples. The campaign placed Italian television chef Simone Rugiati in a delivery truck equipped with a kitchen and a dining table that extended into the square. The pop-up

dining table brought Neapolitans to the table to share food prepared by one of Italy's most recognisable chefs in the way that food is meant to be enjoyed: communally.

POPUPCITY.NET/23167

PHOTO COURTESY: THE COCA-COLA COMPANY

Food-for-Food at Ridley Road
—

Ridley's was a temporary restaurant located at the Ridley Road Market in East London that operated with an admittedly unique scheme: food-for-food. How did it work? At lunchtime, guests ventured out into the neighbouring produce market to purchase raw ingredients in exchange for a lunch from Ridley's. The ingredients collected by the lunch crowd would then be used to make dinner items, while the profits from dinner went into partially funding the lunch. The cycling of the food between providers and preparers stimulated a relationship between Ridley's and the nearby greengrocers on the market, while unconsciously provoking Ridley Road Market visitors to pay more attention towards the selection of fresh produce and how it can be best used in cooking.

POPUPCITY.NET/26756

PHOTO COURTESY: DOSFOTOS

tries are getting in on the pop-up food gathering trend as well. Britain's street food scene is thought by some, including *Guardian* journalist Richard Johnson, to be the by-product of farmer's markets. Eating on-the-go has become fashionable and attractive in fast-paced cities such as London, where living costs are high and time availability is low.

Mobile Food Gains Steam

Multiple factors are behind the emergence of the food truck. In the first place, the modern city demands new spatial concepts that have an inherent adaptability about them. Mobile food is versatile enough to succeed within this landscape. Food trucks are capable of serving the needs of on-the-go urbanites who either want to grab a quick bite at a low cost or even a gourmet meal at a reasonable cost. The adjustability of the food truck also enables cooks to experiment with locations and offerings, meaning that the venture itself is more resilient to tough economic times. Moreover, the barriers to entry for entrepreneurs are significantly lower than the average business venture, considering the lack of a permanent address and many of the facilities seen in an immobile kitchen.

This versatility principle is even reaching other sectors that traditionally have very little to do with culinary culture, including fashion, art, and civic bureaucracy. Axle Contemporary is a contemporary art gallery in Santa Fe that showcases its collection at high schools, festivals, and vacant lots. The Minnesotan city of Stillwater is home to The Fashion Mobile, a boutique clothing shop inside of a repurposed Chevy step van. Finally, the City of Boston has elected to place staffers inside of a truck that visits the city's neighbourhoods, providing essential services and answers to locals. Each of these examples suggests that the food truck spawned the creation of a hyper-flexible space typology that inspires cities to adapt to unforeseen conditions and provide a new format for reaching clientele, more than any form of architecture ever conceived.

The Food Trucks Go Social

The food truck industry ballooned since it began to integrate social media into its marketing arsenal. Facebook and Twitter are crucial channels for attracting the social media savvy to the locations where food trucks temporarily set up shop. A century ago, it would have taken years of dedication to the community from a specific storefront for a business to build a consistent clientele. Many customers are no longer solely bundled according to geographical locations but more along the lines of their online presence. Businesses do not depend on their traditional circle of potential customers living in the neighbourhood or those with the means of transport and a desire to visit: rather, food trucks have the ability to pop up at multiple locations within the city on any given day

▷ CONTINUED ON PAGE 134

Delicious Fieldwork

—

Food trucks are not the only way to reinvent the way we dine in the city. Pop-up restaurants are beginning to dot the urban landscape as ways to bring some temporary life to a place. The Veldkeuken (literally, field kitchen) is a pop-up restaurant that sets up shop for two days in an array of spots such as orchards or industrial plots, serving up seasonal, locally sourced meals for the residents of each town the Veldkeuken visits. The three-person team running the initiative ensures that the Veldkeuken is less about the built structure itself and more about the culinary experience.

POPUPCITY.NET/16225

PHOTO COURTESY: DESIGNSTUDIO BOMM

and utilise social media platforms to inform the hungry masses of their whereabouts. Location-sharing social media platforms, of which Foursquare is the forerunner, enable pop-up initiatives to quickly attract people to a location. In their infancy, the only permanent face of Off the Grid was a Facebook page, showing the reliance of portable eateries on social networks for connecting with their audience.

menus in order to track down precisely whatever it is the hungry urbanite is looking for. Some maintain a specifically local focus and provide accurate information about a city's food trucks, while others are designed for discovering another city's street food culture or even finding a hidden gem right in your own neighbourhood. In the United Kingdom, streetfood.org.uk is a website that maps all popular markets

Off the Grid provides a glimpse of how street food can become a pop-up strategy for neighbourhood revitalisation, and how cooks become city-makers

One mobile restaurant in Los Angeles is making effective use of Twitter in order to promote itself to potentially hungry Angelenos. Kogi, a small army of Korean taco trucks, roams around the City of Angels, informing fans of the restaurant of their truck locations in real time through an interactive website and a Twitter account. Kogi has gained over 110,000 followers due in part to their team that includes not only entrepreneurs and chefs, but also a creative director and a social media manager who are responsible for the pop-up restaurant's online strategy.

There is a rapidly growing collection of websites and smartphone applications that are also helping to serve up an enhanced food truck experience, quickly disseminating the locations and offerings of food trucks in a variety of cities. Many of these applications allow users to track truck locations in real time and read

throughout the country from Brixton to Berwick, while the simply-named Street Food App helps Canadian (and, oddly enough, Bostonian) food truck lovers to keep track of their favourite lunch truck. Countless smartphone applications and platforms, such as FoodCarts, Roaming Hunger, and strEATS are making it easier to keep track of your favourite mobile food purveyors in American cities.

A New Kind of Unconventional Dining

Food trucks are a quicker and cheaper way to start a restaurant than a traditional bricks and mortar space, but that same idea also goes for pop-up restaurants. Pop-up restaurants have no fixed address, but instead operate from a private home, empty office floor, or former factory

▷ CONTINUED ON PAGE 136

The Peer-to-Peer Kitchen

While Airbnb is radically altering the way in which we find accommodation for our travels by renting out an apartment owned by a local, like-minded websites are popping up to change the way we have dinner and making them more social. Two websites in particular, Shareyourmeal and its Dutch counterpart Thuisafgehaald, are mapping the kitchens serving up home-cooked meals in a wide array of cities. Users can browse through the kitchens to see what they offer, at what price points, and how previous diners have reviewed the food. Contrary to the closed-off kitchen of the conventional restaurant, peer-to-peer dining offers an experience that is more convivial, more open, and more social, letting the restaurateurs and customers make new friends in the process of a unique dining experience.

Table for Two in Your Kitchen

"Being a guest in someone's home is a great way to get an authentic local perspective in a different city." That is how the founders of EatWith describe their motivations for creating a platform for a more social dining experience. Registered members can add themselves to a directory of locals offering meals cooked in their own kitchens and served at their own dinner tables, effectively allowing users to turn their house into an informal restaurant. Travellers and locals alike can use the service to engage in the community's food culture, be it local cuisine or the adopted cuisine of a city's incoming cultures. EatWith is a way for the hungry to gain insight, if only briefly, into a whole different world.

 POPUPCITY.NET/26437

PHOTO COURTESY: SHAREYOURMEAL

POPUPCITY.NET/28490

PHOTO COURTESY: EATWITH

on a hyper-temporary basis as a unique one-time event. Similar to urban farms, pop-up restaurants have become increasingly popular in cities all across the world over the past decade. Since pop-up restaurants are rather discreet from the outside, they are even more reliant on social media than their wheeled counterparts. In order to ensure a solid base of customers for a meal in an unusual setting, most pop-up restaurants sell tickets in advance. A ticket gives customers access to a full meal. In the Italian

regulations and open their own one-day restaurants en masse. Restaurant Day encourages everyone to open a restaurant, anywhere, and regardless what the regulations may dictate. The event was organised via Facebook and Helsinki was literally bursting at the seams with fresh food: parks, streets, stores, and homes all became small restaurants for just one day. Since the first forty restaurants popped up in a wide range of re-imagined urban spaces across Finland, Restaurant Day has expanded to numer-

Since pop-up restaurants are rather discreet, they are even more reliant on social media than their wheeled counterparts

city of Ferrara, a secret outdoor pop-up restaurant called Street Dinner mixed dining with a treasure hunt. Customers with a dinner ticket received a series of text messages that revealed the different locations of each course. The Street Dinner created a unique happening, leaving hungry participants running about the city streets, uncovering what tasty morsels may be lurking around the corner. Pop-up restaurants are not solely limited to the city streets: Muru, one of the top restaurants in Finland, created a pop-down restaurant eighty metres below the streets of Tytyri for a decidedly down to earth dining experience.

Helsinki has been taking pop-up dining to a whole new level since Restaurant Day was started in May 2011 by a group of locals who decided to go around the city's bureaucratic

ous cities around the world that have quickly adopted this new Finnish concept. Restaurant Day's website and smartphone application have interactive maps that makes finding pop-up restaurants in your city and around the world easy. Restaurant Day operates at the intersection of culinary culture and pop-up urbanism, encouraging locals to engage with their cities and neighbourhoods creatively and collectively.

Living Room Take-Away

Peer-to-peer platforms can add a new dimension to a more social form of dining. Websites such as Casserole, Shareyourmeal, Super Marmite, and Thuisafgehaald (literally, home take-away in Dutch) give serial cookers the opportunity to share their freshly concocted meals with hungry neighbours. These platforms map nearby kitchens and offer descriptions of what is on the stove, including prices, photos, and reviews. While platforms such as Casserole and Shareyourmeal enable users to turn their homes into take-away windows, Feastly and EatWith are peer-to-peer initiatives that allow home cooks to operate a restaurant from their living room. The website gives people the opportunity to eat with a local in their homes and experience local culinary traditions. Many of the hosts using a platform like EatWith want to nurture their passion for cooking by showing off their cooking skills and hospitality with others in a way that allows them to connect in a more personal manner than in a conventional restaurant. Using EatWith, everyone can be a cook and everyone can be a customer.

Whether it is safely from the confines of your own kitchen or out on the streets, the aforementioned initiatives show that transforming the urban landscape into a more social one can happen by sharing a delicious meal or crossing town to get the take-away you were really craving. These projects make use of technology in order to break down the traditional barriers between restaurateur and customer, and are signs of the exciting and constant evolution of the pop-up food economy.

Shop 'til You Pop!

Shopping in the Pop-Up City

Pop-up shops have been smoking hot over the past decade. New sources of inspiration and fresh concepts were necessary for retailers to keep the experience-hunting clientele happy. Pop-up stores are not the only new retail experiences appearing under a more flexible urban landscape. The rise of online shopping could be considered a massive threat to the traditional shop on the high street as more people are finding their way to online retailers. Meanwhile, cities are left behind with abandoned shopping malls and desolate high streets. The main worry is regarding the liveliness of cities and a dramatic decline in services provided in remote and sparsely populated areas. While no one buys goods at a shop simply to improve the state of their city, new retail methods are putting high streets at risk of being abandoned. It is hard to stop this development, but help is on the way from unexpected angles that are temporary and fusionary.

The Stores Are Popping

Since 2004, the consumer trend analysts at Trendwatching.com have been reporting on a new phenomenon: pop-up retail. This new retail concept has inspired shops to pop up in dense urban areas in order to sell products on a very short-term basis. One is the American discount-chic franchise Target, which launched a temporary 140 square metre store in New York's Rockefeller Center in September 2003 to celebrate a new women's clothing line by fashion designer Isaac Mizrahi. Target was among the world's first brands to open a pop-up store, and, triggered by its success, scores more from other retailers followed in the years

The strength of the pop-up shop lies in its temporality: by existing for a fixed period of time, interim retail locations are able to generate viral interest online, ensuring that locals will be motivated to visit the store while the retailer's brand is simultaneously marketed elsewhere. Today's consumers are hungry for retail experiences that transcend the simplistic relationship between shop and customer. Shopping is no longer simply about acquiring stuff: consumers of all varieties are beginning to look to brands for inspiration and brands are doing all that they can in order to meet consumer expectations. Pop-up shops infuse an element of exclusivity and urgency into the retail experience. There are two types of pop-up stores. First,

> Vacant shopfronts offer limitless opportunities for established brands to create something unique

after. One innovative example in the early days of the pop-up shop was from Japanese fashion label Comme des Garçons. Located in a vacant building in a remote part of East Berlin, the guerrilla store was open for one year only. The shop designers were tasked with transforming a minimal budget and a derelict interior into a raw urban space that shoppers would be inspired by. The shop's location, far from any major shopping district, demanded some extra effort from the trendsetting customers seeking to visit the store. After Berlin, the guerrilla store travelled to a variety of other European cities, offering Comme des Garçons's upmarket collections in unrefined urban settings, creating a unique experience for their clientele.

there are the nomadic pop-up stores that take the entire shop with them, allowing them to be set up anywhere. The mobile pop-up store, which could be housed in anything from a truck to a shipping container, travels easily from location to location as soon as the doors are closed. Major fashion retailers have explored this type of pop-up store, including Adidas, DKNY, Lacoste, Puma, and Uniqlo. The second type of pop-up shop does not have a specific structure associated with it: rather, the store temporarily moves into a vacant space that requires attention. The enormous number of vacant shopfronts in all cities offers limitless opportunities for established brands to create something unique, as well as offering a platform for

▷ CONTINUED ON PAGE 154

Guerrilla Pioneers
—
Japanese fashion house Comme des Garçons were one of the more visible pioneers in pop-up retail. Starting in 2004 with a one-year guerrilla store located in a former bookstore in Berlin, the fashion label created a series of pop-up stores in a variety of locations, including one in a former cigarette factory in The Hague.

PHOTO COURTESY: DOLF LANGERAK

A Roller Rink and a Cube Store

Many pop-up stores seek to breathe life into an underused space. Japanese clothing retailer Uniqlo tweaked the concept to bring a fun, physical activity into one urban area. Opened for one summer under the High Line, a park located in a decommissioned section of railway tracks in Manhattan, the cubic-shaped store was part of a uniquely social fitness experience sponsored by Uniqlo, offering up a place to meet, shop, and enjoy the sun with a retail outlet next door. The company's pop-up shop and temporary roller rink were part of a two-year partnership between Uniqlo and the High Line, which supported the maintenance and operational costs of the Manhattan park.

Boxpark Pop-Up Mall

The roots of pop-up retail lie in single shops appearing for brief amounts of time in unique locations. Contemporary pop-up retail, though, is growing astronomically in size, and Boxpark is one example. Located in London's Shoreditch, Boxpark is the world's first pop-up shopping mall, comprised of sixty shipping containers that are stacked two storeys high, featuring various brands that range from mainstream to niche. Boxpark is a low-cost option for retailers looking for temporary sites to market their products inside of an innovative architectural typology. The concept is attractive to any city with a dead public space that is vast enough to house sixty shipping containers.

Independent Zine Kiosk Pops Up in the New York Subway

—

The Newsstand, an independent zine pop-up kiosk in an empty shop space in a Williamsburg subway station, offers an inspiring selection of independent magazines and publications from around the world. A joint venture between creative agency Alldayeveryday and underground publishing platform 8-Ball Zine Fair, this Brooklyn-based initiative aims to create a temporary physical platform for independent publishing in the city.

POPUPCITY.NET/29635

PHOTO COURTESY: ALLDAYEVERYDAY

Ready-Made Transformation Kit for Empty Shops

A Matchmaking Service for Temporary Spaces

San Francisco's real estate market takes a new turn with SQFT, an online service in the Mid-Market neighbourhood that aims to connect young businesses and organizations with short-term spaces in the city. SQFT allows their clientele to specify the style, size, and time frame of the space necessary for business operations through a sleek online portal, consolidating supply and demand of temporary work spaces. Through this service, underutilised spaces are activated through short-term use and commercial activity while existing businesses are bolstered through increased foot traffic.

The modular miLES system, headed by architect Eric Ho, seeks to utilise the 200 vacant storefronts in Manhattan's Lower East Side and revitalise the area through pop-up ideology. The storefront transformer intends to allow an empty storefront to host a diverse variety of short-term programmes from boutiques to community centres, meant to last for only one month.

POPUPCITY.NET/30257

PHOTO COURTESY: PATRICK KEENAN

PHOTO COURTESY: ERIC HO

Interactive Window Installation Helps Advertise Retail Space

In the Canadian city of Sherbrooke, designer Niklas Roy came up with a unique advertising technique for retail space owners who are vying for the attention of passing potential tenants. His interactive installations use surveillance cameras that track passing pedestrians and moves the sign towards where they are located. Roy's concept is an interesting take on marketing vacant space, revitalising areas plagued by empty retail space by adding a dimension of movement and excitement to advertising.

Pop-Up Shop Opens on the Information Superhighway

The pop-up retail ethos is not only restricted to physical shopfronts. San Francisco-based Quitokeeto represents a new and innovative intersection of the pop-up concept and virtual commerce. This web store offers a wide variety of products, ranging from tableware to food, maintaining a pop-up identity in that it only opens on rare and irregular occasions, notifying its customer base of opening times, new items, and restocking through an online mailing list. Quitokeeto subverts the idea that everything on the Internet should be universally accessible at all times, preserving their product value and quality through exclusivity.

POPUPCITY.NET/29741

PHOTO COURTESY: FRANÇOIS QUÉVILLON

POPUPCITY.NET/27236

PHOTO COURTESY: HEIDI SWANSON

the
gourmet
tea

São Paulo's Secret Tea Shop

—

When closed, this Gourmet Tea Store in São Paulo
is hidden behind a multi-coloured wall. However,
once opened, the wall transforms into a fully-
equipped shop, with different amenities sliding
out from behind each coloured block. Designed
by architect Alan Chu, the tea shop's design is
inspired by the brand's bright packaging for its
different tea blends, adding a hidden layer of
liquid gastronomy behind the urban fabric.

POPUPCITY.NET/21500

the
gourmet
tea

Onedayshop: Flex Retail to the Max

A new shopping initiative, unique in its ultimate flexibility, has recently appeared in the heart of a popular shopping district in Amsterdam. Onedayshop offers customers a retail space that changes concept, products, and brand by the day, while simultaneously allowing retailers to occupy empty but accommodated retail space for a period in between one and three days. This outlet of social selling allows retailers to expose their products to a broader group of potential customers rather than a local group of regulars. With new talent moving in every day, Onedayshop is a revolving door for fresh designs and an opportunity for customer exposure that thrives on its temporality.

POPUPCITY.NET/15529

PHOTO COURTESY: ONEDAYSHOP, STIJN HUPKES

Buy Your Groceries on the Seoul Train

—

A full-service grocery store has appeared in one of the subway trains in Seoul. One tourist waiting to take the subway spotted this train car converted into a fully functional grocery store, complete with a butcher. The subway grocer is an effort to increase convenience for the commuter by placing the necessary parts of the grocery store on the train. This is additional proof that the public transit authorities in the South Korean capital are continuously forward-thinking when it comes to enhancing the passenger experience.

POPUPCITY.NET/30645

PHOTO COURTESY: THE_DAY_MAN (REDDIT)

Pop-Up Clothing for the Homeless

—

Pop-up retail tends to do just that: provide retail items for purchase. One initiative in Cape Town is reversing the concept for the benefit of the city's local homeless population. Dubbed the Street Store, this pop-up shop located on a sidewalk is a place where people can drop off their unwanted clothing and someone in desperate need of some proper clothing can come to pick it up. The project's creators have made the designs available on their website so that anyone can open a Street Store in a community that needs it.

POPUPCITY.NET/32151

budding entrepreneurs to kickstart a project. Fixed-term rental contracts for underused land have created an ample supply of space for creative minds to turn their dream of opening a pop-up shop into a reality, regardless of the type. For brands, it is not simply about sales, but also experiential marketing and brand communication. For small entrepreneurs, however, the main reason to go pop-up are the low entry costs, limited risk, and the opportunity to create momentum for a blooming business.

Changing the City with Retail

In recent years, urban designers and planning professionals have discovered the potential of the pop-up shop for city-making purposes. Pop-up enterprises generate new social energy in derelict areas, filling in the gaps along the high streets and offering entrepreneurs the op-

phenomenon is that it has the power to gather significant digital audiences in the real world. These shops are often started and promoted through online energy. In the past, small shops worked for years with a significant financial and temporal debt in order to build a loyal and local clientele; nowadays, the network of a retailer's potential client base is readily available via social media, just waiting to be poached by the clever entrepreneur or the savvy marketer.

Real estate owners are starting to recognise the value of having a temporary tenant in their empty properties. These sorts of tenancy arrangements help property owners advertise their assets and attract potential long-term tenants. Landlords with open minds for new strategies are also contributing towards the city they are located in by generating short-term activity within their vacant properties. The Pop-Up Hood in Oakland, for instance, is attempting to revitalise an entire neighbourhood by turning vacant storefronts into pop-up retail spaces,

> The pop-up shop's most notable strength is the fact that it looks for unusual assets in a location, manoeuvering through the city's spatial leftovers

portunity to experiment with their retail concepts. The pop-up shop's most notable strength is the fact that it looks for unusual assets in a location; it manoeuvres through the spatial leftovers of the city and has a specific perception of what is appealing. The other main characteristic that makes the pop-up store such a curious

generating energy and interest in an area that had seemingly lost its way. Connecting owners of empty buildings with pop-up businesses has become a business in itself, as well, with a massive rise in the prominence of such agencies. Organised primarily online, firms such as PopUp Republic (Boston), SQFT (San Francisco), Storefront (New York), and We Are Pop Up (London) function as marketplaces that link vacant properties with short-term renters. The rising popularity of pop-up shops has led to rife misuse of the term. Pop-up implies spontaneity and unexpectedness; a pop-up initiative has a time-bound existence with its end always in sight. A photograph of a closed storefront in a Rotterdam's busy Central Station with a sign stating that a pop-up shop will open here soon says quite a bit to the passers-by. Six months later, the pop-up store that all of Rotterdam's commuters were waiting for has still not arrived. In the meantime, all of the surrounding shops in the main hall of the recently renewed station have already opened their doors. A pop-up shop does not remain vacant for months: these retail points are meant to close as briskly as they open, making the brevity of the initiative nearly as important as the initiative itself.

Hyper-Flexible Storefronts

Can retail become even more flexible than the pop-up store? Absolutely. Pop-up retail has the capacity to exist in increasingly extreme forms and shapes. In 2009, Onedayshop opened its doors in Amsterdam with an extreme concept: the shop changes its concept, its products, and its brand *every single day*. Onedayshop enables clients to occupy an empty retail space on a stylish high street in Amsterdam and disappear after one to three days. The concept of hyper-temporary shops that adapt to new products

each day is becoming more prolific along the world's high streets, including Amsterdam's Kalverstraat, which now accommodates a shop that temporarily offers space to brands that want to launch a new product to a considerable audience.

Characteristic for new-style shopping formulas is the centrality of the notion of flexibility. Mama Louise, a self-described 'switch shop,' opened its doors in Amsterdam in 2013, changing its owner and concept every six months and offering local entrepreneurs the chance to hawk their wares in a low-rent space. After a successful campaign at the shop, entrepreneurial sellers are stimulated to rent a more formal shopfront where they can grow further. If the venture fails, the entrepreneurs can stop without any worries or debts.

Some artists and designers take the idea of flexibility in retail to the extreme and cascade it with some of the finest forms of parasitic thinking by using conventional retail space as a hyper-temporary stage for artistic endeavours. Artist Aram Bartholl organised a series of net art exhibitions that all took place inside Internet cafés in cities across the world. Renting all of the computers simultaneously and putting on digital art made by various artists, Bartholl managed to turn ordinary Internet cafés into hyper-temporary art galleries for one night. Amsterdam-based fashion designer Elisa van Joolen chose not to exhibit her new clothing series in an art gallery or other place you would usually stumble upon this kind of work. Instead, she let her pieces infiltrate a dry clean-

▷ CONTINUED ON PAGE 164

WISSELW

Switch Shop Helps Entrepreneurs Kickstart Their Business

–

At Mama Louise in Amsterdam, entrepreneurs are given an opportunity to test drive their business models in the form of a 'switch shop'. The concept of the switch shop is simple: entrepreneurs are given six months to set up their business in a small, flexible space, after which they decide whether to rent a permanent space in the neighbourhood based on initial success, making room for the next entrepreneurial venture. The switch shop concept combines the temporary spirit of the pop-up concept with an infrastructural investment in the neighbourhood. Mama Louise encourages economic activity in an underused neighbourhood by attracting start-up entrepreneurs and clientele in search of a fresh collection of offerings. Mama Louise's first retailer, a bicycle repair shop, has proven to be successful enough for the entrepreneur to rent their own retail space in another part of the street.

De wisselwinkel huisvest ondernemers met lef en geeft ze een nieuwe ondernemer de deuren. In deze periode testen e

POPUPCITY.NET/27070

PHOTO COURTESY: STIJN HUPKES

One Night Only:
An Internet Art Gallery

Using unconventional spaces as exhibition spaces is all the rage these days, but one of the more innovative examples comes from Aram Bartholl. The artist opened his Speed Show exhibitions in Internet cafés in cities around the world, including Milan, Vancouver, and Hong Kong. Using the open browsers of every computer in the space, Bartholl displayed net art for one night only. Speed Show helped take the pop-up principle from public spaces into a private business, generating momentum and interest in a place visitors might otherwise walk straight past.

 POPUPCITY.NET/8730

PHOTO COURTESY: ARAM BARTHOLL, DAM GALLERY AND XPO GALLERY

Fashion Exhibit Infiltrates a Dry Cleaners

Dutch fashion designer and artist Elisa van Joolen displayed her new fashion collection right between the clothes racks at Multi-Clean, a dry cleaners in downtown Amsterdam. Doing so, she transformed a local laundry into a home of fashion design for only one weekend. For her '11" x 17"' series, which was exhibited inside the shop, van Joolen took donations of samples from a wide array of clothing designers, from large to small and from haute couture to mass market. She then cut up and inverted both sweaters and footwear so that the source is barely recognisable. The parasite principle was central to many aspects of the exhibition, including the visual identity and communication. The invitations to the opening event were printed on dry cleaners tickets, and the website of Multi-Clean was tweaked by van Joolen to present the project online.

💻 POPUPCITY.NET/30215

PHOTO COURTESY: GERT-JAN VAN ROOIJ

Not Your Typical Cactus Farm

A new trend in social selling has been spotted in East Asia: box shops. Cactus Farm in Singapore is one such example, featuring displays with multitudes of boxes that serve as small displays for individual designers and vendors. Sellers can select their box and showcase their wares within a 48-hour turnaround, allowing for box rental for as little as a three-month commitment. Entrepreneurs maintain ownership, while paying a basic fee for their cube and consenting to a small commission being taken on each item sold. The Cactus Farm offers rentals for a variety of time periods that are flexible enough for up-and-coming designers as well as established brands. Box shops allow people to showcase their products alongside other temporary renters for reasonable rates in order to test the marketability of new products.

POPUPCITY.NET/17036

PHOTO COURTESY: CACTUS FARM

Rent a Shelf at Flohpalast

In Munich, a new innovative second-hand retail concept called Flohpalast is rapidly gaining popularity. Flohpalast rents shelves to clientele who want to make money by selling their old belongings, but do not have the time to go to a flea market or sell their stuff online. The resulting shop maintains the atmosphere of a second hand store and the diversity of a flea market. This initiative is part of the greater movement in retail of social selling, where retail formulae are based on the joined forces of product providers. Collectively, they create a sales platform, primarily at flexible spaces that are suited to swift changes.

POPUPCITY.NET/14355

PHOTO COURTESY: POP-UP CITY

A London Supermarket Owned by its Customers

—

The People's Supermarket in London is a green-grocer that makes grocery shopping more social and more communal. The People's Supermarket provides a locally-sourced alternative to poor selections or quality at local supermarkets. Organised as a co-operative, this supermarket is exclusive to members, who pay an annual fee and volunteer four hours per month, allowing prices to remain low while maintaining product quality. The members decide collectively on which products the supermarket offers. In doing so, they take back the power in urban food distribution, which is generally in hands of the big supermarket chains.

POPUPCITY.NET/9969

PHOTO COURTESY: DANIEL COOPER

ers in Amsterdam. Displaying art and design in a parasitic way leads to different perceptions of what is being displayed. An exhibition infiltrating a dry cleaners or an Internet café, with pieces of designer clothing hanging in between the freshly steamed suits and digital artwork in a narrow corridor, gives both the artwork and the spaces an enhanced sense of purpose.

Making Selling More Social

Retailers and entrepreneurs alike are creating a new formula for starting a business venture. They join forces in order to attract clientele and to limit expenses. These joint venture shops are not related to one specific retailer any longer, but become a shared place for a number of different small-scale merchants. As a consequence of the economic downturn, young enterprises must be cautious with their capital. Sharing risks and expenses allows retailers to profit from each other's efforts and more easily realise fresh concepts that fit perfectly with a strong online client base.

An interesting trend in the world of hyper-flexible retailing is the box shop. Box shops are shops that are comprised of several boxes stacked on top of one another, usually spacious enough to house one or two products. Each of the boxes functions as a micro-store that displays products that an individual box renter wants to sell. This trend has gained traction in East Asian cities including Hong Kong, Shanghai, Singapore, Taipei, and Tokyo. These cities are characterised by monumental levels of population density and a shortage of developable land and are thus the ideal cities for developing a micro-retailing movement. The Cactus Farm box shop in Singapore, for instance, offers affordable and fully-serviced retail spaces to designers inside of a shopping mall, enabling them to showcase their products together with other temporary co-renters. Renters can get their hands on a cubic micro-shop for a reasonable daily fee for a short time in order to test the market for a new product. The box shop concept infuses a social element into the retail experience and makes the act of selling more accessible to all.

Social selling initiatives are not solely limited to designers and retailers, but to any person with something to sell. Flohpalast is a hyper-flexible social selling initiative located in two German cities. These shopfronts rent out single shelves to individuals looking to sell second-hand items. The well-curated and highly differentiated collections of shelves make it interesting for customers to drop in. A similar initiative from Tokyo is a second-hand store called Pass the Baton. Focussed on style and personal culture, each item for sale is presented alongside a short story by and about its seller. Visiting the store, then, is less about a simplistic relationship between buyer and product and more about transferring stewardship of a unique piece: the object comes with a written history of the individual selling it, and the buyer inherits an object filled with meaning from its previous life.

▷ CONTINUED ON PAGE 169

Self-Service Bicycle Repair Station

—

Bike Fixtation offers a DIY bicycle repair station for cyclists across the Minneapolis-St. Paul metropolitan area, manifesting in the form of a self-service kiosk. The kiosks, installed at temporarily vacant shopfronts, feature vending machines with bicycle repair equipment and tools, as well as bike repair stands and tire pumps for use by any cyclist in need. As the station is unmanned, operational costs can remain low, making it simple and cost-effective to temporarily repurpose a vacant space.

POPUPCITY.NET/13851

PHOTO COURTESY: BIKE FIXTATION

③ 구매할 상품의 바코드/QR코드를 스캔한다
SHOPPING IN THE POP-UP CITY
(Scan the Barcode or QR code of product with smart phone)

Subway Platform Supermarket

—

In South Korea, supermarket chain Tesco has implemented a virtual supermarket shopping system on subway platforms. Groceries are displayed on life-sized posters with QR codes, to be scanned and paid for via mobile devices after which the physical groceries are then sent to a pre-specified address. This concept both utilises customer time spent waiting for the train and decreases Tesco's need for physical space in the way that a conventional supermarket does.

POPUPCITY.NET/18375

③ 선택한 상품을 모바일 장바구니에 담는다
(Add more products to mobile cart)

④ 상품선택이 끝나면 구매버튼을 누른다
(Make a purchase)

HOTO COURTESY: TESCO PLC

Augmented Reality Supermarkets

Yihaodian, China's biggest food specialist E-commerce website, is launching 1,000 virtual stores around China. The project, Unlimited Yihaodian, is based on augmented reality technology and allows smartphone users to wander through dead urban spaces and transform them into retail outlets. The augmented reality shop eliminates the majority of the costs associated with having a store, while also reinvigorating underused urban space. Yihaodian's goal is to build virtual supermarkets that are 1,200 square meters in size and stock around 1,000 products. The virtual stores allow shoppers to order goods directly from their mobile phone and have the goods delivered directly to their door.

POPUPCITY.NET/26508

PHOTO COURTESY: YIHAODIAN

Scanning Your Purchase

The development of the Quick Response Code, or QR code, has exploded since its days as a method of increasing efficiency in the Japanese automotive production lines, becoming a multifunctional tool that serves as a hyperlink to any task that a mobile device can handle. The QR code has led to an experimental wave in retail, facilitating on-the-go shopping using only a mobile device. Online retail not only grows the potential customer base, but it serves as a cost-saving measure for business owners, allowing them to display their product lines without having them displayed in a physical storefront.

In 2012, Tesco and Samsung opened a virtual grocery store in Seoul. Placed inside a subway station, the HomePlus store is a fully stocked grocer with one major difference: none of the products for sale are actually present. The store mimics the look and feel of a grocery store by using cardboard cut-outs of grocery store aisles where each product has an accompanying QR code. When customers want to purchase a product, they scan the QR code using a mobile device and get the items delivered straight to their doorstep. While this might not be the best way to pick out the perfect pepper, it is certainly a convenient way to purchase non-perishable items on the commute home. Another example from the Netherlands, Twiet.nu is a project in The Hague that combines the idea of the box shop with the ease and power of online retail. The company rents out boxes in a shop window to web shop owners, which they can use to display their products offline and promote it to a

new group of potentially interested consumers on the streets of The Hague. By scanning a QR code, shoppers can purchase products immediately with their smartphones. The concept is a stroke of genius: while most retailers simply have an online store and physical storefronts in the city, Twiet.nu ensures that the two are intertwined, giving any designer, regardless of their location, the opportunity to show their wares publicly in a metropolitan setting.

The efficacy of QR codes in an age of augmented reality is questionable: there is no tell-tale sign as to what you will be redirected to when you scan a QR code, with the results being either as harmless as a promotional website or potentially more sinister activities such as running a virus or redirecting to a pornographic website. However, with the strong rise of mobile payment methods, the QR code could become an interesting link between the offline and online world. Offline, one can better showcase a product, while online, one can pay more easily. Every wall, bus stop, and fence can be transformed into digital shopping centres, department stores, or boutiques.

In Toronto, Mattel and Walmart collaborated to open up a pop-up virtual toy store. With two walls of three-dimensional toy images, consumers can simultaneously window-shop and make purchases using their phones. It is not a coincidence that major brands are exploring these forms of combined online-offline sales — they recognise the power of online shopping. Nevertheless, they understand that consumers remain interested in

▷ CONTINUED ON PAGE 172

A 3-D Printing Studio on Wheels

Stuck with a broken car in or around Paris? Help is on the way! French multinational car manufacturer Renault has teamed up with additive manufacturing company leFabShop to offer additive manufacturing services on-the-go and a set of wheels to anyone who may need either or both. The result takes form in an electric vehicle equipped with a mobile 3-D printer that offers mobility to the owners of broken-down vehicles as well as a means of production and delivery for anyone who may need something printed. This combination of product and service stands to cater to a niche market within the rapidly popularizing realm of 3-D printing technology.

Delivery Drones

While aerial drones do not have the best reputation in this day and age, the online retail sector is making strides to use drones in a more utilitarian way. Amazon.com's famous Octocopter has been featured in news reports all over the world, while DHL is experimenting with a smaller drone that can carry packages of up to three kilograms. These innovations could be useful not only for in-city parcel deliveries but also emergency situations. Make sure to add a landing platform to your mailbox!

💻 POPUPCITY.NET/30638

Drive-Through Luxury

Waiting at home for that parcel to be delivered can be a bit of a chore for those of us that have to be at work during weekdays. Selfridges, a luxury retailer in England, has added a Click & Collect service for online shoppers. Instead of having their gifts shipped to their doors, customers are notified when the goods are available for pick-up at a designated drive-through service at a central London location. Who needs home delivery when you can get your goodies on your outbound commute?

POPUPCITY.NET/31352

PHOTO COURTESY: SELFRIDGES

the physical experience of going shopping. Well-known brands often partner up with on-line retail specialists who have the know-how when it comes to online sales and distribution.

lustre with local residents. The physical mani-festation of online commercial enterprises is shifting the negative image of these increasingly abandoned commercial centres. A new shop ty-pology is cmerging here: the hybrid niche store.

Every wall, bus stop, and tence can be transformed into digital shopping centres

Shopping with QR codes leads us to the next logical step in the retail process: how to physi-cally acquire it. For many, having your goods shipped to your home address has been the status quo for years and will remain so for the foreseeable future. However, the notion of hav-ing a permanent mailing address is becoming more cumbersome. The mailbox of the future is less about maintaining an immovable spot where your mail can be dropped off at: rather, it is about having a membership within a net-work where your mail can be shipped to which-ever location is most convenient for you. Secure lockers, parcel machines, and pick-up services are spawning in convenience stores, high-traffic areas, and even pubs. As retailers increase their digital presence, parcel delivery services are re-inventing how we view the concept of a mailing address.

Animating the Hybrid High Street

Many once-vibrant high streets, plagued by high vacancy rates, are beginning to lose their

These stores combine the web shop with a spe-cialised one-man store. In normal circumstanc-es, small niche shops would have major difficul-ties surviving away from streets with high levels of daytime foot traffic, just because their niche is so narrow. As the retail landscape changes with new concepts and a transformed property market, empty shopfronts are becoming desir-able spots for web shop owners to extend their store to the real world. These hybrid shops are accelerating gentrification processes, for better or for worse, in neighbourhoods as they take a pioneering role in underused shopping districts. This new hybrid retail model is also a new way for Web enterprises to reach out to customers in the real world with physical brand experienc-es on top of their online platform. "A physical store offers shoppers the chance to touch, feel, and try on merchandise, and for luxury brands in particular, this is important," writes Lindsay Baker, a business reporter for the BBC.

A great number of examples of this fusion are occurring, for example, in Dutch and British cities. Thisissoul is an Amsterdam-based hy-brid shop that sells in-line skate equipment. The small shop is not necessarily dependent

▷ CONTINUED ON PAGE 175

Making Your Online Reputation Street Visible

A Hybrid Store for Skaters

The web store for in-line skating equipment retailer Thisissoul landed some years ago in an Amsterdam high street facing serious vacancy issues. Thisissoul is a company that one would expect to have more success online than on the street. But low rental rates in this neighbourhood give webshop operators such as Thisissoul the opportunity to open a real shop in a real shopping street, breathing new life into a struggling area. Their shop is small and clients do not necessarily live in the neighbourhood. Instead, the shop focusses on the worldwide market on the web and serves the Amsterdam metropolitan region from its store. The hybrid store thus combines the best of both worlds.

French tech start-up Smiirl has developed Fliike, a real-time counter of Facebook fans that can be displayed in a shop window. The counter demonstrates the presence of a digital community and serves as advertising, tailor-made for small local shop owners. In this way, Fliike helps shop owners create a strong link between their online and offline presence by advertising their digital popularity to the local audience in the street.

POPUPCITY.NET/25617

PHOTO COURTESY: POP-UP CITY

POPUPCITY.NET/29279

PHOTO COURTESY: SMIIRL

Look Mum, No Hands!

—

Think of a bike repairman no longer as an old guy wearing blue overalls, hidden in the back of a dark and decrepit garage. In the London-based bike repair shop Look Mum No Hands, the repair-man is also your barista. Look Mum No Hands is a cycling-themed cafe that functions as the central meeting spot for London's cycling community. Besides drinking coffee, eating sandwiches, and watching the Tour de France, visitors can also use the available equipment to repair their bikes. Shops of this style are a fusion between two completely different functions and are increasingly present in the modern city, offering a niche in the urban retail jungle.

POPUPCITY.NET/10389

PHOTO COURTESY: LOOK MUM NO HANDS

on local customers, realising that their focus is somewhat of a niche business. Instead, the shop focusses on the online worldwide market and serves the Amsterdam metropolitan region from its store. Back in a sleepy residential area of Amsterdam is Salsamentum, a hybrid offline-online shop that carries all kinds of salt. The rise of online shopping is a huge threat for the liveability and economic vitality of shopping streets in urban areas, but there is still

periential retail concepts. Functional fusion turns a conventional shop into a social space in which customers spend extended amounts of time.

Just add coffee: it seems to be a quite successful strategy for prompting customers to extend their visits. Simply ensure that staff know how to sell a shoulder bag in addition to a flat white. Bookstores have a lengthy history of in-

Empty shopfronts are becoming desirable spots for web shop owners to extend their store to the real world

hope for businesses that are able to produce a viable business model that can focus attention simultaneously on the community and the outside world.

This Laundromat Is a Bar, Too

The thought that only the gargantuan department stores can accommodate experimental concepts is becoming increasingly outdated. Shops are choosing to house functional combinations that would normally only be found in separate shopfronts. The motivations for fusing different retail formulae into a single enterprise are plentiful. In doing so, shopkeepers attempt to increase profit levels through a diversified clientele. These cost-effective shops add new space uses to neighbourhoods that might not otherwise benefit from their presence, adding an appealing new space typology based on ex-

cluding a coffee bar in a space to prompt visitors to inspect the literary offerings at greater lengths, but other retail sectors are starting to experiment with this fusion, including print shops, launderettes, and bicycle repair shops. The most successful of these fusions start by offering some variety of a lifestyle-related product line and finish with a caffeinated beverage. Applying a coffee bar formula to existing retail creates a profound connection with the customer base. One creates a community around a brand or a service with specific lifestyle components in it, instead of offering a single take-away service.

One effective example of this trend is Wash & Coffee in Munich, a shop that houses a stylish laundromat and a coffee bar at the same time. While the washing machine is doing the dirty work, customers can relax in the lounge and order espresso-based drinks. Interestingly, Wash & Coffee rethinks the laundromat as a social community place, establishing it as the

▷ CONTINUED ON PAGE 178

Please, Don't Spill Beer on the Laundry

—

Wasbar in the Belgian city of Ghent brings together practicality and recreation by combining a bar and laundromat, giving patrons a means of entertainment as they wait for their wash cycles to finish. Wasbar even invites musicians and DJs to perform at organised events, providing a space of creativity and socialization in a place otherwise known for fostering boredom and unrest. This adds an element of glamour and innovation to completing banal, everyday tasks such as doing the laundry.

 POPUPCITY.NET/29011

PHOTO COURTESY: WASBAR

living room of the global village and a celebration of metropolitan lifestyle. Copenhagen's Fotocaféen is a print shop and coffee bar that combines the arts of photography and printing with a space to sit, hang out, talk, and drink coffee. The place has a bar like atmosphere and design, giving way to a large number of printing devices, and providing services such as complimentary Wi-Fi. The bar also fulfills the role of a meeting place for Copenhagen's photography scene, giving it an artistic touch. A third example is Drink, Shop, & Do, a design shop and café in London that not only sells products from emerging designers alongside vintage furniture and homeware goods, but also organises events and design workshops to give the space an enhanced sense of community. London's Rough Trade record shop on Brick Lane is designed in such a way that all of the furniture can easily be removed in order to transform the space into a hyper-temporary concert hall.

As shopkeepers are facing tough times due to the meteoric rise of e-commerce within a more austere economy, new strategies must be developed to keep the urban core liveable and appealing. Cities can channel the power of trends such as hybrid shopping, flexible shopping concepts, and new technological innovations in order to informally delegate placemaking responsibilities to individual city residents with a tangible interest in contributing to the community. Rethinking retail strategies is not only of use to cities interested in concentrating developments at metropolitan nodes or in reactivating underused streets; a retail rethink is critical for dislocated urban areas and even smaller villages in order to keep the energy on the streets flowing. As urbanites alter their consumption patterns, so too must city planners anticipate temporally-bound shopping experiences for all types of goods and all varieties of consumers by increasing available opportunities for short-term land use changes and flexible leasing arrangements.

Urban Hack-tivism

and the Facebook Generation

Urban Hacktivism and the Facebook Generation
Public Space in the Pop-Up City

That which belongs to everyone also belongs to no one, and there is no part of the city that exemplifies this better than public space. No single entity feels responsible for the provision of public space, and yet many claim temporary possession of it to further their needs. In addition, social media developments are lessening the importance of public space as people gather more efficiently online. We use Facebook and WhatsApp as communication platforms over the town square, we shop on Amazon and leave behind empty shopping streets, and kids prefer their digital playgrounds over physical playgrounds. New strategies must be found to give meaning to our collective places. Urban designers have historically been charged with caring for the public realm of the urban landscape for many years; but, as civic governments surrender their power either consciously or neglectfully, new placemakers are enhancing and even creating the places of public life through space reclamation, urban hacking, and even bottom-up urbanism. There is one element that they have in common: citizens are opening up decision-making processes and taking back control of the public realm.

Hacking the City
Streets

When you open your eyes and look closely at the urban environment, all sorts of micro-level interventions can be found in our public spaces: improvised chairs attached to fences provide seats to tired passers-by and create small spots for social interaction; open-source micro-libraries are found in abandoned phone booths; and urban activists install temporary swing sets at bus stops, bridges or in underground trains to give adults a brief respite from the doldrums of the working life. New social groups engage with the urban environment and develop a fresh generation of forward-thinking city-makers. But where does this renewed interest in taking ownership of the city come from? Cities are certainly not, on the whole, declining in aesthetic value as compared to ten years ago, while city streets are not all suffering from government neglect. Something, though, is pushing the public domain, making it a critical place for broadcasting constructive criticism and testing new concepts.

In 2008, Berlin-based street artist Jan Vormann began repairing cracked urban spaces using LEGO bricks. His small, colourful urban hacks, on the one hand, addressed the issue of public space maintenance, while, on the other hand, it made very minute parts of public space just look a little better and more fun. Vormann's Dispatchwork project turned out to be a remarkable example of an intervention that gets a digital second life, as street art and urbanism

blogs from all over the world covered the project. International acclaim turned Vormann's small-scale repairs of building corners into a major milestone in the urban hacking movement, stimulating urbanites across the globe to repair and decorate public spaces themselves. Their collective efforts can be considered a statement addressing the fact that public consultation for public spaces is, in many cities, inadequate, despite the fact that the responsible authorities are not doing enough to foster high-quality public spaces. As one of the early proponents of the urban hacking, Jan Vormann expressed what many others felt: Why are we not allowed to make the city better ourselves?

While the graffiti artists of the 1980s and the 1990s were primarily interested in publicly exhibiting their artwork on every street object imaginable and expanding their territory through their pieces, contemporary street artists and urban hacktivists do not only take the city as a canvas but use their energy to improve public spaces, without prior solicitation. Architects and urban designers have started to adopt the do-it-yourself principles of urban hackers. In 2008, San Francisco-based design studio Rebar Group started organising public events in their hometown, where artists, designers, and citizens transform metered parking spots into temporary public parks. PARK(ing) Day grew from being a single event in one city into a global movement that regularly reclaims the significant share of space reserved for cars for use by pedestrians, feeding the parking meter with coins in order to use the spaces in a less automobile-centric way. Thanks to PARK(ing)

Day's popularity, the parklet has become a public space typology that has been adopted by cities around the world, including Dublin, where parklets were installed as part of a civic development strategy based on urban hacking principles.

While many designs and projects considered to be urban hacks tend to be more playful in nature and aim to cause a moment of introspection, micro-urbanism inclines towards making any variety of alterations to public space that provides some form of utility in terms of convenience, productivity, or social interaction. Micro-urbanist interventions are cost-effective

It's All About
Momentum

In 2003, flash mobs became a worldwide trend, infusing a breath of fresh air into the public realm. All of a sudden, hundreds of commuters froze in place on cue in New York's Grand Central Terminal; an ordinary shopping mall became the stage for an opera performance; and five-minute pillow fights on quiet afternoons took over the city streets. After each flash mob, the 'actors' walk away in different directions to never see each other again. These hyper-temporary gatherings, driven by collectives

Contemporary street artists not only take the city as a canvas but use their energy to improve public spaces

solutions to a small-scale deficiency, often carried out by individuals to improve their own immediate urban surroundings. New Yorker Alexandra Pulver, for instance, was clearly frustrated by the lack of decent spots to eat lunch on the streets of Manhattan. When she started Pop-Up Lunch, a project that added small tables and seating to sidewalk objects such as fire hydrants, Pulver achieved multiple goals: by providing unique combinations of street furniture and sidewalk objects, the Pop-Up Lunch created a bevy of new social spaces at lunchtime that leads the average passer-by to rethink the function of the sidewalk and the objects located on it.

such as New York-based Improv Everywhere, gave public space a new function as a perpetually open stage for experimentation and performance by anyone willing to stage an event. Flash mobs are so temporary that they hardly exist without the single organising force taking the effort to carefully record and publish the results. Planned online in advance through social media platforms and published online after execution on Flickr or YouTube, these micro-happenings perfectly stress how social media contributes to a reborn public realm.

The combination of hyperflexibility and online collective power has become a critical force in

▷ CONTINUED ON PAGE 204

LEGO Fixes in Berlin

—

Berlin-based artist Jan Vormann is fixing small instances of urban decay by using colourful pieces
of LEGO. The project, known as Dispatchworks,
spread across the planet to over thirty cities including Budapest, Cape Town, Sydney, and Tokyo,
where people repaired broken walls with LEGO.
His project was one of the first to combine the
ideas of street art with a dialogue on the condition of the urban realm.

POPUPCITY.NET/9304

PHOTO COURTESY: MARC PHU (MARC0047 ON FLICKR)

Taking File-Sharing Offline

—

Initiated by Aram Bartholl in 2010, Dead Drops is an anonymous and offline peer-to-peer sharing network comprised of USB drives stuck into the middle of building exteriors across New York. Users can (somewhat awkwardly) stick their laptop into the side of the building to leave or take files with an element of complete surprise. The project creates a secret platform for leaving bits of information in the physical world. What about sharing music or films without the chance of being traced by copyright-protecting organisations? Forget about Netflix, your next video store is in the wall.

 POPUPCITY.NET/9170

PHOTO COURTESY: ARAM BARTHOLL, DAM GALLERY, AND XPO GALLERY

Preventing Recyclable Waste with Pfandring

—

Empty beer bottles and other containers are a common sight in most cities, especially in Germany where beer is sold on nearly every street corner. Empty bottles are strewn across the city and accumulate in numbers. Most mornings, though, the streets tend to be clear of this debris due to individuals collecting them to redeem the recycling deposit. The time-consuming process of searching for these recyclables is made more efficient by Paul Ketz's ring-shaped installation, Pfandring. By placing these attachments around rubbish bins, a collection of returnable recyclables is left by pedestrians in a convenient place for those returning them.

POPUPCITY.NET/18129

PHOTO COURTESY: PAUL KETZ

A Scaffold Hangout

The pedestrian experience in New York, amidst the over 6,000 scaffolds covering the streets, has been pimped by the Softwalks initiative in 2012. New York has recently seen large-scale innovations of the city's public spaces, but Softwalks is a much more humble initiative that ensures that any pedestrian in need of a seat can sit on a pop-up chair on any scaffold from which they would like to watch the city pass them by. Besides seats, the Softwalks toolkit consists of counters, plants, and light reflectors in order to make a complete refurbishment of the ubiquitous scaffold possible. The guerrilla intervention was paid for by the local community through a crowdfunding campaign.

Sharing Page-Turners on a Public Bench

Several benches in Amsterdam's many parks were, during the summer of 2013, transformed into Ruilbanken (literally, barter benches in Dutch) by creative studio Pivot. The signature of these public benches is the red metal clip attached to the bench where people can find books or magazines tucked into the clip. The idea is that strollers can sit down while enjoying something that has been left there by like-minded people who like to share experiences in the urban space.

Build Your Own Bike Lanes

In cities such as Amsterdam and Copenhagen, it is impossible to imagine having to fight for proper cycling infrastructure. However, most cities are not as bicycle-friendly as those in Denmark or the Netherlands. Toronto's Urban Repair Squad are taking matters into their own hands and forcing their city to become a safe haven for cyclists. Through spraying stencils of bike symbols on city streets, these Torontonians are showing how to motivate a citizenry to be open to alternative modes of transportation and to push their civic governments into gear. When a city is not creating bike paths, cyclists can create them on their own, with the hope that, eventually, the city will turn the guerrilla project into real infrastructure.

 POPUPCITY.NET/29716

PHOTO COURTESY: JOSÉ SUBERO AND PAULA COLCHERO

POPUPCITY.NET/621

PHOTO COURTESY: MARTIN REIS

Citizen-Made Wayfinding

Urban designer Matt Tomasulo launched Walk [Your City], a website through which users can generate custom street signs. The main objectives of the platform are building a local sense of community and helping citizens become more engaged with their surroundings.

Focussing on increasing walkability, the attractive signs show the calculated minutes of walking or cycling from one point to another. The signs are somewhat expensive to order, and the sign is always at risk of disappearing when spotted by some enthusiastic policeman. However, street interventions such as these provoke people to make their neighbourhood more accessible and walkable.

POPUPCITY.NET/30193

PHOTO COURTESY: MATT TOMASULO

The World's First Travelling Park

–

Rotterdam-based architecture agency HUNK-Design and artist ID Eddy have created a 36 by 25 metre Persian rug out of artificial grass. Their Flying Grass Carpet has travelled the world since 2010 and lands in places where a temporary impulse in public space is needed. The plug-in landscape has already provided several cities, including Istanbul, Madrid, and Shanghai, with a new, hyper-flexible ground for social gathering and cultural events.

POPUPCITY.NET/55

DIY Toolkit for Urban Hacking

City administrators as well as residents are equally responsible for maintaining quality public spaces. Whenever these spaces need some sort of major improvement, it is the city's responsibility to do so. If these improvements fail to materialise, that is when the citizenry steps in. Interventions such as that by the team behind Fabrique Hacktion twist and turn public spaces at the micro level in order to enhance the user experience, such as coat racks on exterior walls, train ticket reuse dispensers, and mobile phone charging stations in disused phone booths. The interesting idea here is that Fabrique Hacktion provides a toolkit. Their DIY hacks are made instantly available and can easily be exported to other cities. All designs are made according to open design principles, meaning that anyone can access, use, and adapt the files provided online. This way, the global online community works collectively on redesigning the city through micro-interventions.

POPUPCITY.NET/13989

Fertilising Freely with the P-Tree

—

Men prefer trees as places to empty a full bladder. The P-Tree by Rogier Martens is a mobile urinal that is wrapped around a tree. Its simple construction consists of a urinal, hoses, straps, and lashings, and can be connected to a waste pipe joined to a container. During festivals or events, or in public gardens, the P-Tree can be found wrapped around trees in various colours and provides the possibility for those who do not mind standing up during the act to go in the wild with style.

🖥 POPUPCITY.NET/17431

PHOTO COURTESY: ROGIER MARTENS

Lounging in a Parking Spot

—

Valuable urban space tends to be occupied by parking spaces, be they garages, vacant lots, or street-side parking stalls. Parks and spaces for hanging out are not prioritised by many cities, especially in the United States. However, once the meter of a parking space is paid, precious city space is yours to use, so why not use it for PARK(ing)? In 2005, Rebar Group hosted the first PARK(ing) Day in their hometown of San Fran-cisco. During PARK(ing) Day, which has grown into an annual international event, people around the globe transform street parking spaces into temporary microparks. The aim is to improve the quality of public space by enabling people to enjoy nature, seating, sun, and shade, instead of passing yet another public space dedicated to private vehicles.

POPUPCITY.NET/25664

ent This Truck! Call (510) 848-6523

PHOTO COURTESY: REBAR ART & DESIGN STUDIO

No to Petrol, Yes to Film!

Clerkenwell Road's Cineroleum in London is likely the first derelict petrol station ever to be transformed into a cinema. Handcrafted using donated and recycled materials, a group of designers, artists, and architects made an evening cinema that is open four nights per week for a low entrance fee, breathing life into a once-abandoned space. There were around 4,000 abandoned petrol stations in the United Kingdom in 2010, but at least one was temporarily revamped into a cultural hotspot.

POPUPCITY.NET/8638

PHOTO COURTESY: STUDIO DEKKA (FLICKR)

Activating the Streeeeeet

During the International Biennale for Landscape Urbanism in Bat Yam, Israeli designers Guy Königstein and Vincent Wittenberg created a public bench that resembles the place where you pick up a shopping cart at the grocery store. Existing public benches were replaced with individual, moveable seats so that people could choose to sit wherever they preferred. The bench offers passers-by the opportunity to get a seat for a five shekel coin and use it as long as they want. This way, the public bench has become flexible and adaptive to the user's wishes. It can be taken into the sun, or the shade, individual chairs can be set up to be placed opposite of each other or next to each other. The project investigates the meaning of public ownership and creates a complex system within which people find their own way of using their surroundings.

POPUPCITY.NET/10668

PHOTO COURTESY: GUY KÖNIGSTEIN AND VINCENT WITTENBERG

Hanoi's Mobile Skyscraper

—

Bicycles are common in many cities the world over, but it is not very often that you see a building go by on two (or three) wheels. Swiss architecture firm Bureau A designed a seven-storey skyscraper and threw it on top of a tricycle. The structure, made up of steel tubes and a PVC roof, is equipped with a fan and lighting for those hot, late nights in Hanoi. The structure can be used in a variety of ways, including as an exhibition space or a kitchen. A novel concept for taking your public space on the road as long as they are mindful of the bridges overhead!

POPUPCITY.NET/30747

PHOTO COURTESY: BORIS ZULIANI AND BUREAU A

Situationist International Redux

—

Projects such as the inflatable event space
Spacebuster by Berlin-based architects Raumlabor embody a revival of the Situationist International movement of the 1960s and 1970s, an
avant-garde collective that believes in the importance of spectacle as a meaningful element of
daily life. The main goal of Spacebuster is to bring
targeted momentum to a specific location in
order to recalibrate conventional urban spaces.
Raumlabor used a porous and translucent material that inflates from the back of a van, creating
a temporary, portable space for events holding
eighty attendees.

POPUPCITY.NET/2669

Nike Launches On-Demand Street Football Pitch

In 2013, Nike Football Spain launched an on-demand laser beam installation in Madrid that can turn any public space into a street football pitch. The #mipista campaign allows street football players in six different neighbourhoods of Madrid to request a pop-up pitch with a smartphone, after which a team of specialists drive to the location and set up an ad hoc football pitch using a laser projection system and a crane.

POPUPCITY.NET/29799

A Symphonic Swingset

Many designated entertainment districts suffer from an image problem of being overly regulated and too specifically geared towards a specific type of night out. Montréal's Quartier des Spectacles is doing things a little bit differently, though, with 21 multi-coloured swings that have been spread across the district. These swings differ slightly from the ones that you find in your local park: each individual swing is actually a musical instrument. As people swing, recorded noises of pianos and other instruments play. The more people swinging, the greater the symphony that fills the streets of old Montréal.

POPUPCITY.NET/13460

City-Sized Board Games

The spread of flash mobs in most cities around the world has, to some extent, been replaced by another fun urban phenomenon: urban gaming. These experience games are popping up in the public spaces of metropolitan regions and encourage people to use the social realm in alternative ways. Pac-Manhattan was a project organised by students in the Interactive Telecommunications programme at New York University in 2004. Ten players in the game recreate the experience of the 1980s classic, with one Pac Man, four ghosts, and a team of five working in a remote control room to oversee the game. Pac-Manhattan turned public space into a place that is not only used for daily routines but also for excitement and gaming, adding a rather mysterious layer to city life. It must be awkward, though, to see groups of people running in the urban jungle dressed like Pac-Man characters!

urbanism in recent years. Momentum-oriented urban interventions can be considered the architectural equivalent of the flash mob. Some momentum-generating interventions perform a temporary wholesale renovation of how a particular space is used, whether it is through a temporary installation or the temporary use of a particular space for a completely different purpose. In 2008, HUNK-design and Studio ID Eddy, two design agencies from Rotterdam, launched an apt example of the former type of momentum-generating intervention with a 36 by 25 metre Persian carpet made entirely out of artificial grass. The temporary park easily plugs into squares in order to generate a short-term space for social activity that differs from conventional public square use. The gigantic rug has been travelling the world ever since, from Rotterdam to Aachen, Budapest, and Istanbul, offering a poignant example of temporary ur-

ture palace. The temporary cinema was made out of donated materials and was only open for a single summer, but it stimulated a discussion on the perception of the neighbourhood and how Londoners can contribute to a positive image of the area. The motivating ambition of these kinds of projects is not to contribute to long-term urban planning missives, but, rather, to short-term activations with more emotional and psychological aims.

Projects such as these can serve as a unique starting point for local urbanists to take the lead in revitalising a specific area. Official planning frameworks are avoided in this manner due to the temporal nature of pop-up initiatives in public spaces. Temporary interventions, however, possess the power to cause the more static forces of urban change, such as the urban planning departments of civic governments, to

> Momentum-oriented urban interventions can be considered the architectural equivalent of the flash mob

ban design. Other projects in this category have not sought to temporarily alter how people use a popular public space, but simply to breathe some sort of life into a space with the aim of raising awareness of how abandoned structures can be changed for the better. In 2010, a derelict petrol station in London was transformed into a hand-built cinema, celebrating the extravagance and spectacle of the historical pic-

sit up and take notice of a citizenry yearning for change.

The City Is a Game

In recent years, we have discovered an incredible number of playful urban initiatives, projects that, regardless of their size and scale, attempt

▷ CONTINUED ON PAGE 213

Bounce, Bounce, Bounce!

Estonian design studio Salto has built a 50-metre long trampoline sidewalk known as the Fast Track in a forest near Nikola–Lenivets in Russia. Primarily created for the Archstoyanie Festival, the extraordinary trampoline provides an alternative mode of getting through the park, allowing people to bounce amidst the nature. This gigantic trampoline has become an integral part of the park infrastructure as both a pathway and an art installation. The trampoline forces the traveller to reconsider how architecture and landscape interact, all while making for a fun park experience.

POPUPCITY.NET/24884

PHOTO COURTESY: KARLI LUIK

99 Ways to Play London

—

In 2012, Londoners were given nearly a hundred reasons not to be bored, when 99 tiny games could be found in the city's public spaces. The idea,which formed part of the outdoor arts festival Showtime, was to make people enjoy accessible entertainment in the great urban outdoors. Bus stops, bandstands, parks, and shopping malls were equipped with stickers on the walls and pavement, containing the rules of tiny little games that could be played instantly. Although the games were designed specifically for pedestrians, all 99 games were collected on a digital map, so that one could also seek them out. Hidden across London, the small surprises in the urban fabric were provided by the game studio Hide & Seek with a deeper goal in mind; to contribute to the well-being of those playing the games. Thanks to its success during the Showtime Festival, Little Tiny Games was transformed into a crowdfunded smartphone application that provides tiny games on the go.

⌨ POPUPCITY.NET/22577

Fore! From a Parking Lot to a Miniature Golf Course

–

A good game of mini-golf is a fun way for people of all ages to unwind. But have you ever played a round in an abandoned parking lot? NL Architects and Zwirt repurposed one such lot to form a temporary nine-hole mini-golf course in the east of Amsterdam using a limited budget. Installing grass carpet over the dilapidated and unwelcoming lot, the architects reclaimed a space set aside for vehicular use in order to inject life into a rarely visited side of the city.

POPUPCITY.NET/30647

PHOTO COURTESY: NL ARCHITECTS

Re-Inventing a Building with Augmented Reality

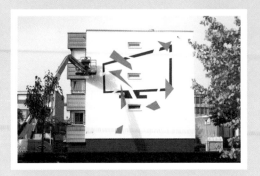

Augmented reality technology provides a new way for individuals to experience real physical spaces in an enhanced way, whether it is productive or playful. Woonbedrijf, a housing corporation in Eindhoven, has spiced up one of its apartment blocks in the city using augmented reality. Studio Maatwerk and Studio 1:1 teamed up to create a smartphone application that presents interactive augmented reality artwork on the apartment building, which is located next to a media and design academy whose students also contributed to the project. The project makes a temporary visual improvement to the building's exterior and gives it a new identity that can consistently reinvent itself through augmented reality artwork.

🖥 POPUPCITY.NET/16558

PHOTO COURTESY: STUDIO MAATWERK AND STUDIO 1:1

Biting Boredom out of Your Commute

Travelling the same route in the city to work or school each day can be dull and tiresome. Daniel Disselkoen, having taken the same tram for his four years at the Royal Academy of Art in The Hague, responded to his tram-bound boredom by creating a game that you can play from the comfort of your tram seat. The aim of the game, called Man Eater, is to 'eat' as many pedestrians' heads as possible between two tram stops while closing one eye and looking through the man-eating character affixed to the window. Differences in perspective mean the player has to keep moving their head in order to succeed. Instructions for the game can be found on the back of the headrests.

POPUPCITY.NET/24369

PHOTO COURTESY: DANIEL DISSELKOEN

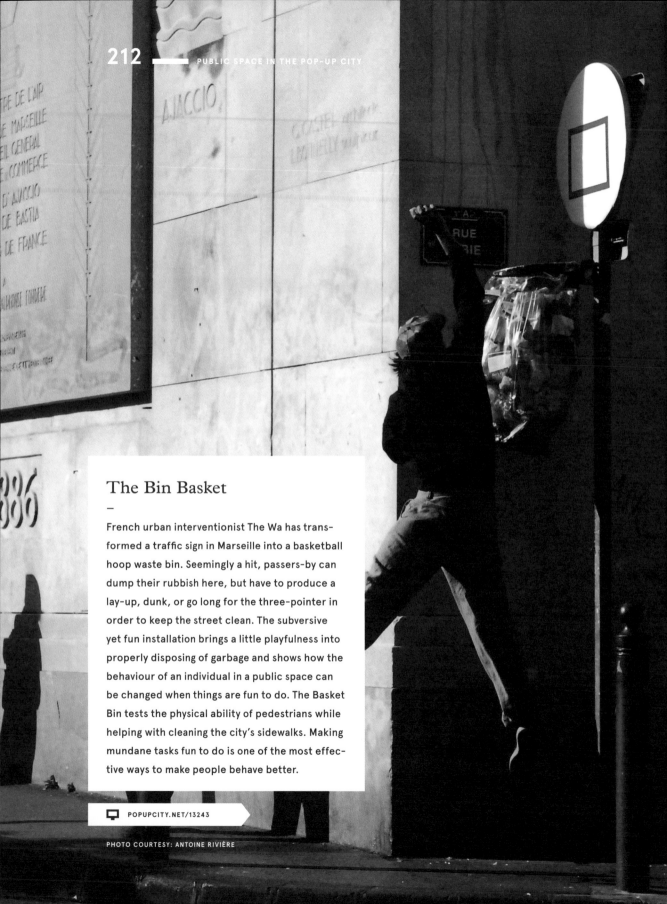

The Bin Basket

—

French urban interventionist The Wa has transformed a traffic sign in Marseille into a basketball
hoop waste bin. Seemingly a hit, passers-by can
dump their rubbish here, but have to produce a
lay-up, dunk, or go long for the three-pointer in
order to keep the street clean. The subversive
yet fun installation brings a little playfulness into
properly disposing of garbage and shows how the
behaviour of an individual in a public space can
be changed when things are fun to do. The Basket
Bin tests the physical ability of pedestrians while
helping with cleaning the city's sidewalks. Making
mundane tasks fun to do is one of the most effective ways to make people behave better.

POPUPCITY.NET/13243

PHOTO COURTESY: ANTOINE RIVIÈRE

to make public spaces less serious and thereby more enjoyable for the user. Many of them are carried out by artists and self-labelled urban interventionists, while others simply come from an individual or group of individuals that perceive a need in their surroundings. In the context of urban development, play means utilising the urban arena as a canvas for human interaction that is predicated not upon productivity but fun, generally in the form of a traditionally well-known game. The streets of Toronto have seen a massive game of Capture the Flag involving 100 participants, while Manhattan was witness to a GPS-powered version of PacMan, complete with the necessary uniforms. Others have started to build slides, swings, baskets, playgrounds, and all kinds of other playful interventions into public space without the assistance of a civic parks department.

Attracted by the success of these playful projects, governments and companies seem to be adopting fun as a principle for urban design, balancing on the thin line between rebellion and positive change. Adidas designed a boxing ball for subway stations, which frustrated commuters can beat to their heart's content in order to reduce their stress level. Nike launched an on-demand street football pitch that could be ordered using a mobile phone application. As massive globalised sporting equipment corporations are producing tools that make exercise in the urban landscape more social, so too must cities consider the lighter side of designing and constructing public spaces.

Mobile communication devices have pushed the urban play phenomenon into a completely new direction. Location-aware applications such as Foursquare have turned gaming into an all-day, everyday experience for over ten million users around the world. Though recently shut down by its creative team, Shadow Cities, an augmented reality game that incorporated the user's real-time location, has an even more competitive element, allowing the gamer to digitally conquer their neighbourhoods using their smartphones. Other urban digital gaming experiences avoid productive and communicative mobile technologies altogether. Mobile gaming consoles have developed significantly in terms of processing power and display capabilities, making augmented reality titles possible and thereby creating a unique gaming experience whenever the user changes her physical location.

Changing Behaviour with Play

Play is becoming increasingly important as a development tactic in urban areas, both formally and informally. Formally, playful urbanism can provoke the behaviour of individuals in public spaces, potentially leading to a positive change. Informally, playful interventions are effective branding strategies for cities and companies seeking to generate viral interest on social media platforms. Many play-oriented projects try to embody a subtle behavioural element. Volkswagen created the Fun Theory campaign, which offered an award to a project

▷ CONTINUED ON PAGE 222

Sliding into the Working Day

—

Officially referred to as a transfer accelerator by Dutch railway maintenance company ProRail, there is no avoiding the fact that this new installation at Utrecht's Overvecht Station is a far more interesting way to start your commute to work: on a slide. The slide does not simply speed up your commute, but it is also a great instrument in making the city a more playful place to be. Designed by Utrecht-based firm HIK Ontwerpers and installed as the final piece of the station's renovation in 2011, commuters at Overvecht are able to reduce their stress levels on the way to catching their train.

POPUPCITY.NET/13906

Whoopdeedoo in Vancouver

What is the best way to get people out of their cars and onto their bicycles? Scores of local governments are fascinated by the question, and Greg Papove might have a fun answer. As part of promoting Vancouver's Bike to Work Week in 2013, the Canadian designer installed a series of Whoopdeedoo Ramps in the city's ever-increasing network of biking infrastructure. The ramps are simple little hills in the middle of the bicycle lanes that give cyclists a similar, but smaller, rush to riding a rollercoaster.

Ready, Steady, Go!

The importance of physical activity is severely neglected by many urbanites, despite the wealth of interesting places to get out and about in. Collectif DC, a group of French designers are looking at the ways in which cities can best be used for workouts and competitions in the city's public spaces. In response to this, they have come up with a series of projects that tries to make urban spaces more active. Utterly simple but thought-provoking are these running tracks between tram rails, ideal for short sprints and races. Simply by painting numbers on the rails, Collectif DC has transformed the standard tramline into a world-class urban racetrack.

POPUPCITY.NET/30123

POPUPCITY.NET/15810

Parasite Cinema in an Auckland Stairway

—

How to do more with the cities' stairwells? In Auckland, the architects at OH.NO.SUMO created a miniature parasite cinema hosted on the stairways of a building. The Stairway Cinema is made out of a timber frame covered with three layers of fabric that provide a waterproof exterior, and a real cinema experience. The construction offers around seven passers-by the opportunity to sit and watch a film alongside a busy Auckland street. The programme of the Stairway Cinema is curated by the audience itself, making use of the constant stream of tips on social media. This ensures the project is embedded in both the physical and the digital world.

POPUPCITY.NET/21796

Reblog This!

Reblog This by Mobstr, found on the streets of London, may seem like a rudimentary piece of street art at first glance, but it comments on the intersection of local and global audiences in the context of street art. While street art is generally seen as a localised, intentionally low-brow form of artistic expression, many street artists have been raised to the level of celebrity and notoriety through the instantaneous and far-reaching network of image sharing through social media. Mobstr plays with the notion that the intended audience for street art has evolved from local to global — from passers-by to Internet users.

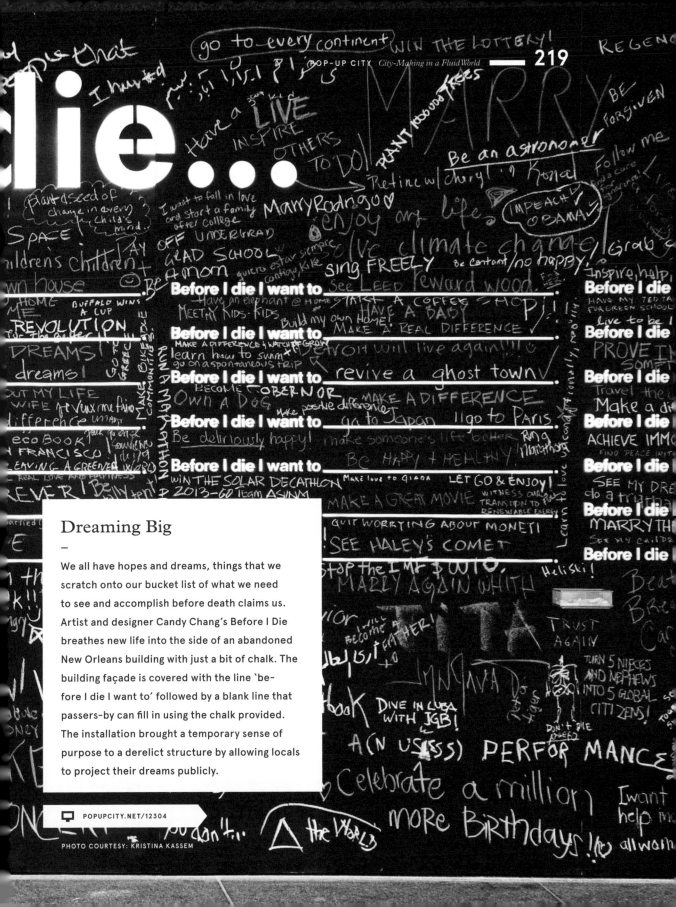

Dreaming Big
–

We all have hopes and dreams, things that we scratch onto our bucket list of what we need to see and accomplish before death claims us. Artist and designer Candy Chang's Before I Die breathes new life into the side of an abandoned New Orleans building with just a bit of chalk. The building façade is covered with the line 'before I die I want to' followed by a blank line that passers-by can fill in using the chalk provided. The installation brought a temporary sense of purpose to a derelict structure by allowing locals to project their dreams publicly.

POPUPCITY.NET/12304

PHOTO COURTESY: KRISTINA KASSEM

A Take-Away Guerrilla Crosswalk

–

Urban hacktivist Florian Rivière offers an entertaining way to get where you want to go. Whenever you would like to cross a street lacking a proper crosswalk, just roll out your very own take-away crosswalk. The recycled black-and-white striped carpet gives you the ability to cross nearly any street you feel like crossing, all for the low cost of only €10.

🖥 POPUPCITY.NET/18287 ➤

PHOTO COURTESY: FLORIAN RIVIÈRE

that best fused fun and positive behavioural change to this end. The main question is: do people improve their detrimental etiquette or languorous behaviour in public space when simple tasks are made more fun to do? The famous piano stairs project at a subway station

Online likeability has become a primary driver behind many urban interventions

in Stockholm, for instance, increased stairwell use in comparison to the adjacent escalator by 66%, because it turned every single step on the stairwell into a piano key.

Over the coming decades, urban play will likely be a foundational component of a more durable, more sustainable, healthier form of urban living. People will be inspired to use less electricity when the meter in their homes turns saving energy into a game that you can play with the neighbours. People will exercise more regularly if the daily commute made by bicycle earns them special points and badges. People will be prompted to eat healthier when they can win fresh produce from gambling automats on the street. One artist, Francisco Camacho, created an energy credit card that locals of one neighbourhood in the Dutch city of Eindhoven can collect credits by engaging in environmentally friendly behaviours such as cycling or collecting energy via solar panels. The project adds a fun, competitive element to positive behaviour change. Brands also appear to be taking note of this trend and are increasingly interested in using the element of fun in combination with

the 'do good' element of their marketing campaigns. Nike, for instance, launched their ubiquitous social running application Nike+ GPS, which enables runners worldwide to share their running data and compete against others on a global level. New York-based interaction designer Cooper Smith used this Nike+ running data to create a series of visualisations that show how Manhattan's public space is experienced by runners. This combination of attentiveness towards play by civic governments, citizens, and the private sector will shape the future city, a city that is more attuned to increasing quality of life. The data generated by play-oriented applications provides unique insight into public space usage and opens up new opportunities for designers to improve the experience of the urban realm.

Facebook Urbanism

All the initiatives, ideas, and designs discussed in this chapter have one thing in common: their impact transcends the level of the street that hosts them. Urban interventions have the potential to become global online hits due to a new, more social media landscape formed by platforms such as Facebook, Twitter, Instagram, and Pinterest. Online likeability has become a primary driver behind many urban interventions. They are tailor-made for a new

▷ CONTINUED ON PAGE 224

Cricklewood, the Town without a Square

Cricklewood is a town with no town hall, no library, and no central square: in short, this northwest London town had no space to call its own. Cricklewood finally received a community space thanks to the arrival of a mobile town square that appeared on the back of a bike containing everything needed to transform some of Cricklewood's unused space into something residents could be proud of. Curated by civic ideas agency Spacemakers and designed by Studio Hato and

Studio Kieren Jones, local residents were built a new sense of community spirit by means of the pop-up town hall at various locations in the town. This facilitated engagement in a variety of activities, including dog shows, film screenings, and dances, reuniting people with the sense of community spirit. Together with Studio Hato, the community created graphics and signage to direct people towards their new town hall and their new community space.

POPUPCITY.NET/30411

online reality with which urban designers and city planners are increasingly confronted. Whether it is building repairs with LEGO bricks, spontaneous improvisational scenes in public squares, or sidewalk hacks for lunching space, these small-scale projects have all turned out to be powerful instruments for generating energy — offline, yes, but even more so online, where the potential audience is significantly larger, leading to broader discussions of major issues such as social cohesion and quality of life in the city. In the Pop-Up City, online media services are city-making tools.

The potential virality of urban interventions in public space is most evident when a project initially meant for bringing energy to a very specific physical location ends up inspiring like-minded individuals in a faraway city who copy and paste the original project, installing a new initiative in their own home city that would otherwise never have the possibility to be transferred there. Candy Chang's Before I Die project, which asks citizens to write their dreams on a neighbourhood chalkboard, was first carried out in Chang's own New Orleans neighbourhood in 2011. Since Before I Die's inauguration, similar chalkboards have popped up in cities such as Amsterdam, Beirut, Berlin, Budapest, Buenos Aires, Johannesburg, and Melbourne. A similar viral spread occurred with PARK(ing) Day, which has inspired so many satellite versions of the event that we can speak of it as a global movement. Local becomes global before becoming local again. Although most of the energy generated by these types of initiatives is predominantly online, this

does not diminish their importance to the communities they were designed for. In an age of mass media, neighbourhood re-activation processes often start with an image shift. This does not merely resonate for brands but also for cities, spaces, and neighbourhoods. A new form of digital city-making is on the rise — a likeable form of city-making that fuses the practice of regenerating urban spaces with a communication appeal that allows an idea to reach citizens farther away than the adjacent street.

Marketing the City

Chocolate with Bars

Marketing the City with Chocolate Bars

Urbanism in the Pop-Up City

Budgets are drying up at all levels of government, leaving countless cities in a difficult position requiring monumental feats of architectural design, infrastructural engineering, and service provision under prohibitive resource constraints. At the same time, groups of all shapes and sizes from both the private and public sectors are beginning to sense a greater potential for helping to shape the city of the future. In the wake of funding shortages and broadened corporate perspectives, cities must seek out creative frameworks for realising projects as an increasing number of individuals and groups define their roles within urban development processes. New ad hoc relationships between the city and city-makers improve both the city and the city's brand image.

228

The manner in which the contemporary city is developed is undergoing a fundamental shift in terms of the source of financial and physical resources: which improvements are made and where the future is happening provides an attractive opportunity to be involved in, not only for the architects and designers that are creating them, but also for firms that want to associate their brand with cutting-edge urban development. Viewing marketing as an inseparable component of urbanism is a bold conception of how brands relate to the urban realm, a type of development that exists in symbiosis with the interests of the private sector and the public good. When a firm conveys a willingness to invest in an initiative, the civic government offers in exchange some variety of public acknowledgment of the funding source or technological provider. In such case, brands do not need logos placed prominently within the city, but a modest yet permanent presence in the background. The firm is thus able to label itself as the provider of a long-term solution to a particular urban problem while meeting their own needs in terms of building a corporate identity. Sponsored planning is thus becoming a new funding stream for cities suffering from constrained budgets.

In recent decades, firms have increased their attention towards corporate social responsibility. The trend transcends the corporate world and now extends to the city, resulting in marketing campaigns that are not merely the canvassing of printed matter but the contribution of something meaningful into everyday urban existence. Companies are increasingly avoiding conventional marketing strategies of highway billboards, print media, and bus stop advertisements. Potential customers are less responsive than they once were to the hyperbolic print advertisements from the glory days

Corporate social responsibility now extends to the city

of post-war American advertising, forcing marketing departments to reinvent their strategies. The birth of guerrilla marketing saw unconventional campaigns that were low in cost and high in efficacy, creating a buzz that was greatly enhanced over time by innovations in social media. Early examples of guerrilla marketing walked the line between brand awareness and bizarre public stunts. An increased awareness of corporate social responsibility has meant that these innovative campaigns end up having a greater embedded meaning that can be seen as a genuine contribution to the public good.

Brands and the Urban Question

Influential global brands are also starting to show how they are reconceptualising the city, ultimately drawing attention to their new

▷ CONTINUED ON PAGE 231

Reclaiming the Social without Wi-Fi

Advertising campaigns in urban environments often try to provide a unique sense of place and utility. In Amsterdam, Kit Kat decided to play with their famous slogan in public space. With the help of JWT Amsterdam and Kyoko Takeshita, Kit Kat offered a Wi-Fi Free Zone with a radius of five metres. Inside of the Zone, a device blocks all wireless signals, serving as a counter-movement to the constant Wi-Fi hunting amongst laptop and smartphone users.

POPUPCITY.NET/25834

PHOTO COURTESY: JWT AMSTERDAM

Concrete Between Your Toes

One of the most common colours for public space is grey, a colour not generally associated with happiness. With this in mind, Coca-Cola's global project, Where Will Happiness Strike Next, hacked the city streets with the help of a Roll-Out Happiness truck.

The temporary pop-up park, shaped like a Coca-Cola bottle, was first rolled out in Vilnius and encouraged people to take off their shoes and enjoy the feeling of grass under their feet (while enjoying a refreshing bottle of Coke, of course).

POPUPCITY.NET/30611

PHOTO COURTESY: THE COCA-COLA COMPANY

product lines: brands are aware that the contemporary city suffers from an array of problems, many of which can be solved using technological solutions produced by a private sector supplier. Automobile manufacturers, for instance, have been tripping over themselves recently to launch collaborative interdisciplinary programmes that showcase how their company vision relates to the city of the future. Three manufacturers in particular have put together temporary urban laboratories to discuss and test ideas and concepts for future urbanism. Likely the most well-known is BMW's collaboration with the Guggenheim Museum to create the BMW Guggenheim Lab, a mobile laboratory that travelled to three cities to address issues of contemporary city living through public lectures and debates. Two other German automobile manufacturers, Audi and Smart, have produced similar public fora for those thinking about a new kind of urbanism in relation to their product lines. Automobile brands are, unsurprisingly, seeking future urban solutions as they are forced to develop alternative options for post-oil mobility.

Brands in other sectors are also flirting openly with urbanism. Siemens is working on an array of sustainable urbanism initiatives under the moniker The Crystal, giving their employees an opportunity to apply their research and technological developments to urban development. IBM's Smarter Cities campaign similarly focusses on the role of computing in building a smart and efficient built environment. Business would not be business if all these future city programs would not be part of long-term company strategies. Brands are, in essence, prepromoting themselves in future urban developments to show their potential in contributing their research and development towards a reconfigured style of planning and design. Influential brands will continue to have a substantial impact on how cities are made, whether it is through their own in-house developments or through partnerships with civic governments. While many of these urbanism-related programs simply appear trendy for the time being, they will likely be the launching point for a new kind of urbanism. Whether it concerns technology companies or automobile manufacturers, each of them attempt to respond to the urban challenge. The city as a future task has never been so popular.

Marketing = Urbanism

The interest of brands in the city not only leads to travelling exhibitions, studies, and branded urban future labs, but also to actual spatial input from the private sector in the city-making process. On the one hand, this can be a detrimental development, inevitably sparking a debate over ownership of the public realm and what entities hold the right to the city in the Lefebvrian sense. Should particular portions of the city be relinquished to private interests, even if it results in gains for the public good? On the other hand, branded urbanism can create unique opportunities for a new framework for how urban development happens, within which both parties are able to benefit through the provision of public projects and meaningful

▷ CONTINUED ON PAGE 241

Sidewalk Billboards Double as Furnished Walls

HomePro, one of the largest hardware store chains in Thailand, has come up with an innovative new advertising campaign: they designed sidewalk billboards that can double as walls for small homes. The campaign, called Other Side, builds upon the widespread phenomenon in Thai cities of urban dwellers recycling sidewalk billboards for the construction of their homes. HomePro designed the back of their billboards as pre-fabricated and pre-furnished walls on one side with a poster advertisement on the other, characterising a new trend in marketing-based urbanism.

PHOTO COURTESY: BBDO BANGKOK

POP-UP CITY City-Making in a Fluid World ━━ 233

Rainbow City

Media and Internet giant AOL has collaborated with Miami-based art collective FriendsWithYou and created an urban playground in New York City, in celebration of the opening of the second section of the High Line. Rainbow City, an environmental installation consisting of a variety of inflated sculptures, encourages both adults and children to explore the immense 16,000 square foot 'happy city.' Inspiring creativity amongst visitors of all ages, the installation was originally commissioned by Luminato Festival of the Arts in Toronto and is expected to host a number of educational programmes.

POPUPCITY.NET/13108

PHOTO COURTESY: FRIENDSWITHYOU.COM

Smart Billboards Are Urban Furniture

—

IBM has launched a clever series of billboards that also serve as furniture as a part of their People for Smarter Cities program. The billboards are strategically designed for passers-by to sit on, take shelter from the elements, or to roll a suitcase up. The design mixes commercial advertising with creative guerrilla urbanism in an effort to encourage people to think smarter about their neighbourhood. IBM's strategy allows them to engage their brand with urban issues and potential solutions.

POPUPCITY.NET/29026

Guggenheim Lab (BMW)

Driving towards a New Kind of Urbanism

Everyone wants to make their urban strategy known, from people to companies to governments. Three German automotive manufacturers have created public platforms that bring together city-makers from a diverse array of disciplines and backgrounds to foster discussions and the sharing of ideas on how to improve the city of the not-too-distant future. The most high profile of these projects is the BMW Guggenheim Lab, a pop-up building designed by Tokyo architecture firm Atelier Bow-Wow which had plans to travel to nine major cities around the world by means of open and inclusive debates. Fellow luxury car manufacturer Audi has an

**Urban Future
Programme
(Audi)**

Smart Urban Stage (Smart)

Urban Future Programme of their own that tracks the trends of today and tomorrow in redefining what it means to move around in the modern metropolis. The third example, the Smart Urban Stage, aims to facilitate dialogue on city-making through exhibitions and an award that offers a launching point for city-makers with innovative ideas. Each of these projects show how a company can reinvent their long-term corporate visions by showing how they can prompt unique projects.

POPUPCITY.NET/22945

PHOTO COURTESY: BDD BANGKOK

POPUPCITY.NET/11409

PHOTO COURTESY: SMART URBAN STAGE

London's Cycle Super-Highways Get Barclays Blue

Nowadays, governments are teaming up with world-leading brands to finance expenditure on urban public spaces in exchange for brand visibility. An example of this is the Barclays Cycle Superhighways initiative in London. British consumer bank Barclays has sponsored the installation of new cycle lanes from outer London to the city centre, painted in the bank's iconic shade of blue. The lanes thus provide a safer and more direct route into central London. Along with the lanes, Barclays has sponsored the launch of 6,000 bicycles and 400 docking stations, emblazoned with the corporate logo and intended to stimulate cycling in London.

POPUPCITY.NET/9099

PHOTO COURTESY: TRANSPORT FOR LONDON

A Football School for Soweto

Nike Global Football and Canadian design agency RIFproject have teamed up to design a football training centre in Soweto, South Africa. The space includes two full-sized synthetic turf football pitches, two junior pitches, a gym, and a first-aid facility. Nike's involvement with the project markets the brand alongside demonstrating commitment to the global growth of football. The project was launched at a strategic moment during the 2010 FIFA World Cup in South Africa.

POPUPCITY.NET/10393

DE KONINCK

UITTBUS

Night Buses, Brought to You by Beer
—

The municipal government of Ghent has collaborated with De Koninck, an Antwerp-based brewery, to maintain public transport services at night, after the primary bus transport company, De Lijn, cut late-night services from its budget. De Lijn buses will continue to run late at night, but the municipal government and the brewery are to cover the costs. The collaboration benefits De Koninck by meeting their corporate social responsibility goals by providing a serious alternative to designated drivers. The city will, in turn, be able to maintain their late-night bus service with the addition of De Koninck advertisements on the buses.

 POPUPCITY.NET/24904

PHOTO COURTESY: DE KONINCK AND DE LIJN

marketing campaigns. In this manner, branded urbanism is less about blatantly programming a message into public space, but rather an integrated message inside of urban policy.

There are many examples of urbanism through marketing, where the role of the relevant actors and the type of investment is, in each case, tailor-made for the scenario. Transportation infrastructure is one area in which these partnerships are occurring at an increasing rate. One example of this strategy is London's bold plan to strengthen the city's cycling infrastructure. Investment bank Barclays, which also sponsors a bike-sharing programme, established twelve long-distance cycling routes together with

on them. A third example of sponsorship of an urban infrastructure comes from the subway systems of Chicago and Dubai, where each respective city organised an auction for the naming rights to stations. Subway station names are integral to how residents experience the city as they enter the collective consciousness of the locals. The auction winners thus produce a branding experience that transcends more simplistic marketing campaigns while generating ten percent of the total construction costs.

Other partnerships of this variety result in branding that is mutually beneficial for both the image of the firm and that of the city. When the Belgian city of Charleroi was chosen as the ug-

A city is no longer just a local canvas that appeals to people in the nearby physical environment, but a place for global promotion of both city and brand

Transport for London, connecting the suburbs with the core. The £50 million sponsorship contract allowed London's government to complete a major infrastructural project for cyclists. Another example comes from the Belgian city of Ghent, which, due to budget cuts, was on the brink of cancelling the city's late-night bus service. De Koninck, a brewery from the nearby city of Antwerp, signed a unique agreement with Ghent's transit authority in which the brewery funds the majority of the costs for the late-night service. The only change noticeable to passengers is the appearance of the buses, which now have De Koninck advertisements

liest city in the world in 2010, the Dutch chemical multinational AkzoNobel offered Charleroi a bright solution to the city's aesthetic dearth: a cost-effective refurbishment of Charleroi's building exteriors with a splash of colour. The Couleurs Carolo project saw AkzoNobel working with the local population, hiring local residents to collaborate with on matters such as which buildings would be painted, how they would be painted, and by whom they would be painted. The direct interaction between a major firm and residents gave the impression of bypassing governmental or bureaucratic entities, leading to swift aesthetic improvements to

▷ CONTINUED ON PAGE 248

A Fresh Coat of Colour in Charleroi

Dutch chemical corporation AkzoNobel seeks to make the ugliest city in the world, Charleroi in Belgium, a bit more colourful through their project Couleurs Carolo. AkzoNobel invested heavily in colouring the city's residential façades, a campaign that promoted the company's paint products and improved the aesthetics and the public perception of Charleroi.

POPUPCITY.NET/14226

PHOTO COURTESY: KING GEORGE

Partyaardvark!
—

In celebration of the centenary of Burgers Zoo in Arnhem, the Zoo wanted to give the city a present. They invited the acclaimed artist Florentijn Hofman to create a special landmark artwork. Hofman created Feestaardvarken (literally, party aardvark), a thirty metre long concrete structure of an aardvark wearing a golden party hat. It did not take long before the Party Aardvark, funded by the Zoo itself, became a playground for children and a gathering place for locals in the heart of the community.

PHOTO COURTESY: THEO KRUSE/KONINKLIJKE BURGERS' ZOO

Trade Your Dog's Poo for Free Wi-Fi

Internet provider Terra collaborated with DDB Mexico to launch a campaign that rewards you for disposing your dog's droppings with free Wi-Fi for everyone in the park. Talk about a treat, and encouragement of good behaviour for the tethered individual. Instead of special signs or the threat of a fine, Poo Wi-Fi tries to make those poo-littered parks in Mexico City a little bit cleaner through positive reinforcement.

POPUPCITY.NET/19766

PHOTO COURTESY: DDB MEXICO

To Repeat:
Bucharest Is Not Budapest!

Romanian candy brand ROM is now producing candy bars emblazoned with the phrase "Bucharest not Budapest," wrapped in packaging coloured to match the Romanian flag. Their campaign aims to clear up the difference between the Romanian capital, Bucharest, and the Hungarian capital, Budapest, as well as to connect with the many Romanians who tire of correcting foreign visitors. Aside from chocolate, ROM has also installed billboards throughout both cities in addition to an online campaign. ROM's campaign demonstrates an innovative strategy for raising Bucharest's own image in the eyes of tourists while simultaneously giving a subtle reminder to locals of their own city's unique character.

POPUPCITY.NET/29591

PHOTO COURTESY: MRM WORLDWIDE

the city achieved in a bottom-up manner. This collaborative style of development arises from a lack of resources in public authorities as well as the emergence of new forms of social media. Due to the global reach of social media, a city is no longer just a local canvas that appeals to people in the nearby physical environment, but a place for global promotion of both city and brand.

While there is a greater tradition of private contributions to public affairs in Anglo-Saxon countries, these partnerships are less prevalent in other societies. Policymakers in other contexts, and even from the Anglo-Saxon countries as well, generally have cold feet for this form of co-financing. Due to unfamiliarity with public-private partnerships, a negative connotation seems to exist around fusing for-profit marketing with urban development. Relinquishing complete governmental autonomy in the public realm is often seen as an undesirable means towards an end, and the concerns raised by citizens and policymakers alike are legitimate. There is, however, much to be said for letting the private sector contribute towards, without dominating, the public domain in a balanced way. External financial flows have historically been part of the realisation of urban policy, such as from philanthropic entrepreneurs or other levels of government with larger budgets. Within the framework of public-private partnerships, private investment picks up the slack where civic budgets are tightened and inflexible to accommodate new development projects, with the price to be paid by the city generally being advertising space.

The possibilities for marketing-powered urbanism in confluence with an urbanised corporate social responsibility are strong. However, there is a gap in the market in terms of mechanisms that bring together the creative and strategic visions of all relevant parties. This is both a challenge and an opportunity: institutionalising a role for the private sector within planning decisions may prove risky, but developing tangible ties with the business community and simultaneously with the citizenry ensures that development is better attuned to the needs and desires of all city users.

Subscribing to the City

One trend that is altering the way that we live is the shift from ownership to access. Spotify, the subscription-based music streaming service, is perhaps one of the most well-known examples of this change that is gradually transforming the economy. Most music, for instance, is not purchased: streaming and file-sharing services, ranging on a wide scale of legality, have resulted in music aficionados no longer investing ownership in a tangible product that they can place on the turntable, radically altering the way we experience cultural products as a whole. This focus shift is affecting the way cities are designed and developed.

Nomadic lifestyles allow people to live their lives free from the heavy burden of ownership. Comparable to leasing a car or a smartphone, fashion label Mud Jeans offers jeans for lease. For a monthly subscription of a paltry €5, customers get a pair of jeans to wear. When they get sick of that particular pair, they simply return it and others will use it, or the store can return it to the manufacturer in order to recycle the materials into new jeans. During the leasing period, a complimentary repair service is included. This enables the subscriber to be fashionable with little hassle. Other rental services exist in the realm of productivity. At Drexel University's library in Philadelphia, a vending machine dispenses MacBooks for students to borrow. Since the library is open 24 hours per day, one student government representative foresaw a potential safety problem for students walking around with their laptop late at night, prompting the library to install the laptop dispenser.

Consumers are not the only ones attracted to this lightweight lifestyle; cities are beginning to see the advantages of more flexible ways to deal with their city-making tasks. The modern city need not provide every imaginable service to locals, perhaps exploring the options for service rental. Dutch technology giant Philips, for instance, is working on plans that enable cities to lease lamps instead of investing in expen-

ensure that the most environmentally friendly light bulbs are used to light the city streets. Philips remains the owner of all of the hardware, while the city merely rents light from the provider. With a pay-for-use model, Philips rethinks the way it offers its products and tries to establish new markets for its services. The market for this service is not limited to cities, either: German architect Thomas Rau similarly rents light from Philips for his office, leaving maintenance, replacement, and recycling up to the owner. Rau has similar leasing contracts for the carpets and furniture suppliers for his office, as well.

Crowdfunded Indie Architecture

A new approach to urban planning and service provision is rising in concurrence with a fresh approach to architecture, in which architects and urban designers are adopting a do-it-yourself mentality. They do not need a project developer or local government approval to start a

Indie architects do not need a project developer or local government approval, but rather start a project entirely at their own risk

sive lighting infrastructure. In doing so, cities benefit from being able to use the latest technologies available, while saving on maintenance costs and allowing the technological experts to

project, but rather start projects entirely at their own risk and even out of their own pockets. These are the new indie architects. Similar to the meteoric rise of independent record labels

▷ CONTINUED ON PAGE 259

Detroit's Power House of Arts

As the city struggles with a shrinking population and civic bankruptcy, one pair of Detroiters are trying to lure in creative locals and outsiders to try to breathe some life into a neighbourhood on life support. The Power House started when Mitch and Gina Cope bought a foreclosed house for $1,900 and single-handedly transformed the house into a home for local and visiting artists, providing space to create and live. The project is bottom-up at heart, having motivated other artistic types to move to the area to rebuild a community.

A Crowd-Funded Elevated Pedestrian Bridge

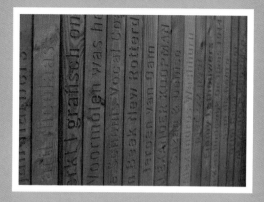

In 2012, Dutch architecture firm ZUS started to work on an elevated footpath connecting the area near Rotterdam's Central Station with two difficult-to-reach districts nearby. Not commissioned by local authorities, the Luchtsingel project is one of the best examples of indie architecture. Starting with a crowd-funding campaign, the Luchtsingel connects multiple neighbourhoods separated by busy railway tracks, busy streets, and the building that ZUS calls home. The project won a local bottom-up urbanism award, making it financially feasible to complete the yellow-wood road.

🖥 POPUPCITY.NET/17046

PHOTO COURTESY: ADAM NOWEK, OSSIP VAN DUIVENBODE

Dumpster-to-Dumpster Design

–

The Dutch designers of Stortplaats van Dromen have unleashed an innovative little design to repurpose trash dumpsters in Utrecht. The recycling kiosks are dumpsters renovated using found and donated materials. These former dumpsters are then transformed into various public and social venues, breathing life into any neighbourhood in the city.

▭ POPUPCITY.NET/21522 ➤

PHOTO COURTESY: HEIN LAGERWEIJ

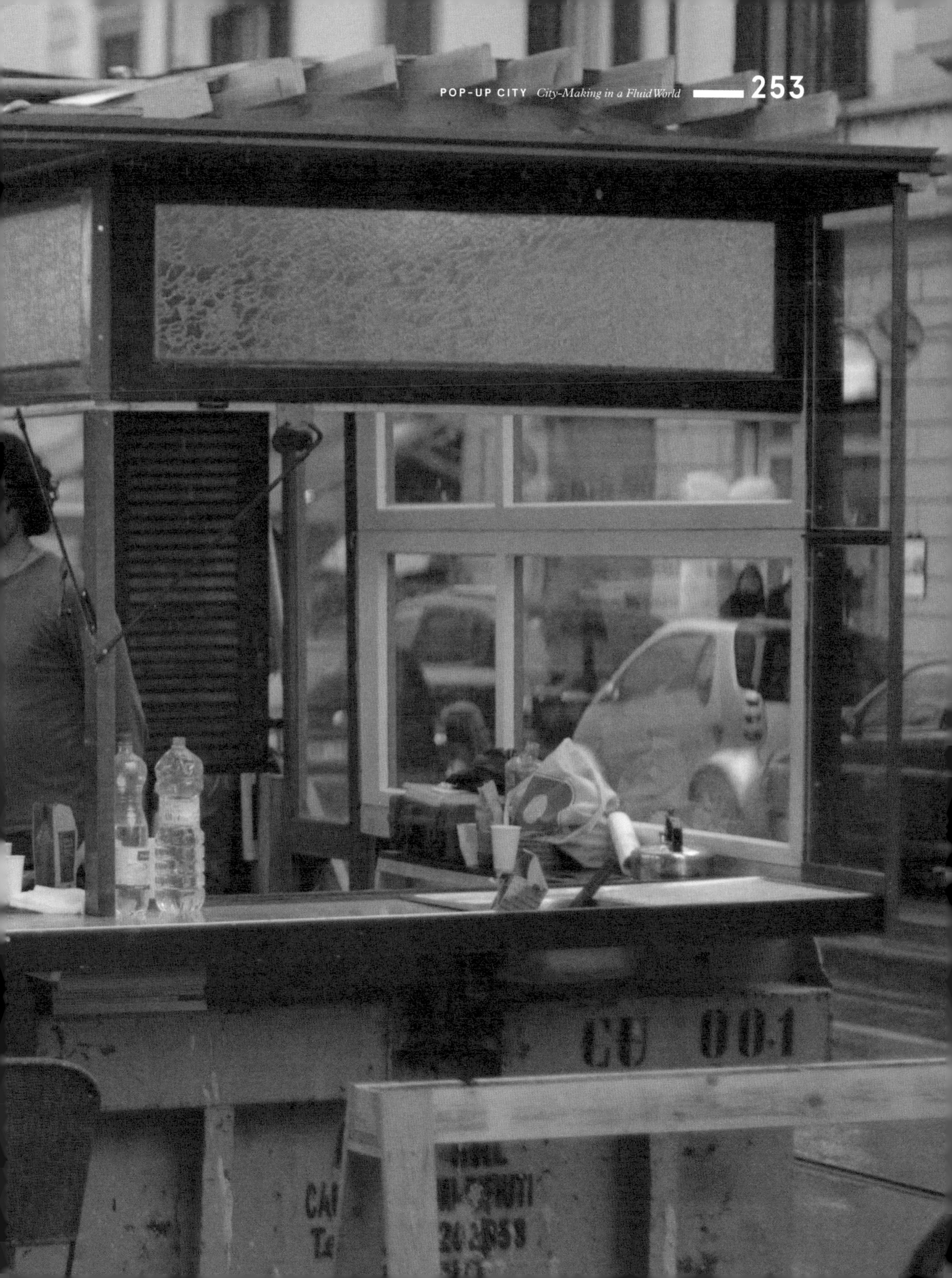
CO 001

The Modular Bike Lane Kit

Bikway has launched a pre-fabricated recycled modular bike lane system that helps any city to test the feasibility of bicycle lanes in a simple, cost-effective manner. The system can be installed easily into a street, creating a separated, adjustable bike lane of any width or length. The design enables local cycling enthusiasts to showcase what effect that proper cycling infrastructure would have on a city. No construction crews are necessary, as the modular system can be assembled and taken apart as easily as LEGO. Bikway can serve as a useful tool to prompt infrastructural planners to consider permanent bike lane installations.

Visualising a Better City

Many American cities are struggling with image problems and hearing repeatedly about how they are a city in decline. The residents of one city in northern California are trying to change this perception through visual storytelling. This Is Vallejo is a blog featuring photographs and visual essays that shows Vallejo, a city in San Francisco's metropolitan region, through the eyes of locals. By offering a visual digital platform for residents, This Is Vallejo not only challenges negative perceptions perpetuated by major news publications but also helps to build community pride.

A New Way to Let You Pay

Neighbor.ly brings crowdfunding to the next level by providing a service that allows citizens to play a hand in selecting and financing urban projects and services. Local governments, companies, and residents alike can submit proposals to the website, to be funded at the behest of anyone willing to donate to the cause. Neighbor.ly's platform brings about a new form of privatisation in city-making of which the consequences remain to be seen. While the notion of crowdfunded urbanization simultaneously includes everyday citizens in the decision to change their surroundings, it can potentially add a layer of financial privilege to formerly public projects.

 POPUPCITY.NET/32309

PHOTO COURTESY: ROSHANDA CUMMINGS

PHOTO COURTESY: AMANDA GEHIN

Pointing towards Positive Urban Change

In 2011, Eve Mosher introduced her project Insert Here to New York, enabling people to voice their opinions on improvements to the city's public spaces. In cooperation with 350.org, large yellow arrows are available to those who want to display their support for environmental protection in their area. Mosher's project has proven to be a success, with several arrows appearing across all five boroughs of New York, sparking a new discourse on how the city is planned.

POPUPCITY.NET/15530

PHOTO COURTESY: EVE MOSHER

Bloggers: The New Agenda Setters

City blogging is an effective tool for sharing the interesting happenings in a city or a neighbourhood with locals and visitors alike, but it is also a potent tool for hyper-local community development. In cities across the world, community blogs are a relatively new phenomenon that is being taken more seriously, also by urban authorities. They are the promoters, ambassadors, and defenders of the neighbourhoods they represent, taking the social pulse of their respective communities. With many of them representing gentrifying neighbourhoods, these community blogs are addressing a need for participation and inclusivity in formal planning initiatives for all locals. Amsterdam Noord, a short ferry trip across the lake from Amsterdam's city centre, is the frontier of gentrification in the Dutch capital, home to a mixture of hipster artists and immigrant communities. Founded by designer Luc Harings, ilovenoord was one of the first neighbourhood blogs in the Netherlands, featuring daily news on the area. The blog's heart-shaped logo can be found everywhere in the northern side of Amsterdam. It could be said that the blog has been a catalyst for gentrification in the area, but it also has established an important forum for all locals to express their experiences and concerns regarding neighbourhood development. The high visibility of ilovenoord has meant that the views expressed on the platform have reached the ears of the formal policymakers and have actually influenced decision-making processes. For now, gentrification in Amsterdam Noord has become more inclusive, with planning becoming increasingly participatory.

🖵 POPUPCITY.NET/28277

PHOTO COURTESY: ILOVENOORD

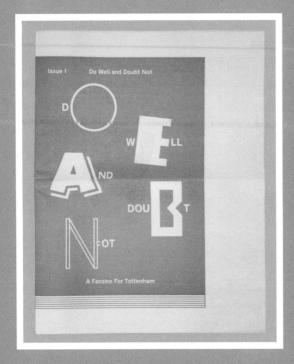

Doing Well and Doubting Not in Tottenham

Many non-central neighbourhoods suffer from urban blight and poor public perceptions, and, historically, London's Tottenham has been no different. One civic ideas agency, Spacemakers, is trying to change that with a truly local fanzine called Do Well and Doubt Not. Taking its name from the district motto, the zine is full of impromptu interviews with area residents and typography borrowed directly from local business frontages. Do Well and Doubt Not is a project that challenges the negative stereotypes that plague Tottenham while provoking a love for the little things that make Tottenham unique.

POPUPCITY.NET/30435

PHOTO COURTESY: THEO SIMPSON

and the subsequent diversification of the popular musical landscape, so too are architects and city-makers working in an independent manner, searching for freedom in their artistic and programmatic choices, bypassing the effects of financial and building crises. This does not solely concern small architectural developments, but also large-scale challenges and public structures. Indie urbanism has swiftly devel-

The Luchtsingel in Rotterdam is one apt example of a project realised by means of crowd-funding, where an eye-catching elevated footpath built by local architecture office ZUS was constructed with crowdfunded support for every last piece of wood. The architects themselves came up with the idea to create a new layer of public space that crosses roads and, impressively, railway tracks in order to connect

Crowdfunding makes projects possible that would otherwise not be of interest to government agencies

oped into a subtype of urban design. It gives less-than-official actors in the urban development sector the opportunity to help make the city and produce ideas that would otherwise never have a chance of realised through more formal decision-making processes.

One predominant characteristic of indie urbanism is how funds are raised. Rather than having a typical unitary source of funding or submitting a proposal for a tendered project, indie urbanists use crowdfunding platforms to directly involve locals. A host of general crowdfunding platforms exist, such as Kickstarter and Indiegogo, and have achieved great popularity. Other crowdfunding websites that are specific to urbanism projects have started appearing in order to directly connect those seeking to realise a project with locals, examples of which include Neighbor.ly (United States), Peoplefund.it (United Kingdom), Space-hive (United Kingdom), Brickstarter (Finland), and Voor Je Buurt (the Netherlands).

Rotterdam Centraal Station with two derelict regions of the inner-city that desperately need a spark of interest. The local government began supporting the Luchtsingel after the successful crowdfunding campaign that enabled citizens to buy a small portion of the infrastructure and, in return, get their names engraved on the wooden planks that the bridge is comprised of.

The appeal of crowdfunding is that it is citizen-oriented and a very real example of the forces of the free market, depending on your theoretical stance: crowdfunding makes projects possible that would otherwise not be of interest to government agencies by giving the audience the choice to support whichever project they want. An early example of crowdfunded urbanism comes from New York, where designers proposed a public swimming pool that floats in the Hudson River. Enough New Yorkers, as well as non-New Yorkers, liked the idea so much that they wanted to be part of the process of making it possible, raising $41,647 from 1,203 backers on crowdfunding platform Kickstarter in order to realise the project. Some urban agricultural projects are being made possible via crowdfunding, such as the Whitelock Community Farm in Baltimore and the Atwater Village organic farmers market in Los Angeles.

Some indie urbanists have the wherewithal to undertake a civic project completely at their own risk. Helsinki-based architect Tuomas Toivonen took the initiative to build a public sauna for the Finnish capital. While Finland still maintains its strong sauna culture, the number of public saunas has decreased dramatically in recent decades due to many new housing developments having their own built-in saunas. Toivonen's NOW OFFICE built the public sauna without being contracted by the local government, a sauna company, or a project developer. Toivonen assumes all of the risk in the project, and will manage the building, from the accounting down to the towels, for the next three decades in order to ensure that the sauna becomes a viable operation.

Bottom-Up Place Marketing

Beyond simply building something, local written coverage of a city or a neighbourhood can also help the image of an area, leading to increased interest and civic pride. This Is Vallejo is one city blog that covers the Bay Area city of Vallejo in a very visual way, featuring high-quality photography that documents the perspective of residents and the spaces that they live, work, and play in. The project tries to avoid the prototypical narrative of the American city in decline and rather tries to focus on the vitality and resiliency of the population. Shifting north of the border, Vancouver Is Awesome reports only on positive developments in Canada's Terminal City, choosing to avoid negative reportage in order to emphasise what it is about Vancouver that locals love about their home city. In Zürich, a collective of documentary makers built a beautiful promotional website that enables everyone in the world to virtually stroll along Langstrasse and take a look into the life of local entrepreneurs, families, and other urbanites that inhabit Switzerland's most vibrant district. Here in our home city of Amsterdam, the authors behind BoLoBoost cover the developments of the Bos en Lommer neighbourhood, an area of the city's west side that has long battled with a negative stereotype fuelled by higher crime rates. By highlighting the tightly-knit community that exists in Bos en Lommer, BoLoBoost is helping locals foster a sense of pride in their neighbourhood as well as showing other Amsterdammers that their view of Bos en Lommer as being a bad part of town is far from the truth. City blogging does not contribute to the physical built environment but rather helps shift the discourse about a neighbourhood or the city as a whole, setting the agenda for future discussions of how the city ought to be run.

Printed publications can also have a similar effect on the brand of a city or a neighbourhood. Bottom-up changemakers are generating momentum simply by provoking discussions. Do Well and Doubt Not, a zine from North London's Tottenham district, is entirely by, for, and about all things Tottenham. Interviews arise from conversations on the streets and the typography is borrowed from area signage, giving the zine an extremely local flair. Another example comes from the Dutch village of Barchem,

has very clearly emerged from the financial crisis in the construction industry from 2008 onwards, it has also shown to be a more adaptable form of city-making that is here to stay. Indie urbanism is a more inclusive urbanism, where designers and citizens alike can autonomously take the lead in fostering high-quality civic projects and guiding public discussions of policy

City blogging does not contribute to the physical built environment but rather helps shift the discourse about a neighbourhood or the city as a whole

which suffers from a shrinking population. To counter this, locals place signs in their yard displaying the price of the house and photographs of these homes are collected in a magazine, Barchem Centraal, alongside essays on the merits of quotidian life. By producing a tangible product that places the neighbourhood on a pedestal, both locals and non-locals can gain an insight into a place that they might otherwise have a negative perception of.

Each of these projects change their neighbourhoods for the better, raising interest and fostering a sense of civic pride, whether it is in the broader metropolitan region or the immediate neighbourhood. People are increasingly disillusioned by the glacial pace of city planning departments when it comes to installing an innovative project. Residents would rather use their intimate knowledge of the neighbourhood context in order to address a deficiency. While this bottom-up indie urbanism and city branding

and practice in the urban realm, regardless of whether or not civic governments and their respective planning authorities are able and willing to support them.

New
Strategies
for
New
Urbanscapes

New Strategies for New Urbanscapes

Five Messages for Pop-Up City-Makers

Cities are organisms: they live, breathe, and endure the occasional midlife crisis. This is precisely why spontaneity and temporality are important for ensuring the health of the city: temporary initiatives help to refresh an urban area, infusing it with an energy that may have been displaced or even evaporated altogether. As the world's urban regions continue to expand and become ever more interconnected with each other, urban practice must adapt to new land uses, new space typologies, and new city users. The pop-up ideology is an effective and appropriate way for locals and businesses to harness the principles and strategies of urban development in order to build better cities.

We are not living, as many have argued, in a transition period in which society is moving from an old economy to a new economy. There is no new economy. Rather, transition itself has become a permanent state of being. Change is the new status quo, and cities must prepare themselves for this new reality. Pop-up is frequently considered to be merely a trend that has emerged over the past decade. But the true meaning of flexibilisation goes far beyond pop-up stores, plug-in parks, and container houses. In this book, we have tried to shed a light on the wide variety of projects that have embraced this new condition.

Of course, there are more elements of urbanity than the ones that we have presented in the previous chapters: we, the urbanites, are not merely bound to the spaces and places that we use and how we organise them. There are endless ways to conceive of what the city is and how it ought to be, and there are infinite sources for how the city has become this way. The Pop-Up City does not look a particular way, nor does it utilise a specific set of spatial typologies. The Pop-Up City is not designed for a specific sub-section of society or for a predetermined set of activities. The Pop-Up City is a new style of city that is driven largely by what is rapidly becoming a less radical concept: anyone can be a city-maker. Collectively making cities with a diversity of backgrounds and capacities is advantageous in the sense that it will prompt micro-level development that actively recognises this diversity. This is not urbanism in a cohesive, master-planned sense: this is making a city, gradually and collectively.

Cities are being urged to think of new strategies that prepare them for a fast and flexible age where urban dwellers are less and less attached to the place they live in. Civic governments across the world must embed adaptability in their policy frameworks in order to prevent inflexible planning that prohibits rapid land use changes. Pop-up thinking may seem volatile and unsustainable at first glance, but flexible policy and practice can help prevent the increase of derelict structures and abandoned districts that have suffered under inflexibility. Urban regions are meant for perpetuity, but they are not designed as such and nor should they be.

Since establishing Pop-Up City in 2008, we, alongside our army of Pop-Up Citizens, have researched and documented a smorgasbord of individuals and initiatives that are prompting those in their native setting to rethink what it means to build and use a city. Every instance of pop-up thinking that we have documented is indicative of cities and societies in transition and can serve as inspiration to practitioners and policymakers keen to make their cities more responsive and resilient to change.

#1: Embed Pop-Up Thinking

In the late 2000s, few urban professionals viewed temporary space use as a legitimate response to a growing collection of vacant lots or abandoned structures. As we approach the mid-2010s, pop-up is not just a momentum-generating retail strategy but a widely accepted strategy for urban development and regeneration. Contemporary built environments are increasingly subject to pop-up strategies: while the term implies DIY ethics and aesthetics that provides ad hoc strategies of city-making, the experimentation evident in the early days of pop-up is starting to become more professional and strategic. This is not to say that pop-up urbanism is becoming routine, but rather that more and more people see the city as a living laboratory where each individual can try to realise an interesting project that contributes to city living for a short amount of time. A pop-up initiative can be made up of recycled materials and have shoddy aesthetics, but it can also have a shine and a gloss. Pop-up solutions were once thought of as temporary, band-aid approaches towards problems in the city, but now that pop-up thinking is maturing, pop-up thought is also becoming more oriented towards quality.

The prevalence of pop-up initiatives in cities is making them a more natural part of urban life to the extent that they can hardly be referred to as a trend any longer. The average urbanite is less surprised by parasite architecture or spontaneous public spaces than they would have been pre-crisis, resulting in urban populations that are receptive to temporary interventions in their immediate surroundings. As exposure to pop-up city-making increases, so too does the level of professionalisation. Pop-up pioneers used to face tremendous obstacles that are simply not present anymore as cities strive to be more adaptive. While civic policy frameworks have become more welcoming to spontaneity, pop-up city-makers need to recognise how to channel the methods of architecture, art, and design to create projects that add value to urban space. Making a pop-up project for the sake of making a pop-up project is unproductive: the pop-up city is awash in temporary initiatives that contribute to any one of the six realms of urbanity by recognising a need.

#2: Design to Add Value

How, then, to add value to the urban realm through pop-up principles? The truly effective projects that we have featured here arise out of strong concepts, decision-oriented design, and temporal thinking.

In conceiving the form and process of a design, many projects lose sight of their initial concept, resulting in an ambiguous project for which the purpose is unclear. In failing to maintain the idea through the design process, any project, especially one with a brief, pop-up shelf life, can seem pointless and disorganised if the concept is not in balance with form and process. Maintaining sight of the original inspiration to create a pop-up initiative in the first place shows that the inspiration can be a problem, a need, or even just a space for increased convenience. Keeping a strong focus on the concept shows those that encounter the project that it has a fundamental purpose.

Facilitating decision-making during the design process is another necessary element of creating an effective pop-up project. While the architects and planners of the twentieth century often pursued perfection in form or function, bottom-up and open-source tactics of city-making are primarily interested in process, often resulting in mediocre forms and functions. Excessive attention to a democratic design process results in uninteresting developments that are collections of concessions rather than the realisations of good ideas. This is not to say that democratic elements of the design of an urban intervention ought to be removed entirely; rather, it is crucial to strategically assign tasks to those most capable. Decision-oriented design thinking is necessary for the pop-up city-maker: including creative direction as a task to be delegated in developing such projects, as a growing number of pop-up city-makers are doing, is one strategy for ensuring that quality is not lost within the design process.

Architecture and urbanism as design disciplines have historically addressed three dimensions: height, length, and width. Each and every design tool and method used by scholars and practitioners are based on these three dimensions, whether it is sketching, modelling, or CAD drawing. A fourth dimension has started playing a more important role in urban practice: time. Many of the city-making projects and ideas that we have presented during our existence are selected based on their use of time as a design element. Time is what sets a pop-up shop apart from a conventional shop and what sets a co-working space apart from a conventional office. Operating in this relatively new mode is extremely difficult for urban design professionals,

as time is difficult to capture on paper or in a blue foam model. Pop-up projects typically invest in understanding and harnessing the temporal dimension in the design process.

#3: Generate Momentum

Momentum is one of the key elements of the pop-up movement, manifesting in both social and physical ways. In a media-driven society where digital communication has become more prevalent than physical communication, it is difficult to stand out in the endless stream of information. In generating social momentum, the pop-up urbanist does not need to necessarily focus on an intervention in situ, but rather inspire other city dwellers. In this way, how people perceive an urban project can become even more important than what the project actually is. Making an idea or an intervention successful means publicising it well, demanding promotional skills from the pop-up urbanist that touch the hearts and minds of people.

Creating or using physical momentum demands specific skills and intuition that is not very well distributed amongst professionals in the urban disciplines. A project that temporarily enters a public space exemplifies how momentum can regenerate a dead space, public or private, and transform it into a distinctive place where things happen and where people want to be. The same happens when a food truck rolls in or a pop-up shop launches in a vacant store space: the situation is created for a very short term, but the impact can reach far beyond that timeframe. Momentum as an instrument is much more communicative and intuitive compared to conventional urban design methods, and in this sense we would do well to learn from advertising and communications professionals whose sole profession is based upon generating momentum. Momentum hacks into social constructions and taken-for-granted environments, toying with the emotions and psychologies of people rather than with the composition of bricks, ultimately creating social energy for a brief period that, under ideal circumstances, spawns new initiatives.

From a broader perspective, these social energies characterise contemporary cities. With the maturation of the footloose generation, many are becoming less drawn to a city by the traditional connections to a place but rather because they are attracted by the social energies they seek to belong to. The exponential rise of the festival economy is but one piece of evidence of this generational eagerness to dive into short-term social gatherings to offer a kind of collective human experience. The generators of momentum, from event organisers to shopkeepers, help curate the tastes of city dwellers. They design the route through the concrete jungle. They perfectly understand the new media landscape and are aware of how best to utilise new city-making tools. These curators give our cities an influx of energy that helps to shape its identity.

#4: Design Your City Digitally

An essential element of the Pop-Up City is digital media, which generates new flows of fluctuating activity in cities and makes cities work in a more efficient and variable mode. An army of service-oriented digital platforms is capable of filling in the spatial gaps and tying together different social realities. They turn living rooms into pop-up restaurants for one night, link together supply and demand of hyper-temporary retail spaces, and fill the empty seats in taxis and private cars. Ideas such as these were not designed with grand ambitions to improve the urban condition, but simply to make everyday things in the city work better.

Whether it is in the process of design, consultation, production, or promotion, an array of digital technological developments are lowering the barriers to entry to urbanism at a breakneck pace. Digital media makes social and productive interaction more efficient, more flexible, and more productive. New technological developments are making it easier than ever before to collaborate, design, and build a project of any size and scope. Rather than relying on individuals working in a sterile and closed office alone, a greater number of city-makers with an extreme diversity of professional and creative backgrounds can pool together their ideas to ensure for a more inclusive and collaborative decision-making process that is based upon the best ideas. Digital media platforms are making it simpler to generate ideas in the first place. The fact that local ways of thinking can go viral and galvanise similar efforts in faraway lands is a testament to the heightened presence of global interactivity and its role in promoting a Do-It-Together ethic. In a sense, local culture goes global, inspiring pop-up urbanists the world over.

Recent developments are similarly aiding the process of promotion and engagement of finished projects, as well. Marketing-savvy pop-up urbanists commonly use social media platforms in order to spark interest in locals and non-locals alike, hoping that projects go viral and subsequently sparking similar initiatives in other cities. Projects that require additional funding are finding crowdfunding to be a simple yet effective strategy for acquiring capital and interest in their initiatives, regardless of the length of their existence. As cities and neighbourhoods begin to teem with pop-up activities, city bloggers document the vibrancy of the places they live in, giving locals insight into what happens in their neighbourhood and offering non-locals a glimpse of the area's character. This generation of momentum-building online activities not only boost the impact of urban initiatives but also help to set the long-term agenda for urban planning.

#5: Don't Do It Yourself, Do It Together

We are not crisis economists with a fascination with the urban realm, though many of the examples on the previous pages might suggest otherwise: we are urbanists attuned to how practitioners, regardless of their background and training, create effective and meaningful interventions under resource constraints. The new urbanist does not sit back and wait for clients to ask them to commit architecture; the indie architect of tomorrow takes the initiative on their own volition and assumes the risks in addressing the issues extant in the city, showing a simultaneously entrepreneurial and philanthropic ethos. This type of urbanist need not even be a trained architect or planner, but can come from an endless variety of disciplines and is willing to bypass formal authorisation from civic governing bodies to create something exciting. New public and private spaces are popping up across the urban landscape from an ever-increasing array of non-traditional sources, helping to build a better and more inclusive city.

A new way of realising projects means that there is a shift in how projects are realised. As the DIY ethic inspired alternative perspectives to flourish in music during the heyday of punk ideology, it is clear that the time is right for a DIT ethic: Do-It-Together. Open-source design communities permit collaboration, creating platforms that are inherently democratic but allow good concepts to flourish. Ad hoc relationships between cities and service providers create flexible arrangements that cater to the needs of both parties, avoiding the institutionalised baggage of conventional public-private partnerships. Pop-up thinking breaks open the predefined set of spatial development partners, creating room for short-term, issue-centered collaborations between governments and un-usual parties that lead to surprising results. Short-term coalitions within projects promote a more responsive urbanism that recognises the needs and desires of the populace, creating a customised and inclusive urban realm for all.

popupcity.net

References

Chapter One:
Flexible Cities with Fluid Citizens

Gerbaudo, Paolo. *Tweets and the Streets: Social Media and Contemporary Activism.* London: Pluto Press, 2012.

International Telecommunication Union. "ICT Facts and Figures 2013." http://www.itu.int/en/ITU-D/Statistics/Documents/statistics/2013/ITU_Key_2005-2013_ICT_data.xls.

Kotz, David M. "The Financial and Economic Crisis of 2008: A Systemic Crisis of Neoliberal Capitalism." *Review of Radical Political Economics* 41, no. 3 (September 2009): 305 - 317.

Krumideck, Susan, Shannon Page, and André Dantas. "Urban Form and Long-Term Fuel Supply Decline: A Method to Investigate the Peak Oil Risks to Essential Activities." *Transportation Research Part A: Policy and Practice* 44, no. 5 (June 2010): 306 - 322.

Kuymulu, Mehmet Barış. "Reclaiming the Right to the City: Reflections on the Urban Uprisings in Turkey." *City* 17, no. 3 (June 2013): 274 - 278.

Martinez-Fernandez, Cristina, Ivonne Audirac, Sylvie Fol, and Emmanuèle Cunningham-Sabot. "Shrinking Cities: Urban Challenges of Globalization." *International Journal of Urban and Regional Research* 36, no. 2 (March 2012): 213 - 225.

Self, Will and Ralph Steadman. *Psychogeography: Disentangling the Modern Conundrum of Psyche and Place.* New York: Bloomsbury, 2007.

Tillman, Karen. "How Many Internet Connections Are in the World? Right. Now." *Cisco Blog: The Platform*, 29 July 2013. https://blogs.cisco.com/news/cisco-connections-counter/.

Williams, Patricia A. H. "Information Warfare: Time for a Redefinition." *Proceedings of the 11th Australian Information Warfare and Security Conference.* Perth, Australia. 30 November - 2 December 2010. 37 - 44.

Chapter Two:
Container Homes, Plastic Cocoons, and Lofts with Legs

American Hotel and Lodging Association. 2012 *Lodging Industry Profile.* http://www.ahla.com/content.aspx?id=34706.

Economist, The. "City Rankings: Hong Kong's Best." 3 July 2012. http://www.economist.com/blogs/gulliver/2012/07/city-rankings.

Hackethal, Anita. "Vacant NL Dutch Pavilion at Venice Architecture Biennale 2010." *Designboom.* 30 August 2010. http://www.designboom.com/architecture/vacant-nl-dutch-pavilion-at-venice-architecture-biennale-2010/.

Harris, Elizabeth A. "Short-Term Rentals via

the Web: Lucrative but Often Illegal." *The New York Times*. 5 November 2013. A22.

Haverkort, Heleen. "Airbnb mag wel in Amsterdam." *Nu.nl*. 7 June 2013. http://www.nu.nl/economie/3494485/airbnb-mag-wel-in-amsterdam.html.

InterNations. "Expat Neighborhoods in Singapore." http://www.internations.org/singapore-expats/guide/16063-housing-accommodation/expat-neighborhoods-in-singapore-16058.

Isaacs, Ken. *How to Build Your Own Living Structures*. New York: Harmony Books, 1974.

Stallwood, Oliver. "How Berlin Is Fighting Back Against Growing Anti-Tourist Feeling in the City." *The Guardian*. 4 December 2012.

Tiny Life, The. "What Is the Tiny House Movement?" http://www.thetinylife.com/what-is-the-tiny-house-movement/.

Urban Dictionary. "Modern Nomad." 2 February 2012. http://www.urbandictionary.com/define.php?term=modern+nomad.

Wu, Rufina and Stefan Canham. *Portraits from Above: Hong Kong's Informal Rooftop Communities*. Berlin: Peperoni Books, 2008.

Zhao, Yaohui. "Leaving the Countryside: Rural-to-Urban Migration Decisions in China." *The American Economic Review* 89, no. 2 (May 1999): 281 - 286.

Chapter Three:
Co-Working in a Nightclub

Accenture. "Flexible Work Arrangements." http://careers.accenture.com/gb-en/your-future/work-environment/flexible-work/Pages/index.aspx.

Economist, The. "The Great American Slowdown." 12 April 2008.

Flint, Anthony. "The Next Workplace Revolution." *The Atlantic Cities*. 15 November 2012. http://www.theatlanticcities.com/jobs-and-economy/2012/11/next-workplace-revolution/3904/.

Oldenburg, Ray. *The Great Good Place: Cafés, Coffee Shops, Community Centers, Beauty Parlors, General Stores, Bars, Hangouts, and How They Get You through the Day*. New York: Marlow & Company, 1997.

Singer, Michael. "PC Milestone: Notebooks Outsell Desktops." *CNET News*. 3 June 2005. http://news.cnet.com/PC-milestone--notebooks-outsell-desktops/2100-1047_3-5731417.html.

SinglePoint Communications. "Benefits of Mobile WiFi for Mass Transit, Motorcoach, and Private Charter Agencies." *MoovBox*. 8 October 2013. http://www.yoursinglepoint.com/moovbox/benefits-of-mobile-wifi-for-mass-transit-motorcoach-private-charter-agencies/.

———. "Bus WiFi and the Changing Face

of Public Transportation [Infographic]." *MoovBox*. 10 January 2013. http://www.yoursinglepoint.com/moovbox/bus-wifi-transportation/.

Centraal Bureau voor de Statistiek. "Aantal jongeren met flexibele arbeidsrelatie neemt toe." 30 October 2013. http://www.cbs.nl/nl-NL/menu/themas/dossiers/jongeren/publicaties/artikelen/archief/2013/2013-3923-wm.htm.

Chapter Four:
Shop 'til You Pop!

Baker, Lindsay. "Online Retailers Move into Bricks and Mortar Stores." *BBC*. 2 November 2013. http://www.bbc.co.uk/news/business-24728406.

Niehm, Linda S., Ann Marie Fiore, Miyoung Jeong, and Hye-Jeong Kim. "Pop-Up Retail's Acceptability as an Innovative Business Strategy and Enhancer of the Consumer Shopping Experience." *Journal of Shopping Center Research* 13, no. 2 (2006): 1 - 30.

Page, Stephen J. and Rachel Hardyman. "Place Marketing and Town Centre Management: A New Tool for Urban Revitalization." *Cities* 13, no. 3 (June 1996): 153 - 164.

Shepherd, Ifan D. H. "From Cattle to Coke to Charlie: Meeting the Challenge of Self-Marketing and Personal Branding." *Journal of Marketing Management* 21, nos. 5 - 6 (2005): 589 - 606.

Surchi, Micaela. "The Temporary Store: A New Marketing Tool for Fashion Brands." *Journal of Fashion Marketing and Management* 15, no. 2 (2011): 257 - 270.

Trendwatching.com. "Trend Briefing: Pop-Up Retail." January 2004. http://www.trendwatching.com/trends/popup_retail.htm.

Chapter Five:
Can Cooks Become City-Makers?

Ahrendt, Jana. Historische Gründächer: *Ihr Entwicklungsgang bis zur Erfindung des Eisenbetons*. Technical University of Berlin: PhD Dissertation, 2007.

Bloomberg News. "Detroit's Urban Farmers Fight to Save City." *Financial Post*. 9 August 2013. http://business.financialpost.com/2013/08/09/detroits-urban-farmers-fight-to-save-city/.

Center for Automotive Research. *Beyond the Big Leave: The Future of US Automotive Human Resources*. http://cargroup.org/?module=Publications&event=View&pubID=80.

Chynoweth, Carly. "The New Food Businesses Helping to Revive Urban Communities." *The Guardian*. 9 July 2013. http://www.theguardian.com/sustainable-business/food-business-revive-urban-communities.

City of Helsinki. *Helsinki Foodism*. http://www.helsinkifoodism.com/en/.

City of Melbourne. *City of Melbourne Food Policy: Planning for the Future of Our Food.* http://www.melbourne.vic.gov.au/CommunityServices/Health/FoodPolicy/Documents/CoM_Food_Policy.DOC.

Detroit Future City. *The Land and Buildings Assets Element: A Strategic Approach to Public Assets.* http://detroitworksproject.com/wp-content/uploads/2013/01/DFC_Plan_Public-Land.pdf.

Falling Fruit. "About." http://fallingfruit.org/about.

Fashion Mobile, The. "Are Fashion Trucks the Next Food Trucks?" http://www.thefashionmobile.com/are-fashion-trucks-the-next-food-trucks.

Hunt, Nigel. "Agriculture in Cuba Today." *Cuba Agriculture.* 2008. http://www.cubaagriculture.com/agriculture-today.htm.

Johnson, Richard. "Street Food: The Latest Rage." *The Guardian.* 19 June 2011. http://www.theguardian.com/lifeandstyle/2011/jun/19/street-food-recipes.

Millstone, Erik and Tim Lang. *The Atlas of Food: Who Eats What, Where, and Why.* Berkeley: University of California Press, 2008.

Palmer, Charles H. Night-Lunch Wagon. United States Patent 458,738. Filed 6 June 1891. Issued 1 September 1891.

Petsinis, Steven. "Mobile Activation: How Melbourne's Food Vans Can Stimulate the City's Disconnected Docklands Area." *Global Site Plans.* 27 March 2013. http://globalsiteplans.com/environmental-design/landscape-architecture/mobile-activation-how-melbournes-food-vans-can-stimulate-the-city%E2%80%99s-disconnected-docklands-area/.

Reynolds, Ben. "Feeding a World City: The London Food Strategy." *International Planning Studies* 14, no. 4 (2009): 417 - 424.

Shuman, Michael H. "Economic Impact of Localizing Detroit's Food System." *Fair Food Foundation.* http://www.fairfoodnetwork.org/sites/default/files/Economic%20Impact%20of%20Localizing%20Detroit%20Food%20System.pdf.

Sniderman, Zachary. "How Social Media Is Fueling the Food Truck Phenomenon." *Mashable.* 16 June 2011. http://mashable.com/2011/06/16/food-trucks-social-media/.

Tyson, Richard V., Danielle D. Treadwell, and Eric H. Simonne. "Opportunities and Challenges to Sustainability in Aquaponic Systems." *HortTechnology* 21, no. 1 (February 2011): 6 - 13.

Zeeuw, Henk de and Marielle Dubbeling. "Cities, Food, and Agriculture: Challenges and the Way Forward." *Working Paper* No. 3. Leiden, the Netherlands: RUAF Foundation, 2012.

Chapter Six:
Urban Hacktivism and the Facebook Generation

Ford, Simon. *The Situationist International: A User's Guide*. London: Black Dog, 2004.

Foursquare. "10,000,000 Strong." June 2011. https://foursquare.com/infographics/10million.

Ganz, Nicholas and Tristan Manco. *Graffiti World: Street Art from Five Continents*. London: Thames & Hudson, 2004.

Goldstein, Lauren. "The Mob Rules." *Time Europe* 162, no. 7 (18 April 2003).

Hofmann, Romy, Martina Mehren, and Rainer Uphues. "Hacking the City: A Somewhat Different Mode of Field Work." *European Journal of Geography* 3, no. 3 (2012): 23 - 32.

Quirk, Vanessa. "Can You Crowdsource a City?" *ArchDaily*. 10 May 2012. http://www.archdaily.com/233194/can-you-crowdsource-a-city/.

Chapter Seven:
Marketing the City with Chocolate Bars

Ashworth, G. J. and Henk Voogd. *Selling the City: Marketing Approaches in Public Sector Urban Planning*. New York: Belhaven Press, 1990.

Gutzmer, Alexander. *New Media Urbanism: How Brand-Driven City Building is Virtualising*

the Actual of Space. Doctoral thesis. Goldsmiths, University of London. 2011.

Heurkens, Erwin. "Changing Public and Private Roles in Urban Area Development in the Netherlands." In *The Urban Question: Urbanism Beyond Neo-Liberalism*. Proceedings of the 4th International Conference of the International Forum on Urbanism. Delft, the Netherlands. 26 - 28 November 2009.

Lefebvre, Henri. *Le droit à la ville*. Paris: Anthropos, 1968.

Paddison, Ronan. "City Marketing, Image Reconstruction, and Urban Regeneration." *Urban Studies* 30, no. 2 (March 1993): 339 - 349.

Special thanks to the amazing people who have supported this book on Kickstarter:

@andrewecoulson — abgc architecture/andróid design — Ad Hupkes — Adam Beck — Adriaan

Wormgoor — Adventure Movie Club — Afaina de Jong / AFARAI — Alain Tack — Alberto Boido -

oldwallsproject.com — Alessandra Maljers — Alexander Opper — Alexander Thong — Alice Lilian

Suckling — Amy Grey — andARCHITECTURE | André Günther — Andrea Paolini — Andrew — Andrew

Luft — Andy de Freitas — Andy James — Andy Wayro — Anke Hendriks — Ann Light — Anna Dekker

— Antoine Talon — Arianna Allahyar — Aris & Vivian — Arlene Etchen — Attilio Romano — Bart

Hoekstra — Bart Meyskens — Ben Young — Bernadette van Lankveld & Niek Beekmans — Betina

Gomes — Bianca Benjamin — Blaž Lokar — Brian Driscoll — Bruce Sterling — Bureau.Donald —

C-Light-Wise, Carlijn Timmermans — Carla Link Federizzi — Carlos Pedro Sant'Ana — Carlton

Solle — Carolijn Slottje — Carolina Georgatou — Caroline Knappers — Carolyn W — Cathrine

Frederiksen — Cees Kamp — Charlene Leibel — Charles Woolford - @charleswoolford — cheryl

eng — CHERYL PAPOVE — Chia-Hsing Lin — Ching S. — Christian Caravante — Christoph Funk

— Christopher Bowns — Christopher M. Weir — Christopher Woodward — CITIES Foundation —

CitiesInOneWord.com — Claudia Ray-Centeno — Claudio A. Sarmiento-Casas — Colleen Kaman

— D1 Design v/ Annemette — Borreschmidt Kruse — Daan van Rossum — Dan Acher (42prod) —

Daniel Cooper — Daniel Seyde — Daniel Wiegand (@wiegimania) — Daniela Vieli — David E Lackey

— David Heyburn — David van Moppes — De Stedenfabriek - co-creatie katalysator — Dear Human — Diego Fagundes and Erica Mattos (Nimbu) — Dmitry Kalinychev — Dominic Rodgers — Doug Mirams — Duncan Geere — Edial Dekker — Edward 'Edbull' G-Jones — Edwin Oostmeijer — Edwin van Onna — El Desafío Foundation — Elizabeth Krasner — Emanualle Wright — Emile Forest — Emily Case — Emily Sivich — Emma Fenton - Australia — Emma Petersen — Emmet Blackwell — Ennio Emmanuel — Erlend Hsj — Ernst-Jan Pfauth — Eva Kritharelli — Everett Guerny — Ewa Spohn — Felipe Rocha — Félix Drouet — Fool on the Hill — Francien van Westrenen — Frédéric Maupin — Frederiek Dijkstra — Fredo De Smet — FreshAirWorking.com — Frieda Barneveld — Friso Wiersum — Gabrielle Marks — Gavin Watt — Gijsbert Hanekroot — Giulia De Vita — Giulia Domeniconi — Grant Stevens — gravitymax — Guillaume Bailey — Guus Witteveen — Hackity — Harry van der Velde — Hector Tan — Heidi Sinclair — Howard Chambers — HUNK-design — ilovenoord — Ingeborg Bruinewoud — Iris Kruijen — Iryanie Suhardi — Issara Twiltermsup — Jaime Izurieta-Varea — Jakub Knera — James Deeley — Jan en Wilma Rademaker — Jasper J. Kort — Jeanet van Antwerpen — Jennifer Yip — Jens Flammann (Mannheim/Germany) — Jeremy DiPaolo — Jeroen van der Zwan — Jess Baker — Jesse | We The City — Jiwon Park — Joe Seliga — John Griffin — John H Locke — Jon Doughty — Jon Tuley — Jons Janssens — Joost van Nuland — Jordi Buskermolen — Jorge Brandão Pereira — José Pérez IV — Julia Nowek — Julie de Weger — Julien Thomas — Kacper Jarecki — Kathleen Laylle — Kenneth Cochanco Go — Kim van der Leeuw — Kristina Cooke — Lacey Smith — Laura Bruns — Leanne Wijnsma Studio — Leigh

Abernethy — Liesbeth Brackel — Linda Lowe — Lindsay Kinkade / Design Re:Public Studio — Lisa

Gansky — Locodomo, from Amsterdam with love — Lucas C. Ross — Lucas Lindsey — Lucien

Coy — Luis Monteiro — Luisa Bravo — Maartje ter Veen — Machteld en Lot — Maciej Szafraniec —

Mads Pålsrud — Magda Sadowska — Margot Lefranc — Marie-Andrée Poisson — Mariken

Gaanderse — Marissa Villeneuve — Marjolein Dekker — Mark Donovan — Mark Richardson —

Markus Schäfer — Marleen Rademaker — Martijn de Waal — Martijn van der Hijden — Martine &

Joris & Pia — Martine Nicolay — Marvin Schwark — Matt Pickersgill — Matthijs Bouw — Meghan

Albert — mekala v — Menno Dudok van Heel — Michael — Michael M. Kroeker — Michael Sharman

— Michael Smyth — Michael T — Michal Broda — Miguel Rodriguez Montes — Milan van den

Bovenkamp — Mina Hanna — Ministry of World Domination - Polle de Maagt — Molly de Aguiar

— Monika Kanokova — Nalden — Neil Galway — Nicholas Wooyoung Park — Nicola Borgmann,

Architekturgalerie München — Niek Immers — Nina Martin — Patrice Fleurquin - Spacified.com

— Patrick & Tina Keenan — Paul Kozak — Pete Mummert — Peter Davis — Peter Feldkamp — Petra

Jyrkäs — Philippe Cordeau — Pierre Mallet — Pin-Ji Tang — Piyachai Karnasuta — POWERHOUSE

COMPANY & Being Development — R Rajani — Rebekka Keuss — Reinier Mees & Michiel Mees

— Rene Vullings — Ria Havinga — Rick Lindeman — Rick Taintor — Ricky Harris — Rik Adamski —

Rikkert Paauw — Robbie Rainbow — Robert Gaal — Roderik Schaepman — Roeland Rengelink

— Roland Reen — Ronald van der Steen - MMiV — Ross Duncan — Ross Gilbert - Spiritus

Development — Ruben Koster — Ruben Sissing — Rudolf van Wezel — Rukesh Patel (Smart Levers)

— Salomé Galjaard — Sam Maloney — Samuel Hansen — Samuel Weiffenbach — Sandra Larson — Sanne van der Beek — Scott Burnett — Scott Elliott-Brand — Sebastiaan Capel — Sebastiaan van Dam - Being Development — SETEPÉS, Portugal — Shawn McCann — Sietske Voorn - Siets & the City — Simon Whatley — Siobhan Hanlon — Sipke Visser — Sjerk de Groot — Sjors de Vries — Stadler Reini — Stefan Al — Stephanie Erwin — Stephanie Goodson, Founder NOMADgardens — Stephanie Jenkinson — Stephanie Koenen — Steve Swiggers — Steven Goldman — Susan Conklu — Sven Lohmeyer — Tamar Barneveld — tart2000 — Ted Pouls — Teresa Lee & Keenan Jackson — Teresa N Yn — Tessa Steenkamp — The Urban Conga — Thijs van Exel — Thomas — Thomas Joie — Thomas Spratt, USN — Tim de Boer — Times Square Art Square Foundation — Toby Anstruther of that Ilk — Tony Gatner — Tony Mangels — Tracy Metz — Unpleasant Design (Gordan Savicic, Selena Savic) — UPLAND | Urban Planning + Design Studio — Vanessa De Luca, urban flâneuse — Vera Pache — Vera Rademaker en Jeroen Meijers — Vincent Luyendijk — Vincent Muller [ontwerpburo MULLER] — Vruchtvlees — Walter Tempst — We Landscape — Wendy Winder — Wigger Verschoor — Wijnand de Boer — Willemijn Schmitz — www.kapteinbolt.nl — Yegor Korobeynikov — Yu Lan van Alphen — Yuki Kho — Yuriko Jewett — Zinnebeeld / Bart Driessen

Colophon

A Publication by
Pop-Up City

Authors
Jeroen Beekmans
Joop de Boer

Editor
Adam Nowek

Contributing Editors
Hannah Cook
Melody Moon

Image Researchers
Hannah Cook
Rebekka Keuss
Melody Moon

Graphic Design
Vruchtvlees
vruchtvlees.com

Publisher
BIS Publishers

Find Us Online
Web: popupcity.net
E-mail: mail@popupcity.net

Special Thanks to
Tamar Barneveld, Daniel Cooper, Michael Danker,
Vivian Doumpa, Rindor Golverdingen, Stijn Hupkes,
Margot van der Kroon, Teresa Lee, Rachel Lissner,
Marleen Rademaker, Sofie Rådestad, Daniel Rotsztain,
Roman Stikkelorum, Rudolf van Wezel, Bob Wiebes

This publication was made possible through the
generous support of

creative industries fund NL